The Pindar Diamond

The Pindar Diamond

A Novel

KATIE HICKMAN

BLOOMSBURY
NEW YORK · BERLIN · LONDON

Published by Bloomsbury USA, New York

All papers used by Bloomsbury USA are natural, recyclable products made from wood
grown in well-managed forests. The manufacturing processes conform to the
environmental regulations of the country of origin.

LIBRARY OF CONGRESS CATALOGING-IN-PUBLICATION DATA

Hickman, Katie.
The Pindar diamond : a novel / Katie Hickman. — 1st U.S. ed.
p. cm.
ISBN: 978-1-60819-213-7
1. Merchants—Fiction. 2. Diamonds—Fiction.
3. Venice (Italy) —History—17th century—Fiction. I. Title.
PR6058.I27P56 2010
823'.914—dc22
2010002581

First U.S. edition 2010

1 3 5 7 9 10 8 6 4 2

Typeset by Hewer Text UK Ltd, Edinburgh
Printed in the United States of America by Worldcolor Fairfield

This book is for my daughter
Maddie

A'az ma yutlab
my heart's desire

Part I

Chapter One

1603

They say lots of things – don't they? – about what it's like to drown.

.That it's a slow and dreamy way to die. That you will see the whole of your life flash before you as you pass into nothingness, or into the next world, although, afterwards, when it was all over, how anyone had ever possibly thought either of these things was quite beyond her.

No, what they don't tell you about what it's like to drown is the sound. Not the sound of the waves beating overhead, or the dip and crack of the boat, or even the muffled voices of the oarsmen – '*Come along, you boys, get on with it, the sooner we finish the job, the sooner we can get home*' – not even the terrible deafening rush of the water roaring in your ears. It is the sound of your own voice that you never forget. The sound of your own voice begging, pleading, crying – *not this, not like this, not the sack, please, please, kill me now* – on and on, even in the water, until it seems to be the very sound of your own voice that chokes and suffocates you. Perhaps that's why she never spoke now. Had never spoken again since. Not now that it was all over; not now that she had passed over into the next world.

Chapter Two

The coast of southern Italy, 1604

The village, when they came to it, seemed to the women to be one of the poorest they had yet encountered in an already bitingly poor land.

Even though they had travelled through the night, when they came to it early that morning they knew immediately that they had made a mistake. The village was not so much a village as a collection of fishermen's huts that clung to the bleak shore like molluscs. From the sea the huts must have seemed more like piles of driftwood, boned and bleached, accidentally spooled together by the tides, which is what they were, really, when you looked at them more closely. Not much more than driftwood and rags.

Through long habit the women stopped at the edge of the village, and regarded their destination warily. There was no church, not even a chapel that they could see, although a stone cross by the wayside just at the entrance to the village had been decorated like a rudimentary shrine with flowers and a picture of the Madonna painted crudely on a piece of tin. A handful of votive charms, fashioned like women with crowns on their heads, had been strung together overhead. They made a tinkling sound in the breeze. Nearby there were the ruins of some buildings which looked as if they had once been more substantial dwellings. The roofs had collapsed, blackened rafters sticking up through the rotted thatch like splinters of bone; but here and there, in amongst the crumbled walls, you could see a stone lintel here, a carved door jamb there, evidence of considerable prosperity in some long-ago and long-forgotten time.

Two of the children, twin girls of about eight or nine, jumped down from the back of the cart where they had been riding, running one after the other, threading their way like quicksilver through the ruined courtyards. In their brightly coloured dresses they looked like butterflies. Maryam, the leader, called them back sharply.

'What are you thinking, letting them run off like that?' She turned to their mother, a woman with the sad, pale face of a pierrot sitting next to her at the front of the cart.

'What harm can it do? Let them run around for a bit,' the other woman said mildly.

'Just call them back,' Maryam's expression was grim, 'we're leaving.'

'But we've only just arrived –'

'Look there.' Maryam pointed to a wooden doorframe tipping from its hinges.

Elena saw it straight away, the cross painted crudely in lime. Her heart lurched. 'They've brought us to a plague village?'

'That would explain a good deal, wouldn't you say.' Maryam jerked her chin in the direction of the deserted village.

'But I thought they said –'

'Never mind what they said, we're not staying here.' Maryam jumped down from the front of the cart. Even in her bare feet she was a whole head taller than most men, with a chest and shoulders to match. The horse's heavy leather reins seemed no thicker than those of a child's hobby-horse in her hands.

'But we can't go on, we've been travelling for days.' A hot wind was whipping Elena's hair into gritty tangles. 'The children are so tired – we're all so tired.' She gestured to the motley group of women who were gathered behind them, and then at the horse. 'And this poor old nag can't keep going for ever, either.'

The creature, so painfully thin that each individual rib jutted out, stood with its head hanging so low it almost touched the ground.

'I don't care, we're not staying here and that's that.'

Signalling to the rest of the small caravan, Maryam pulled the reins of the horse over its head and began to lead it away from the village, through a patch of scrubby, sandy ground between the fishermen's huts and the sea.

At the edge of the dunes the horse stumbled and fell. Although Maryam beat it with her whip until she thought her shoulder would break, it was clear that the horse was never getting up again.

Later, as the others had begun to set up their camp in the shade of two crooked olive trees on the windswept hinterland, Elena found Maryam sitting with her back against a patch of grass. For a while they sat together in silence, looking out to sea. The wind had dropped a little, and there was no sound except the tiny hiss of wavelets breaking on the beach. There was no sand here, only a thin strip of shingle. There was a strong smell of decay, of seaweed and rotting pine.

'Here, I've brought you this,' Elena handed her a piece of bread and cheese.

Maryam took a bite. There was a taste of salt on her lips. She put the rest in the leather pouch that hung from her belt.

'Well, looks as if we're going to be staying here after all,' she said after a while. Her voice was gruff. Neither of them mentioned the dead horse.

'We need the work, you know.'

'Work? *Panayia mou!* By Our Lady, there's no work here.' Maryam sounded as if she had tasted something sour.

'But – I thought you said –' Elena glanced at her. 'What about the village feast day?'

'There's no feast day.'

'What d'you mean, no feast day?' Elena tried to leaven Maryam's gloomy tone. 'There's always a feast day.'

'What, here? In this ghost town? How can there be a feast day, when there are no people?' Maryam nodded towards the huts. 'It's time to face it – we've been duped. Wouldn't be the first time. A troupe of tumblers on their own is bad enough, no better than thieving gypsies. But a troupe of *women* tumblers, no husbands, no fathers to keep them in order – well, that's against nature, that is.' She spoke bitterly. 'What better jest than to send them off somewhere with a wild goose between their legs? Reckon he must have thought we'd got off lucky, that man from Messina –'

'That man, Maryam –'

But Maryam was not listening. All she could think about was the horse, putrefying already in this heat, she shouldn't wonder. Maryam hid her head in her hands. Should they try to eat it? Sell it? She pressed her fingers into her eyes, so hard that she made sparks of light dance there. The loss of their only horse was a catastrophe so great she knew she had not yet even begun to comprehend it.

6

They'd have to get back to Messina first, and the only way to do that would be to walk. It had taken them three days to get here. She was the strongwoman of the troupe after all, stronger than three men . . . But even with her great strength she doubted whether she could pull their cart all that way. Perhaps if she tied herself to the shafts . . . As if to shut out the thought, she dug her fingers in still harder.

'Maryam!' Elena was shaking her by the arm. 'Maryam, are you listening to me?'

'What –?'

'He's here.'

'Who's here?' Maryam lifted her face from her hands, her eyes watering.

'The man who hired us. The one in Messina.'

'He's here?'

'Yes, I've seen him.'

'Now you're the one seeing ghosts.'

'He's no ghost,' Elena smiled. 'I've spoken to him, too. He came to the camp. He's there now, waiting for us. That's what I came to tell you.'

They found the man, a Signor Bocelli, sitting at his ease, eating heartily a piece of dried cured bacon between two slices of bread. Maryam, a woman of few words, did not waste her breath on useless reproaches.

'I don't know why you brought us to this plague village, and I don't care. But, see here, we want to be paid for our trouble anyway, *capito?*' She hoped he would not hear the note of desperation in her voice.

Signor Bocelli did not reply immediately. It seemed to amuse him to keep her standing in front of him. He took a large raw onion out of a leather knapsack at his side, the bulb roughly the size and colour of an ostrich egg, and bit into it with relish.

'*Hew!* I'd forgotten!' He grinned up at her at last, shaking his head, his mouth still full. 'You really are *big*, aren't you, giantess.' Maryam watched as a piece of unchewed onion flew out of his mouth and landed on her foot. He followed her gaze. '*Hew!* Feet as big as a Cyclops, hands to match . . .' still grinning, he sighed, '*hew!* And ugly, too, by God.'

You think I haven't heard all this before? Maryam regarded him steadily, watched as the juice from the onion trickled down his chin. *This and worse. Far worse. Is this really the best you can do, you lying, cheating, squirming little tick? Do you know that I could crush your skull with my bare hands?* But she said nothing. Just stood there, in her shapeless man's leather jerkin and boots, staring down at him, until at last he stopped his silly grinning and seemed almost discomfited, quelled by the sheer force of her silence.

'All right, all right.' He let out a belch and threw the rest of the half-eaten onion back in his knapsack.

'Why've you brought us to this plague village?' Maryam was growing tired of Signor Bocelli. 'There's no *festa* here.'

'Well, you're right about that, there's no *festa*. But this is no plague village.' He regarded her with his head cocked to one side.

'What then? I don't like it –' Maryam watched as a lone dog sniffed in the dust amongst the deserted huts '– there's something . . . strange about this place.'

'Did no one tell you? In Messina, I mean?'

'Tell me what?'

'What this village is.'

There was a pause. 'Now you're speaking in riddles, Signor Bocelli.' Maryam's eyes glittered. 'Perhaps you would be so good as to get to the point?'

'Have you ever seen one of these before?' From his knapsack the man brought out a small shiny object and held it out to her on the palm of his hand. Maryam took it, turned it over carefully.

'What is it? A charm? Looks like a fish of some kind –'

'An amulet. Look more closely.'

Maryam looked again. The amulet was made of silver, and showed not a fish, she now saw, but –

'A mermaid!'

The mermaid hung from a silver chain. She was swimming on her back, blowing a horn. She wore a crown on her head; tiny bells hung from her tail.

'I've seen some like these,' she said, remembering the tinkling sound, 'at the entrance to the village, at the stone cross. Only I didn't realise what they were.'

'In these parts mermaids have always been thought to bring luck. You can find these amulets almost anywhere along the coast – I'm surprised you've never seen one before. And this village especially has always been dedicated to the cult. Trouble is –' he shifted uncomfortably '– now they've actually got one. A real one, I mean.'

Chapter Three

She lay in a stall in one of the stables, a thin bundle with matted hair. A second bundle, tinier and more matted still, lay by her side. At first, Maryam thought she must be dead, she lay so still, but when they had been watching her for a while in silence, the bundle lifted a hand, so pale it seemed made from paper, and stirred the fetid air. A cloud of fat black flies rose lazily from where they had been feasting on the open wounds along her wrists and ankles, then sank down again to gorge. There was a stench of faeces and rotted fish.

Maryam pulled away from the stall, her face impassive. She had seen enough.

'If that were a horse, I'd shoot it.'

She tried to get round Bocelli but he was blocking her way.

'Let me past –'

'Take her with you,' he was so close she could smell the onion on his breath, 'she could be part of your show –'

'How, exactly?' Maryam could feel the bile rising in her throat. 'We're a troupe of tumblers – acrobats – Signor Bocelli.'

'You can show her. Like, well, an attraction . . .' When he put his hand on her arm she had to resist the instinct to beat it away.

'A freak show, you mean?' She paused, as if considering this idea.

'A sideshow! Yes! Now you're seeing sense. That's just what I thought.' For the first time Bocelli's face cracked into what Maryam supposed was a smile. 'You'll make a *fortune*.' He rubbed the tips of his fingers together meaningfully.

Maryam looked down at him. When standing she was a full two heads taller than him. Could he see the expression in her eyes? She hoped so.

'No, I don't think so.' One by one, she peeled his fingers from her arm. 'Thanks all the same.'

Bocelli followed her out into the dusty street. The sun was well risen now and the heat, reflected off the white houses, hit her like a wall.

'But – she's a mermaid, a real live mermaid –' she could hear him calling out after her. 'You're making a mistake, a big mistake –' his voice rose plaintively.

With a sinking heart Maryam realised that he had probably not even considered the fact that she might refuse his offer.

'If it's such a mistake, why don't you do it?'

The words were out of her mouth before she could stop them. *And no, she's not a mermaid. You know that as well as I do. She's a young woman whose legs have been broken. God alone knows how she ended up in this Godforsaken place.*

Maryam strode down the street thinking hard. She knew the Bocellis of this world. He was pleading with her now, almost craven, but it would not last long. Even as she walked, Maryam knew that she would be making a mistake to cross him too obviously, that she must get them all away quickly. Before he turned on her – on them all – which he surely would. She searched around for a sop to his pride. She felt rather than saw him at her heels.

'Besides, Signor Bocelli, we don't have the money to buy her from you.'

'Money? We don't want money.' She could hear him struggling to keep up with her. 'She's yours for nothing –'

'I'm sorry, but I don't want her –'

'We'll give you a horse.'

Maryam stopped dead in her tracks. 'What?'

'I said, we'll give you a horse. If you take her away from here –' he was panting at her side now. 'That's all we ask.'

She stared at him, not daring to believe what she had heard. 'You'll give me a horse?' Vaguely she wondered who he meant by 'we'.

'Your horse is dead –' there was a pause '– isn't it?' Maryam could feel a trickle of sweat running down one side of her face. 'How else are you going to get away from here?'

She could feel the scales shifting in his favour. Exercising all her self-control, she said nothing; had the satisfaction of seeing the quick gleam in Bocelli's eyes gutter again.

'Where are you heading?' Conversational now, he fell into step beside her.

'Up the coast,' she answered him grudgingly, 'to the Serenissima.'

'To Venice?' He seemed to hear this with satisfaction.

'In our business, all roads lead to the Serenissima,' Maryam replied coldly.

'Look –' he tried another tack, confidential now '– the villagers are frightened, that's all.' He gestured up and down the deserted street. 'They won't come back till she's gone.'

'Frightened of a girl with broken legs?'

'A girl with . . . ?' For a moment she caught an expression in Bocelli's eyes that she could not read. 'Oh, yes, of course the girl . . .' He shifted uncomfortably. 'They caught the girl in a fishing net. We all thought she was drowned, but –' he shook his head '– she didn't die. Not even after it . . . after the baby was born.'

'After the baby . . . ? She had a *baby*?' Maryam remembered the tiny bundle at the girl's side. So that's what it was. *Panayia mou!* By the Blessed Virgin! They'd be better off dead, both of them, than at the mercy of men like Bocelli. She wiped her fist over her sweating forehead. 'The poor wretches . . .'

'Nothing short of a miracle, if you ask me.' Bocelli shifted again, would not meet her gaze. 'Either that, or the devil's work, more like. Is it a wonder they're all so frightened? How did she get here, in her condition, it doesn't seem possible . . .'

But Maryam had heard enough. 'So?' She was beginning to tire of this conversation. 'She can swim, that's all. It's not hard to understand.'

'Swim?' Bocelli spread his fingers in a disbelieving gesture. 'In her condition? And from where? The nearest island is more than a hundred leagues from here.'

'Well, I don't suppose anyone has tried asking her?' Maryam allowed a tinge of sarcasm to enter her voice.

'She doesn't speak.' Bocelli lowered his eyes. 'She – can't speak.'

'I thought you said mermaids were supposed to be lucky in these parts. Why don't you just keep her?' She was curious now.

'Keep her? How? I know the amulets are supposed to bring luck – and they say there's a sacred grove dedicated to them further up the coast – but a *real* mermaid . . .' He shrugged. 'No one knows what to do with her, they're afraid even to go near her. They'd have killed her by now if they didn't think it would bring even worse catastrophe on themselves.'

'So that's why you brought us here? So that we would take her away with us?'

'Yes.'

Maryam was silenced. From the corner of her eye, she could see a tiny dust-devil, a whirlwind of sand and dirt, dance up the baking street. Beyond the fishermen's huts the sea was so blue it was almost black.

'Take her with you. Take her to Venice.'

Their eyes met.

'I'll give you my horse.'

Maryam's jerkin was sticking to her back as she turned and walked towards the women's camp, crouched in the burning sun beneath the two bent olive trees.

'My price is two horses, Signor Bocelli,' she called out to him over her shoulder.

'*Two* horses . . . ?'

'I suppose you want me to take the baby too?'

Signor Bocelli had the grace to look discomfited, mumbled something that she could not hear.

'Two horses then.' Maryam gave a curt nod. 'And I'll take them away this very night.'

There were many things that Elena thought when she first saw the girl, but she said none of them. They put her on a bed of cushions on the floor, where she lay very still, cradling the bundle of filthy rags to her thin chest. The bundle gave out a tiny sound, like a kitten mewing.

Elena glanced up at Maryam. 'There's a baby?'

'Seems so.'

'Poor creature.' Elena's face looked even longer and sadder as she contemplated the girl. 'What happened to her?'

'No one knows. They caught her in one of their nets, somewhere out to sea. Or so he says.'

'And you believe him?'

'Believe Bocelli? Of course not. She was probably just abandoned, by her husband, by the father of the child, who knows. Now they're saying she's a mermaid, or some such nonsense –'

'And they are afraid?'

'Too afraid to keep her, that's for sure. Too afraid to do anything other than throw raw fish at her –'

Elena crouched down. 'You poor creature.' She stroked the girl's head, spoke to her softly, gentling her with her voice as though she were a snared animal. 'I won't hurt you.' But she need not have worried. The girl kept perfectly still, even when they took her filthy rags from her, bathed the lesions around her wrists and ankles, her crooked legs, dressed her in a clean linen shift. She made no protest, no attempt to evade their ministrations, but lay there passively, saying not a word.

'Bless her,' Elena said when they had finished, 'she's got no more wits than her own infant.'

'And these rags are only fit to burn.' Maryam picked up the bundle from the floor, and as she did so something fell out from amongst the folds. When she bent to retrieve it, she saw that it was a small pouch, made of rose-pink velvet. 'Where did this come from?' She held it out for Elena to see.

Elena shrugged. 'It must have been hidden under her clothes somewhere, sewed into her linen – I don't know. Open it, it might tell us something.'

Maryam opened the pouch and pulled out a hard round object about the size of a bantam's egg, wrapped in a piece of cloth.

'What is it?'

'I'm not sure.' She unwrapped the cloth, looked at it in puzzlement. 'It looks like a stone.'

'What sort of stone?'

'Just a stone. An ordinary stone, like something you might pick up on the beach.' She weighed it in her hand. 'In fact, it looks like a stone someone's picked up from the beach just here – why, Elena, what's the matter?'

While Maryam had been inspecting the contents of the pocket, Elena had taken the baby on to her knee and had started to unwrap it from its filthy swaddling. Now she was staring at the infant. Her face was pale.

'Elena – what is it?'

'Look at this –' Elena's voice was hoarse. 'She is – it is – Signor Bocelli was not lying after all!'

She held the baby out for Maryam to see.

The infant was so tiny and weak that at first the only thing Maryam could think was that it was a miracle it was still alive. It lay quite still in the cupped palms of Elena's hands. At first its eyes – the dark blue eyes of the newborn, as blue and dark as the sea it had come from – seemed the only living thing about the creature. That, and the tiny ribcage, rising and falling, rising and falling, struggling for breath like a wounded bird.

It was only then that Maryam saw that in place of two legs the child had but a single limb which stuck out in front. And where two feet should have been was a single web of flapping flesh.

'You see! It *is* a mermaid. Bocelli didn't mean the mother, he meant the baby! It is a real mermaid, after all.'

Chapter Four

Venice, 1604

'He will come, you know.'

'Oh yes.'

'Will he be drunk?'

'What do you think?'

'That's what they call a rhetorical question, I suppose?' The courtesan, Constanza Fabia, spoke from the shadows.

'I don't know what they call it.' John Carew leant out of the window a little further, scowled down into the canal below. 'I know I could call it a number of things – ah, look now, here he is.'

Carew watched as further up, on the curve of the canal, an approaching gondola parted the water like black oil. Its lamp threw out gleaming sparks of light, but as it came closer, he saw that the gondola did not bear the Levant Company coat of arms after all. 'But no, no, I'm mistaken,' he drew back into the room on the first floor of Constanza's *palazzo*, 'drunk or no, it's not him.'

The room was one of the most extraordinary Carew had ever seen. The walls were three times as high as they were wide, the space beneath almost naked of furniture except for a massive bed. Over the bed was a half-tester canopy hung with silver brocade. Although the walls were covered with tapestries, the rest of the room had an empty feel. A pair of painted and carved *cassoni* had been pushed against two of the walls; while against a third was a huge sideboard also of carved wood. A folding table covered with a Turkey carpet had been placed at the foot of the bed at which Constanza sat. She seemed very small, Carew thought, in the echoing room.

'For pity's sake, come and sit down, John Carew.' Constanza

held a game of triumphs in her hand. Expertly she shuffled the cards together, dealing them with swift, well-practised movements on to the table in front of her.

'It never does any good,' her voice was light, unconcerned, 'you know that.'

'What never does any good?'

Aware of Carew's gaze, she glanced up at him with her sleepy, cat-like half-smile, but did not reply. Instead she said, 'Let me read the cards for you.'

'You'd tell my fortune?' Reluctant to move from his vantage point by the window, Carew put his hand up absently to feel his scar, a long silver cicatrice which stretched from his cheekbone to the corner of his mouth. 'The pity is I already know what my fortune is. And yours, Constanza, if we all carry on like this.'

But still Constanza said nothing, and for a long while there was no sound except the susurration of the cards and the small hissing of the candles which had been fixed in their heavy silver sconces on either side of the windows.

'Where did he go this time?' she asked eventually.

'Somewhere above some wine shop. At the Sign of the Pierrot.'

Constanza's eyes flickered briefly towards Carew.

'The Sign of the Pierrot?'

'Yes. Why, do you know it?' For the first time Carew could sense a change in Constanza's until now unruffled demeanour.

They looked at one another across the dimly lit room, a brief moment of understanding.

'He's in deep then,' was all she said.

Carew turned away again, fixed his eyes on the canal where the mist was now rising, hanging in wisps over the water.

'He's going to kill himself, you know,' he said, his back to her. 'Either that, or someone's going to do it for him,' he went on evenly, 'and that someone just might be me.'

'Oh come now.' Constanza made a small clicking sound with her tongue against her teeth.

'He has no money left. Or almost none. Night after night, Constanza . . . not games of skill – which he could win – but games of chance. He has thrown it all away, his whole fortune, with the roll of dice; and for what?'

Constanza shuffled the cards again, spreading them out with one swift movement on the table in front of her: the Tower, the Sun, the Magician. Nine of Coins.

'He is not happy,' she said at last.

'Not *happy*?' Carew almost spat the word at her. 'You think I give a piss in a pot for his happiness? I'll tell you what, Constanza, I really think he is mad, quite mad.'

'How long –?' Constanza began.

'How long before I kill him?'

'No!' She smiled, despite herself. 'I meant, how long has he been this way?'

'You know that as well as I do. Three years, more . . . I don't know exactly. As long as we've been in Venice, certainly. Since we came back from Constantinople.'

'Since he lost the girl, you mean?'

'The girl, yes.'

'The one they thought was shipwrecked?'

'Yes.' He sounded sombre.

'What happened to her?'

Carew was aware that Constanza already knew the story, had probably heard it a thousand times from Pindar himself, and was only asking him now out of pity; but he told her anyway.

'Her name was Celia Lamprey. Her father was the captain of one of the Company's merchantmen. As you say, we thought it was shipwrecked, in the Adriatic. But it seems it was attacked by corsairs. They killed the father, and everyone on board, but the girl was taken and sold as a slave. We believe – no, we are sure – she became a concubine in the Sultan's palace.' Carew pressed his fingers against his eyes until spots of light danced. 'I saw her there once –'

'You saw her?' Constanza looked up from her cards. 'I thought that was impossible. I've heard that the Turks keep their women closer than our nuns.'

'I saw her, yes – although there have been many times since then when I think it must have been a dream – but Paul, well, Paul never did. We tried, we tried a lot of things . . .' He paused. 'Then the Valide – that's the Sultan's mother – discovered it, and – well, it's a long story.'

'So she's still alive?'

'Oh no, she is dead. Dead to him anyway.'

'It's grief, then, Carew,' Constanza said slowly. 'That's what all this is about.'

'Grief? No.'

'What then?'

'Rage, I'd say.'

'Rage? How so?'

'He rages at himself,' Carew said, and the words were out before he had even thought them, 'because he could not save her.'

'Carew – would you please come and sit down.' Even Constanza sounded weary now. 'I've told you before, it never does any good.'

He pressed his forehead against the jamb of the window and closed his eyes briefly. 'What never does any good?' Hadn't they had this conversation before? He was too exhausted to care. Absently, he squeezed the ball of one hand into the fist of the other. There was a series of sharp retorts.

'The watching, the waiting –' Constanza glanced up at him '– the cracking of the finger knuckles. For pity's sake, Carew –' She put the cards down and went over to one of the *cassoni* where a silver flask of wine and two long-stemmed glass beakers had been set out on a linen napkin. 'Some wine?'

'Thank you, no,' Carew's eyes were still closed, 'I seem to have lost my taste for it of late.'

She poured out a glass for herself, studying him over the rim of the beaker. Some wine would do you good, *carissime* Carew, she wanted to say. She looked at him carefully, at his wiry frame, the dishevelled hair hanging to his shoulders, the quick, suspicious gaze – the figure of a rogue, that's how most people would see him – if it were not for his hands. The surprisingly beautiful hands, for all that they were covered – silvered over, you might say – with cuts and burns. You could always tell a man by his hands. There was a time, not so very long ago, my friend, when you were the one out whoring and gambling, Constanza thought, half-amused. You were the one always in a scrape of one kind or another. And now look at you, who would have believed it? Playing nursemaid to your own master. *Well, well* – but Constanza knew better than to say any of these things.

'He will come, you know,' she said again.

'He has to come. If he doesn't get here before Ambrose, I'm completely . . .' The words were out before he could stop them.

'Completely –?' Constanza raised one perfectly arched eyebrow.

'Completely undone, that's what, Constanza.' Without opening his eyes, Carew gave a groan. 'Completely and utterly undone –'

But Constanza's second question, 'And who, in God's name, is Ambrose?' died on her lips, because through the open window now came the scraping of a gondola coming to rest against the landing steps; then the sound of men's voices, querulous but not quite yet quarrelling, the splash of some heavy object landing in the canal.

Constanza went back to the table, began to deal the cards again: cups, swords, money, clubs. The Magician, again. In every hand she had dealt, always the same card. If Carew noticed that her hands seemed less dexterous this time, he said nothing. But the voices receded. It was no one looking for them.

'*Dio buono . . . !*'

'I thought that must be him.'

'And I . . .'

The two looked at one another, and each saw a shadow of apprehension in the other's eyes.

'You have nothing to fear, Constanza –' he began.

She looked away quickly. 'I know –'

'I won't let him –'

'Paul? He never would. Not with me.'

Carew began to say something, and then thought better of it. More than anything, he did not want her to start asking questions about Ambrose again. He had already said too much. Ambrose Jones was part of his own private scheme; he'd be in a whole peck of trouble if it came out too soon. Too late to go back on it now, Carew thought with a shiver. Ambrose was either his salvation or his ruin, he reckoned. And knowing his luck, quite possibly both.

How much longer they waited, he could not tell. From time to time he could hear the familiar clear sound of the bell of the new church on the island on the other side of the Grand Canal, San Giorgio Maggiore, strike the quarter-hour. At one point, in the very dead of night, he had the impression that he had, after all, been asleep. When he came to, he was still standing at the window, aware, suddenly, of the darkness all around him. The candles were no more than stubs. Wax hung like cobwebs from the heavy silver sconces on the walls on either side of the windows; had gathered in pools of pearly lava on the flag-stoned floor beneath.

Across the room from him Constanza was still sitting at her game of triumphs. Did she ever sleep? Carew regarded the courtesan in the guttering light. How old was she? It was hard to tell. His master, the Levant Company merchant Paul Pindar, called her a sphinx, said she had no age. John Carew, who was nothing if not a practical man, knew that she must be a woman well into her thirties by now, perhaps older. Old, then. But not old. He watched her as she dealt the cards again. She was dressed in the robe that Pindar had given her when they first came back from Constantinople: the sleeveless garment of an Ottoman lady of high rank, blood-red damask embellished with tulips in pure gold thread which she wore open to the waist. Below it was a shirt of lawn cambric, so fine it was like a cloud of gauze, embroidered around the neck and sleeves with seed pearls. No jewels. Her dark hair loose around her shoulders. She was, he thought to himself, the only woman in Christendom for whom Carew had had, from the first moment of meeting her, something approaching respect. So much so that he had not even wondered what it would be like, what she would be like – her taste, her smell – well, not much, anyway, not often.

Constanza caught his gaze. 'You look as if you've been asleep.'

'I'm not sure.' He stretched. 'You?'

'Me? No.' She smiled at him.

'Why are we doing this, d'you suppose?' His own question caught him by surprise.

'Who knows?' Constanza shrugged. 'Because we love him?' She put her head to one side. 'Because, despite appearances, you and I are rather alike?'

If Carew caught her mocking look, he did not rise to it. 'Don't flatter yourself.' His tone was gloomy.

Constanza's mouth opened a little with surprise, then she threw back her head suddenly and laughed, a real hearty sound of genuine mirth. 'You see. I rest my case. For that, Carew, I *will* tell your cards.'

21

She dealt them again, and he watched her looking with fierce intent at the cards on the little folding table in front of her. *Tsk.* She made that sound again, tongue against her teeth.

'What is it?'

'What . . . ?' Sweeping the cards together, she brought herself back as if from some deep dream. 'No, no . . . it's nothing. Let's try again. Here, you shuffle them this time.'

She handed him the pack and when he had finished she spread them out into a fan shape, held it out for him. 'Pick one, and give it back to me. But don't look at it, not yet.'

He did as she commanded. 'Don't tell me, it's the Fool.' An attempt at a levity that he did not feel.

'The Fool?' She gave him one of her slow sideways smiles. 'The Fool denotes innocence, and folly. Not really you, John Carew. Not the innocent part anyway.' A dimple appeared at the corner of her mouth. 'Curious . . .' She looked back at the cards, frowning now.

'All right then. If not the Fool, then the Hanged Man,' Carew said, more gloomy still. For that's how I feel now, he thought to himself, like a man about to be hanged.

'No, not the Hanged Man,' Constanza said slowly, 'although that might not be so bad as you think.' She held the card that he had chosen, tilting it away from him so he could not see the face. 'The Hanged Man often denotes a change; in life, in circumstances.'

'A change for the better?'

'Well, that depends –'

'Not much could be worse. Here, let me see it.' He put his hand out to take the card, but she held it away from him.

'No, not yet, I'm trying to decide.'

'Decide?'

'What it means.'

For a while there was silence while Constanza considered the cards.

'You say Paul's gone to the Sign of the Pierrot . . .' she said thoughtfully at last. 'Are you sure that's where he's gone?'

Carew looked at her. 'I'm not sure about anything any more.'

'Ach, it's probably nothing.' She gathered the cards together again. 'Did you ever hear him mention the name of Zuanne Memmo?'

'Zuanne Memmo? No, I'd remember a name like that.' Carew shook his head. 'Why, is he a friend of yours?'

'A friend?' Constanza gave a small laugh. 'I very much doubt if Memmo has any friends. He runs a high-stakes *ridotto*. And when I say high, I mean *very* high. Men – young boys – even women sometimes too – he takes all types. I've heard he *specialises* in foreigners –' She gave Carew a warning look. 'I've heard that never a week goes by without some blood being shed at one of Memmo's games.'

'And is that who you've seen in your cards?' Carew jerked his chin towards the pack, now closed, that she had placed face down on her table. He had no very great opinion of fortune telling, by Constanza or anyone else.

'I'm not sure, it's still not clear,' she frowned. And then, musingly, as if to herself, 'But why it should be you, and not Paul . . . and why do I see Zuanne Memmo, of all people –'

Constanza looked up at Carew again. 'I heard that there was to be a big game at his new *ridotto*, perhaps it is that which is confusing me. They say the prize is this diamond that everyone's talking about.'

'A diamond?'

'Yes, you've heard about it surely: the latest wonder of the Serenissima. I believe they have been talking about nothing else in the Rialto,' Constanza said. 'The Sultan's Blue. It's supposed to have belonged to the Ottoman Grand Seignor, or was it some king in the Indies, I don't remember now,' she shrugged. 'Anyway, whichever, it was some dealer from Aleppo is said to have brought it here, and then lost it at cards. There was some story, you know how it is in this city –'

Just then there was the sound of someone banging on the door. They had been so intent on the cards that they had not, despite Carew's long vigil, seen the gondola approach, nor heard any footfall upon the stairs. When they looked up it was to see the figure of a man standing on the threshold. He wore a travelling cloak; his face was in shadows.

'*Salve?*'

When the man did not answer, or make any move towards them, Constanza half-rose from her seat.

'*Salve?*' she repeated. 'Paul, is that you . . . ?'

Carew made an inarticulate sound under his breath.

'No, it's not him –' he began, but before he could say any more the stranger spoke at last.

'Is this the house of Constanza Fabia?'

'Who wants to know?'

'And I should like to know the same of you.' A cheerful English voice, clipped, precise. There was a pause. 'I was told I would find a man named Pindar here. Paul Pindar, merchant of the Honourable Levant Company.'

'Mr – Jones? Ambrose Jones?' Carew seemed to have something stuck in his throat. 'We – *ahem* – we weren't expecting you so soon.'

'We?' Sounding encouraged, the man in the travelling cloak took a step into the room. 'And with whom do I have the honour . . . ?'

At that moment two of the candles flared briefly to life. For the first time Constanza and Carew could see the stranger standing before them. An older man, in his fifties perhaps, greying hair swept back from a high forehead, beady blue eyes the colour of periwinkles, a turban of egg-yolk yellow silk wrapped, Ottoman style, around his head. And a nose . . . well, quite the most extraordinary nose that either of them had ever seen. A nose that swelled and rippled from the middle of his face, a nose so improbable in its size and shape it gave him, Carew would later recall, the air of a fabulous beast.

In the same flare of light the stranger took one quick look about the room and his cheerful expression faded.

'What's all this?' He put down a small wooden chest that he had been carrying and surveyed the scene in front of him with a grave air. 'Is this some kind of a joke, sirrah?'

'Carew?' It was Constanza who spoke. And when Carew, who seemed stunned into unaccustomed silence, did not answer her, she said, more sharply now, 'Who's your friend, John Carew? Is this the person you were speaking of so – so colourfully – before? I would like to welcome you, sir,' she turned to him with all the fabled courtesy of the Venetian courtesan, 'but I find myself at a disadvantage . . .'

The turbaned stranger did not reply. He seemed immune, both to beauty and to charm. Instead, his bright, searching gaze swept over the room like the beam of a lighthouse: the immense space, naked of any furniture except the cavernous bed, the empty wine cups;

24

the courtesan with her loose hair and bare neck. His lips narrowed ominously.

'Well, well,' he turned to Carew, 'John Carew, is it? I know who you are at least. So this is where your master spends his time? Which would explain a number of things. And just what does he mean by bringing me to this bawdy house?'

'Bawdy house?' Now it was Constanza's turn to look ominous. 'What's the meaning of this, Carew? Who is this – this – this –' she rounded on him.

'I'm sorry, Constanza.' In the dim light of the guttering candles the blades of the knives Carew carried at his belt glinted. 'Truly, I am.'

Constanza seemed to grow taller suddenly.

'What do you mean by this? You've brought him here on purpose, haven't you?'

'Please believe me, Constanza, it was the only way.'

'What do you mean it was the only way? Will someone please tell me what's going on?' Ambrose Jones was shouting now, too, over the two of them.

'Gentlemen, gentlemen – Constanza – please!' A smooth dark voice was speaking from the doorway.

'Paul –!'

'Pindar –!'

All three turned to see a tall slim man, dressed from head to toe in black. To an untutored eye his appearance was gentleman-like, even fashionable. He wore a short cloak and doublet made of velvet, a high-crowned hat. But to anyone who knew him well the change in his appearance was terrible. His cheeks were sunken, his eyes glittered strangely, his skin had the cadaverous pallor of someone who rarely sees the light of day.

'Con-*stan*-za.' Paul Pindar spoke her name with exaggerated care, enunciating as if his tongue and lips were foreign bodies stuck on to the middle of his face. 'And you, sir, if I am not mistaken, must be Ambro-*se* Jon-*es*.' Despite the fact that his tongue seemed to be glued to the roof of his mouth with molasses, he got the words out eventually. Paul was not looking at Ambrose but beyond him into the shadows by the bed, to where Carew in the confusion had made a nimble retreat.

25

'Ah! And yes, of course. Carew.' Pindar, who had begun to list slowly to one side, caught hold of the door jamb for support.

Carew said nothing, but stood watching him in silence. Every so often his eyes flickered between Ambrose and Paul.

'Don't think I can't see you over there, you bastard rat-catcher,' Paul hissed at him. 'I can see the whites of your eyes.'

Still Carew did not respond. And as if enraged by this, with a sudden, not altogether smooth movement, Pindar pulled a short dagger out of the belt he wore around his waist. 'Noise, trouble, confusion, and there he always is, you know,' he said, looking round unsteadily at the others. Swaying slightly, he pointed the tip of it towards his servant. 'And now, Carew. You damned. Bastard. Rat-catcher. I'm going to kill you.'

With that he tipped forward, falling with an almighty crash, like a felled tree trunk, on to his face in front of them.

As he fell, a hard round object, about the size of a baby's fist, dropped on to the floor at his side. Unseen by any of them, it flashed briefly, dazzlingly, and then rolled under the bed.

Chapter Five

An Island on the Venetian Lagoon, 1604

Annetta stood listening to the bells.

From her window she could see the full length of the garden: the neat box hedges, the carefully marshalled flowers and herbs, each in their own compartment. Soon even this green haven would be swimming with heat, but in the early morning everything was still fresh, as sweet-smelling as if it had been new-minted. She could see Annunciata walking below her, as she did every morning, with her little wooden watering can, a white figure, slipping in and out between the fruit trees. Beyond her were the walls of the convent's famous physic garden, a row of cypresses, a distant sliver of the lagoon. The best view to be had, Annetta thought to herself with satisfaction, now that she was rich. The best view that money could buy.

She stretched, sniffed the still-cool and perfumed air. It was a great day today – Francesca's niece was bringing her wedding party on a visit, and they were all invited, would have a high old time together, with wine and cakes and all manner of other sweetmeats with which to feast the happy couple. None of your snooty *contessas* among them, insisting on having the parlour to themselves, and everyone else could go hang. 'Isn't that so, my little pippet?' Annetta reached into a jar of seed on the windowsill and carefully sprinkled a palmful into the birdcage that hung from the lintel above her. The sparrow hopped down from its perch, its black eyes like tiny pieces of jet.

Despite the festivities ahead, Annetta was reluctant to get dressed just yet. At her feet was a basin of water, and the linen cloth with which she had just washed herself. The others thought she was half-crazed to wash herself so often, but, well, old habits died hard. And, besides, the breeze against her damp skin felt almost cold, ruffled her naked flesh and made her shiver with pleasure.

Some distance from the convent's island, the bells of San Giorgio Maggiore on a neighbouring island near the Giudecca were still ringing: a hollow, coppery sound; a green sound, she thought, inconsequentially. She had not realised how much she missed the bells all those years that she had been away. The bells, and the view. At the other place, no one had ever been allowed a view.

Annetta sighed. She must get dressed, but it was so pleasant to stand here; pleasant, and not a little dangerous, given her state of undress. Annunciata was making her way back across the garden, stopping from time to time to pull a dead head from one of the roses. She had a basket over her arm, full of cuttings from the herbarium. If she looked up now, Annetta calculated, she would be able to see her standing at the window. More to the point, would be able to see her standing completely naked at the window. She knew quite well that Annunciata knew she was there, wanted to look, was determined not to. A dimple appeared at the corner of Annetta's mouth. She had forgotten what wonderfully good sport it was to shock the convent sisters.

On the bed behind her lay her clothes for the day. Even though the weather promised hot, in honour of the festivities later on she had already decided on the silk stockings with the embroidered clocks. Her best *camisa* was, as good fortune would have it, made of the finest lawn, so thin it was almost transparent – like wearing air next to the skin, she had once told Eufemia – with the most fashionable black-stitched embroidery along the neck and sleeves. Over the *camisa* came her new bodice, plainer than she would have liked, but with a double layer of *point de Venise* lace around the neck. Annetta did up the laces at the back of the bodice herself, pulling it down at the front as far as she dared, showing the definite curve of her breasts. She could have got one of the *conversas* who normally waited on her to come and lace her, but on the whole Annetta preferred not to have them snooping around in her room. Then for the *pièce de résistance*: her petticoat of silk-gauze shot with gold, which she tied to the bodice with points, so beautiful it grieved her heart to have to conceal it beneath her everyday robe. She looked at the pattens – four inches high and inlaid with mother-of-pearl – that she had brought back with her, but decided against them, swapping them at the last moment for a pair of brocaded slippers.

Last of all Annetta arranged her hair, carefully pulling out two little curls from beneath her headdress, one on either side of her forehead, fashioning them expertly with spit and pinched fingers. Round her neck went two heavy chains of gold. At her waist she fastened a chain girdle, at the end of which dangled her fan and prayer book.

From a tiny space in the wall above the bed-head Annetta drew out a round object wrapped in an old cloth and uncovered a piece of silvered glass in a frame. She held it up so that she could see herself in its reflection. There! The use of a looking-glass was absolutely forbidden, but why should she care? In her short but eventful life she was beginning to think that she really had had enough of rules. The sin of vanity, they said. Far graver than any of the other sins she had committed recently. If she had cared to, she could have enumerated them all: keeping a sparrow in her room as a pet, not to mention the chickens, lodged in a wicker coop just outside her door, which she kept for her own personal supply of eggs; the wearing of silks and brocades, the gold chains, the immodesty of standing naked at the window; of tempting another to lustful thoughts. But it was the sin of vanity, she always thought, as she held up the looking-glass, that was by far the most satisfying. For several minutes Suor Annetta, soon to be professed nun of the Convent of Santa Clara, continued to gaze, with untroubled delight, into the forbidden glass.

At some point the bells must have stopped ringing, for suddenly Annetta was aware that they had started again. She was late now, for sure. And so taking up the last object on the bed – a small pouch of embroidered rose-pink velvet – and placing it carefully in her pocket, she made her leisurely way down to join her fellow sisters for prayers.

Chapter Six

For a few moments, when he first woke, Paul could not remember where he was. It was very dark. He was lying in a canopied bed, in a high-ceilinged room; panels of tooled leather lined the walls, and heavy damask drapes had been pulled against the windows to block out the daylight. He realised suddenly that he was not alone, that there was someone standing looking at him from the foot of the bed.

'Constanza?'

'Paul, you're awake?'

'Yes.'

He tried to turn over, became aware of a scorching pain between his eyes.

'How do you feel?'

He heard the sound of water in a basin, felt a cool cloth against his forehead.

'Ah, don't do that!'

He put his hand up to his forehead, his fingers met a lump the size of a tennis ball.

'*Christos!*'

'Does it hurt?'

He ran his fingers over the rest of his face.

'My nose! Dear God, I think I've broken it.'

'I expect you have.' Constanza did not sound sympathetic. 'You fell face down flat, right here on the floor.'

'I fell –?'

Paul ran his tongue over his lips. They were so parched they felt as if they were full of cracks, and there was a strange metallic taste in his mouth, a taste he recognised as blood. Flakes of something dried and black clung to his beard; were stuck in his hair. *Oh, Christos.*

He lay back and closed his eyes; slowly, painfully, the events of the previous night were coming back to him.

'I have a message for you, from your John Carew.' She held up some water for him to drink.

'Carew?' Instantly, Paul's eyes were open again. He turned his head more quickly than he intended, and it was all he could do to stop himself yelping with pain. 'Did I kill him?'

'No.'

'Pity.' Paul's eyes flickered shut again. 'Next time then.'

Constanza, surprisingly, said nothing to this. So Paul added slowly, 'He always was ... a ... conniving ... lying ... little bastard, don't you think?' He could not at this moment remember very precisely why he had wanted to kill Carew, but the feeling of rage against him was still there, like a red stain pressing against the backs of his eyes.

Still Constanza did not reply. *Oh, well, damn the both of them.* Paul lay in the darkness. Talking had tired him out, but his head hurt too much to sleep. Perhaps if he had some wine? Even the thought of it, appealing though it usually was, was enough to make his stomach heave. Constanza had been going to tell him something, but he could not now for the life of him remember what it was. In the darkness, where he lay in a waking sleep, slivers of the previous night's events fluttered, unbidden, to the surface of his mind.

Christos! Suddenly, he was very much awake again.

'Constanza?'

'Yes?'

Paul turned slowly and painfully on to his side. 'Was – was there someone here last night? Not Carew; someone else, I mean?'

'Ambrose Jones?'

'Oh God!'

'Don't you remember speaking with him? He gave you a letter.'

'A letter? Yes – a letter –' Paul was searching feverishly now in amongst the crumpled linen on the bed. 'Yes, here it is. Give me some light, can't you.'

Constanza pulled the drapes over the windows open, and kneeling on the bed, Paul read the letter quickly. Then he lay back down again. He lay like that for a long time, staring up at the ceiling.

31

'He was very angry with you.' Constanza came and sat beside him. 'Why was he so angry, Paul?'

She had a glass of wine in one hand.

'No, thank you,' Paul said. He felt empty suddenly: dried up as a bleached bone.

'It's not for you,' Constanza said, her voice mocking; then, in a slightly softer tone, 'So who is this man, then? This Ambrose Jones, of whom you both seem so frightened.'

'Ambrose?' Paul was still staring up at the ceiling. 'I'm not really sure what you'd call Ambrose. Ambrose is many things. I suppose you could call him . . . a collector.'

'A collector?'

'Amongst other things. He works for someone I know, a Levant Company merchant in London. A man named Parvish. Collects things for him, anything that is beautiful and rare, for his cabinet of curiosities.'

'Ah,' Constanza thought she was beginning to understand. 'Haven't I heard you mention him before? You were apprenticed to him once, weren't you?'

'Yes, I was his apprentice. It was a long time ago.' Paul put a hand up to his face, tracing the swollen contours of his nose and eyes. For a moment he was eighteen again, back in London, snow seeping in through his boots, his nose bloody . . .

They sat in silence for several moments.

'He's done this to shame me.'

'Who? Parvish?'

'No. Carew, of course.' Paul lay back among the bolsters on Constanza's bed. 'He knows that Ambrose reports everything back to London – he wants to shame me in front of Parvish.' With a sudden movement he caught hold of her wrist, circling it between his thumb and forefinger. 'But he must have told you that, didn't he? You must have known . . .' As he spoke he twisted his fingers still tighter around her wrist until she winced. 'That's why you sent for me, isn't it? You'd both have known I'd always come here.'

'He didn't give me a reason –' Constanza tried to pull away from him, but he held her fast, his fingers biting into her skin '– and I did not know about Ambrose, I swear it –' He had a surprising strength, she remembered now, for such an educated man.

'Are you sure about that?'

'But if I'd have known, I'd have done it anyway. Gladly –'

'Is that so?' He let go of her wrist so suddenly that she fell backwards, striking her head against the bedstead.

'He's always been clever, I'll grant him that.' Paul was no longer looking at her. 'Too damn clever for his own good.'

Paul got up from the bed and went over to Constanza's little balcony, a row of pointed arches giving out over a bend in the canal. Ambrose. *Christos!* What was Carew thinking of? Paul ran his fingers nervously through his hair, over the stubble on his cheeks. It was still early, but already the sun was striking hard on to the walls of the *palazzo* opposite. Its stuccoed walls were washed with that pinkish colour so peculiar to Venice – in his trade, he mused, they might call it anything between lady's blush and pimpillo – but he never could find the right word to describe it. He breathed in the familiar smell of the canal beneath him. It would be stinking hot today. He looked down: the water looked invitingly cool and green. Usually Paul was charmed by it – the reflections of the arched windows in the water, the cry of the gondoliers as they went by, the play of light and shadow – but now all he could think about, with extreme irritation, was that his gondola had gone; no prizes for guessing where. There was, of course, no sign of Carew.

'Carew says you're all but ruined.' As if reading his mind, Constanza spoke from the bed behind him.

'That's what he says, is it?' Still standing at the balcony, Paul did not turn round. 'And what else does he say?'

'That everyone in Venice knows it. All the merchants.'

'Go on.'

'That you have stopped trading. That you've gambled your money away instead. Or drunk it.' Constanza went on, reckless now. 'That you are a disgrace to the Honourable Company.'

At this Paul's eyebrows shot up. '*Carew* said that?'

'Well, no. I believe it was your friend Ambrose Jones who said that.' Constanza's voice was brittle.

'*Hmm.*' Paul closed his eyes again as another wave of nausea passed over him.

'*Hmm?* Is that all you can say?'

33

'Well, if you ask me, Ambrose was laying it on a bit thick,' he said mildly. And then, curiously, 'So what else did Ambrose say?'

'Variations on that theme, I think you might call it. There's talk, he says, of expelling you from the Company.'

'Really?'

'For God sake, how drunk were you last night?' Constanza said, unable to keep the exasperation from her voice. 'Don't you remember *any* of this?'

Paul did not reply.

'He was very angry.'

'That much has become clear.'

'Angry that a wastrel and a drunk such as yourself had no business in the company of respectable merchants. That a wastrel, a drunk and a whoremonger had no business in the company of respectable merchants,' she added, warming to the theme.

'A whoremonger?'

'I believe that's what he said.'

'Ah, Constanza.' Paul turned to her at last. 'I'm sorry, Ambrose goes too far.'

He went over to the bed again, took her by the arms, more gently this time, and pulled her to him. She did not resist, but lay down and put her cheek against his chest. She felt his hand on her hair, stroking it absently, just as he always used to do, all those years ago; smelt his familiar smell.

'That was a mighty sigh.'

'Was that me?' Now it was Constanza's turn to close her eyes.

It was only now that she realised how tired she was, tired as a dog. It was a whole day and almost two nights since she had slept. *And I would go to sleep now for all eternity*, she thought; *and gladly, if you, my beloved, were by my side*. But she said nothing. Instead, after a while, in a more musing voice: 'What will you do now? About Ambrose, I mean?'

'Ambrose? I wouldn't worry about him. It's Carew I'm going to have to deal with.' She felt his fingers tighten on her scalp, pulling her hair sharply.

'Carew loves you –'

'Alas, the only thing Carew loves is Carew.'

There was another pause.

'He thinks you are half mad with grief,' she ventured after a while.

'Is that so?'

'Half mad with grief and rage.'

To this Paul said nothing.

'About the girl. The one you left behind in Constantinople.'

'Carew is my servant,' Paul replied softly. 'What would he know about these things?'

'You've no idea, he waited here all night. I don't think he meant to shame you. I think he believes he'll save you –'

'Save me? His own scrawny skin is the only thing he wants to save. If I am ruined, he loses his livelihood, it's a simple calculation. You don't know him as I do. Where is he, anyway?'

'John? There was to be a wedding party going out to the Giudecca, or one of the islands, I don't remember,' Constanza suppressed a yawn, 'to some convent or other.'

'A wedding party?'

She shrugged. 'There was some girl, I believe.'

'There's always some girl,' he murmured sleepily.

With her head on his chest Constanza listened to his breathing, felt his hand slacken on her hair, until she too fell into sleep.

He must have slept for a long time for when he opened his eyes again, his head felt clear, the only pain was in his bladder. Someone had closed the curtains and the only light was coming from a single blade of sun piercing through the heavy drapes. From the strength of the light Paul guessed that it must be late, past noon. Normally Constanza's maid would have been in by now, pulling the curtains, clearing away the glasses and discarded chicken bones from the night before, bringing clean linen and hot water for her mistress's ablutions – Constanza was always fastidious – but no one had come. Perhaps, as she sometimes did, she had asked not to be disturbed; he thought it highly probable. But there was something that troubled him, a thought, like a blown leaf, that snagged on the corner of his mind. He listened for her servants moving about in the rest of the *palazzo*, for a whispered admonition, the creak of a floorboard or a dropped pail; but there was nothing, not a sound. A profound silence rang in his ears. In the distance he heard a church bell ringing the hour.

35

He wondered vaguely if Carew were still at the wedding, whether he had churched the girl.

Paul looked around the room. He took in the table at the foot of the bed covered with a Turkey carpet, the empty wine glass, the discarded pack of cards. The wooden wainscotting on the walls was interspersed with panels made from leather, each one tooled and painted intricately with flowers and birds of paradise; their edges scrolled with leaf of gold. Over one of the *cassoni* pushed against the wall his eyes lit on a patch of panelling that seemed paler than the rest. He remembered now that an immense glass, its frame richly worked and gilded, had once hung there, wondered vaguely to where Constanza had had it moved.

He remembered when he had first come here as a young man, recalled this very room, which seemed exactly the same to him now as it had been then, the room from which she always seemed indivisible. No pilgrimage madonna could have been more sumptuously staged. He remembered, too, the agony of anticipation that had accompanied his first sight of her, as if she were a creature so rare – a mythological beast, a siren or a sphinx – too fine for most mortal eyes.

It had been the mother – herself, in her youth, one of Venice's most fabled courtesans – who had attended them when they first arrived, gave them sweetmeats and wine in golden goblets. He remembered how she had put them – him and his companion, Francesco – to wait in the antechamber, time enough for them to repent, if they had been inclined to do so, the immense sum they had paid for an introduction to Venice's most celebrated courtesan. Paul could almost laugh at his younger, foolish self – at the caprice, the arrogance, of two young men, newly rich. For it had been a sum so reckless that for the three weeks they had been made to wait for their first introduction the mere recollection of it caused a feeling of nausea, made a film break out on his brow as if he had the sweating sickness.

He had been with common women before, it was true. They were easy enough to find around the Southwark theatres that he and his fellow apprentices frequented, but if he had thought to find another such, he was much mistaken. He and Francesco had stood in the antechamber, got up like a couple of apes in their new-fangled velvet pantaloons. What an absurd pair they must have seemed, he could not help smiling to himself. How long they had waited to make their

36

entry he could not remember, only that after what had seemed like an eternity, the doors had opened to a room full of candles, so many the room blazed like the day. And there she was at last, in the full dawn of her dazzling beauty: her dark hair loose about her shoulders, dressed in the finest cloth of tissue of gold, with rings on her fingers and jewels at her neck, rising to greet them. When she looked at him, she made him feel he had the beauty of Paris, the strength and wits of Odysseus. That he, and he alone, was the only man on earth she might desire.

Had she played for them that day? He could not recall, but he remembered that she had spoken with them in a way that he had never before heard a woman speak, about poetry – Dante and Ariosto, and even the scurrilous Aretino. And the two of them, he and Francesco, had just stood there – their legs turned to syllabubs – dashing out their eyes at the sight of her.

But he had been young then; Paul shook himself out of his reverie. Warm in the crook of his elbow lay the still-sleeping form of Constanza. He leant down, breathed her hair. She smelt of musk, and of something else, something sweet – violets, perhaps? – mixed with the stronger female odours, skin and sweat.

He felt himself stirring, kissed her shoulder, felt his lips, still rough with dried blood, pass over the smoothness of her skin. She lay with her back to him. He thought about enjoying her right then, just as he always used to, when she was warm and soft and still pliant. He felt himself begin to swell at the thought of it, the flesh of her buttocks felt cool against his heat – had even begun to push her *camisa* up over her thigh – but it was no good, the pain in his bladder was urgent now, he knew he needed to piss first, before anything else was possible. He stumbled out of bed and went to where the *po* was always kept, behind a screen in one corner of the room. As he did so he trod upon something large and hard.

Constanza woke to the sound of Paul's curse.

'*Cosa?*' She watched him as he came hobbling back from behind the arras on stockinged feet. 'What is it?'

'Nothing, I just trod on something, that's all. Did I drop anything last night?' He climbed back on to the bed and pulled her to him.

'I don't think so, why?'

'I think I just found something that belongs to me.' He started to draw the *camisa* from her shoulder, exposing one of her breasts.

'Paul –'

'Lie, let me look at you,' he commanded her.

She lay for a moment, obediently, gazing at him with thoughtful eyes.

'Where's the glass?' he said, his mouth on her breast. 'The one that used to be on that wall.'

'What? Oh, that,' Constanza shrugged, 'it's being re-gilded, that's all.' There was a pause. 'You can't just walk in like this, you know, and just expect . . . after all this time.'

She pulled away from him and then sat up. The two faced one another. Then suddenly her mood seemed to shift. With one smooth movement she rolled over on to the far side of the bed, laughing at him over one shoulder. 'After all this time, Paul Pindar,' she said, 'aren't you at the very least going to ask after my health?' Against the dark coverlets on the bed her body was voluptuous, golden. On either buttock, he saw, was a small dimple.

'I can see you are perfectly well, Signora Constanza,' he countered. His hands felt pleasingly warm and dry as he traced the dimples with his fingers. 'As well as ever, if I might make so bold.'

She reached up and put her hand tenderly to his cheek.

'Are you quite sure – about this, I mean?'

'This?'

'You know quite well what I mean . . . *la négociation entière.*'

'Just lie. Let me look at you.'

'You know very well you want to do more than just look at me.' She pulled away from him again, and sat up, facing him across the bed, her arms crossed over her breasts.

'You want to know, will I be able to pay you?'

'Well?' Constanza, unabashed, held his gaze.

'Will this do, my lady?' Between his fingers he held up a small round object.

'What's this?'

'A jewel.'

'A jewel?' Constanza became very still. 'What kind of jewel?'

'Open it and see.' Paul placed the stone, which he had wrapped in a piece of cloth, carefully on to her upturned palm. She held it there for a while as though reluctant to touch it.

'Don't worry, it's not going to bite you,' he laughed when he saw Constanza's expression. 'I won it at cards.'

Constanza went pale. 'You didn't? You won it in a card game?'

'Yes.' Paul looked at her, puzzled now.

'*Madonna mia!* I can't believe it.' Carefully she unwrapped the cloth, sat looking at the stone inside, which glowed dark red in the still-dim room. 'Oh –'

'Oh? Is that all you can say?'

'A spinel,' Constanza announced politely.

'Yes, a spinel, and a very fine one too. I don't know why you should find that so very funny.'

'It's just that I thought for one moment, for one extraordinary moment . . .' Constanza put her hand to her throat. 'Oh, never mind.'

'What then?'

'Nothing, nothing, really.' Constanza was still laughing. 'It's just that there has been all this talk of late, you know.'

'Talk of what?'

'Of the great diamond. The Sultan's Blue. The one Zuanne Memmo is giving as a prize in the big card game –' The moment the words were out of her mouth Constanza knew she had made a mistake.

'The Sultan's Blue? The Ottoman Sultan's Blue? Are you sure that's what it's called?'

'Sultan – Shah – I don't know, something beginning with an "s" –' She tried to shrug it off. 'It probably doesn't even exist, just Rialto gossip anyway, you know how it is. But *this* one certainly does.' In an attempt to change the subject Constanza held the red jewel up to catch the light. 'A spinel so it is – and a very pretty one – table cut.' She ran her thumb carefully over the top of the gem. 'Not the finest I've seen,' she said consideringly, 'but by no means the worst either. And I thought Carew said you always lost at cards these days?'

'Well . . .' Paul seemed about to say something, and then thought better of it. 'Let's just say I've been very interested recently in foreign exchange.'

'Bah! Why do you have to talk to me in riddles?'

'It's simple. Our trade is not as certain as it once was, for many reasons. But jewels always keep their value.'

'You'd trade a stake in your precious Levant Company for a jewel?'

'You catch on fast, Signora Constanza. Do you like it?'

'It's beautiful. What a colour, like the finest red wine.'

'I'm going to take it to Prospero later today, he will value it for you more precisely. You remember Prospero Mendoza?'

'The jewel merchant? *Ma certo*, everyone knows him.'

'I'll ask him about that diamond too. He'll know.'

Constanza watched Paul's naked buttocks as he climbed down from her bed and went across to the window – were all Englishmen so very white? She was here with him, he had stayed, he was coming to her now, was going to lie with her the way he always used to, and her heart was singing, singing with joy.

She put the spinel down at last, and with every last ounce of strength tried to compose herself. She knew that this was the moment when she should tell him to forget about the diamond, to warn him about having anything to do with Zuanne Memmo; but now all that mattered to Constanza was that she must not let him see her joy, must never let him know: how she wanted to cry out, to weep at the very sight of him. This was the lesson her mother had taught her, all those years ago, that had been learnt at such cost, but was impossible now to unlearn. Desire for a man, or disgust, whatever you felt for him must never been shown, but must be concealed always; disguised behind the courtesan's mask. On this rested everything.

And so it was for this reason that the one person to whom Paul might have listened, who might have saved him, said nothing. Composing her face instead into a lazy smile, Constanza lay back against the bolsters. 'I accept your spinel with great pleasure.' She patted the mattress beside her. 'Now, *viene*, my darling.' She stretched her arms out behind her head, allowing one beautiful breast to fall naked from her *camisa*, watched him watching her. '*Viene*, Paul, my darling, I think you'll find that I too am very good at trades.'

Chapter Seven

The wedding party was come at last.

Annetta and two of the other choir nuns, Suor Ursia and Suor Francesca, and the *conversa* Eufemia, watched the little flotilla of gondolas as they made their way slowly across the lagoon.

'D'you think that's them?'

'Yes, look, here they come!'

'There are so many of them, it must be!'

The four had taken themselves to one of the top dormitories usually occupied by the *educande*. By placing three benches, one on top of the other, it was just possible to see out of a window set high in the wall, the only ones which gave out on to the outside world. From here, as it was well known amongst the younger nuns of Santa Clara, the most extensive view of the lagoon was to be had, north towards the Giudecca and the City of Venice itself; and most particularly of any boats or gondola approaching the convent.

'Here, get down all of you, let me look now.' Annetta pushed the others away. 'Let me look with this.'

From her pocket she brought out a small cylinder, about the size of a fairground penny whistle, covered in shagreen; shooing the others away she took up her position at the window.

'What is it? What is it tha's got there?' Suor Eufemia, the youngest of them, a child of no more than twelve or thirteen, was hopping from one foot to the other.

'It's called a spyglass, and keep your voice down, can't you? Suor Margaretta will be up here in a trice if she hears us.' Annetta put the cylinder to one eye and squinted through it. At first all she could see was the dazzling refraction of light on the green lagoon waters.

'You've been in Suor Purificacion's room again, haven't you?' whispered Ursia.

'Stolen it, more like,' Francesca said, her plain face taking on a disgruntled expression.

'Not stolen – only borrowed –' slowly Annetta scanned the lagoon horizon '– I'll give it back to old Pure Face tomorr – *oh*!'

'What?'

'It works – I can see them, I really can –'

'Oh, glory! Tha's made me half leap out of my skin.' Suor Eufemia put her hand to her breast. 'Look, my heart is jumping.'

'Let me look, after all she is my niece.' Suor Francesca was tugging at Annetta's gown.

'Have patience, can't you?'

In the tiny circle afforded by the spyglass Annetta could now see a flotilla of boats fluttering festively with coloured ribbons. A group of about twenty people was crowded into them. In one Annetta could see the bride – Francesca's niece, Ottavia, formerly one of the convent's *educande* – and her two maids of honour, easily recognisable by their hair hanging loose down their backs. In the others were the rest of the bridal party, a group of mostly young men and women, accompanying the bride and groom on their wedding visits.

'They're here!' At the sight of them a feeling of excitement gripped Annetta's stomach, but the next minute she almost dropped the spyglass. 'But – oh!'

'What? What's it now?' little Eufemia, one hand still to her chest, piped in her curious high-pitched voice.

'Oh, do be quiet, Eufemia, no one is going to catch us; and will you stop pawing me, Franca.' Annetta gave Francesca an impatient kick. 'You'll get your turn in a moment. It's just – *Madonna!*' She ducked down below the level of the window, flattening herself against the whitewashed wall. 'He's looking right at me –'

'Who is? Who can possibly be looking at you? I thought tha' said –'

' 'Femia! In a moment I'm going to slap your face,' Annetta hissed, 'but no, this is absurd –'

She stood up again and fixed the spyglass to her eye, searching for the little flotilla of gondolas on the lagoon.

The wedding party, in all its finery, was closer now; could be clearly seen from the convent window even with the naked eye.

Annetta fixed the spyglass to her eye again, and this time she could be in no doubt. A man standing towards the back of the very last gondola was holding to his eye a spyglass exactly like her own. He had a thin wiry body, and a shock of unkempt curly hair which hung to his shoulders. How long his spyglass had been trained on the upper dormitory windows she could not tell. Now, still looking in her direction, he lifted his arm and gave a slow wave of his hand. And then, as if now sure of her attention, slowly and deliberately he put his hand between his legs, rolling his hips lasciviously.

Annetta dropped the spyglass as though she had been stung. It fell to the floor with a clatter. She scrambled down from the window. Her face felt hot.

'Why? What is it?' The others crowded round her.

'Nothing, it's nothing . . . I – I – just think I should return the spyglass to Suor Purificacion, that's all,' and with that she fled the room, leaving the other sisters behind her, twittering like sparrows.

The wedding party had been shown into the parlour, where the traditional nuptial-visit refreshments – wine from the convent's own vines, cakes and biscuits made by the nuns themselves – had been laid out. The guests, in a boisterous mood which suggested that this was not their first visit of the day, milled in the hall, eating the cakes and drinking the wine that had been provided for them. The nuns, as they were required by the rules of the convent, sat on their own in a second parlour which was separated from the public parlour by an iron grille. The younger ones, particularly, Suor Francesca and Suor Ursia among them, clustered at the front, calling to the bride, fingering the lace at her neck, the brocaded cloth of her wedding gown. After a little while a door in the wall opposite the nuns' grille opened and a third group, the convent's *educande*, young girls who were not destined to take holy orders but had been sent by their families to board, and to pick up some skills at needlework and cate-chism until a husband could be found for them, came in to join the wedding party. When she saw them the young bride, Ottavia, who until just a few weeks before had been among their number, gave a little shriek, and with much laughing and crying they fell upon each other's necks, hugging and kissing one another, much to the amuse-ment of the assembled company.

Only one of the group seemed reluctant to join in the holiday mood. Annetta sat on her own at the back of the nuns' parlour, a sour expression on her face. She refused both the wine and the cakes that were offered her. After a while Ursia came over.

'May I sit here?'

Annetta shrugged, but slid along the bench she was sitting on to make a space for her.

'What's the matter?' Ursia saw her glum face. 'Did Suor Purificacion catch you putting back the spyglass?'

'Old Pure Face catch me? Never.'

'Something you saw then? Through the spyglass, I mean,' Ursia probed, a little too shrewdly for Annetta's liking.

She thought of the man again, and of where he had put his hand, saw again the strength and curve of his hips.

'That's none of your business?' Annetta stood up and violently shook out some invisible crumbs from her skirts.

Although the light was dim where they were sitting at the back of the nuns' parlour she saw Ursia give her a sharp look, and then turn away. She had a strong face, with high cheekbones, not quite pretty; beautiful lips that turned up at the very edges when she smiled. Annetta wondered what colour her hair was beneath the tight veil. Blondish, perhaps; it was hard to say. Not dark, anyway. She thought briefly about telling Ursia the truth about what she had seen. She sometimes thought she liked Ursia, whose irreverence about convent life and whose sharp wits almost matched her own. There were times when she could almost think of her as a friend, for she had been lonelier than she had imagined here, since her return from the other place. Besides, Annetta was morally certain Ursia would find her story funny rather than shocking. And how she herself would have laughed – would no doubt have almost died laughing – if it had happened to one of the others; but for some reason she could not quite bring herself to confess it.

Eventually, when she could glean no more from Annetta, Ursia drifted off back into the refectory, leaving Annetta to her own thoughts.

He can't possibly have seen my face, can he? She peered out at the wedding guests in the communal hall. *No, that's impossible, I was holding up the spyglass all the time. He must have seen it catch the light, that's all; must have seen the glass flashing.*

44

She tucked the two curls she had so carefully pinched out on to her forehead that morning back beneath her veil, nervously scanning the group again for any sign of the man in the gondola. But no, he was not there. Perhaps she was mistaken, perhaps he was not part of the wedding party after all, perhaps he was on another boat that had just got mixed up with theirs. And with this comforting thought, she gradually regained her composure, grew brave enough to approach the front of the parlour and be with the others again.

At one corner of the communal parlour one of the wedding guests had set up a kind of booth, made of yellow and red striped canvas, where a puppet show was now in progress. Annetta sat down ready to enjoy the spectacle.

And then suddenly she caught her breath. It was him. Yes, it was definitely him, emerging from behind the puppet booth. So that's where he had been skulking! Brown eyes and a surly look – somehow she thought she would know that look anywhere – curly dark brown hair dangling to his shoulders. On his belt was a collection of sharp kitchen knives. It was these that she had seen flashing at his waist. As she watched, he drew away to the back of the crowd, gave a quick glance around the expectant throng, and when he was sure no one was looking slipped silently through the *educandes'* door, into the convent garden behind.

With so many of the nuns fully occupied with the wedding visit, and now the puppet show in the parlour, the garden was quite empty when Annetta reached it.

She had not, of course, been able to follow the intruder through the *educandes'* door: the metal grille separating the nuns' parlour from the visitors' parlour prevented that. Instead, without really stopping to wonder what she would say or do if she ever caught up with him, Annetta had doubled back along the corridor that led to the refectory, and then out through the kitchens, the numerous sculleries and storerooms which all backed on to the convent's vegetable garden.

She had run so fast that when she reached the kitchens she was quite out of breath. Apart from Fat Anna, the scullery maid – deaf, dumb, and so slow-witted that even the puppet show was thought to be beyond her – sitting peeling carrots on one of the steps, until now

Annetta had seen no one. In the courtyard beyond the kitchens she stopped, leant against a water butt to catch her breath.

This was a part of the convent that she hardly ever had cause to visit these days, but it was exactly the same as she remembered it. A gaggle of white geese made small hissing sounds at her as they passed by, and a cat lay licking its fur in the sun, black against the red-brick flagstones. How strange it was: she had almost lived in the kitchens in the old days, when she had been a *conversa*, or a lay nun, and therefore no better than a servant really; but now that she had returned to the convent with her own dowry, and was to be professed, everything had changed. She was every bit as good as those snooty *contessas* now – and certainly as rich.

From the courtyard she made her way cautiously to the vegetable garden beyond and stood there for a moment to get her bearings. It was noon, or thereabouts, and it was hot and silent in the garden. Even the cypress trees around the convent walls cast no shadows. A little way off, to one side of the main bulk of the convent building, she could just see the beginnings of the physic garden, with its neat box hedges, the intricate, symmetrical knots and shapes of the raised beds in which grew the rare and medicinal plants for which the island convent was famed. But it was too easy to be seen there, so she decided to remain in the ornamental part of the garden. She entered the rose garden, the colours of the flowers – red, white and pink – flattened to a silvery haze in the midday heat; then started to walk down an avenue of pleached lime trees. And now a faint humming sound reminded her that she was near the beehives. She started back, hiding herself behind a hedge. Suor Virginia, one of the eldest of their number, was walking among the hives; her back was stooped, and turned towards Annetta, her face hidden by an enormous net. Annetta decided that she was unlikely to be seen by her, and carried on walking cautiously down the avenue.

Although she had only seen him at a distance, and through a spyglass, there was no doubt at all in Annetta's mind that the man she had seen slipping into the garden was the man from the gondola. What did he think he was doing? Annetta thought of him, of the look of him. She thought she knew that look, surly and arrogant at the same time, thinking he could get in among them, and then boast about it to his friends. There were times when she could almost think that they had all been better off at the other place, where from one year to the next they had had no sight of a man at all, unless you counted the ones without *coglioni*, the eunuchs, the gelded men, although some of the girls she had known there fell in love with them all the same.

As she hurried along Annetta grew hotter and hotter. Wisps of hair had come creeping out from beneath her headdress, and she could feel her *camisa* sticking to her back. Apart from Suor Virginia in her beekeeper's hat, there was no sign of anyone in this part of the garden. At the far end, nearest the walls abutting the lagoon, she came to a path between two high hedges; at the end of it she saw a small, overgrown arbour, and in it a stone seat. Feeling almost faint with heat, Annetta sat down gratefully in the green shade. Even through her thick skirts the stone felt cool. From somewhere on the other side of the box hedge she became aware of the sound of water – a fountain or a spring, just out of sight. And it was then that she heard it: the sound of two voices, a man's and a woman's, laughing softly together.

Instantly, Annetta ran back down the path again, lifting her skirts up as she went. She rounded the corner of the hedge, found herself in a circular grotto, in the centre of which was a statue, a thin jet of water cascading from it. But no, she was mistaken, there was no one here. She was just beginning to persuade herself that it was the effects of the heat, when out of the corner of one eye she saw, unmistakably, a flash of something – something coloured – flit past the entrance to the grotto. She ran out again, headed first one way back down the path, then changed her mind and ran the other way round the hedge, only to find herself back at the arbour once more. There was still no sign of anyone.

Annetta went back to the stone seat and sat down heavily. As she did so she felt a hand come round her neck; rough fingers clamping themselves to her mouth. She leapt up at once, or tried to, but it was no good, she was held fast. Even when she tried twisting her head, turning it this way and that to see who her captor was, whoever it was held her easily, keeping always somehow just out of reach, and the more she struggled the tighter their grip on her. Were those his fingers she could feel on her throat?

Not able to move her head, Annetta took her chance and with her right leg delivered a kick as hard as she could to the person standing behind her.

'*Ow!*' The arms let go immediately. Annetta half-stumbled, half-ran, out of the arbour.

'*Suora!*' a voice called out behind her.

'What . . . ?'

'It's me!'

Annetta turned. 'Ursia!'

There was no man, only Suor Ursia, doubled up with laughter.

'What in the name of all the saints possessed you to do that?' Annetta said furiously.

For a moment or two Ursia seemed unable to speak, she was laughing so much. 'It was a joke of course, you should see your face!' Wiping tears from her eyes, Ursia struggled out from behind the stone seat. There were crushed leaves and cobwebs clinging to her robe.

'You think that's funny?' Annetta put her hands to her throat. 'You frightened me half to death.' She slumped down into the shade of the hedge and pulled off her headdress.

'I'm sorry if I frightened you.' Looking rather more contrite, Ursia came and sat down next to her. Annetta's face was scarlet. 'You look hot – are you all right?'

'Yes, I'll be fine, I just need to rest for a moment.' Annetta ran her fingers through her hair; it felt good to get the air to her scalp and the back of her neck. '*Madonna!* I never imagined you would be so strong!'

'And you were struggling like a drowning cat.'

'I thought –'

'What did you think?'

'I thought you were that man.'

'What man?'

'The one from the gondola. He had a spyglass, remember, just like Old Pure Face's.'

'And you thought he was here?'

'I saw him go through the *educandes'* door into the garden, I'm sure I did. And so I followed him.'

'Did you see him?'

'No. I heard him, though, I'm sure of it, a man and a woman's voice talking together. In the little grotto, where the fountain is.' Annetta motioned to the other side of the hedge. 'You were here too, didn't you hear them?'

'Me? No. I was looking for you.' Ursia shrugged. 'I think you must be hearing things – the heat, it does that sometimes.' She patted Annetta's arm. 'Here, look –' she handed Annetta back her head-dress, 'better put this on, the bell for prayers went ages ago, and you know what Old Pure Face will have to say if we're late. Here – shall we go inside?'

Chapter Eight

Annetta knew full well what Suor Purificacion was like. She was to find out again later that day when the under-Abbess sent for her.

'Do you know why I have asked to see you?'

'No, *suora.*'

'No *Reverend Suora.*'

'No . . . Suor Purificacion –'

Annetta kept her eyes fixed upon the small crucifix on the wall just to the right of the nun's head. There was a small pause, and then she added, 'Forgive me, *suora*, but you see I was always given to understand that it was only our most revered Abbess herself who was to be addressed as *reverend* – but perhaps,' she added humbly, 'perhaps I am mistaken?' She lowered her eyes to the floor. 'And if so I do most humbly beg your pardon.'

For a few minutes the older woman said nothing. Annetta heard a soft sibilant sound, a slow inhalation of breath as if she were sucking the air in through her teeth – such teeth as remained in that aristocratic mouth of hers, Annetta thought with satisfaction. When she glanced up, and then away again, quickly, she saw Suor Purificacion's mouth working silently. But no amount of praying, Annetta vowed to herself in that moment, was ever going to help Old Pure Face get the better of her.

For her part Suor Purificacion remained contemplating Annetta in this way for some time. After a while, she got to her feet, walked stiffly round until she was standing behind her. Still she said nothing. The only sound in the room was the silver-topped cane tapping, with some impatience now, on the floor.

'It seems we had an intruder earlier today.'

After the long silence, Annetta almost jumped when Suor Purificacion spoke.

'Oh?'

'In the garden.'

'Oh.'

'This would not have anything to do with you, would it, by any chance, *suora*?'

When Annetta did not reply she added, 'We know he was in the garden – this *monarchino* – because he trampled over one of Suor Annunciata's flower-beds, broke several branches of her best pleached pear tree climbing over the wall. Left us a gift, indeed, of one of his shoes . . .'

A man's leather sandal landed on the flagstones at Annetta's feet.

'*Monarchino*?'

'Yes, I'm sure you've heard the term many times before, *suora*. A man who makes it his pastime to try to have carnal relations with nuns.'

'Oh . . .'

'Do I shock you?' Suor Purificacion's lips arranged themselves in something that might have been a smile. 'Surely not, *suora*. *You* of all people . . .'

As she spoke Annetta felt a movement at her feet. She looked down to see that Suor Purificacion had hooked the silver top of her cane beneath Annetta's robe, and had lifted her skirts a fraction, just enough to reveal the forbidden embroidered slippers. For a moment there was complete silence in the room. Somewhere outside the parlour walls Annetta could hear the bells in some far-distant campanile on the other side of the lagoon strike the hour.

Suor Purificacion walked round until she was facing Annetta again. Her face, tightly framed by her veil, was a perfect oval; her skin, despite her age, was very pale, almost miraculously unlined. She must have been beautiful once, Annetta surprised herself with the thought. The black Spanish eyes were hooded; their strange and heavy lids, so thick and white that she seemed to struggle sometimes to keep them open.

'The . . . *monarchino*, as you call him, was nothing to do with me,' she said at last.

51

'You were seen.'

'Seen where?'

'In the garden.'

'I visit the garden for contemplation and prayer – as we all do.' Annetta flashed her a look. 'I saw no one – no intruder – while I was there. And if anyone says otherwise they are lying.'

There was another long silence.

'It was against my wishes, but you probably know that.'

'I don't understand you. What was against your wishes?'

For the time being, at least, Annetta decided that she would not be goaded.

'To allow you back here on such favourable terms.'

'Favourable terms?'

'You know quite well what I mean. When you first came to this convent you were merely a *conversa*, a servant nun. And now, well, I hear you wish to become professed; a choir nun on a par with those of us here who are ladies of rank, ladies from the best families in all of Venice.' Suor Purificacion's voice sank till it was no more than a whisper. 'You! Who are no better than a common . . .'

'I'm sorry if I offend you, *suora*,' Annetta, who had no desire to hear herself abused, interjected. 'As you surely know, it was the Abbess herself who agreed to it. I do, after all, bring a very considerable dowry, which this convent needs. And the Patriarch himself decided . . .' Annetta searched for the words '. . . well, the Patriarch himself reminded our most revered Abbess that we are all equal in the sight of God.'

'The size of your dowry is quite irrelevant. It is your knowledge of the world, *suora*, that is quite inappropriate –'

'Inappropriate? How so?' Annetta looked up at her with furrowed brows; this conversation had taken a turn that neither of them had expected. 'What else would you have had me do? I was brought up here since I was a child. You know quite well I had nowhere else to go.'

'You break the rule of poverty –'

'In that I do not think that I am alone.' Annetta looked pointedly at Suor Purificacion's silver-topped cane.

'And you lead the other young ones astray – they are quite wild, quite insubordinate since you came back. Even Eufemia, who is but a *conversa*. You lead and they follow.'

52

'But I –'

'Against our rules you keep food and drink in your cell, and they come to sew and read there, all of you together. You sleep through prayers, and gossip together in the chapter. As you know quite well all these things are against the rules of our communal life. Friendship, Suor Annetta, may have been possible in the other place,' and with this she gave a little bow in Annetta's direction, 'but you must realise that here it is not.'

'You would forbid friendship?'

'Friendship with individuals is forbidden, yes of course. If you favour any one or other individual it is always inimical to friendship with the whole; that universal benevolence which is our ideal. Surely you can see that?'

'But our revered Abbess has always –'

Suor Purificacion held up her hand for silence. 'Our Reverend Abbess is old, very old – and not much longer for this world. And when she's gone, I think you will find that many things will change.'

For another long moment the two women stood together in silence. Above her Annetta could see that a small bird, a sparrow, had flown into the room; was crouching down, watching them from one of the blackened rafters.

'So tell me, *suora* –' Suor Purificacion spoke at last, and this time there was just the faintest hint of hesitation in her voice '– what was it like?'

'What was what like?'

'The other place.'

Annetta thought for a moment.

'It was . . . big,' she said after a while.

'Big?'

'Yes, it was big.'

Suor Purificacion's black eyes watched her expressionlessly; then she said, 'What do you mean, big?'

'I mean that there were more of us there, Suor Purificacion. More of us there than here,' she added helpfully.

'I see.'

'And the food.'

'The food?'

'It was different.'

'Different?' In her eagerness to try to elicit information, Suor Purificacion was beginning to sound almost simple-minded. 'How so?'

'Well,' Annetta dug her nails into the palms of her hands to stop herself from laughing, 'it was different from the food we have here –'

'Yes, yes, I see what you are saying,' the under-Abbess interrupted her with an impatient wave of her hand. 'I see that, of course.'

Oh no you don't. You don't see at all, Annetta thought to herself, *although you'd like to, wouldn't you? I think I have a good idea of just what it is that you'd like to see.*

'Anything else?'

'I'm not sure I quite understand you, Suor Purificacion.' Annetta's face was a shining blank. 'What kind of thing was it that you wanted to know?' For the first time Annetta turned her gaze towards her, all innocence. 'What – exactly?'

And all at once she knew she had gone too far. For a moment she had the older nun in her power, but something indefinable had shifted; something that had been just within her grasp had fallen away from her, out of her hands. Closing her eyes as though it pained her to see the girl standing in front of her, Suor Purificacion took a step backwards. 'You will wait here, please, *suora*.'

'But I've been standing here for an hour already, I . . .'

'You will wait here, Suor Annetta,' the older nun cut in, 'for as long as I wish you to.' And with no further explanation she left the room, her cane tapping softly against the stone floor.

With the other younger nuns, the simple ruse of making them stand and wait, in silence, for as long as it pleased Suor Purificacion to keep them there if she wanted a confession, was often enough. *Madonna!* Annetta wanted to stamp her foot with rage. Why, sometimes she even got them to own up to things that they had *not* done. It was a scandal, but Old Pure Face was dreaming if she thought she would ever get anything from Annetta that way. Four years of training as one of the Valide's handmaids had taught her that, at least. Annetta tried not to think too much about the other place these days, but now a memory came to her.

In her mind's eye she saw the Valide again, as she had last seen her. She had been on duty that night, and had gone to the Valide's sleeping chamber to check that all was well, to find her lying on her divan.

Face upwards, eyes open; her hands folded neatly, one on top of the other, across her breast, as though she had been fully prepared for this very moment, had perhaps – Annetta could not help wondering – even willed it. For, to those who knew her, there was nothing within the harem walls that the Valide did not control. Safiye Sultan, the most powerful woman in the Ottoman empire, the mother of God's Shadow Upon Earth, the Ottoman Sultan himself, and the woman whose personal slave Annetta had once been.

They say that the dead look as though they are asleep, but this had not been Annetta's experience. She remembered how she had contemplated the woman lying there; the curious sensation that she was seeing her as if for the first time. There had been a mole on her left earlobe, a light sprinkling of freckles on one cheek, a brown birthmark on her hand – imperfections that Annetta had never noticed before.

When she found her, Safiye had not been dead long, but the skin was already yellowing, the mouth slack, one eye slightly open so that it looked at first as though she were just waking from a long sleep. Annetta could almost hear her voice – *well, what are you waiting for*, caryie? *Bring me my shawl – my coffee – my cat – at once* – but no; strange to think that miraculous voice was now silenced for ever. Her presence, in all their minds, was so strong that when Annetta had finally called the eunuchs, none of them at first could be persuaded to touch her. But for the moment, for one long moment, she had stood there on her own, contemplating the dead queen.

Standing in the convent parlour, Annetta shivered. The Valide, dead! She remembered the profound feeling that this was merely a husk, a shell; all beauty gone, all strength. The body, lying very straight beneath the heavy fur coverlets, was so much more frail in death than it had ever seemed in life, Annetta found it almost shocking; as if the person whom she thought she knew had been simply an illusion. A magician's trick. An act of will. Or, knowing the Valide, perhaps all three.

Her hair, unbound, streamed out around the head, like mermaid's tresses in the strange blue-green light of her sleeping chamber. Annetta had reached out, touched her hand. The skin was soft, but beneath it the flesh was already hard and cold, like a bird's claw. She felt no fear, standing there all on her own, only a kind of curiosity. So this was death. Was that all?

And it was then that Annetta saw it. In the hand beneath the one she had just touched she became aware that the Valide was holding something in her fist. What was it? How strange. She bent down to look more closely. A jewel of some kind – but not just any jewel, a diamond! And not just any diamond. This was a diamond so big that it could not properly fit into the Valide's fist. Annetta's mouth – which had been half-open, on the brink of calling out for help – snapped shut.

The Valide had many jewels, *parures* of exquisite workmanship and beauty – emeralds from the New World, pearls and rubies from Persia and the Indies, great lumps of green turquoise from the mountains of the north, the spoils of her long career as the old Sultan's favourite – but Annetta had never seen anything like this before. For a start, it was a single stone, cut, but not as far as she could see set into any kind of fastening, and was in any case perhaps too big to be worn, even by the Valide.

It was simple curiosity at first that made Annetta reach down and try to pluck it from the dead woman's hand. Just one quick look, she thought to herself, and then I'll put it back. But the dead woman's fingers had closed around the stone so tightly she could not loosen it. The palms of Annetta's hands were sweating now. There were two candles guttering in their holders – the two candles it had been her duty that night to come in and replace – and even in the mysterious flickering light of the little sleeping chamber the diamond seemed to her like a living thing, glittering in the dark. She cocked her head, listening for any unusual sounds, but the silence in the palace was so profound that all Annetta could hear was her own breath catching in her throat, the blood drumming in her ears.

Nothing, no one.

She tried again, pulling at the diamond more roughly this time, trying to shake it loose. Then, when that did not work, she grasped the Valide's fist between her own two hands, and pressed, trying to squeeze the stone out, like a pip out of an orange, but still to no avail. The Valide's hand was closed tight around the diamond as though her life depended on it, and who knew, Annetta thought . . . perhaps it had. Stranger things had happened within the shadowy confines of the harem, as she herself knew only too well.

Annetta began to feel the panic rising in her. The dead Valide, so peaceful when she had first found her, was starting to take on a more sinister mien. Her hair was dishevelled, hanging over her face, and in the tussle her head had somehow become jammed to one side. She was facing Annetta now, the candlelight catching the white of her half-open eye. The skin of her lips and jaw had begun to pull more tightly across her face, so that her teeth were bared slightly, arranging her features into a strange grimace.

By now Annetta could hardly breathe. Her whole body began to sweat. What was she thinking? At any minute someone was going to come, and if they found her like this . . . Well, there was only one thing for it. She knelt down on the floor, and with both hands grasping the Valide's fist as before, she bit down on to the dead woman's fingers, unpeeling them one by one with her teeth. There was a taste of something sweet – some fruit the Valide had eaten, or honey from a pastry, perhaps – and then, at last! Annetta could feel one of the fingers begin to loosen. And then suddenly, sickeningly, a snap.

A piercing, demonic yowl broke the silence of the sleeping chamber, and at the same time the body beneath the fur coverlets began to seethe and thrash violently about. Annetta opened her mouth to scream but her terror was so great that it seemed to knock all the wind from her lungs, and the only sound that came out was a hoarse little gasp, like the squeak of a frightened mouse. And then an all-too-familiar form, something soft and white, came shooting out from beneath the coverlets.

'Cat! You sneaky, mangy, good-for-nothing, verminous little . . .' Annetta made a grab for the Valide's pet, but it streaked past her, just out of reach, and disappeared into the night.

The cat's yowls had been heard. Annetta could hear the sound of some of the women approaching the Valide's antechamber, guessed that they would hesitate, but only for a few moments, outside the door. Swiftly, she plucked the diamond from the Valide's now opened fist, rearranged her arms, one on top of the other, so they were resting on her breast as before, the hand with the broken finger carefully concealed beneath the other, and slipped the stolen jewel into her pocket, where it lay, heavy as a stone in a drowning sack.

Chapter Nine

That night, in the dead hours sometime before prime, Annetta became aware of someone shaking her awake.

'What –? Who's that?'

'Tha's been talking in tha' sleep, *suora*.'

'Eufemia, what are you doing here?'

Even in her half-dream state, Annetta recognised the distinctly musty, unwashed smell of the little *conversa*. Eufemia's clothes, unlike Annetta's own finery, right down to her body linen, came from the infrequently cleansed communal wardrobe.

'Tha' mun be having that dream again.' Eufemia's thick, working dialect was unmistakable. 'Here, let me in.' Without waiting for an invitation, she climbed over Annetta and under the covers, lying with her back to the wall so that they lay cupped together like two spoons in a box. In the darkness Annetta could just make out the silhouette of her uncovered head. Eufemia's dark hair, which had once been closely cropped, was growing out in feathery clumps, giving her, Annetta sometimes thought, the comical air of a baby bird.

In accordance with the convent rule, the door of Annetta's cell, like those of all the choir nuns, had been left ajar. No locks were allowed, and the corridor outside was always lit, with candles burning throughout the night. Suor Virginia, one of the *discrete*, the oldest and most venerable of the convent's number, had been given the duty of patrolling the cells every hour to make sure that nothing untoward was happening amongst the youngest nuns, but by the second hour after sunset she was usually so sound asleep that, as Ursia liked to say, she would have slept through Judgment Day itself, quite drunk on the barrel of wine that she kept in her cell.

'Were it that dream again?'

'I don't know.' Annetta could feel Eufemia stroking her hair. 'I suppose it was.'

'Can't tha' remember?'

'No, I can never remember. I just wake with this . . . feeling.'

'What kind of feeling?'

'I don't know . . .' Gazing into the darkness, Annetta searched for the right words to describe the desolation that she was feeling, something that she could not put a name to, something dark and black pressing down on her. 'It's as if I've . . . lost something, something that I'll never find again.'

'It's over now, don' tha' think about it no more.'

'You're right, I must try not to.' Annetta could feel the warmth of Eufemia's small body gradually begin to seep into her own. 'It was probably that pudding we had last night, enough to give anyone bad dreams.'

'I gave mine to Suo' Caterina, tha' knows how she likes sweet things.'

'And I gave mine to Suor Margaretta's cat, although Lord knows it's fat enough already.' Annetta smiled. 'Don't stop doing that, it's nice.' She stretched a little, searched for a more comfortable position on the thin convent mattress.

Gradually, as her eyes became accustomed to the darkness, the familiar contours of her room began to take form. Annetta's cell, which she had secured with her dowry money on her return from Constantinople, was in fact two rooms knocked into one at the far end of the dormitory corridor, and the largest in the convent apart from the Abbess's own. The walls were plainly whitewashed, the rafters of the ceiling high and black, but apart from these communal features it bore little resemblance to an ordinary cell. Against the walls were pushed two painted *cassoni* in which she kept her clothes; in the corner a tall wooden cabinet in which – it was true – she kept plates and knives and jugs, and all her own supplies of food and drink. At the window her sparrow was asleep in its little cage.

'Were it so very different there – the other place – from here, I mean?' Eufemia asked hesitantly after a while.

Annetta thought for a moment. Ever since she had come back to Venice she had managed to preserve an almost total silence about her experiences in the harem. At first it had not been intentional. The shock of being back in the convent again – for all that it had been her choice to return – had made it difficult at first to speak about it at all; but gradually she became aware that the air of mystery that her silence lent her was something she could exploit. But now – perhaps it was the dream, perhaps it was because at lonely moments such as these the little servant nun seemed to be the closest thing she had to a friend – the urge to confide was suddenly overwhelming.

'You know,' she found herself saying, 'when I was in the Ottoman Sultan's harem for all those years – four years in all – there was someone there who reminded me of you –'

'Who were she?'

'Oh –' Annetta gave a sigh, and her voice sounded sad '– an English girl. They used to call her Kaya, but it wasn't her real name.'

From the corridor outside, where some of the nuns kept the hen coops which produced their own personal supplies of eggs, came the occasional disgruntled cluck.

'You know, it's strange, but when I was a *conversa* like you, sleeping in those little rooms behind the kitchens, I used to think that the choir nuns were all so grand living up here, but now –' Annetta smiled to herself '– but now, with all these chickens everywhere, it feels more like living in a barnyard.'

'*Shh!*' Eufemia put her finger to her lips. 'Old Suo' Virginia will hear tha'.'

'Suor Virginia? Not she! Why, I sometimes think you can do anything here.'

'Tha' told me once that there was more rules in the other place.'

'Oh, yes, many more rules. Why, you couldn't even speak in the presence of the Sultan without permission. Nor even sometimes in the presence of his mother, either. And there were guards everywhere.'

'The gelded men?'

'The eunuchs, yes. Black ones as well as white,' Annetta said, knowing full well how much Eufemia would like to hear about them.

'Black men, and gelded!' Annetta could feel the girl give a shiver of fascination. 'What was they like?' she breathed into the darkness.

'Men without *coglioni*?' Annetta gave a derisive snort. 'Fat mostly, as if their chests had dropped down into their bellies. Ugh! And they had this strange way of speaking,' she piped, in falsetto voice. 'But for all that, some of the girls liked them,' she added. 'Would fall in love with them sometimes. One girl I knew even married one, after she left the harem.'

'Left the harem? But tha' were all captives, weren't tha'?'

'Yes, that's true. But girls left the harem all the time. If they didn't get on well in their work, or if they were never likely to be in the Sultan's eye, they were let go. Besides, what do you think happened to me? I didn't exactly jump over the harem wall, you know.' Annetta smiled. 'We were all slaves, it's true; Christian girls, each and every one of us. Each of us had our story of how we came to be there. As for me and my friend Kaya, we were taken by corsairs when they attacked our boat in the Adriatic. I was with some of the other nuns from Santa Clara, we were on our way to our sister convent in Ragusa – you probably heard about it?' She felt Eufemia nod, wrap her arms around her a little more tightly. 'We'd been given passage on this English boat, a merchantman, whose captain had agreed to stop in there on his way to Constantinople. When Turks attacked us they threw the other sisters overboard. The ship had hit some rocks and was going down anyway – so they couldn't have taken all of us, even if they'd wanted to, and by then the captain and his men were mostly dead –' Annetta's voice was matter-of-fact – 'but they took Kaya and me, and eventually we ended up in the House of Felicity.'

'A slave amongst them infidels! Our Lady preserve us! It would have been better if tha'd been drowned too!' Eufemia's pious words were somewhat betrayed by the crackle of excitement in her voice.

'Better off dead! What nonsense! Better off than as a *conversa*, I can tell you.'

'*Suo*'!'

'Well it's true. Or even a choir nun, for all our privileges. There were some women who chose that life; chose to be sold into slavery in the hope of ending up in some rich man's harem. Better than a life in the fields. And how many of us, after all, might not say the same?'

'So how did tha' escape?'

'I didn't have to escape, you silly. When the Valide died, we were all set free, all of us who were her personal slaves that is –'

'The Valide?'

'The Sultan's mother.'

'I see – and then what?'

'Well, some women chose to stay, others were given dowries, and married off. Any woman who had been trained up in the House of Felicity was considered a special catch, you know.'

'*Suo*'!' Eufemia giggled. 'And tha' wouldn't have liked a husband for tha'self?'

'What, are you mad?' Annetta's voice was withering. 'Some paunchy old pasha to service? Not me! When I was very young my mother tried to sell me to a fat old man – little girls' maidenheads were what he liked, the disgusting old goat.' Annetta had the satisfaction of feeling Eufemia, still lying behind her, shudder with horror, so she went on, slightly intoxicated now by her own narrative.

'I was only ten, 'Femia. Just a little child, younger than you. But old enough. I swore to myself then that I would never have anything to do with any man, not ever again.'

'What did tha' do?'

'What did I do? *Ha!* I bit him so hard I swear he'll never have tried to touch young *culo* ever again.' Behind her she could feel Eufemia quivering with laughter. 'I told Kaya once that if the Sultan ever laid a finger on me I'd do the same to him. *Madonna!* I remember how angry she was with me when I said that. She said one day my tongue would get us both killed . . .' Annetta broke off.

Eufemia waited for her to go on, and when she did not she nudged her gently.

'And tha' friend?' she prompted. 'What happened to her? To tha' friend Kaya, I mean?'

For a moment or two Annetta said nothing, then, in a muffled voice, she answered grumpily, 'Kaya? I don't want to talk about her, understand?' and Eufemia was left wondering what it was that she had said to offend her.

Annetta lay so still that Eufemia thought she had gone back to sleep, but Annetta was very much awake, her eyes wide open, staring into the darkness.

What had happened to Kaya? Not a day went by, not an hour, when she did not wonder the same. In the end she had given everything to save her friend, even her most valuable possession.

A single tear rolled down Annetta's cheek. There was only one question that remained, one question to which she knew she might never learn the answer: had the Valide's diamond been enough to save Celia Lamprey?

62

Chapter Ten

Annetta and Eufemia were still lying there, side by side, when they heard the noise.

For a moment or two they both kept very still, listening.

'What were that?' Eufemia whispered eventually.

'*Shh!* I don't know.'

'Listen! There it is again.'

A sound like a small sigh came from somewhere at the other end of the dormitory corridor.

'*Madonna!* It's Suo' Virginia! Or worse, Suo' Purificacion . . . ! What will they do if they catch me in here . . . Quick, let me hide in one of your *cassoni*.' Eufemia was half out of the bed in her panic not to be caught, but Annetta, putting her finger to her lips, held her back.

No, she mouthed the words absolutely silently, *wait*. And signalling Eufemia to hide under the coverlets, she got out of bed and slipped silently into the corridor.

Outside her cell door the candles were guttering, burnt down almost to the wick. At the end of the corridor, closest to her own door, she could make out the form of the chicken coops, smell the familiar acrid smell. It occurred to her that what they had heard was probably only one of the chickens, and she was just about to turn and go back to bed when she heard the same sound again: only lower this time, not so much a sigh as a grunt.

Silently, on naked feet, Annetta made her way down the corridor, peering left and right into each of the nuns' cells. Each woman was lying face up, arms along their sides and over the coverlets; in each a cropped head lay upon a straw-filled bolster. A faint odour of stale wine came from old Suor Virginia's cell, but apart from this, Annetta saw that all was well, all was as it should be.

Even so, she could not account for a faint feeling of unease. Perhaps it was the lingering effects of her dream, but there was a strange quality to the silence in the dormitory that night. It was *too* silent, *too* still. The nuns all went to sleep in the same position – the correct position as strictly prescribed by their order – but no one ever stayed that way. Tonight, they looked like marble statues on the top of tombs, as though they had not so much as moved a muscle the whole night through. Did not Suor Virginia always snore? She was famous for it: it was a well-worn joke amongst the younger nuns, but tonight there was not even the faintest fibrillation coming from her cell. Annetta padded silently back and listened again. But there was nothing.

And it was then that she heard it for the third time. Unmistakable now: first a sigh, then a grunt, then another, slightly louder sigh. An at once Annetta realised where the sound was coming from: not from the dormitory at all, but from one of the cells that stood a little apart from the rest. This cell, which was usually kept for the convent's rare visitors, was positioned on a half-landing at the top of the stairs. Annetta crept silently down the three stairs, found the cell door open a crack, and peered cautiously inside.

The room was small and whitewashed. It had no windows, and was bare of decoration other than a plain wooden crucifix hanging on one wall. Most of the space was taken up by a narrow truckle bed. Lying face down on it, her head jammed at an awkward angle up against the bolster, her hands gripping the bed-head as though to steady herself, was the figure of a woman. It was from her that the sound was coming: a kind of whimpering.

Her naked buttocks, round and pale, were raised in the air, while behind her, naked from the waist down, stood the figure of a man. His hips were thrust forwards, his hands gripping the tops of her thighs so that the soft flesh spilled through his fingers like butter. Since he was positioned sideways to the door, Annetta felt rather than saw the expression on his face: a look of such intensity it would have taken ten men to pull him off her at that moment. As he moved, slowly at first, then gradually increasing in pace, the whimpering from the woman increased. Not a sound of pain after all; but the sound of pleasure. At first, as if watching himself, his face was looking down over the woman's naked back, but after a few moments he threw his head back suddenly, turned his face to the ceiling and out of his mouth came a small sob.

Annetta drew back into the shadows behind the door; leaning heavily against the wall. Could that woman she had just seen coupling like an animal possibly be one of the nuns? *Santissima Madonna!* Annetta's hand flew to her mouth, and found that she was smiling. But it was! She did not know what to think. The scene she had just witnessed was ... absolutely scandalous, of course. She waited for a suitably pious sensation of outrage to overcome her but found, to her surprise, that it did not; found, in fact, that she was more curious than shocked. Never one to obey the rules herself, Annetta had little use for moralising. There were other questions that were far more interesting. Which of the nuns was so reckless, so desperate, as to take a lover right under their noses? That was the question; that and how she might put this knowledge to good use. Annetta had not spent four years as the Valide's handmaid for nothing.

Still hiding behind the door of the little cell, she could now hear whispered voices: the woman's barely audible, his a little louder. She struggled to make out the words, but could not; only his tone, and was surprised to find that it was reassuring, tender even. Then, without warning, the door was opened quickly and the man came out, and ran silently down the stairs.

Had he seen her? No, it was impossible. It was still so dark, and he would not have expected anyone to be hiding behind the door. Annetta hesitated. Her heart was beating so hard she could almost hear it. But in the dormitory, so far as she could tell, there was utter silence still: not a sound, not a sign of life. Finding out who the nun was would be easy enough: not for a moment did Annetta doubt her ability to winkle the offender out. But her lover? If she were to have any chance at all of finding out who he was, she knew she had to act quickly. Annetta ran silently down the stairs after him.

At the bottom of the stairs a corridor led off in two directions, one towards the refectory and the kitchens, the other towards the two parlours and the main entrance gates to the convent. Annetta headed first in the direction of the two parlours, and beyond them, across the courtyard, to the gatehouse. This was the most obvious and the easiest route by which a stranger would be able to find his way into the convent. If he had been able to bribe the gatekeeper to leave the door unlocked nothing could be easier. Annetta arrived there with a pain in her side – and saw at once that the great metal studded gate, with its elaborate system of brass locks, was firmly shut and bolted.

Without giving herself time to catch her breath, she turned and began to run again, back the way she had come. She sprinted across the courtyard, through the grilled gateway separating the nuns' from the visitors' parlour, then turned right down the corridor towards the refectory and, beyond it, the kitchens. She knew now for sure how he had found his way in: through the garden, of course! Just like the other one. Why hadn't she thought of it immediately? At the entrance to the kitchens she paused. And there, sure enough, the door out into the kitchen courtyard was standing ajar.

She ran out into the night.

Except it was no longer night. The first thing Annetta noticed was that the sky was now several shades lighter than it had been when she had at first gone to investigate the strange noises. The row of poplar trees that lined one of the convent's perimeters, and which she could see from her cell, stood like black paper cut-outs against a sky that was no longer black, nor even dark blue, but distinctly pearly and grey. Annetta shivered, and sniffed the chill air.

It smelt sweet, of damp earth and bitter herbs. From somewhere amongst the trees a solitary bird began to pipe its morning song.

Annetta had never been in the garden at dawn before. Usually the bell for prime rang in the very early hours of the morning summoning the nuns to the first prayers of the day, after which those who had been bothered to get out of bed often found good reasons to return there (Sister Virginia was notoriously lenient, and almost any pretext – *Suora, I have a headache*, or *Suora, I have my courses* – would satisfy her). There had been a heavy dew in the night and droplets of water, white as frost, clung to every leaf, every flower, every blade of grass, transforming the convent's famed botanical garden into something quite other, a strange, dream-like place fit more for fairies or sprites than for ordinary mortals.

She began to walk, slowly this time, taking it all in, so entranced by the beauty of the silent garden that she barely noticed the fact that her bare feet were numb, or that the hem of her linen nightshift was already wet. Like a lonely ghost, Annetta flittered on. She passed the avenue of pleached lime trees, the box hedges of the herb garden. At the end of this avenue she found herself at the carp pond.

Faint skeins of mist hung motionless over the dark green water. At the centre there was a fountain in the shape of a small boy holding an upturned amphora, his body covered with moss. A barely perceptible stream of water came from the open top of the amphora, fell with a small bubbling sound into the pond below.

It was almost light now. The sky, reflecting the distant lagoon, was so soft it seemed almost colourless. The garden was stirring. More birds had joined their shrill voices to the lone piper in the trees. Annetta sat down on the side of the pond. What was she doing, running around the garden for a second time? It was as though a kind of madness had possessed her. She looked down into the water, trying to make out the black forms of the carp which hung there, motionless in the weed below; instead she saw the reflection of another face, the reflection of a man standing just behind her.

Annetta leapt up so suddenly she almost fell into the water.

'You!'

Instinctively, she threw her arm out to steady herself, but as she did so he caught her wrist and before she knew it he was holding her to him, pinning her arms to her sides with one hand, his other hand over her mouth.

'*You?*' he repeated after her, his breath in her ear; and then, mockingly, 'Why, *suora*, have we met before?'

Of course not, she wanted to say, but I know you all the same. You are the *monarchino*, the man with the spyglass, but it was no use, she could not make a sound. Annetta struggled to free herself, but the harder she tried the tighter his grip. She bit at the fingers covering her mouth, but his hand was clamped over her jaw so fiercely that she could not get her jaw open wide enough. For a moment they wrestled together in silence. And then, just as suddenly as he had caught her, he let her go. Annetta fell forwards on to the wet grass, a faint metallic taste of blood in her mouth.

'What did you do that for? You made me cut my lip.' She glanced up at him, and then quickly away. Yes, there was no doubt: it was he. The same dishevelled locks, the same insolent demeanour. From the clothes he was wearing, sober but of good quality, and especially from the knives she could see sheathed on to a leather strap at his waist, she guessed he must work in the household of some noble or rich merchant family living in Venice itself.

'Well, aren't you going to help me up?' she said after a while. But Carew, naturally, had no intention of helping her. He stood looking down at the dark-haired woman at his feet, her nightshift now covered with dirt and damp, apparently quite unfazed either by being seen by her, or by the necessity – surely quite urgent now – of escaping from the garden before anyone else should discover them.

'No,' he continued to stare at her, his eyes hard as stones, 'why should I help you when you've been spying on me.'

Annetta spat, as hard as she could, in his direction; saw, with satisfaction, a pinkish-coloured gobbet land on his shoe.

Carew looked at her levelly; he seemed neither dismayed nor amused by her action. Then he slowly wagged his head from side to side as if reproving a naughty child; *tsk, tsk*, he made a small sound with his tongue against his teeth.

'But, wait a moment, of course I *do* know you, don't I? You were the one who came chasing after me last time. Quite the little busybody, aren't you, *suora*? Or do you fancy a nice bit of *monarchino* yourself?' He saw the look on Annetta's face. 'Ah-ah! I see that I've found you out, you've got the itch, just like the other one. We-e-ll, let's see . . .' He looked around the still-deserted garden consideringly, and then back at her again. '*Hmm*, just as I thought, no one about,' he said cheerfully, 'no one at all. How about it? You can get up now if you like.'

He put his hand out to her at last as if to pull her up, but Annetta shied away from him. 'Get away from me, *stronzo*! Don't you dare touch me.'

'I'm not asking you,' Carew said, 'I'm telling you,' and with the same quickness as before he grasped her wrist and pulled her to her feet. Suddenly Annetta found that he was holding her in his arms, pressing her wet body up against his, his mouth against her ear.

'I'd be happy to oblige you right now,' he whispered, 'if you like.'

'No!' Annetta's eyes were smarting with rage.

'But isn't that what you want?' He was rocking her now, to and fro, to and fro, so that she could feel his hips knocking oh-so-delicately, first one then the other, against her body. 'I know that's the real reason you followed me here.' He was so close to her that she could feel his breath against her neck, feel his lips brush the soft skin just below her ear.

'No!'

There was a pause, as though he were considering something. 'All right, then, this time I'll let you off,' he said, still holding her fast against him, 'but in return I want you to promise me something.'

'Promise what?'

'Promise you won't tell anyone what you saw last night.'

Annetta considered her options; she felt she would rather have her head boiled in oil than promise anything to this man, but pragmatism soon got the better of her. Of course she would promise him anything he liked, the stupid fool. And as soon as she got safely away from him she would tell everyone, but *everyone*, what she had seen, scream it from the convent rooftops if necessary.

'All right, I won't,' she answered him meekly, 'I promise I won't tell anyone what I saw –' but immediately the words were out of her mouth she knew that she had fallen into his trap.

'*Ah!* So you did see something!'

Stronzo! She detected a change in his tone of voice: could it be that he was smiling, or worse, actually laughing at her?

'You're wrong, I didn't see anything, not really!' Annetta was floundering now, but she knew it was no good.

'Oh, yes you did. Describe to me what you saw.'

'*What?*'

'It's not hard to understand. I said, describe to me what you saw.'

'No!'

'Oh go on. Which bit did you like best? Was it just a bit of kissing, or . . . something a bit more exciting? She's very eager to please, that little nun, but then you usually are, you know.'

'*Stronzo, stronzo, stronzo!*'

'Language, please!' Carew was really laughing now. 'Well, I'd wager that *you* haven't been a nun all your life. Which particular gutter did they pluck you from, I wonder?' Loosening his grip on her at last, Carew held Annetta out at arm's length, looking at her with an expression of distaste.

At that moment, the sound of a bell being rung, rather inexpertly, came from somewhere in the convent buildings. 'Oh, well, I imagine I'll never know the answer to that now, will I?' he said cheerfully.

And then, just as suddenly he had appeared, he was gone from her, running swiftly towards the far end of the garden and out of view.

Chapter Eleven

Her bare feet raw and red with cold, her shift wet through and covered in leaves and grass stains, a dishevelled Annetta made her way slowly back inside.

She heard the ringing bell with dread: it was not the sound of the regular summons to chapel. Had they noticed her absence, she wondered, and felt her stomach lurch. Judging by the sight of the sun just now coming up over the garden wall, she realised that she had not only missed prime, but quite possibly even matins too. In the past she had always been able to talk her way out of all-too-frequent absences from chapel, but even Annetta, usually so quick-witted and resourceful, was somewhat quailed by the prospect of finding a plausible explanation of how she came to be wandering about in the garden, in wringing wet nightclothes, and at this hour in the morning.

But when she did finally creep in through the kitchen court-yard it was to find the entire convent in an uproar. Nuns with their headdresses awry were running backwards and forwards along the corridor as if a swarm of hornets had been set loose among them. When she reached the staircase up to the younger nuns' dormitories she met Suor Purificacion coming down the stairs towards her. She at least was fully dressed, Annetta noted. Her first instinct was to turn and run in the opposite direction, but it was too late: there were already others coming up the stairs behind her; she was well and truly trapped. Annetta gave herself up to her inevitable fate. But, no. To her amazement, Suor Purificacion seemed barely to register Annetta's presence, let alone her extraordinary and dishevelled state. She looked at her, and then through her, almost blankly, but said nothing, merely walked on past in the direction of the nuns' parlour, her silver-topped stick tapping on the flagstones.

Back in the dormitory she found Ursia in her cell wrestling with her headdress.

'What's going on?'

'What do you mean, what's going on? We've overslept, that's what.' Ursia gave an enormous yawn. 'Can't you see how late it is? Here, can you help me with this, I'm all thumbs today.'

'Overslept? What, everyone?'

'Seems like it. You're one to talk, look at you still in your night things. Can't you hear the bell?' Ursia sat back down on her bed with her back to Annetta. 'Oh, what's wrong with me?' she lamented. 'I tell you, for two pins I'd go straight back to sleep.'

Annetta helped Ursia as quickly as she could with her headdress, then ran back to her own cell at the far end of the dormitory and closed the door. She was shivering as she stripped off her wet night-shift and pulled on a dry one. From one of her chests she took out a pile of shawls, and finally a sable rug, one of her most prized dowry possessions, and wrapping them round her, climbed into bed. She had only been there a few moments when another thought occurred to her. She got out of bed again and, sitting down on the floor, placed her feet up against the end of one of the heavy wooden *cassoni*, pushing it with her legs until it was blocking the doorway. Then, still shivering, she climbed into bed again, where she could think at last.

Even with the sable rug on top of her, she still felt cold.

Who was the man in the garden? There was no doubt that he was the same man she had seen through the spyglass the afternoon of the wedding visit; she had tried to follow him into the garden then, and he had left his shoe behind in a flower-bed.

The *monarchino*, as Suor Purificacion had described him. Annetta had pretended to Suor Purificacion that she did not understand the term, but that was not strictly true. She had of course often heard talk of these men among the other nuns. There were always stories, lots of stories. Men who thought it good sport to try to – how had Suor Purificacion put it exactly? – have carnal relations with nuns. And the good Lord knew that in this city of convents – nearly half the women in Venice, it was sometimes said, were confined behind convent walls – there would always be enough of them willing to take the risk.

Carnal relations. Well, she reflected, whoever he was he had certainly managed that. In her mind's eye she could see the two figures, as if in a tableau, in their peculiar geometries, their colours. The pale flanks of the woman, like two moons raised to her lover. The look of extraordinary intensity on the man's face; the way his head had fallen back, and that sound, like a little sob, more of grief than of ecstasy.

It was – she could hardly believe that she thought this – it was, well, beautiful.

But then came other thoughts that troubled her far more. She had set out to follow him, but in fact it was he who had followed and lain in wait for her. Over and over she played the scene in her mind: remembered his face looking over her shoulder in the carp pond, the moment he had caught at her wrist, the easy strength with which he had overpowered her. At the thought of it, such violent emotion consumed her that the tears sprang into her eyes.

Why had she not struggled harder?

But that had been impossible. Hadn't it?

At some point she must have slept, because when she next became aware it was past midday, judging by the strength of the sun shining into her cell, and there was someone banging on her door.

'*Suora . . . suora?*' She could hear the querelous and slightly reedy voice of old Suor Virginia, and then the dull sound of her cell door knocking against the wooden chest. 'What's happening? Are you indisposed? You must come out now, you know, you must . . .'

But Annetta had no intention of opening her door just yet, and when she did not reply the old nun soon gave up, as Annetta knew she would, and she could hear her shuffling footsteps receding down the whitewashed corridor outside.

Annetta continued to lie where she was, staring at the ceiling. She did not think she could get up even if she wanted to. She needed more time to think, more time to assimilate what she had seen and heard – and not done. Did the fact that she had not immediately raised the alarm, but rather followed the intruder back into the garden, conversed with him there, albeit against her will – but even then not raise the alarm; did that not make her complicit in some way?

It was only by the purest good fortune that the convent had been in such disarray that morning, and that her dishevelled return had not been noticed – or had it? How could she be sure? Suor Purificacion had seemed to look straight through her, as though she, like Ursia, had been still half-asleep, but that did not mean that every other nun had been similarly unvigilant. And besides, there was at least one of their number who would surely come to know the part she, Annetta, had played that night: the *monarchino*'s lover, whoever she was.

At that moment there was another loud banging sound at her door. 'Suor Annetta?' This time it was the stern Spanish-accented tones of Suor Purificacion. 'Suor Virginia says that you are unwell.'

There was a pause while Annetta, lying silently in her bed, wondered what to do.

'Open this door at once, you know it is against the rules for any sister to lock her cell door.'

'We are anxious about you, *suora*,' Suor Virginia's bird-like vernacular chimed in.

Anxious? No, you are not, you are a couple of intefering old busybodies, and I am not listening to you. She would stay silent as a fish. Rolling over, Annetta turned her face to the wall and pulled the sable rug over her head.

It was dark under the coverlets and the fur of the rug tickled her nose, but for the first time she began to feel warm. Vaguely, in the background, she could hear the sound of her cell door being rattled against the wooden chest again, but she did not care. They could go hang, the whole lot of them, so far as she was concerned.

Shutting out the sound of their voices, the rattling and banging at her cell door, Annetta turned her thoughts to the intruder again. Why was it so hard to get the memory of the *monarchino* out of her head? It had been startling, the feel of a man's body. His flesh had been absolutely spare, not an ounce of fat anywhere. How curious it was, she thought – how very strange – how troubling – the touch of a man after all these years – almost her whole lifetime, now she came to thinking about it – living among women.

As she had told Eufemia just the night before, Annetta had sworn to herself that she would never have any use for a man. She remembered her mother's client, an old man with a paunch; remembered the way he smelt. *Faugh!* No amount of pomade could disguise the

73

decaying odour of rotting teeth and sour skin. She remembered his fumbling hands and quickness of breath, how he had pinched her little nipples beneath her chemise, tried to force his hardness into her secret place. The thought of him, even now, made her gag.

But this – this had been different. Annetta could not explain it. It really was the strangest thing, she found herself musing, that she had not been frightened of him at all. Even when he had held her against her will, he had made her angry, but not afraid. In some part of herself she allowed herself to feel once more his breath against her neck, the feel of his lips in her hair, his smell, the hardness of his body against hers.

And yet, and yet. Straight away a more troubling thought took its place. The way he had laughed at her as if she were of no account. And then the look in his eye: was it really disgust that she had seen there? Annetta felt her toes curl with mortification. He had depised her. She could feel the rage rising in her again, until she was almost writhing with fury against this man, this intruder. She should be the one despising *him*, a common *monarchino*, no better than a servant, judging by his clothes, and – remembering the way he had talked – a foreign one at that.

Her mind, which had been opened a crack, sprang shut again like a trap.

Chapter Twelve

Prospero Mendoza's workshop was on the top floor of a seven-storeyed house in the Jewish ghetto, a tiny slip of a room barely bigger than a ship's cabin. Paul was usually accompanied by Carew on these occasions; but Carew had not been seen since the night at Constanza's *palazzo*, and so, with the spinel he had won at cards in his pocket, he had walked there, alone, across the canals.

Although it was two hours after sunset, and the ghetto was already closed for the night, Paul was well known to the watchmen and a few coins easily secured him entry. Climbing the narrow stairs to Prospero's little eyrie at the top of the building, Paul gave the prearranged knock – four short raps, followed by two longer ones – pushed the door open and went in.

Despite the lateness of the hour, he found the old man at his workbench: a jeweller's loupe was fixed into one eye, and his long beard, which when standing fell almost to his knees, was flung over one shoulder. Prospero did not look up when Paul came in, but carried on squinting at the gemstone he was holding.

'So, English, what can I do for you?'

'And good evening to you too, my friend –?'

'Friend? Since when was I your friend?' Prospero took a length of gold wire from the workbench beside him and, pulling out a measure, snipped off a piece with a pair of tiny scissors. 'You come here, just like everyone else, for a purpose, to buy and sell your jewels, am I right? You are no friend of mine,' he looked up at Paul, one eye twinkling through the loupe, 'and let no one say otherwise.'

'If you insist.' Paul smiled at the tiny man, who with his long beard and beady eyes seemed like some creature from the underworld.

'So, then, English,' Prospero went on in a milder vein, 'what have you got for me today?'

Paul took the red stone from his pocket and put it down in front of the jeweller.

'Very well, I'll look at it later if you like.' Prospero jerked his chin in the direction of the curtain which hung across the entrance to a second room. 'You're late, he's waiting for you in there.'

Paul pushed aside the curtain and stepped into the room leading off the workshop. At the window was a man standing with his back to him: short, barrel-chested, resplendent in an egg-yolk yellow turban. Paul took in the oriental robes, the extraordinary nose the size of two tulip bulbs nestling unapologetically in the middle of his face. Ambrose Jones.

'Well, well, Ambrose.'

'Ah, there you are, Pindar. It's not like you to keep a man waiting.'

The two men regarded one another across the room.

'That's a nasty swelling you've got there,' Ambrose said at last. 'Here let me look at it. Is it broken?'

'No,' Paul fingered his still-tender nose, 'just bruised.'

'You play the part well,' Ambrose took in the pallor of Paul's skin, the shadows underneath his eyes, 'a little too well, if you want my opinion.'

'I could say the same thing of you.'

'You are too kind, sirrah.'

There was an uncomfortable pause.

'I gather I am a disgrace to the Honourable Company.'

'Alas, it was the best I could do at such short notice,' Ambrose said drily, 'although I have to confess, I'm quite impressed by your John Carew; it must have been quite a job of work to bring that little scene about. Inventive.'

'Inventive!' Paul said bitterly. 'Carew goes too far, as usual. I'm done with him.'

'He has no idea then, I surmise, of the real state of our affairs?'

'He has no idea you are a Levant Company intelligencer, if that's what you mean. Or that I've known you as long as I've known Parvish.'

'But of the rest – he knows nothing?'

'Nothing at all.'

76

'You are quite sure about that?'

'He knows something of the Levant Company's most recent troubles, it's true. But he knows nothing about you. He thinks you are merely one of Parvish's factors – a collector for his cabinet of curiosities. He does not know that you are also here to meet me, and at my request, on secret Levant Company business. How could he? His little game would not have worked otherwise.'

'Really? It might have worked even better.'

'No, with Carew the element of surprise is usually part of it, you can depend on that.'

'But you are angry.' Paul could feel Ambrose's small blue eyes boring into him '. . . very angry with him. Why so?'

'Do you have to ask? He sent you a message, telling you to meet me at Constanza's house, when he knew full well –'

'When he knew full well what?'

'– that those nights can be very long ones.'

'Oh, so that's what it's called, is it? A long night. Very pretty. In my day it was called being in your cups.'

'That's not the point; you know that perfectly well. Carew is a conniving, treacherous little –'

'But my good Pindar,' Ambrose interrupted him, 'you have made him believe you are on the point of ruin! How is he to know that you are merely, how shall we put it –?'

'– diversifying.'

'Ah, so that's what we are to call it, are we?' Ambrose said, looking at Paul with a lugubrious expression.

Paul let this pass. 'Letting my interests in the current Levant Company stock . . . go,' he chose his words with care, 'and acquiring in its place something more solid; something – unlike our stock in these present conditions – that will hold its value. Gemstones, to be precise.'

'I see. That part of it, anyway.' Ambrose took out a large square of silk and mopped his brow with it. 'And if none of the merchants in all of Venice are yet apprised of what you are doing, then how can you expect him to be?'

'What I expect him to do is not to stick his nose in where it's not wanted.' Paul looked as though he would like to wring Carew's neck. 'He's on the next boat back to London – in the galleys if I have my way.'

'You are too harsh.'

'That's what Constanza said. But you are mistaken, both of you. If I have been at fault, it is for not being hard enough on him. He thinks he has the licence of a . . .' Paul seemed about to say something and then stopped. 'But he is nothing, nothing to me,' he said bitterly. 'He's a servant! It's not up to him to think.'

'Well, well, never mind about him now –' Ambrose pushed back his turban a little and mopped his brow again. Now it was his turn to look displeased. 'So I am *merely* one of Parvish's factors, am I? I like that! I'll have you know that Parvish's cabinet has given me more uncomfortable moments than any intelligence collecting for the Honourable Company ever has, unless you count the time when they sawed a hole in the ceiling of the Doge's audience chamber, but that's another story – and a state of affairs which – believe me – is quite likely to get much worse with this next venture . . .'

'Come, Ambrose,' Paul could see that the older man was about to become thoroughly worked up, 'we're getting ahead of ourselves, don't you think? Let us sit. Let us put our differences aside for a moment. What news have you brought me.'

'I fear the news I have is not good. As you already know, the Dutch continue to bring their vessels round the new sea route most successfully.' Ambrose took out a roll of paper from a bundle at his side on which was drawn a rudimentary map. 'They buy their spices here –' he pointed with his thumb at the scattered mass of the spice islands on the far right-hand side of the paper, 'and then instead of bringing them back overland, thus –' he traced a loop round the roughly triangular landmass of India, and then a trajectory to the port of Ormuz, up the gulf to Basra, and then across the Persian deserts, 'where the caravans bring them to Aleppo, and then on to Venice and Constantinople, which is where our trade lies. Instead, they sail south, thus,' with the same thumb he drew a second trajectory down the page and round the far greater landmass of Africa, 'round what they are pleased to call Buena Esperanza – the Cape of Good Hope – although much hope it is likely to bring us. For even though this new Cape journey is ten times longer, it has proved to be ten times safer than the old overland routes to the Levant. And we all know what this has already done to our prices.'

'Parvish sent the figures for me?'

'Indeed he did.' Ambrose fumbled in the bundle again and brought out a second piece of paper. He put on a pair of green-tinted spectacles, perching them on the bridge of his enormous nose, and squinted through them at the figures. 'Let me see, ah, yes, here they are: in Aleppo the last consignment of pepper was bought at two shillings per pound; in the east the same amount is bought for only two and a half pence.'

'May I see that?' Paul took the piece of paper from him. 'It's the same with cloves. Lately we have been buying them at four shillings a pound in Aleppo, but in the east they cost just nine pence for the same amount.' Paul ran his eye swiftly down the list. 'Cinnamon, nutmeg . . . it's the same story.'

'There's no doubt, we are most soundly trounced,' Ambrose frowned.

'We are, aren't we?' Looking thoughtful, Paul handed the paper back to Ambrose. 'The prices are even lower than I had anticipated.'

'And soon it won't be only the Dutch who are our competitors. You read Parvish's letter about our own East India Company, the one I left at the . . . er . . . the lady's house?'

Paul nodded. 'Yes, I read it.'

'If our own merchants are ever to become even half as well established as the Dutch –' Ambrose let the thought hang in the air between them.

'Like owls to Athens.' Paul stood up and went restlessly over to the window. In the house opposite he could see the lights flickering in the windows overlooking the courtyard.

'Owls to Athens?'

'It's a Greek expression. Owls abounded there in ancient times, and so became its emblem. When there is already a superfluity of a certain thing in a certain place, it does not make sense to take any more there.'

'Well I'm on my way to Athens just now,' Ambrose said gloomily. 'I'll let you know if I meet any owls.'

'Athens? What's taking you there?'

'Parvish's cabinet. There are stories that there is a mermaid there just come on the market and I am sent to acquire it for him.'

'I thought he already has a mermaid.'

'He has a mermaid's *purse*,' Ambrose said tetchily, 'not the same thing at all. A mermaid's *purse* is no better than a scrap of seaweed – you should know that – and besides everyone's got one. This, they tell me, is the real thing.'

'Ho! And you believe them? That it will not turn out to be a monkey skull stitched on to a dried fish tail, or I don't know what other unnatural monstrosity.' Paul looked cynical. 'Wherever did you hear of such a thing?'

'You know I never divulge my sources. I have an exceedingly large network of informants – of which our good friend Prospero here is a part – all the way from here to Lime Street.' Ambrose, who was packing his papers away in his bundle, stopped and regarded Paul severely over the top of his spectacles. 'Who are you, pray, to cast doubt on it? Who found him the crocodile from Egypt, *hmmm*? His entire collection of Strange Beaks of Birds from the East? Not to mention a *genuine* unicorn horn. I'm told only the Medici Dukes have one of those.'

'Ambrose, Ambrose!' Paul could see that he was about to work himself up again. 'Come, I don't doubt you! We all know that if anyone could find such a thing it would be you. You have created the *ne plus ultra* of *wunderkammen* for Parvish, quite the best in England, everyone knows that.'

'The best in England? The best in Europe!'

'The best in Europe,' Paul said soothingly. 'So tell me, how is the old man?'

'How do you think he is?' Ambrose adjusted his turban. 'Old.'

'No, really,' Paul said, more gently now. 'Tell me how he is: how is Parvish?'

'I've told you, he's old. Like me. There is too much that's new in this world. First a new king; now new trading routes. What next? Neither of us like it. We prefer the old ones. Besides, I am getting too old for all this running around.'

Paul laughed. 'You have been saying that these last twenty years, ever since I have known you, anyhow.'

'Well, this time I mean it. Too many leaky ships. Too many leaky merchants, come to that.' Ambrose put his hand on Paul's shoulder. 'It would break his heart if he could see you like this. And if you ask me – which I know you don't want to – *that* is why you are so angry with your John Carew. Because you know that this is not just a pretence, much as you would like me to think it. He holds up a mirror to you, Pindar, and you do not like what you see.'

'I know what I'm doing.'

'Do you?' Ambrose pointed to the little paned window beside them. Paul turned and found himself looking at his own reflection. A bruise was beginning to form across the bridge of his nose; his eyes were rimmed with red. Despite his night at Constanza's, he looked exhausted, his normally pale skin pallid as though he had not slept at all.

' "Shrewd, gentleman-like, a man of good counsel," ' Ambrose said severely. 'That's what our honourable merchants used to say about you. That was the man they chose for the Constantinople job.' Ambrose's surprisingly strong fingers dug into Paul's shoulder. 'But I know something rotten when I see it,' he added softly. 'What's happened to you, Pindar? Have you taken a look at yourself recently? Do not tell me that you did this to yourself a-purpose.'

'I know what I am doing.' Paul tried to pull away, but Ambrose kept his grip. 'I know what I'm doing – and so does Parvish,' Paul insisted. 'If the new East India Company should succeed in their ventures, then they will be buying the same spices as us, but almost at source. If they can successfully combine that with the new sea route, as the Dutch have done, the Levant trade will collapse and we face certain ruin. We agreed that we would sell whatever stock we still had . . . Transfer it for the moment into something that would keep its value, until we could see more clearly what to do next.'

'Gemstones. Yes, you told me that already, very clever. Small, portable, and much more likely to keep their value, in this current climate, than pepper or cloves. You always were the one for clever ideas. But the gaming?'

'What of it?'

From his pocket Paul took a shining round object about the size and shape of a timepiece; he ran the tip of his finger along the gilded brass lid of the compendium, tracing the pattern that was engraved there: two eel-like creatures, or lampreys, entwined.

'You know quite well what I mean,' Ambrose was saying. 'Does Parvish know about the gaming?' His face had become hard suddenly. 'What? Cat got your tongue? No, I thought not. You've got the gamester's sickness, Pindar, I can feel it in my bones.'

'Sickness? I don't know what you're talking about –' Paul began to flick open the top of the compendium and close it again with his thumb abstractedly.

'Oh but I think you do,' Ambrose said. 'You can't help yourself any more, can you, Pindar? You can't stop.'

'That's a lie –'

'Then why are you fiddling with your compendium? You always were one to fiddle, even as a boy. Parvish used to say he could always find you out. Let me see that.' Ambrose took the compendium from Paul, looked it over with a collector's practised eye. 'What a very inferior piece of work, I'm surprised at you. Humphrey Cole would be turning in his grave. Where's your old one?'

'I gave it away.' Paul returned Ambrose's gaze impassively. 'To a friend.'

'To a friend?' Ambrose held the lid up, squinted at the engraving of the two creatures. 'Lampreys, if I am not much mistaken – ah, well –'

Giving the compendium back to Paul, Ambrose sat down heavily. He took his turban off, flung it angrily into one dusty wainscotted corner of the tiny room. 'Listen,' he said, in a softer tone, scratching the top of his great bald pate. 'I know all about your losses, Pindar,' he sighed. 'I know they are real.'

'You are a fool if you believe everything John Carew tells you.' Paul could feel the palms of his hands beginning to sweat.

'And you are a fool if you think I would rely only on a mere servant for my intelligence,' Ambrose snapped back. 'It's what I *do*, Pindar. Collect things: unicorn horns, mermaids, intelligence. It is why I am here.'

'To collect intelligence about me?' Paul began to laugh, but his ribs hurt too much where he had fallen on them the night before. 'Parvish sent you to collect information about *me*?' He rubbed his chest gingerly. 'You're dreaming, Ambrose.'

But when he looked up, Ambrose's expression told him he was very far from dreaming. 'Well, do your worst,' he decided to bluff his way through. 'Who – exactly – are your informants?'

82

'I told you before, I never divulge my sources.' Ambrose looked at him severely. 'Part of the reason I am here is to get your assurance that you will give up the gaming, either with your money, or Parvish's, or anyone else's. You say you don't have the gamester's sickness, so that should be easy enough for you, shouldn't it?' For such a short, fat man, Ambrose's presence seemed to fill the little room. 'Well,' he snapped, 'do I have it?'

Paul hesitated, and then gave a curt nod.

'So I have your word?'

'You have my word.'

Just then the curtain was pulled aside and Prospero came in looking flustered. 'Forgive the intrusion, gentlemen, but I'm afraid you have a visitor,' he began, 'a most importunate young man who would not take no for an answer –' but before he could finish Carew pushed past him into the room.

'Ah so here you are, Constanza said she thought you might be, I've been looking high and low –' he stopped when he saw Ambrose.

There was a short silence while the three of them looked at each other.

'Well, well,' taking in the scene, Carew's eyes glittered, 'this *is* cosy.'

'It's no matter, Prospero,' Paul said, 'the gentleman and I were just finishing.'

'You go, Pindar. I still have some business with Prospero here.' Stiffly, Ambrose turned to retrieve his turban out of the dusty corner. 'And I still have some things I'd like to ask you,' he looked at Paul thoughtfully, 'but it's nothing that won't keep.'

Outside, back in the workshop, Prospero handed Paul the spinel. 'Here's your stone. It's a pretty one, I grant you, but I couldn't offer you much.' He named a price in ducats.

'Is that all?'

'I'm sorry, English. There's been a flood of jewels on the market recently. A spinel's not worth much these days.'

'How so?'

'They say that it's a lady who's been selling them, a woman from one of the convents.'

'One of the nuns?'

'Maybe, maybe not,' Prospero shrugged. 'What would I know about your nuns and your convents? It sounds unlikely to me; after all what would a religious be doing with all those jewels?'

'Some rich widow seeking refuge there in all likelihood – or part of some poor novice's dowry,' Paul began to speculate, and then a thought occurred to him. 'Would she by any chance also be the seller of this great diamond everyone's been telling me about, the Sultan's Blue. Have you heard of it?'

'The Sultan's Blue? Of course I've heard of it! Now if you can bring me *that*, English, that's another story,' Prospero's eyes gleamed. 'I'd pay good money just to hold it in my hand. Nearly a hundred carats they say. Do you know how big that is?' He held out a clenched hand. 'Nearly as big as my fist. And then the colour: a true blue-white, by which we mean the finest white but with a light blue tint. Think of it, English, what beauty: a diamond the colour of moonlight!' Prospero gave a mighty sigh. 'But that's not why the gem dealers are all talking about it. Over the years there have been many big stones that have made their way in and out of the lagoon. The most remarkable thing about this stone is the brilliance of its cut: they say it has nearly double the number of facets that anyone else we know has been able to produce. What light! What lustre! What unknown genius has been able to create this marvel?' Prospero shrugged. 'No one knows.'

'So where d'you think the diamond has come from?'

'The stone itself? Almost certainly from India, from the great mines of Golconda; some say it was once set in the eye of an idol in a sacred temple there –' Prospero shrugged again '– but of course, with these great stones,' he spread the fingers of both hands expressively, 'they come, they go – they change their name – no one can ever know for sure.'

'Old women's tales, Prospero.'

'No, English!' Although there was no one around to hear him Prospero lowered his voice. '*Not* old women's tales. Diamonds have many mystical properties, so much has always been known. But the Sultan's Blue is – different. They say that never in the whole world has there been a diamond – or any kind of gemstone – quite like it.' Prospero was whispering now, as if half-afraid of what he was saying. 'I've heard it tell that this diamond has many properties: that the stone, freely given, gives great protection to the wearer; that it does great good for the good man – but that quite the opposite is true for the bad. They say it bears a magical inscription on it in the language of the Moghuls –' He looked up at Paul and saw the sceptical expression on his face. '*Bah!*' He made a gesture of disgust with his hand as if pushing Paul away. 'You never listen to me, English, why am I wasting my breath?'

'So you'd give me a good price for it, Prospero, if I come across it on my travels?'

But Prospero was not in the mood to be teased.

'No, English, I don't want the Sultan's Blue. Never!' He was vehement. 'And you won't find many dealers who'll touch it. A stone like that, we would all do well to leave it alone.'

'Why do you say that?'

Prospero shuffled uncomfortably. 'The stone is moving on.' He did not meet Paul's eye.

'What?'

'I said the stone is moving on.' Prospero flung his long beard over his shoulder impatiently. 'Haven't you understood a word I've been saying?' He was almost shouting at Paul now. 'A magical stone like this one, you think it can be bought and sold? No, I tell you, and no good will come to anyone who tries.'

Prospero was about to make his way back into his workshop behind the curtain but he hesitated in the doorway.

'If you are really interested, it was a man, not a lady, who was selling the Blue, I'm told. They say he'd come from Constantinople.'

'What happened to him?'

'No one knows where he went. He brought the diamond here to the ghetto to be valued – but a stone like that,' Prospero shrugged, 'no single gem dealer would have had the money to buy it from him, even if they'd wanted to. I don't think he'd bargained on that. A man I know offered to keep the jewel safe for him – you don't want to be walking round the city with something like that in your pocket – offered to put out the word amongst our people in Antwerp and Amsterdam. There's always a fool to be found eventually who'll try to buy a gemstone like that one, it just takes time to find him, that's all. He said he'd come back, but –'

'He never did?'

'I heard he lost the stone at cards, may his name be blotted out for ever.' Prospero turned and spat on to the floor behind him. 'You see? It's as I told you, English, the stone is moving on. There's no point asking why, or trying to prevent it.'

Chapter Thirteen

It was almost midnight by the time Paul and Carew left Prospero's workshop. The moon was bright. For extra secrecy, Paul had taken no gondola that night so in order to avoid the watch they made their way together on foot through the back canals.

Paul eventually broke the silence between them. 'I don't suppose there's any point my asking where you've been for the last two days?' Despite keeping his voice low so as not to attract the unwanted attentions of the watch, his tone was venomous. 'But, no, on second thoughts, don't tell me,' he put his hand up, 'I really don't want to know. From now on you're on your own, Carew. *Basta*. I don't care what you do.'

'Make your mind quite easy, I'm going,' Carew said. 'But before I go, I don't suppose there's any point asking you what you were doing closeted with Ambrose Jones?'

'Is that any of your business?' Paul replied; and then, contradictory, 'I thought that's what you wanted? To *introduce* us. Well you certainly succeeded in doing that.'

Carew ignored the taunt. 'Who is he? Who is Ambrose?' When Paul did not answer this, he went on: 'You already knew him, didn't you? I don't believe he's a collector for Parvish at all.'

'Oh yes, he's Parvish's collector, just as he says he is.' Paul was walking so fast that his ribs were beginning to hurt him again. 'But he's also a Levant Company intelligencer, you scrawny, fornicating little want-wit!' Paul stopped to catch his breath. 'Do you have any idea of what you have done? To blacken me in Parvish's eyes would have been bad enough, but now –'

'I never meant to blacken you,' Carew interrupted him, 'I just wanted you to *wake up*!'

'– but *now* you have put it in Ambrose Jones's power to expose me to the whole of the Levant Company!'

'But don't you see? Can't you get it into your head? You already *are* exposed! Everyone knows about you, about this – this – madness – this melancholy –' Carew was almost shouting, the sound of his voice ricocheting off the walls of the narrow *calle*. 'You are not yourself . . .'

'Quiet, fool!' Grabbing Carew by the shoulder, Paul drew them both back into the shadows. 'I have licence to be abroad at this hour, but I'll remind you that you do not. And if the watch should find us here, don't think I won't throw you to them like a rat.'

They had come to a little bridge at the end of the narrow passageway. Paul was panting now, his breath jagged, a screaming pain in his chest. He laid his head back against the wall, trying to catch his breath, trying to get his bearings. Somewhere in the labyrinth of tiny *calles* they had taken a wrong turning, and he realised that he no longer knew where they were.

The canal in front of them was very narrow. It led off in two directions; to the left of the bridge it doubled back into the labyrinth of the back streets of Cannaregio; to the right it led almost immediately into another, slightly bigger waterway. The moon hung low between the rooftops of two merchants' houses, refracted in the silent, gleaming black ribbons of water on either side of them. In an arched window overlooking the water a solitary candle burned.

Was there anywhere more beautiful, or more melancholy? Paul had lived here, on and off, for more than half his life, but it was only now, at this very moment, that he realised how much he hated it. What had possessed him to come back? Was it because Celia had once lived here too? It was here that he had first known her; here that they had fallen in love, become betrothed. Then he had gone to Constantinople on Levant Company business, and the ship bringing Celia to him had been shipwrecked – or so they had thought. In Constantinople Carew believed he had seen her once, that she had somehow found her way into the Sultan's harem, but they had never managed to reach her, and he – he had been left perpetually wondering.

Perhaps Carew was right? He hardly seemed to know himself any more. Celia was gone from this place now, was lost to him for ever, and yet, in his mind, the city was haunted by her. Whenever he walked these streets he had the curious premonition that she would one day come round the corner towards him. He could not get the idea out of his head. Once or twice he had even thought he had seen her: a young woman with pale skin and red-gold hair sitting at a window, her face bent over some sewing or a book; at other times she floated past him in a gondola, her face half-turned towards him, her fingers trailing in the water. But then she would turn, or speak, and he would realise that it was not her after all, but another, and he would never see her again. All around him there was nothing now but dampness and decay.

Suddenly something moved in the shadows on the other side of the bridge.

'Did you see that,' a voice, the faintest of murmurs, in his ear, 'in the archway, to the left?'

So Carew had seen it too. Paul nodded; he turned and put his lips to Carew's ear, and was about to say something, when a figure of a man, his face hidden by the hood of his cloak, emerged from the shadowy archway and began to walk towards them. When he got to the middle of the bridge he stopped, and a voice enquired softly:

'Paul Pindar?'

Motioning Carew to stay where he was, Paul stepped out of the shadows towards the stranger. 'Who wants to know?'

Instinctively he had put his hand on the short sword at his belt, but the man put both his hands up to show that he was unarmed. 'Paul? Do you not know me?'

As he said this the man removed his hood and Paul saw that there was indeed something familiar about the form standing before him in the moonlight.

'It is I, Francesco.'

'Francesco?' Paul said, amazed. 'Dear God! As I live, it *is* you!'

He crossed the bridge to meet him and the two men embraced.

'Francesco! How long has it been?'

'Too long, much too long.'

'Years.' Paul looked into his old friend's face with as much curiosity as delight. 'Francesco Contarini! Why it must be ten years, more.'

'Ten, fifteen, who cares?' the other man smiled. 'Too many to count.'

They stood looking at one another.

'You look just the same.'

'And you.'

But even as they spoke the words, each knew that the other was lying. Paul, with the bruises coming up around his nose and eyes, had streaks of grey in his black hair and beard; Francesco's once handsome face had become thin; the linen at his neck and sleeves so grimy and threadbare it looked as though it had not been changed for several months. But still they carried on smiling.

'I heard you'd left Venice.' Francesco clapped Paul awkwardly on the shoulder.

'It's true. I was living in Constantinople for a few years. The Levant Company sent me to do business there – an embassy to the Great Turk. Trading rights, you know the kind of thing –'

'But of course: Paul Pindar, the great merchant.' Despite the flattering words, there was tincture of irony in Francesco's voice. When he smiled Paul saw that his lower teeth were now no more than blackened stumps. 'Why does that not surprise me? You were always destined for great things. Always found favour in Fortune's eyes.'

'Fortune?' Now it was Paul's turn to smile. 'A fickle mistress, I fear.'

'I heard about Tom Lamprey and his daughter.' Francesco gave a sympathetic nod. 'I'm sorry.'

'Thank you,' Paul said, 'it was a long time ago.' And then, anxious to change the subject, 'But you, Francesco? Tell me about you.'

'Me? I've been away, too –' Francesco made a small dry noise, more like a cough than a laugh, in the back of his throat. 'You probably heard?'

'I had heard, yes.'

What was it? Paul struggled to remember. Something about a woman, a fight over dice or cards? He had killed someone, of that much he was sure.

Francesco saw what he was thinking, and gave a small shrug. 'Some whore, she was nothing.' To Paul he seemed nonchalant enough, but in the moonlight his eyes were hard and unblinking. 'You know how it is. Four years, she cost me, four whole years in exile. And do you know, I can't even remember her name now. Like that other one, d'you remember, when we were young? What was her name –?'

There was a small, uncomfortable pause.

'Constanza?'

'Constanza. Of course. I had forgotten.'

'Forgotten Constanza?' Was it really possible that he had forgotten? They had come to blows over Constanza all those years ago, a battle for her affections so bitter that their friendship had never really recovered.

'Do you still see her?'

'From time to time.'

'She must be old by now. Nothing so detestable as an old whore, wouldn't you say?'

When Paul did not reply, Francesco gave another small shrug. 'Well, as you say, it's a long time ago. Come, will you walk with me?'

He took Paul's arm, and Paul found himself falling into step beside his one-time companion. The twisting narrow streets and *calles* were deserted, the only sound was their own hushed voices echoing back to them. In the canals, the moonlight gleamed on water the colour and texture of black oil.

'Where are you going at this time of night?'

'You have to ask that?' Francesco gave the same hoarse little cough as before. 'Where do you think? Where else is there to go?'

'I'm done with gaming, Francesco, if that's what you had in mind.' Paul was surprised by how convincing he sounded.

'Done with gaming?' Francesco gave him a quick sideways glance. 'That's not what I heard –' He looked as if he could go on, but he did not.

'Well, it's true.'

'Since when?'

A pause.

'Since tonight.'

'Since tonight?' Francesco laughed. 'Oh I see, is that what the bruises are all about?' When Paul did not reply he laughed again. 'It's all right, you don't have to tell me if you don't want to, I know how it is.' He was close enough now for Paul to smell the wine on his breath; his body gave off the rank, unwashed odour of someone who has not slept or washed for many days. 'Just some wine then?'

'I've given up drinking, too.' The prospect of another night such as he had recently had made Paul's stomach churn. But Francesco appeared not to have heard him.

'I know just the place. An acquaintance of mine – the Cavaliere – has recently set up a little *ridotto* near here. Have you met the Cavaliere yet?'

'No, I don't think I have.'

When Francesco saw Paul hesitate he seemed anxious to reassure him. 'I assure you, it's a very good establishment, not like some of these new *casini*. The Cavaliere admits all comers, so long as they have an introduction to him – and provided their credit's good. Come,' Francesco grinned, showing his blackened teeth, 'let me give you an introduction? After all these years, it's the least I can do.'

Paul could only think two things at that moment. One was to wonder how much Carew, who was still waiting for him in the shadows of the little *passaggio*, had heard of this conversation; the other was how he could be rid of Francesco. There was something about him – something feverish, almost feral – that he could not quite put his finger on. He could deal with Carew later, he decided; extracting himself from Francesco was going to be far harder. He had given Ambrose his word about gaming, that was true, but he would take some wine, a very little, with Francesco, then he could leave with courtesy.

'For you, my old friend,' he said, suddenly cheerful again, 'just one drink, for old time's sake.'

Just one drink at the new *ridotto*. That could not hurt anyone, Paul thought, now could it?

Chapter Fourteen

The *ridotto* was over a wine shop in the Calle dell'Asrologo, just behind the Grand Canal.

As a young man, acting as Parvish's factor in Venice all those years ago, Paul had been in dozens of places just like this: temporary gaming dens fitted up in rooms above inns or shops in which men played cards, games of hazard or chance, often losing large sums of money in the process. So he was not at all surprised when Francesco took them through to the back of the deserted shop, to a door behind the counter, from which led a flight of narrow stairs.

With Paul and Carew following behind him, Francesco made his way up the stairs, at the top of which was a large first-floor room. They could see at once that the room, which was flooded by moonlight, was completely empty except, in the chipped wainscotting at its far side, for a single step leading to a tiny door. The door was so small, however, that at first Paul could not believe that it led anywhere other than a store cupboard, or an attic room at best. But when Francesco gave his knock, it opened silently, as if on oiled springs, and the three stepped over the raised lintel to find themselves in some kind of antechamber, no more than a few yards long, at the end of which was a second doorway, much bigger this time: a secret entranceway which led from the first floor of the wine shop into what Paul immediately understood must be an adjoining house.

As the three stood together at the second door, Francesco nodded towards Carew, acknowledging him for the first time. 'Your servant, can he keep his tongue?'

'Yes, I can vouch for him,' Paul nodded, 'but what is this, Francesco? Where are we?'

There was no sound at all coming from the other side of the door. In fact the whole place was so eerily silent that Paul began to think, for one crazed moment, that this was not a *ridotto* at all. Crammed into the little antechamber, he and Carew were like nothing so much as two rats in a trap. Paul felt his pulse begin to quicken. It was quite clear that they were all alone in this strange place.

But just as Paul was wondering what kind of madness it was that had made him agree to come here, he heard Francesco's voice in his ear: 'You ask me what this is? This, my friend, is like no other *ridotto* you have ever been to in your life.'

And as he spoke the second door swung silently open, just like the first, only this time they found themselves dazzled by a blaze of candlelight.

They were standing on the threshold of the *piano nobile* of some great mansion or *palazzo*. The walls were covered in painted panels; at the windows fell heavy drapes of the most sumptuous, tasselled velvet; and from the ceiling hung a vast chandelier made from the finest spun Murano glass. But the most curious thing about this silent place was that the room was crowded with people.

Men and women, some of them masked, stood in groups or moved without speaking in between the several tables. The men seemed to Paul to be a mixture of young nobles and merchants; the women almost exclusively courtesans, their lips and cheeks enhanced with carmine, as was the outlandish custom of the city.

Despite the closeness of the room they were dressed at the height of fashion: stiff brocades, in jewel-like colours, rippled in simple folds from their padded and pointed stomachers; their bodices were low, exposing their breasts to the nipple, but their collars were outrageously high; made from stiffly starched *point de Venise* lace, so fine it was almost transparent, which fanned out behind them in ruffs like peacock tails. Their hair was parted in the middle and gathered up at either side in two strange horn-like shapes. One of them, Paul recognised as a friend of Constanza's. When she saw him she kissed the top of her fan and tipped it laughingly in his direction.

Each one of the tables was covered in a thick velvet cloth, at which four or more players sat carefully masked; at the head of each table was a man who took it upon himself to deal the cards. Beside him were two candles, several packs of playing cards, and two cups, one full of gold ducats, the other full of silver. The spectators, Paul noticed, grouped themselves behind the players, watched for a little while, and then moved on to the next table. Occasionally there was a muffled whisper or a cough, the chinking of two glasses knocking together, the soft rasping sound of a woman's gown trailing over the wooden floor, but apart from this utter silence filled the room, and only served to enhance the strange, dream-like atmosphere.

A servant came up with a tray set out with cups of wine. Paul took one and followed Francesco in. At times the crush was so great that they had to squeeze past the other spectators in order to move from one part of the room to another. At each table a different game was being played, at one *primero*, at another *bessano*: from the amount of gold and silver pieces on the cloth, Paul could see straight away that the stakes were very high.

At the centre of the room was one game which was attracting a particular crowd, and although Francesco seemed determined not to stop, Paul paused for a moment to watch. There were only four men at this table, but all eyes were on one player. His mask showed a smiling face, but from the studied fashionableness of his clothes and his physical slenderness Paul guessed he must be a youth of no more than eighteen or nineteen years old. From the hungry look on the faces of the onlookers, Paul guessed too that the stakes here had risen particularly high, but despite this fact the young man was playing with extraordinary detachment and studied nonchalance, as if the fortune slipping through his fingers was of no greater importance to him than chips of coloured glass.

Paul watched, fascinated. He drained his glass, barely noticed when a servant replaced it with another full one. He had sworn he would not play, and he had no doubt at that moment that he would stick to his word, but all the same he was sorry when he felt Francesco tapping him on his arm, leading him on through the crowd to what looked like a second, smaller room at the far end of the *piano nobile*.

The second door led, not into a room, as Paul had thought, but into an antechamber, across the back of which was a heavy curtain, black velvet embroidered with gold thread. Just as Paul was about to follow Francesco through the door he felt a hand on his shoulder.

'Signor Pindar?'

'Who wants to know?'

Paul turned and saw a swarthy-looking individual with pock-marks, or scarring of some kind, etched deeply into both cheeks.

'Cavaliere Memmo, at your service.' The man gave Paul a smile that did not reach his eyes.

Memmo? Something stirred in Paul's memory. Where had he heard that name before?

'Cavaliere.' Paul made his bow.

'You are most welcome; please –' he made an elaborate sweeping gesture into the room in front of them, 'it will be an honour to have you take a place among us.'

'Thank you but I'm not a gaming man.'

'Forgive me, but that's not what I've heard, Signor Pindar.'

'Well then I regret that you have been misinformed, Cavaliere Memmo,' and as he pronounced the name for the second time Paul remembered. Memmo. Of course! Hadn't Constanza talked to him about someone called Zuanne Memmo? She had, he was sure of it.

'As you say,' the Cavaliere spread his fingers, the palms of his hands upwards, a gesture that seemed to imply that this was of no importance to him one way or another. Then he nodded towards the black velvet drapes. 'But you should know that this room is where our most –' he hesitated, as though wishing to choose his words with care, 'our most – interesting, shall we say? – games are played. But, no matter. Some wine before you go?'

In the antechamber was a sideboard with some jugs of wine laid out on it. Memmo went over and came back with one. Paul held out his glass to be filled. He knew he must not appear to be too interested.

'What are they playing for?'

'They are playing for the chance to take part in an even bigger game.' Memmo smiled, and as before the smile did not reach his eyes. 'But I'd better be careful what I say, I might waken the gaming man in you yet.' He turned to put the jug back on the sideboard.

'It is as I said, I am no longer a gaming man,' Paul repeated. How those words seemed to stick in his throat! A feeling of restlessness was beginning to come over him. 'But tell me, I'm curious, is this the game that I've been told about, is this the game for the Sultan's Blue?'

At the sideboard Memmo still had his back to Paul. The hesitation in his reply lasted no more than a fraction of a second.

'The Sultan's Blue?'

'I heard there was a diamond called the Sultan's Blue which was to be the prize in a big game.'

'And from whom, if I might ask, did you hear that?'

The glass stopper, as Memmo replaced it in the wine jug, gave a faint chink.

Should he mention Constanza? Some sixth sense decided Paul against it.

'I thought every merchant on the Rialto knew about it,' he answered as casually as he could. 'A gem dealer I know told me that the man who brought it to Venice lost it at cards before he could find a buyer. So I'm guessing that was here.'

Had Memmo given an almost imperceptible shake of his head in Francesco's direction? Paul could not be sure because at that moment a servant came up and whispered something in Memmo's ear.

'Excuse me, gentlemen, this will not take long.'

Another man, a masked player from the main saloon, now entered the little antechamber. Memmo pulled the black velvet drapes to one side and ushered him in, drawing them again firmly behind him.

There came a small cough from the doorway. Paul looked up and was surprised to find Carew standing there; he had been so intent on his conversation with the Cavaliere that he had almost forgotten about him.

'Well?' Paul looked at him impatiently. 'What in God's name are you doing still here?'

'Waiting for you, sir,' Carew said with studied politeness, 'waiting to attend you home.'

Paul turned to Francesco again, his desire to escape from the *ridotto*, and from his old friend's clutches, now utterly forgotten.

'It's true then, about the diamond?'

'Yes, it's true.' Francesco, who was slouched in a chair, drained his glass of wine.

'I heard it was a man from Constantinople who brought it here.' Prospero's stories came flooding back to him. The Sultan's Blue, that magical stone. One hundred carats of moonlight.

'I don't know. He didn't look like any Turk that I've ever seen. A runaway slave, more like. Although, now I come to think of it, there was some talk –' Francesco tailed off.

'Some talk of what?'

'– that he had once been in the service of the Sultan's mother.'

'The Sultan's mother? Do you mean the old queen?' Paul's mind was on fire. 'The one who died last year?'

'I believe so. There was a name for her, I seem to remember –'

'The Valide?'

'Yes, that was it. The Valide.'

'And the diamond –' Paul ran his hands nervously through his hair, 'have you seen it?'

'Yes.' Francesco glanced towards the closed drapes, and then quickly away again. 'Yes, I've seen it.'

Paul followed his gaze. 'What, is it here?' The thought of the diamond, and of its proximity, the thought that it could be won in a card game, was beginning to give him the most unbearable feelings of excitement. But no, he must not; he must not even contemplate it; he had given his word. Paul felt a constriction in his larynx, as though someone were squeezing him round the throat. 'It's here, isn't it?'

'Yes.' Francesco nodded.

For reasons that Paul did not quite understand they were both speaking in whispers now. There was a cough again from the doorway. Dear God, was Carew still there? It was one of life's great imponderables: why was Carew always there when you didn't want him, and never around when you did? Ignoring him Paul turned to Francesco again. 'Would the Cavaliere let me see it?' Somehow, seeing the diamond had taken on the greatest possible importance in Paul's mind.

'This is for high stakes, the highest that have ever been played in Venice.' Even in the candlelight Francesco's face looked almost grey with fatigue. 'I don't think you quite understand what it means. Entire fortunes will change hands, will be lost for ever. The authorities are already trying to close the *ridotto* down, but if they got to hear of this . . . Zuanne would face prosecution, perhaps even exile.'

Paul felt a kind of roaring in his ears. 'But supposing I wanted to play?' By now he did not care if Carew heard him or not. 'Would he let me see it then?'

Francesco shook his head. 'He'll never let you play, not in this game.'

'Why not?' The palms of Paul's hands had begun to sweat, he could feel his heart pounding.

'Don't be a fool, Pindar, you've already lost one fortune. Everyone knows it.'

He seemed even more feverish now than before. Paul had his hand on Francesco's arm, but he pulled away from him impatiently. 'Go on, go home while you still can. Your servant's waiting for you.'

At Francesco's signal, Carew stepped into the room and tried to take Paul by the arm, but the wine he had drunk was beginning to take effect; Paul shook him off roughly.

'Please! Francesco, can you talk to him? Talk to Memmo for me.' He gripped Francesco by the arm. Francesco was about to pull away from him again, when suddenly he seemed to relent.

'If I let you see the diamond, will you go home?'

'Yes.'

Francesco looked at him doubtfully. 'Do I have your word?'

'You have my word.'

'You promise me faithfully, and on your honour?'

'Faithfully, and on my honour. *Christos*, Francesco, what more do you want?'

'Then come with me.'

Francesco beckoned Paul over to the closed velvet drapes, and pulled them silently aside.

With Carew following close behind him, Paul stepped through. He found himself in a room shaped like an octagon. There were no windows, so anyone playing here would have had little idea whether it was day or night; instead, hanging from floor to ceiling on each of the walls was a long glass mirror, in which candlelight from the sconces fixed to the mirrors was reflected. The effect was small and womb-like, a magnificently jewelled box.

In the middle was a table where the players sat: two men and a woman; a fourth player, apparently asleep, lay on the floor, wrapped up in his cloak. The table was made from a wood so dark it was almost black, and richly inlaid with mother-of-pearl; the chairs the same.

Zuanne Memmo was standing with his back to the players. He turned round when he heard Paul come in, and instead of indicating his displeasure, as Paul half-thought he might, silently nodded his assent. The masked man, who had accompanied him inside, stood to one side, watching the play. Unlike the main saloon, where almost total silence reigned, in this room some talking, albeit in hushed tones, seemed permissible.

'Watch,' Paul heard Francesco murmur into his ear. 'Watch Memmo.'

Memmo brought out a small pouch from a cabinet behind him: a pouch like a woman's pocket, made from pink velvet embroidered with silver brocade. He opened it and then shook it gently, and as he did so a round object the size of a child's fist rolled out into the palm of his outstretched hand.

'So it's true, after all,' Paul heard the masked man say in a whisper.

'What did you expect?' Memmo answered him. 'The Sultan's Blue. Of course it's true.'

And holding it between his finger and thumb he raised it up for them all to see. The players stopped their game, and there was a sudden silence. The stone shone dazzlingly in the candlelight, blue fire and blue ice together, was reflected a hundred times over in the mirrors on the walls. As mysterious and beautiful and as rare, Paul thought, as something from another world.

The masked man bent forward to look at it more closely.

'Why, there's something written on it –'

'An inscription. I'm told it's in the language of the Moghuls.'

'What does it say?'

'Who knows?' Memmo smiled. 'I've never found any gamester yet who could speak that tongue.'

He turned and was about to replace the stone in the cabinet when Paul spoke up from the doorway.

'Let me try.'

That same roaring sensation in his ears.

Memmo looked over to him enquiringly, as if he had not quite understood what had been said.

'I said, will you let me try?'

For a moment Memmo seemed to hesitate, but then, with a sudden easy grace, held the stone out for him to examine.

'By all means, Signor Pindar. This is rare indeed, I did not know we had a scholar in our midst.'

100

Paul went over and took the diamond from him. The skin of his fingers seemed to tingle slightly at its touch, as though it were alive. He felt its size and weight, felt the way it fitted perfectly into his fist, as though his hand were a glove specially fashioned. Paul held the stone up to the candlelight as he had seen Memmo do, watched as it glittered with its strange pale fire. Up close he could see now the extraordinary skill with which the stone had been faceted, and the fact that there was one among them, along the upper side, which was larger than the others. And there indeed, in tiny writing, was carved an inscription, just as Prospero had said there would be.

Slowly he spelt out the words; felt the hairs rise on the back of his neck.

'What does it say?'

'It says *A'az ma yutlab*.'

'What does it mean?'

'It means "my heart's desire".'

Whoever had the stone would have their heart's desire.

In that moment Paul knew he had to have it, no matter what the cost.

Chapter Fifteen

As a punishment for locking herself in her cell, Annetta was to be dealt with not by Suor Virginia, or even by Suor Purificacion who usually took on such disciplinary matters as these, but, it was decided, by the Reverend Abbess, Suor Bonifacia herself.

Annetta had conversed with Suor Bonifacia only once since she had re-entered the convent, when she had been formally welcomed on the day of her arrival. Since that day she had seen her on a handful of occasions, usually feast days, when the old nun was deemed well enough to attend prayers in the chapel. Despite her position as Abbess, Suor Bonifacia was so old now, and so often unwell – feeble-minded, some said – that she rarely left her rooms at all, and she appeared, to the younger nuns at any rate, to have little if anything to do with the running of the convent. And yet the esteem in which she was held by the nuns was considerable, although as Annetta had very soon discovered this had far more to do with the size of the dowry she had brought, and the fact that she could claim at least four doges in her family, than with any great claim to spiritual riches.

The Abbess's private rooms were located at the very far end of the convent, on the opposite side to Annetta's dormitory. When she knocked, she was admitted at once by a woman who, to Annetta's surprise, was not dressed in nuns' clothes at all, nor even the robes of a *conversa*, but in the livery of an ordinary servant. The room was large and had several long windows overlooking the garden. In one corner was a huge fireplace in which, despite the season, a fire had been lit.

'Come in please, *suora*.'

A voice spoke, and it was only then that Annetta became aware of the Abbess herself. Small and bird-like, she was sitting at the other end of the room, at one of the open windows where a chair had been placed for her. Her servant had clearly been helping the old woman with her toilette, for although she was fully dressed the old nun's head was bare, and her hair fell loose around her shoulders. Annetta saw that far from being cropped close to her head, as their order required, Suor Bonifacia's hair was still long. It hung in a silver sheet, as fine and thin as spider's thread, all the way to the middle of her back.

'Don't be afraid, come in, come in and sit by me.' Seemingly quite unperturbed to be seen in this state, the old woman patted a second chair that had been placed opposite her own. Annetta approached respectfully; sat as she had been asked. The servant took up her position behind Suor Bonifacia and began to comb her hair again.

Annetta looked around. The room was decorated like a noble-woman's private parlour. Various tapestries and hangings in jewel-coloured damasks and velvets decorated the walls. A painting of the annunciation, the angel's wings decorated in shining gold leaf, hung over the mantel. On a table next to the fireplace were a number of leatherbound books, their spines tooled in gold leaf, several pens and papers, seals and sealing wax. Two *cassoni*, bigger and heavier than Annetta's, and beautifully painted with hunting scenes, stood at either end of the room.

'You are looking at my *cassoni*, I see.' Although Suor Bonifacia uttered this in grave tones, Annetta thought she saw a look of amusement pass between the two women. And despite her great age, her voice was both clear and gentle, the voice of a woman who had never been in the slightest doubt of her ability to command. 'I am told that you have one just like them, is that so?'

Annetta had been prepared to argue her case vigorously, but the Abbess's gentleness disarmed her so completely that instead, she found herself saying, with unaccustomed meekness, 'Yes, Reverend Abbess.'

'Suor Purificacion seems most distressed by it.'

Annetta was unsure how to interpret this remark so all she said, again, was 'Yes, Reverend Abbess,' bracing herself for the lecture on pride and disobedience that she was sure was to follow.

But to her surprise the Abbess seemed quite unmoved by the thought of Annetta's disobedience, and did not seem to want to refer to it again. Instead, the old lady turned her gaze towards the window.

'Look at my view, it's beautiful, is it not? If you know where to look, through the poplar trees over there, you can see the lagoon from here.'

Annetta looked and admired, wondering if Suor Bonifacia knew that she also enjoyed a room with a view. But whereas the view from her own window gave out south over the island, over the vegetable and herb gardens attached to the kitchens, from the Abbess's windows one could see the more formal physic garden, with its geometrical-shaped beds. A little to one side she could also see the avenue of pleached lime trees, the pathway surrounded by high hedges, the grotto with the fountain, the carp pond in whose reflection she had seen the *monarchino* for the first time. At the unexpected reminder of him her heart gave a lurch.

'Do you know how long I've been sitting here?'

The Abbess gave a wave with one hand, so gnarled it looked more like a piece of oak than human flesh, towards the window and the garden beyond.

Did that question require an answer? Annetta was not sure; when she said nothing the Abbess smiled at her.

'Sixty years!' The old woman gave a little laugh. 'Sixty years is how long I've been sitting here. I was here before anyone, except perhaps Virginia and Margaretta, and they've been here since they were eight. Imagine that, a whole life spent within these walls. No husband, no children, just the garden.' And as if on cue, Suor Annunciata and some of her helpers came into view: some were carrying baskets on their arms, others were armed with hoes and spades. Watching them, Suor Bonifacia gave a sigh.

'There was nothing here when I first came. But I was here at the very beginning, you know. It was my brother, the count, who brought us our very first plants. Our merchants travelled far, even in those days. A merchant he knew gave him some specimens, and he brought them to me. He'd seen the botanical garden in Padua, and he thought we could make one here. Rare plants changing hands all the time, from the Adriatic and the Black Sea; from the Ottoman lands, Syria, Greece, Alexandria, Tripoli, Tunis, even the New World. The *Fritillaria imperialis*. You see, I remember it. That was the first – I think we still have a grafting – and then others brought more, and gradually we became known for it. So you see I've watched this garden grow, right from the beginning,' the Abbess gave a sigh, 'and Suor Purificacion thinks I should be exercised about one girl and her *cassoni*! Really, they are like children these days, all of them. The things they think up to worry about.' She seemed to find genuine amusement in the idea.

For a while there was silence in the room. All that could be heard was the crackling of logs on the fire, and the soft rhythmic sound of the servant combing the Abbess's hair. When Annetta finally looked up, she saw that Suor Bonifacia seemed to have fallen asleep. Although her face was turned towards the sun which came streaming in through the window, her eyes were closed, as though lost to the sun's warmth. She sat there for so long like this that Annetta began to think that she had forgotten her completely. But then, just as Annetta was wondering whether she should get up and leave, the Abbess's eyes opened again.

'*Basta*, Giovanna.'

With her long silver hair still streaming over her shoulders she looked more like a seer or a prophetess than an old nun of their order.

'*Si, Contessa.*'

The servant withdrew silently, and the two were left alone together.

'There's something I would like to ask you, *suora*.'

Annetta felt her chest tighten. Was it possible after all that someone – perhaps even Suor Bonifacia herself? – had seen her in the garden yesterday morning?

'Yes, Reverend Abbess?'

'Did they put you in here against your will?' Annetta could feel the Abbess's full gaze on her. 'I'm told they are not supposed to do that any more, but –' she shrugged, 'well, only you know the answer to that. Please, speak frankly, *suora*, Giovanna cannot hear us. Consider this room as you would a confessional.'

When Annetta did not reply at once she said: 'They put me in here against my will, you know.' She gave Annetta a quizzical look. 'Did they do that to you?'

'The first time I was here, I was just a child, I didn't know any different,' Annetta replied, unsure how much of her own strange story the old Abbess would remember. 'But the second time, no, *suora* . . . I mean Reverend Abbess. I asked to come here.'

'Did you?' The old woman's brow puckered suddenly, and for the first time Annetta was struck by how smooth her face was, her cheeks like the roughened skin of a country apple. But as before, she seemed to lose interest in Annetta quite quickly.

'In my day there were so many of us. Most of the nuns I grew up with here are dead now. Except me, of course, although I too shall be gone quite soon. Sixty years is enough time for anyone to wait, no?' She smiled at Annetta again. 'Not enough husbands to go round. Or not enough husbands from the right families, or of the right rank, that is, because of course our families would rather we were dead than that we married beneath us,' she added, 'so they put us in here instead, locked the door and threw away the key.' She saw the look on Annetta's face at this pronouncement, and laughed. 'Don't look so shocked, *suora*. I am old. I speak my mind. It is my right – no matter what Old – how do you young nuns call her? – Old Pure Face says.'

At this, Annetta laughed out loud. Suor Bonifacia's eyes glittered. 'Giovanna,' she whispered, 'tells me everything.'

She sat back in her chair, and Annetta could see that the old woman was beginning to tire, exhausted by their conversation. She shut her eyes again, seemingly oblivious to Annetta, turning her face to the sun's rays once more.

'Should I go now, Reverend Abbess?'

'*Hmm*? Yes, I think that would be best,' the old woman murmured, her eyes still shut. 'Would you be so good as to call Giovanna on your way out?'

When Annetta reached the door, she turned to make the customary courtesy, and saw that the old nun was watching her after all, her back still ramrod straight, her hair still flowing over her shoulders like a girl's. With the sun behind her Annetta had the vivid impression that she was looking at a woman suddenly grown young again.

'And *suora* –'

'Yes?'

'I believe I am going to tell Suor Purificacion that from now on you will go to work with Annunciata in the garden. She'll find you something useful to do.'

Annetta looked at her with consternation, not quite believing what she had heard.

'Reverend Abbess?'

'I think you heard me, *suora*.'

'But –'

'The spiritual life that you have chosen as a choir nun is not always as . . . sustaining, shall we say? . . . as it might be. Or if I may put it another way: sixty years is a long time just to sit looking out of your window, however pretty the view. You must put your trust in me, I should know.'

'But I didn't think I –'

'That will be all, Suor Annetta.' A steely note had crept into the Abbess's voice. 'I believe this is the best way to satisfy everybody in this case. I am after all still the Abbess of this convent. Or so I'm told.'

Chapter Sixteen

'So how did you find our most Reverend Abbess?'

Suor Annunciata, cheerful, vigorous and round-cheeked, her skin browned and coarsened by long hours in the garden, seemed not to notice Annetta's sulky face when she presented herself for duty in the garden the following morning.

'She is in good health, *suora*,' Annetta replied glumly, 'all things considered.'

'Ah, really?' Suor Annunciata cocked her head to one side sympathetically. 'Well, of course, the poor thing, she is really *very* old now, and, well ...' Annunciata tapped the side of her head meaningly with one finger '... you know.'

'No, *suora*, I said she seemed *very well*,' Annetta repeated, raising her voice a fraction, 'and not nearly as simple-minded as everyone seems to think,' she muttered, half to herself.

'Ah, really?' Annunciata shook her head. 'Well, that's only to be expected, given her age.'

'No, no, *suora*, what I said was –' Annetta began, but Suor Annunciata was already bustling ahead of her, apparently delighted to have a new helper.

'Now, you were the one who came to us as a *conversa* all those years ago, is that right?' Suor Annunciata beamed at her, displaying a pair of large and slightly prominent front teeth. 'So you must have helped out in our garden before, I'm sure?'

'Yes, *suora*.' Annetta's tone was arctic. She had indeed often been obliged to work in the garden – as all the *conversas* did – and it was something she had much rather forget. But Suor Annunciata rattled on obliviously.

'Splendid, splendid, now follow me.'

They reached the kitchen garden where a large pile of squash and pumpkins were stacked up against the wall.

'Just a moment, *suora*, I'm just having a little difficulty...' Annetta raised her skirts with one hand, revealing for the first time the little embroidered slippers beneath her robes.

'*Hmm*, I see.' Annunciata watched her for a moment. She looked doubtfully at the velvet slippers, the lace at Annetta's neck, the little embroidered velvet pouch she always wore at her waist. 'Dear me, dear me, this won't do at all. I can see we must get you proper gardening clothes, *suora*.'

'I'll be all right, really.' Her skirts in her hands, Annetta picked her way precariously across the cobbled courtyard. She could easily have worn a pair of plain shoes, she had some perfectly serviceable ones in her chest, but she was determined to make this as awkward as possible, for herself as well as everybody else.

'Well, well,' Suor Annunciata said kindly, 'perhaps we can leave the garden just for today. Suor Veronica is in the herbarium, I am sure she can give you something to do. Let's go and find her, shall we?'

The work in the convent's herbarium had always been considered specialised, and although she knew where it was, in all her time living here before Annetta had only rarely visited it: a long, low-ceilinged building on the far side of the kitchen courtyard, where the medicinal plants from the convent's physic garden were dried and sorted. The floor of the herbarium was made of beaten earth; the air inside was cool and had a pleasant aromatic smell, of lavender and rosemary, chamomile and rue.

Several of the nuns were already there busily sorting the different herbs and flowers; some they hung in bunches from the rafters, others they laid flat on sheets of paper on shallow shelves along the walls. A second group was carefully dividing the ready-dried plants into their component parts. Some extracted the seeds from pods and flower heads, others collected the still-closed buds, or selected the petals, stems and even the bulbs and roots of the different plants; while a third group had been given the task of labelling and packaging them, placing each parcel in wooden boxes ready to be sold to the herbalists and apothecaries of the Veneto.

As she walked along with Annetta behind her, Suor Annunciata stopped occasionally to pinch a leaf or a bud from one of the hanging bunches of plants, sniffing it between her fingers. Sometimes she would nod with evident satisfaction; at other times she clicked her tongue with displeasure and signalled for the bunch to be taken down and thrown away.

The nuns did her bidding eagerly and efficiently. Although most, Annetta noticed, were *conversas*, a fair few were choir nuns, such as herself, although they too were wearing the same thick homespun habits and wooden clogs as the *conversas*. All of them went silently about their business, but with an air of such purposefulness and calm that it felt like balm to Annetta's ruffled nerves. How different this was from the strained atmosphere of the nuns' parlour, the snubbing looks and comments of Suor Purification and the *contessas*. And yet, the probability was that it was one of these – her head bent innocently beneath her wide-brimmed gardening hat – whose secret lover she had disturbed, the intruder she had pursued into the garden, the man whose breath and lips she had felt on her neck and in her hair. The thought of him, even now, gave her a feeling of anger so intense she thought she might faint.

'Ah, look, bless you, *suora*.' Noticing the expression on Annetta's face, Suor Annunciata's ruddy features broke into a beam of delight. 'I can see you are going to like working with us here after all.'

Annetta, who had no intention of working in this place, or indeed any other in the convent, for any longer than she could help it, dragged her gaze away from the drying plants in the rafters.

'I am not here at my own pleasure, but at the Abbess's,' she said stiffly, discomfited at having let her guard down.

Suor Annunciata seemed not in the least put out by her tone.

'Well, well, we all do God's work here, after all,' she said kindly, 'and Suor Veronica, I think you will find, is no exception. Go on, my dear,' she gave Annetta a little shove, 'tell her it was Annunciata who sent you.'

Suor Veronica's room was attached to the herbarium, but also separated from it, by a small covered porch.

Annetta entered the doorway at right-angles, and found herself in a large high-ceilinged room, which had perhaps once been an old

110

barn. A wooden gallery, reached by a miniature spiral staircase, had been fitted to its upper storey, and was filled on three sides by shelves full of books. The fourth side of the gallery was given over to a large window which, judging by the watery sunlight which Annetta could see dancing on the ceiling above them, must give out directly on to the lagoon. In the middle of the room was a strange wooden structure, like a pulpit. There was a sharp smell in the air that Annetta could not identify.

At first the room appeared to be empty, but after a few moments Annetta noticed that there was a person sitting behind the pulpit, her back to the window. Suor Veronica, with her long horse's face and Roman nose, was of indeterminate age, neither old nor yet particularly young. She had a pair of spectacles perched precariously on the high bridge of her nose, and between the fingers of one hand she was holding up what looked to Annetta like a pen. In the other she held a curious object, like a globe made of glass. She was gazing so intently at something on the desk in front of her that at first Annetta did not think she had seen her come in, but after a while the nun said, without looking up: 'Yes, what is it?'

'I'm sorry to disturb you . . . Suor Annunciata sent me.'

'Annunciata sent you? What for?'

The nun dipped her pen in one of several pots of ink on the desk and began scratching carefully, making little hatching marks on the paper in front of her.

'I am to work in the garden. The Reverend Abbess said so,' Annetta added. The nun's attitude was beginning to make her feel somewhat awkward.

'Bonifacia said so? But this is not the garden,' Suor Veronica said. Her voice sounded dreamy, as though she were speaking from some faraway place, and without looking up she continued her writing for a while, for so long in fact that Annetta began to think that she had forgotten all about her. She glanced up at last, and was evidently surprised to see Annetta still standing there.

'I am sorry, you are in the wrong place. As you can see, this is not the garden, *suora*,' she repeated patiently. Her voice was low and pleasant, but somehow dry, as though she did not have enough moisture in her mouth.

111

Looking round, Annetta could only agree. The room looked more like a library, or a *scriptorum*, than anything connected to herbs or vegetables or flowers; and yet, despite her reluctance to have anything to do with the workings of the garden, she was beginning to feel a curiosity about Suor Veronica, and what she might be doing in this strange light-filled, book-lined room.

'Annunciata said you might need my help, *suora*,' she ventured.

Suor Veronica looked up from her work at last. She put down her pen and peered at Annetta over the rim of her spectacles.

'I know you. You are the one who used to be a *conversa*, and who now is to be professed. The one who survived the shipwreck, and lived for all those years in Ottoman lands.'

Usually Annetta's instinct was immediately to repel all talk of her past adventures, but something about Suor Veronica's directness caught her by surprise.

'Yes,' she replied simply; and then, 'May I see what you are doing?'

'Indeed, of course you may. Many of the objects I paint have come to us from Ottoman lands.'

When Annetta approached the pulpit she saw immediately that Veronica had not been writing at all, but painting. It was not a pen that she held between her fingers, but a brush. On the sloping desk in front of her were two pieces of paper of the same size, on each of which two flowers had been painted. Their long, thin spindle-like stems took up most of the page. Balanced at the top of the stems, like turbans preposterously swollen by the rain, were the flowers. Their petals glowed in the watery lagoon light in an explosion of colour: crimson and vermilion; orange and magenta; shocking pinks through to the palest coral hues.

The first flower that Annetta's eyes lit on was almost completely round in shape like a bowl, its petals fully blown exposing the fragile stamen within; its companion was even more delicate, with thin, almost wispy petals shaped like a mandolin. Veronica had painted it as though it had been picked at dawn, its petals still lightly furled, one inside the other.

'But these are *beautiful*,' Annetta said, amazed.

Suor Veronica seemed pleased.

'Do you recognise them?'

'Of course,' Annetta nodded, 'in the Sultan's gardens there were many flowers like these, although I never learnt what they were called.'

'They are called tulips.' Suor Veronica seemed gratified by Annetta's interest. 'And you are quite right, like many of the most beautiful plants from our garden, these ones come from Ottoman lands.'

'Suor Bonifacia started to tell me something about them,' Annetta said, remembering her conversation with the Abbess. 'It was her brother who first brought them here, wasn't it?'

'That is how this garden started, certainly. But our merchants have been bringing new plants to Venice for many, many years now. Some of the finest come from Ottoman lands, to be sure – hyacinths, anemones, crown imperials – but others come from India, China, the spice islands, the New World,' Veronica said, wiping her brush on an old cloth, 'from all corners of the world. At first they were just curiosities, but now there are many who desire them. Many are rich men who want to create gardens for their own glory and magnificence. Others, like the count, our convent's first benefactor and Bonifacia's brother, who wanted to create a botanical garden for its own sake, like the ones at Pisa and Padua.'

Annetta turned to examine the paintings again.

'I like this one.' She pointed with her finger to the fourth and last tulip. Its colours were pink and white; the undersides of the petals, nearest to the stem of the plant, had been tinted the palest silvery green.

'All are valuable. But these ones, where the colours have variegated –' she indicated a flower that was red and white striped '– are the most costly of all. Here, look through this,' Veronica handed Annetta the glass globe she had been holding in her hand, 'you can see more clearly when you use this. It is what our lacemakers use.'

Annetta peered through the glass globe, and sure enough, before her very eyes the painting appeared suddenly enlarged. 'Oh look!' she said with excitement. 'Ants!' There, climbing up the stem of the pink and white tulip, were two tiny ants, perfectly observed.

She moved the glass globe carefully over the other paintings, marvelling at the details that she had not been able to see before. In one Suor Veronica had painted two shining drops of dew trapped within the single leaf which encased the stem. In another a winged insect like a tiny jewelled butterfly hovered over the wispy petals; in a third the minutely haired and arched back of a tiny caterpillar.

'They are so lifelike, I feel as though I could pick them.' Annetta looked up, delighted. 'But aren't these spring flowers, *suora*?'

'Yes, you are right. I painted these many months ago. A collector from England, a merchant, commissioned them from me – his agent came to see me when he was last in Venice, a few years ago now. Now he's in Venice again. He visited a few days ago and requested one more painting. He wants to take delivery of them today. I was just putting the finishing touches to them when you arrived.'

Suor Veronica took off her spectacles and rubbed the bridge of her nose. Without her glasses on, she looked much younger suddenly, even though her eyes had a strained look about them.

'Truly, *suora*, Annunciata was right, you do God's work here.' Annetta meant the words sincerely, but Suor Veronica looked up sharply, as though she had been stung.

'We all do the work that we can,' she said, cramming her spectacles back on to her nose. 'And I for one believe that it is God's work that I do here, whatever some of our number would say.'

'But, *suora*, I did not mean –'

'Some of us work in the garden and grow the plants, some of us work in the herbarium to sort and dry them. I . . . I . . . paint them.' She glared at Annetta over her spectacles. 'It is not vanity, no matter what she says . . .'

'Wait, wait, *suora*, please; no matter what who says?' Annetta stared at her, bewildered.

But Veronica was not listening, 'It is *God's* work, I tell you, and I will not let anyone say otherwise.'

'Of course, of course,' Annetta said, but the older nun was not to be mollified.

Ranged along the top of the pulpit was a collection of small pots and phials containing the mineral pigments needed to prepare her colours. The older nun reached up for one of them, but in her haste she dropped it. The glass bottle smashed, and the red powder – ground cinnabar – that had been stored inside spilt, like a stain of blood, all over the floor.

'Oh, now look what you've done!' she cried out, shooing Annetta away with her hand. 'Go away from here, go, go!'

'But . . . I am supposed to be here to help you.'

'You can't help me, no one can.' Suor Veronica was on her hands and knees now, picking up pieces of glass.

'Please, let me help you with that.' Annetta knelt down beside her. 'You'll cut yourself if you are not careful.'

'No, I'll do it.' Suor Veronica sat back on her knees, and passed the back of her hand over her forehead. 'Go up to the gallery,' she said, her voice returning to its dry precise tones, and she gestured in the direction of the little spiral staircase. 'My visitor will be here soon, see if you can see anyone coming. I'll clear this mess up.'

Annetta made her way up the spiral stairs to the gallery. Although it was forbidden for any individual to possess books in the convent, there were plenty of them here. She did not think she had ever seen so many all in one place. Some were old, others looked as though they had been newly bound, with their covers of pale calfskin, their spines tooled in gold.

She bent her head to read the titles as she passed by. *De Historia Stirpium*, *Der Gart der Gesundheit*, *Herbarum vivae eicones*; she read out the foreign-sounding names with difficulty, curious as to how they might have got there. Perhaps the rich men who commissioned Suor Veronica's paintings brought them for her as gifts. Were they valuable? She did not know. Although she had been taught to read, Annetta had never had much use for books, and those that she had seen were usually written in Latin, which she could not in any case understand.

Below her, in the main body of the room, she saw Veronica still kneeling amongst the spilt paint and the shards of broken glass. As she dabbed at the floor with a cloth, her hands had become red and bloodied with the pigment, and so was a corner of her robe. Annetta looked at her thoughtfully: what had that outburst really been about? She had seen how absorbed the nun had been when she had first entered the room: no wonder she had been so angry at the thought that someone might try to stop her painting; and yet, she mused, it was an unusual occupation for a nun. In the harem – a world, like the convent, populated and run entirely by women – they might have been physically constrained, but their minds were free. In the convent, it was different. She thought of Suor Purificacion and Suor

115

Bonifacia, of the unknown nun and her lover, of Suor Annunciata in her garden, and now Suor Veronica with her paintings. There were currents and pressures, rivalries and ambitions here that even Annetta, with her considerable facility for navigating such waters, was only just beginning to understand.

Just then she heard a familiar sound, the cry of a boatman. Remembering that she was supposed to be on the lookout for the collector's agent, Annetta went over to the window.

Sunlight came flooding through the glass, so strong at first it dazzled her eyes. The water of the lagoon was pale green; in the near distance she could see the gardens and cupola of San Giorgio Maggiore, and beyond it the city of Venice itself, like a pink and gold cloud on the horizon. All manner of boats – merchant galleys and smaller skiffs – plied the busy waters.

And there, sure enough, was a small boat being rowed towards the convent. There were two men sitting in it. One was old and stocky, wearing a yellow turban on his head. While the other . . .

Annetta stared. *Santa Madonna!* The other was – surely not? For a moment or two she could not quite believe her eyes. Not him again! By all the saints, it was impossible. But it *was* possible: the same curly brown hair reaching to his shoulders, the same eyes like two cold stones, even the very same posture, now she came to think of it, one leg resting on the side of the boat, as when she had first seen him, on the day of the wedding visit, through the spyglass from the dormitory window.

It was the intruder again.

Chapter Seventeen

It was the morning after their night at Zuanne Memmo's *ridotto* that Carew went back to the convent again. Only this time, with Ambrose Jones in tow, it was with the expectation of a very different kind of adventure.

The pale green water of the lagoon sparkled so it hurt his eyes to look, and so it was with a narrowed gaze that Carew watched the walls of the convent garden grow steadily closer. Here and there he could see the tops of the trees, poplar and cypress, the avenue of pleached limes, could picture with ease now the famous physic garden within those walls; a topography that he had come to know so well over the last few weeks, he could have made his way round it blindfolded.

Carew shifted restlessly at the back of the boat. The thought of his previous adventures there should have brought a smile to his lips, but it did not. In fact, the thought of her, of the nun he had churched, brought him no pleasure now the deed was done. She had been grateful, that went without saying. Compliant, too; a little too much so for his taste. They had done it, at his insistence, right under the noses of the younger nuns, practically in their dormitory, and yet, even with this added piquancy, the memory caused him not a stir, not a *frisson* of pleasure. Instead he was aware only of a faint, unsatisfied feeling seeping into him, of what he could hardly tell. Boredom? Disgust? Carew gazed down moodily into the green depths, who cared anyway? Not him. He would do what he had agreed to do – help Ambrose make some enquiries about the harem lady – and then he would be done – with Pindar, with Ambrose, with Zuanne Memmo and Francesco, even Constanza – done with the lot of them.

117

He had a yearning, suddenly, to be gone, to be off, to go home.

It was a while before he became aware that, from his seat at the front of the boat, Ambrose was trying to say something to him. 'Mr Ambrose?'

'Well it's obvious you can't hear me from over there, can you?' Ambrose motioned Carew to make his way forward. 'And try not to set us all into one another's laps, while you're doing it.'

But Carew, nimble as a cat, was already at his side. 'Sir?'

'Do sit down, John, you rock the boat lamentably, with all that jumping about.' Ambrose clutched his collecting boxes to him as the boat wavered.

Carew sat as he was bidden, and regarded Ambrose without enthusiasm. Already he was regretting his decision to accompany him back to the convent. In his yellow turban and oriental robes, he looked like nothing so much as a giant hatchling nestling in the prow of the boat. Close to, his nose was even larger than Carew remembered it: a spectacular fluorescence, worthy of one of the cabinets he collected for so assiduously. Carew studied Ambrose's nose for a few moments, and then looked away again. The silhouette of the city of Venice, in a pink nimbus, glowed on the horizon behind them.

'I expect you're wondering why I've brought you with me, John?'

Carew gave an inward sigh: the last thing on earth he needed right now was a grilling by Ambrose. 'Damned if I knows, sir.'

'How uncharacteristically incurious of you.' Ambrose gave him a beady look, and then went on evenly: 'Go on, hazard a guess.'

'I heard there's a nun there that paints.' Carew stared straight ahead of him.

'Well, that's one reason. Sister Veronica. I've known her a long time, paints and draws plants like an angel, exquisite work, absolutely exquisite –' Ambrose, warming to his subject, rubbed his hands together as he often did when discussing his treasures. 'All the paper collectors use her these days, although of course I was the first –'

'She is one of your informants, then?' Carew, never one to mince his words, cut in flatly. And then, in an undertone to himself, 'expect she knows a thing or two and all.'

If Ambrose was aware of the taunt, he gave no sign of it. 'You are a sharp one, aren't you, John?'

'Years of practice, Mr Ambrose,' Carew said, his face expressionless, 'trying to keep up with the master.'

He looked over Ambrose's shoulder towards the crescent-shaped spit of land they called the Giudecca where the nobility built their pleasure houses; gardens and orchards spilt down to the waterfront, and on a little bank of sand some boys were hunting for crabs. Sweet Jesus, he knew he shouldn't have come; but there was no going back now.

'The master, eh?' Ambrose put his hand up to shield his eyes from the sun. 'I'd like to come back to that subject in a minute, but first –'

'So do you think your painter nun – whatever she's called – might know something about the lady from the harem?' Carew interrupted.

'She might.' Ambrose settled further back into his seat, arranging himself more comfortably among the cushions. 'If anyone has knowledge of this mysterious lady and her jewels, it will be Sister Veronica. People visit her all the time and she seems to know everything that goes on in the lagoon, but I have to tell you that I very much doubt she exists, no matter what Pindar is hoping for.'

'Who, the harem lady with the jewels?'

'Yes of course.'

'But I thought Prospero said –'

'Oh those gem dealers!' Ambrose waved his hand airily. 'Fabulists to a man. They're stolen stones, I shouldn't wonder; and this is just a story that they've invented to explain a sudden influx on the market. There's always some story or other going round the Rialto, and hardly any of them are true,' he glanced away, 'surely you know that.'

'Maybe.' Maybe not. Had Ambrose been in the room when Prospero had told them about the diamond? Carew realised he could not remember. What he did remember very clearly was the scene only an hour or so later in Zuanne Memmo's *ridotto*. The Sultan's Blue had been real enough, hadn't it? Could Ambrose with his apparently infinite capacity to glean information, to suck it up from the gutter, have heard about their illicit visit there? His curiosity was piqued. 'And the Sultan's Blue? Is that just a Rialto story?' he ventured, trying not to look too interested.

'Almost certainly.' Ambrose's tone was firm. 'Although I know Pindar doesn't think so. He's like a man possessed. The last thing we want him believing is that this jewel – if it exists at all – might have some sort of connection to Celia Lamprey, however remote.' Ambrose gave Carew a sly look, as though trying to gauge his reaction.

There was a small pause while Carew digested this.

'So you know all about that then, do you?'

'Do I know about Celia Lamprey?' When he saw Carew's face Ambrose gave a satisfied chuckle. 'Lord love you, I knew her when she was a little girl; I knew her father, the good captain, too, may their souls rest in peace. We heard all about the shipwreck, every merchant in London did. A great deal of money was lost when the *Celia* went down. But if Pindar thinks this harem lady might be Celia Lamprey, he is deluding himself.' Ambrose gave Carew one of his long, unblinking gazes. 'They say you saw her, John. Is it true?'

'Yes, I saw her,' Carew said, and then he added, 'or I think I did.'

'So you can't be sure?'

'Yes I am sure. Of course I'm sure. At least –' and for the first time he hesitated '– I was sure at the time.'

'How long is it now?'

'Four years ago, seems longer, what with . . . well, what with one thing and another.' Carew looked away. But it was true, wasn't it, that whenever he thought about it, the memory seemed to get more remote, until it dissolved, like moonshine on water. 'I was with Tom Dallam at the time,' he found himself saying.

'The organ maker?'

'Yes,' Carew nodded.

Tom Dallam! He hadn't thought about him in years. Carew remembered how he had gone with him one day to the palace. There had been a little courtyard paved with marble in which Dallam was building an organ, a present to the Sultan from the Levant Company merchants. The guards had made signs to them that they should go over to a place in the wall where there was a little grille. He remembered how they had looked through and glimpsed a second secret courtyard, and in it about thirty of the Great Turk's concubines playing with a ball; remembered the guard stamping his foot on the ground to make them come away.

'But I couldn't move. I'd seen this one girl, you see,' Carew hesitated, 'this girl who was different from all the rest.'

120

He could picture her clearly in his mind's eye now. She was sitting a little apart from the others, and very richly dressed. Jewels, pearls perhaps, at her neck. Pale skin and beautiful hair, reddish-gold. Tom Dallam pulling at his arm, begging him to hurry. But he could not, for it was then that he had realised who she was. Carew rubbed a hand over his eyes. Remembered the catch in his own voice. '*God help us, it's Celia, Celia Lamprey! We all thought she was dead.*'

'*I* knew it was her. I'd have known her anywhere . . .'

'Well, well, all very pretty, but if you ask me, one wench in breeches must look very much like another wench in breeches.' Ambrose, who had been sitting silently, let out a curious high-pitched giggle. 'What a can of worms! Pindar's dead betrothed turning up in the Sultan's chicken coop!' He seemed to find the whole scenario highly amusing. 'Don't suppose it occurred to you that it might have been better if you'd kept that information to yourself? But no matter,' he sighed, 'the damage is done now.'

He sat up in the boat, serious again suddenly. 'There was another reason I thought to bring you with me and now I can see I've got the right man for the job. Someone who's good at sneaking about. Pindar tells me you know your way around there.' He nodded in the direction of the convent island, which was drawing ever nearer.

'Knows my way around?' Carew bent the fingers of his hands back until the knuckles cracked. 'Not quite sure I get your meaning, sir?'

'Oh, I know all about your fornicating ways,' Ambrose said smoothly, 'but you need not worry, it's of absolutely no concern to me. A houseful of women, left to their own devices – heretics and Catholics into the bargain –' Ambrose's tone was withering, 'what does anyone expect? I don't hold with any of it myself. You're too young, but I can just remember the great Dissolution under old King Henry, and a good thing too. If you were my servant, of course, I'd have you horsewhipped,' he went on cheerfully, 'but luckily you're no concern of mine. So tell me, John,' Ambrose trailed his fingers in the water, 'why doesn't he?'

'What, have me horsewhipped?'

Ambrose smiled at him benignly. 'You are sharp, aren't you?'

Carew glanced at Ambrose and then looked away again quickly. This was an unexpected turn to the conversation, and he was not at all sure that he liked it.

'A servant who does not serve,' Ambrose went on meditatively. 'A cook who does not cook. All the licence of a Fool. And that's just the beginning of it,' he stared at Carew. 'It's like locking a lot of women up together in a convent, it's against nature. Not *na-tu-ral*,' he spelt the word out slowly, 'not natural at all. Well, come on, man,' impatient now, 'cat got your tongue?'

If Carew had felt at all inclined to exchange any more confidences with Ambrose, which he did not, even the threat of hellfire and eternal damnation was not about to wrestle one from him now.

'I don't knows, Mr Ambrose,' Carew spoke slowly, returned Ambrose's unblinking blue gaze, 'but I expect you're going to tell me.'

But Ambrose seemed, of a sudden, to lose interest. 'Well, well, it will keep,' he said mildly. 'I'll find out eventually, I always do, you know.' He took his turban off and scratched his enormous nose with it thoughtfully. 'The fact is, your master has fallen into a melancholy. And we must get him out of it before he does any more harm to himself.'

They were nearly at the island now. Ambrose sniffed the air reflectively. 'They say there'll be another plague here this summer, and dear Lord it's going to be hot enough. But you'll be gone by then, won't you, John. Or that's what I've heard?'

'On the next merchantman that will take me.'

This, at least, was information that Carew did not mind sharing with Ambrose.

'So you really are done with Pindar? Your mind is quite made up?'

When Carew did not respond he added, quite kindly, 'He may have kept you in the dark about certain things, John, but it's really he who is in the dark.'

Chapter Eighteen

They reached the island at last. As instructed, the boatman rowed them not to the main gatehouse, but to a secondary *riva d'acqua* on the garden side which led directly into Suor Veronica's workshop.

Until now Carew had believed that this secondary mooring was completely disused, and had made free use of it during his escapades over the last few weeks, but now he saw that it was the means by which Suor Veronica's clients made their occasional visits to her workshop, without intruding on the main part of the convent. He had seen the painter nun's workshop from the outside many times, an old building, far older than the more modern part of the convent, and roofed like a barn, but now, as he made his way in behind Ambrose, he found himself in a cool, book-lined room. Light from the lagoon spilled in through a window.

The nun, whom Ambrose greeted as Suor Veronica, came towards them, a paint-stained cloth in her hands with which she had apparently been wiping up some spilled pigment from the floor; a brilliant crimson coloured her fingers, and the hem of her robe.

'Good morning, sister, I hope you haven't cut yourself,' Ambrose said after he had greeted her.

'No, no, it's nothing, just spilled paint – please, please.' Dabbing ineffectually at her robe, she seemed almost displeased that he had mentioned it. 'Please come in, Signor Jones, I was just collecting the last of your paintings together.' She led Ambrose off to the middle of the room.

From the doorway, Carew settled down to wait. He watched the nun from behind as she moved. Why was it, he wondered idly, that nuns always held such a peculiar fascination? Young, not so young, plump, thin, short, tall … there was no accounting for it. Despite his earlier feelings – of disgust and boredom – he found his interest piqued again.

Carew looked Suor Veronica over, trying to imagine what she was really like. Ambrose might think her a painter of genius, but no, there was nothing here to stir his imagination: beneath the robes and the headdress covering her hair, Suor Veronica was neither old nor yet particularly young; slender, it was true, but probably felt like a sack of old bones without her shift on; a pleasant, intelligent face, but long … like a horse.

His fantasy was interrupted by a sudden sharp pain in his ribs. When he looked up it was to see Ambrose glaring down at him, the toe of his boot jabbed again in the direction of Carew's ribcage.

'Don't stand there gawping, man. My business won't take long. Go on, go and make yourself useful somewhere else.'

Carew stood up slowly. 'You knows best, sir.' He gave Ambrose a bow of exaggerated respect. 'I'll go and wait by the boat then, shall I, sir?'

'He can go and look at the garden if he likes,' Suor Veronica called out from inside the workshop.

As she spoke a small clear bell rang from somewhere within the apparently sleepy midday convent.

'Well, if you are quite sure,' Ambrose frowned. 'I wouldn't want my servant here –' he gave Carew a meaning stare – 'to be guilty of any impropriety.'

'Quite sure, quite sure. He won't disturb anyone. That was the bell for *pranzo*, my sisters will all be in the refectory. *Suora!* Where are you, *suora!*' she called to another as-yet-unseen person. 'Strange, she was there a minute ago,' Veronica muttered to herself, and then: 'Ah, no, there she is – what are you doing still hiding up there, *suora*? You should be going off to the refectory now with the others,' the nun's tone was brisk, 'come down now, there's no need to be shy.' Turning to Carew, she pointed to a second nun, who was now slowly making her way from the gallery down the library ladder.

'There you go, young man, just don't go picking anything, that's all,' she gave Carew a beatific smile, 'Suor Annetta will show you the way.'

Carew followed the second nun out of the room. After her cautious descent of the ladder, she now almost ran ahead of him; so fast, in fact, that he barely had time to catch a glimpse of her as she rushed past.

'Wait, sister, not so fast!'

But the nun sped on, walking briskly so as to keep herself several paces in front of him, head bent demurely to the ground, her hands folded inside her sleeves.

'I won't bite you, you know . . .' Carew had almost to run to catch up with her. This nun seemed, if anything, even more flustered than the painter nun had been when they first arrived.

'What did you say your name was? Benadetta, was it?' At this she half-glanced over her shoulder, but still would not answer him.

'Oh well,' Carew gave a sigh, 'not very godly of you, Sister Benadetta, to ignore a guest of the convent.'

For a while Carew amused himself by examining the nun's back view: young, or at least much younger than the other one, he guessed; a slender waist, but a good rump on her all the same; she had a strange undulating walk which showed it off to some advantage. Not much mortification of the flesh had gone on with this one, that was for sure.

The thought was energising. That vague, dissatisfied feeling that he had experienced in the gondola, the resolution to give up these dangerous escapades once and for all, was now, like morning mist on the lagoon, thoroughly dispersed; and Carew found himself sniffing the scent of a new adventure in the air.

They had passed the herbarium and were in the physic garden itself now, rows of neatly clipped box hedges fanned out from one another in symmetrical shapes. The young nun stopped unexpectedly, and with her hand over her face to shield it from the blaze of the midday sun, she half-turned towards him.

'This is the garden,' she said, and her voice he noticed was unexpectedly warm and low. 'The bell will go again at the end of *pranzo*, so when you hear it you'd better make yourself scarce – no matter what Suor Veronica may have told you.'

The way she said this gave Carew the impression that Ambrose's painter nun was somehow not quite party to the rest of the convent rules. He had the distinct feeling, growing by the minute, that he should not be here at all. But why should he care? He was here as Ambrose's servant, let him take the blame for once. So Carew stood, waiting for her to elaborate – most of the nuns he had come into

125

contact with had seemed only too pleased for the excuse to chat to someone new – but evidently not this one. Nonetheless, when she made as if to walk past him, he placed himself firmly in her pathway.

'But stay! Please, not so fast.' Carew, deciding on a change of tack, put on his most caressing voice. 'Aren't you going to tell me . . .' he searched around for an excuse and finally his eyes lit upon one of the flower-beds '. . . tell me what these plants are?'

'Tell you what these plants are?' This time the nun's tone was neither low nor warm. And then: 'And don't think that your little games are going to work on me!'

If Carew were surprised by this sudden change in her he soon recovered himself; and then almost immediately a memory stirred. 'Wait, sister, we've spoken before, haven't we?'

When she did not reply he put his hand up as if to draw her shielding palm from her face, but she snatched her arm away and turned her back to him again.

'You were told not to touch anything, remember?' The words came out breathlessly, as if she had been running; as if it were an effort to get them out.

'Ho!'

Carew stood there looking at her; and realised what he should have seen all along: that the girl was frightened of him. Unbidden, an image came to him of a rabbit he had once snared as a boy. It had sat in front of him without moving, as though quite tame, and it was only after a while that he had become aware of its small ribcage rising and falling, as though its heart would at any moment burst with terror.

He looked around him; to one side lay the garden and the wall facing the lagoon, to the other one wing of the convent. His eyes cast a practised glance up at the windows, searching for signs that someone might be spying on them, but as far as he could tell there was no one there.

The girl must have followed his gaze, for now she said quickly, 'Our Reverend Abbess – she lives up there – so you'd better not try to touch me – *capito*?' and once again the words came out breathlessly, as if it hurt her to speak.

And now he was sure of it. 'But I *do* know you, don't I?' Even by his standards, it seemed an amazing coincidence. 'You're the one who was running around the garden in her nightshift –'

The one I nearly strangled; the one I offered to church right there and then, because I wanted to frighten her. Sweet Jesus, no wonder –

She stood staring at the ground, but still he could not see her face. And then she glanced up again, looking up at the north wing of the convent, as though searching for a face at one of the windows. Might she have been telling the truth about the Abbess?

Her profile was turned towards him and all he could see now was that a wisp of long dark hair had escaped from beneath her tight head-dress. He saw too the pure high bridge of her nose, the nostrils slightly flared, a small mole, like a beauty mark, on her right cheekbone. Suddenly it seemed imperative that she should not leave, not just yet. He was assailed by the feeling that there was something he needed to say to her, although he was not quite sure what exactly it might be.

The sun beat down. Carew could feel its heat, like the blade of a knife, on his back, on his neck, on his hatless head; and all around him, in the midday heat, the garden shimmered. The colours of the flowers seemed to bleed into one another in a dream-like haze. The garden had that silence peculiar to hot still places in the middle of the day, as though it were holding its breath. He tried to remember what she had looked like that other morning, but found that he had no particular recollection. Only that she had felt small, vulnerable, in his arms.

Then she turned to face him at last, and they were looking into one another's eyes.

'Benadetta . . .' he heard himself say.

But she shook her head. 'No,' she said fiercely, 'it's *Annetta*. My name is Annetta.'

And Carew, for possibly the first time in his life, could think of nothing to say.

In the next instant she was walking past him, and he, like the great dolt he was, was standing to one side and doing nothing to stop her go, although she passed so close that – had he imagined it? – the back of her hand brushed lightly against his palm, her fingers curling briefly, hooking themselves into his.

Carew watched her go. That same strange undulating walk again. Where had he seen that walk before? It struck him now as oddly familiar, although he could not for the life of him think why.

But the next moment all that was forgotten as he saw that she had dropped something on the path. He knelt down to retrieve it, and found himself holding a small pink velvet pouch embroidered with silver thread. An exact replica, unless he was very much mistaken, of the one in which the great diamond, the Sultan's Blue, had been kept in Zuanne Memmo's *ridotto*.

Chapter Nineteen

For the whole of that summer, through the searing heat, the women travelled north, stopping in the villages and hamlets along the way to perform their tumbling acts at fairs and feast days. They travelled at night, mostly, as was their custom during the summer months, to avoid the worst of the sun. A few times, when their route took them to the littoral, they found a boat willing to carry them – horses, cart and all – for a short stretch along the coast. Maryam grumbled at the cost, but after the furnace of the land – a land grown so hot that an egg left on rocks on the ground would cook in its own shell – the proximity of the sea, and its cool breezes, was like a small paradise.

They were a fine sight to behold as they paraded around the village squares; heralding their arrival in a strange cacophony of cymbals, drums, tambourines and reed pipes. One of their number, Ilkai, who had a voice even louder than Maryam's booming baritone, went ahead of them, shouting out their wears like a town crier: *the Women from Salonika, the world's Most Famous Tumbling Troupe, as favoured by Pashas, Viziers, even by the Sultan, the Great Turk himself. For one night only . . .*

In great leaps and bounds the other women tumblers would follow her, six of them in all, in their brightly coloured jackets, and strange voluminous garments that clung to their legs like a man's breeches. After them came Maryam – *the giantess of Salonika* – a red bandana tied across her forehead, a leather belt around her shapeless jerkin. Sometimes Maryam carried Elena's two little girls, Nana and Leya, one on each of her shoulders. Sometimes they ran ahead of her, walking on their hands, throwing themselves backwards, arching themselves into strange crab-like shapes, while Maryam herself pulled a trolley on which was displayed a strange variety of objects – pots and pans, logs of wood, a set of cannon balls – the props of her strongwoman act. Behind them all walked Elena, her gentle features whitened into a sad mask with chalk, her costume a strange robe of striped motley covered in sequins which made her glitter as she moved, a magical being covered in hoar frost.

Mostly the villages welcomed their arrival, the glamour and excitement of their outlandish appearance outweighing their dubious status as outsiders. But at other times, when the priests turned against them, the people seemed fearful. They rang the bells from the church campanile, threw stones and set their dogs on them, so that the women were often forced to march, through the blazing heat of the day, on to the next village.

Against all the odds, the mermaid woman and her baby seemed to thrive at first. Not knowing what to call her, Maryam named the young woman Thessala, after the sea from which she had come, but somehow the name never fitted her. She seemed never to inhabit it, in the same way that she seemed not to inhabit properly the clothes they found for her to wear, nor the space in which she slept. The other women – who from the beginning were suspicious of this mysterious sea cuckoo, this broken nymph, who had landed so inauspiciously amongst them – rarely referred to her as anything, even amongst themselves, other than 'she' or 'her'.

Still weak after the birth, the mermaid woman lay with her infant in a makeshift shelter at the back of the troupe's cart, a place from which she showed no sign of wanting to move. Her wounds, the lesions on her wrists and ankles, healed slowly, but she was mercifully free from any fever, which would almost certainly have killed her. As for her legs – well, although it was discovered that the breaks were old and the bones had knitted again, no one thought it likely that she would walk again.

The woman never spoke, not even to the infant, with which she seemed to have very little idea of what to do, beyond wrapping it in swaddling and carrying it by her side. It soon became clear that she had no milk, or so little that the child could not flourish on it, and if it had not been for the fact that Maryam was able to barter one of the horses that Signor Bocelli had given them for a milking goat, it would not have survived. Elena tried all the languages she knew – Venetian, Spanish, Greek, even the language of the Ottomans – but she had no luck with any of them. The mermaid woman merely stared at her, uncomprehending, with her strange unblinking eyes.

'Is she deaf? A deaf mute, perhaps?' Maryam said. 'Or perhaps she's just half-witted?'

'No,' Elena frowned, 'I don't think so. I don't think she is any of those things, she is more like . . . I don't know.' She had been going to say 'a ghost', but it seemed an unlucky thing to suggest, so instead she said, 'It's as if she's simply – not there.'

It was a night with no moon and it was too dark to travel, so the women had pitched their tents – small, round, brightly coloured pavilions such as nomads use – in a half circle in the lee of whatever trees they could find.

After the two little girls had gone to sleep, Maryam and Elena were lying together outside under the stars, just their hands touching, their little fingers linked together, listening to the familiar sounds of the women's voices coming from the other tents.

'Are you sure?'

'Yes, I'm sure. And it's not true that she can't speak. I have heard her speak, just the other day, but only one word.'

'What did she say?'

'Just one word: *No!*'

'Just that?' Maryam stared into the darkness. 'Just "no". Well, that doesn't get us very far, does it. That could be anything: Italian, Spanish, French . . .' She shrugged. 'What was she saying "no" to, anyway?'

'You remember that little velvet pouch? The one we found hidden inside her clothing? The one she opens and closes all the time?'

'Yes, I know it.'

'Well one of my girls, Nana, had got hold of it somehow and was playing with it, but when she realised what had happened she seemed very agitated. She raised herself up on one elbow and just cried out "No!" – like that. Nana heard it, too. If she had not been there, I might have thought I had imagined it.'

For a while the two women lay in silence. From some distant hill, they could hear the sound of a shepherd's dog barking; the faint tinkling of sheep's bells.

'Where can she have come from?'

How often in the last few weeks had they had this conversation?

'How did she end up in that plague village, that's what I want to know.'

'She's no country girl, that much is for sure. Her hands, have you seen them? And that skin, so pale. She's never done a day's work in her life, not village work at any rate.'

'So she's a lady then?'

'A lady? *Panayia mou!* Not now, bless her.' Elena sounded sad. 'Nor likely to be ever again.'

'That man Bocelli told me that the fishermen had drawn her out of the water in their nets.'

'And you think he was telling you the truth?' Elena turned towards Maryam in the darkness.

'I think that men like Bocelli would not know the truth if it reared up and kicked them in the balls.' Maryam gave a contemptuous laugh. 'My guess is that someone must have abandoned her somewhere near there when they thought she was about to give birth. And Bocelli found her . . . I suppose . . .' But the more she thought about it, the more improbable the whole story sounded.

'What brutes, how could anyone do such a thing? Imagine what she must have gone through, all on her own, with no friend to help her.' Elena shook her head. 'But where does Bocelli come into it? And why was he so anxious to get rid of her? That's what I don't understand. *Two horses*, Maryam . . .' Two weeks after the event there was still wonder in Elena's voice. 'It's more than the Sultan himself gave us when we played in the House of Felicity.'

'I got a high price from him, that's for sure, the man's a fool,' but even as she said the words, Maryam felt a twinge of disquiet.

Had the price, in fact, not been *too* high? It was not the first time that the thought had crossed her mind. Things had been happening in the villages since they had the mermaid woman with them. At first it was nothing she could quite put her finger on, a feeling in the air, a gust of wind, a dust-devil dancing down a deserted street; but then a few nights ago they had found food placed outside their camp: a basket of eggs, some fruit, small loaves of unleavened bread, olives still on the branch. They were laid out carefully, on leaves. Had it been her imagination, or had they been left not so much as gifts, but as offerings? Perhaps Bocelli was not such a fool after all. In the darkness Maryam felt in the pocket of her leather jerkin; her strong fingers closed around the mermaid amulet that he had shown her in the plague village. She supposed she would have to tell Elena and the others what Bocelli had said, but not yet . . .

In these parts mermaids have always been thought to bring luck. You can find them almost everywhere along the coast . . . I'm surprised you've never seen one before. She could almost smell that stench of onion on his breath. *But a real mermaid . . . ! No one knows what to do with her, they're afraid even to go near her. They'd have killed her by now if they didn't think it would bring even worse catastrophe on themselves . . .* Well, it looked like they were going to need all the luck they could find to get themselves to Venice in one piece.

Elena looked up at the sky. In the absence of any light from the moon, the stars blazed across the firmament, so bright and in such numbers that it gave her the vertiginous feeling that she was flying up towards them. This was the moment she had been dreading, but she knew that she had to speak.

She closed her eyes. 'Maryam?'

'Yes?'

Elena decided that there was nothing for it but to plunge in. 'The others think she is unlucky.'

'*Un*-lucky?'

If there were something discordant in Maryam's voice, Elena did not notice it.

'They won't go near her or the child, haven't you noticed?'

'*Hmm.*' Maryam gave a non-committal grunt.

'And if that were not bad enough, we've so little work . . . the villages seem more . . .' Elena struggled to express herself. 'Well, the people seem strange, I can't really explain it.'

So, Elena had noticed it too.

'They're poor, that's all,' Maryam said gruffly. 'It's my fault, we shouldn't have come this way.'

'Look, she's going to have to pay for her keep somehow. I know you don't want to hear this, but . . .'

'Why say it then?' Maryam said so sharply Elena felt herself recoil, but she knew she must speak out.

'The others say she is a burden on us, she and the child.'

'And you? What do you say?' When Elena did not reply she added, 'We were paid for taking her, handsomely paid, you said so yourself.'

'She can't work, probably never will. We don't have enough food –'

'But she eats no more than a bird!'

'– and we can't eat the horse or the goat,' Elena went on patiently. 'But if you would only consider –'

'Consider what?'

Elena opened her eyes again, willed herself to continue. 'We have discussed this before.'

'Put her on show? No, I tell you.'

'Look, I know you have your own particular reasons . . .'

'Reasons? Yes, I have my reasons. And you – of all people, Elena – should know why. You are no better than that little tick Bocelli.'

For several minutes they lay without speaking; but after a while Maryam felt Elena's hand, thin and bony, being slipped into her own calloused paw, and held there until Maryam's own fingers relaxed round it.

'It does not have to be like . . . like . . .' Elena found it difficult to say the words '. . . like how it was.'

'You think?'

Maryam stared blankly up into the night sky. Even now, after all these years together, Elena's innocence about the world amazed her. 'They broke her mother's legs, in case you hadn't noticed, Elena.' She shook her head, as if to rid herself of some thought, and pulling her hand away from Elena's, ran her fingers up and down her bare forearms, feeling the familiar scars that peppered and disfigured them, raised cicatrices the size of bullet holes. 'You have no idea what men can do.'

That night Maryam could not sleep. So many thoughts in her head, they were like dervishes, spinning and spinning until she thought she would go mad.

As the leader of a woman's troupe she was quite used to carrying the full weight of their vulnerability on her own shoulders. She was used to the task, second nature now, of having always to be on guard, to second guess what everyone around them was thinking; to interpret a look here, a gesture there; to demur, to placate, to be ready to move on, *on the instant*, if she felt a sea change in the air. Ever since the troupe had been formed, seven years ago now, they had been compensating for the inestimable offence of their being women with no man to herd and control them. But in all her experience nothing was equal to the sense of foreboding she had now.

Ever since they had left Messina, Maryam had been plagued by a feeling of almost constant danger. Was it simply that the country-side was always more dangerous than the towns? The people more sullen, more superstitious, more likely to turn on them. Maryam knew only too well the consequences of misjudgement. She shifted uncomfortably on her blanket.

In the darkened hills behind them the shepherd's dog was still barking. There was silence now in their own camp; beside her Elena had fallen asleep at last. That too, was disquieting, for it was rare for them to leave their differences unresolved before sleeping. She could hear the sound of the horse chewing at his feeding bag; the goat rustling at its post. Normally she was comforted by these small noises, but not tonight. She stood up, shifting her ungainly bulk slowly, and with difficulty, trying not to notice the aching, almost constant these days, in her joints; the numbness in her fingers.

In her makeshift shelter at the back of the cart, Thessala the mermaid woman lay asleep, her infant beside her. In her hand she held the pink velvet pocket, her fingers clasped around it like a talisman. The child lay so still, and so quietly, that at first Maryam presumed that it was asleep too; she was just about to turn away when she caught a small glint, and saw that its eyes were open, staring up into the night sky.

Beside them there was a sudden sound of the horse blowing softly through its nose, and as Maryam watched she saw the baby turn its head slowly, wonderingly, towards the animal, its little brow wrinkling as though this were the first noise in the whole universe. As the baby moved, part of the cloth wrapping it came undone, exposing the lower part of its body: the two tiny legs fused together, two perfect feet splayed outwards. She put out her finger, felt the child's tiny fist close round it, the touch of it against her skin, no more substantial than gossamer. Maryam felt her heart contract.

Had she been right to take them on? Probably not, Maryam gave a sigh; but, under the circumstances, how could she have said no? Even so, her soul felt heavy at the thought of what might lie ahead.

What were the chances that the child would survive? Not for long surely; and perhaps it would be better that way. The fact was the mermaid baby was worth a fortune. Elena knew it, they all did.

Under the spinning firmament, the giantess and the baby stared into each other's eyes. A lesser woman might have prayed to God at that point, prayed to Our Lady and all the blessed saints to protect them, but Maryam's life had not led her to have much faith in the efficacy of prayer. God, like man, was a distant tormentor, far beyond the reach of women such as she.

Chapter Twenty

When Maryam lay down to sleep finally she dreamt the dream again.

She was fifteen years old, and they were leading her into the bear pit. Behind a palisade of sharpened sticks she could hear the dogs snarling . . .

Just two years earlier, when she was already the height and weight of a burly young man, her parents had been glad to sell their freakish daughter to the first person who offered to take her off their hands. The man, a travelling salesman from the south whose name she had never learnt, had claimed that he wanted her as his wife; but it soon became clear to Maryam that this was not his intention at all.

As soon as he had tired of the novelty of coupling with a child-bride the size of a prize fighter, the salesman's plan was to lend her out to any friend, neighbour or passer-by who would pay for the privilege. Thus began, for her keeper at any rate, a life of relative ease. He gave up his trade in fairground toys and trinkets, and bought a booth instead, which he would set up here and there on his travels, at the various fairs and markets they attended.

The booth was a simple affair, not much more than a screen with a straw pallet inside it on which Maryam lay with his customers. After a few years of this bitter life, the salesman, who was getting on in years, had woken up one morning seized by the desire to return to his real wife and children somewhere in the Peloponnese. His idea had been simply to abandon Maryam now she was no longer any use to him – would have not given a second thought to leaving her to shift for herself without so much as a few *soldi* to her name – but as his good fortune would have it, his last customer was the leader of

an itinerant troupe of acrobats, and when they left town the following day, Maryam found that she was to go with them. She had been
sold again.

Now, at the age of fifteen, Maryam was several heads taller than
she had been at thirteen, towering over even the tallest of men. She
had a barrel chest like a man's, forearms like two hams, hands and
feet the size of trenchers: a great bull of a young woman, with fierce
black looks to match: black hair, black eyes, a powdering of fine
black hair on her upper lip like an adolescent boy's.

The first time the leader of the troupe saw her he knew he would
easily recoup his money. He would put her on display as a freak of
nature – the Minotaur's Daughter, they would call her – and he set
her to work at once, knowing full well that this time it would not
only be the men who would pay.

The next few years were, if possible, an even more wretched exist-
ence for Maryam than the previous two. Like the salesman before
them, the acrobat troupe – a family from Genoa called Grissani –
followed a well-worn route. The difference was that the fairs were
bigger, the distances greater, and instead of a booth this time Maryam
had a cage. It was a real cage with iron bars, still bearing the traces,
the smells, and even the dried faeces, of the troupe's recently deceased
dancing bear, in which she had to sit for long hours every day, a pair
of cow horns fastened to her head, while people paid a few coins for
the pleasure of laughing and throwing stones and rotten fruit at her,
or poking her with sticks.

She did not know how long it was before they came to the place:
a mountainous region where they no longer spoke Greek, or the
language of their Ottoman overlords, but some more guttural dialect
that Maryam could not at first understand. The town, encircled by
pine forests, was poor, and much smaller than their usual destina-
tions; the women were not much in evidence, the children too timid
to do more than peer at them from the windows.

As was their custom, the troupe made their camp on the outskirts
of the town, at the edge of the dripping forest. A good crowd gathered that afternoon to watch the tumbling, but the sight of Maryam
behind bars seemed to make the men angry, and on a few occasions she caught sight of one or more of them offering the troupe
leader money, which at first he appeared adamantly to refuse. The

faint flutter of hope that she allowed herself at the sight of this was confirmed by the appearance at dusk, several hours earlier than usual, of Signor Grissani at the bear-cage door.

'What is it, what's happening?'

'You'll find out soon enough.' He took the key from the belt at his waist and unlocked the cage.

'Have they paid you to let me go?'

For years afterwards, when Maryam thought of that remark, she found it hard not to shed tears of pity at the innocence of her younger self. Had she really learnt nothing about the nature of men?

'Let you go?' Signor Grissani, who seemed very intent on his keys suddenly, did not raise his head. When he looked up at last, his expression was so sad that it was all she could do to stop herself throwing her arms around his neck.

'They have, haven't they, oh thank you, *thank you*, signore . . .' Maryam had dreamed so long of this moment, the moment of her delivery; had wanted it so badly, had willed it every minute of every hour of her wretched vigils in the bear cage, that she was almost stupefied with joy.

Just then Signor Grissani's wife, a hard-eyed woman with the wiry body of an acrobat, came running up to him.

'Sergio, is it true?' She, too, seemed stricken. 'You can't do it, Sergio, you can't let them take her.'

'She'll be all right.' Grissani answered gruffly.

'What do you mean? She may be big, but she's a girl still, not much more than a child.'

Maryam could still remember her sense of absolute amazement at the emotion in the woman's voice: this woman who had begrudged every last crust of bread that they were obliged to feed her, every last spoonful of watery soup.

'I'll be all right, signora, really I will.' Maryam felt almost sorry for her. She did not know how she would manage on her own, but she would, somehow.

'Shut up, you blubbering great idiot, I'm not talking to you.' The signora shot her a venomous look. 'Sergio! Have you gone mad? Are you listening to me?' she shouted at him, pulling at his sleeve. 'The dogs'll rip her to shreds . . .'

'But, signora –' The happy words that had been bubbling up inside her curdled on Maryam's tongue. '*Dogs?*'

A strange vertiginous sensation, as if all the blood had suddenly drained from her head, came over her. She clutched on to the bars of the cage to steady herself. '*What dogs?*' she repeated faintly, but no one was listening to her.

'They'll rip her to shreds,' the wife shrieked; she was lashing out at her husband now, trying to box his ears with her clenched fists. 'And then what'll we do?'

Maryam was standing outside the bear cage, looking down on them: a pathetic, shambling creature in her soiled leather jerkin and trousers, the fake cow horns slipping over her eyes. She knew, with a sensation that was more weary than anything else, that the men she had seen had not meant her any good after all. The town, which a few moments ago had seemed like a place of liberation, now had a sinister air. Its cobbled streets were mean and dark, the ill-kept houses, with their rotting thatched roofs, were too close together. Behind them a thin mist was descending from the mountains, threading its way through the pine forests like spirit matter.

Maryam knew then that they were going to kill her.

'*Basta*! We have no choice, *capito*?' Signor Grissani, looking very white, gave his wife a shove that sent her flying. 'And you,' he jerked his chin at Maryam, 'come with me.' In his hands she saw that he held a stick with a sharp metal point, of the kind that farmers use to herd their cattle.

'Where are we going?' she asked him with a feeling of dread. But he did not reply, merely poked her with the stick in the direction of the town. His hands, she saw, were trembling. Why had she not run, right there and then, made a dash for the dark of the forests while she still could?

Why not, why not?

But all the years of slavery – of being a child, a woman, a freak – had taken their toll. Maryam did not think it had even occurred to her. Head bowed, she walked meekly on.

She had walked through the town as though on a tumbrel, so dazed with fear she hardly saw where she was going. The women watched her silently from doorways and behind shuttered windows, recoiling if she turned her great lumbering head, still in its cow-horn headdress, towards them, pulling their children to them as though she might at any moment bite. *Do they really think I'm some sort of beast?* And from their faces she knew then, in her very soul, that they did. She was the monster who ate their sheep and stole their children. She was the creature who lived in the dark heart of their deepest forests; who hid on the most desolate mountaintops, in caves full of bones. She was the monster their grandfathers had told them stories about by the fireside on dark winter nights, never seen except in dreams.

By the time they reached the bear pit it was almost dark. There was a palisade of sharpened sticks all the way around the edge; and the men, with their closed hard faces, were waiting. From somewhere she could hear the sound of dogs snarling.

Signor Grissani gave the terrified girl a shove.

'You'll be all right,' he said gruffly.

The men who had come to take delivery of her were crowding all around them now. Maryam turned to him, gave him one last supplicating look, but it was no good. All was noise and confusion, a cacophony of dogs barking, men shouting, when suddenly, at some still moment through the press of bodies, she felt a hand slip something cold and hard into her own. A knife.

And then before she knew it she found herself in the pit, and they had let the dogs in on her. There were three of them. The first came for her straight away. It was not a big dog, but heavy and square-set, of the kind which she knew men trained for fighting. Through a blur of terror she saw it jump, as though on a spring, two or three feet in the air, aiming for her throat, but she was so tall that it could not get near her upper body. She raised her arm to defend herself, felt the animal's teeth tear at her flesh, but she hit it away with such force, that first time, that it let go, and fell yelping to the floor on the other side of the pit.

Before she had a chance to recover herself the other two dogs flung themselves at her, too. She tried to beat them away with her fists, as she had done with the first dog, but this time, the sheer weight of their combined impact made her stagger backwards, and she dropped the knife. Instantly, before she could pick it up, the first dog was on her again. It did not jump up at her this time, but went for her legs, was making little lunges at her, snapping and snarling at her ankles. And

141

all this time, from somewhere outside the pit, she was aware of the sound of the men howling and shouting as she capered and skipped, trying to kick the animal out of the way, thankful that this part of her, at least, was protected by her heavy leather boots.

A searing pain, first in one buttock and then in her thigh, told her that the other two dogs had attacked her from behind. She spun round but the two animals held on. They clung fast as she lashed out at them with her fists, but it was too awkward an angle for her blows to have any real force. Her hands glanced off their heads, and so instead, in a moment of inspiration, she tried to feel for the first dog's weak places, its ears and eyes, gouging into them with her fingers with all her might. Her thumb found one finally, she was scarcely aware which; she pushed as hard as she could, and with a strange sensation, like a tough-skinned grape bursting, she knew she had hit home. With a yelp the creature fell off her. It hit the floor and ran cringing and whimpering to the barricade, blood gushing from one eye.

There were only two dogs left now, but already Maryam was tiring. The surge of almost superhuman strength that had run through her when she first entered the pit was slowly beginning to ebb. Blood was flowing freely from her buttock and thigh where the dogs had clung to her, and was now seeping from the lacerations on her arms as well. Having tasted blood at last, the two remaining dogs were hurling themselves at her in a kind of frenzy. When she put up her arms to defend herself their teeth ripped into her flesh. With a grunt Maryam managed to hurl one of them away from her, but, sensing that its prey was weakening, it came back, with renewed ferocity this time, flinging itself at her from behind.

Maryam's legs buckled. She fell heavily, painfully, on to her knees on the hard ground. *This is it*, she remembered thinking to herself, *they'll kill me now for sure*. It was almost a relief. The jeering, shouting crowd could sense that the end was near now too; faintly, above the sound of her own heart hammering, Maryam heard their cries. She could sense rather than see their faces: the eyes filled with hatred; malnourished skin stretched taut over their cheekbones, mouths open, spittle flying; the blackened stumps of teeth.

Her limbs felt heavy now, as though they did not belong to her any more; it was an effort to move them at all. But somehow, she was not quite sure how, she must have managed to land a blow on one of the remaining dogs, because the smaller of the two slunk off, limping and trying to lick one of its paws.

Only one dog remained now: the largest and most ferocious of the three. With one last, futile attempt to save herself, she tried to stagger to her feet, but she was too slow, too clumsy for it. The dog jumped. Like a felled tree trunk, Maryam crashed to the ground; lay, half-winded, with her arms clasped protectively around her head. She was not aware of any pain, only the sound of the animal as it closed in for the kill, the foul-smelling warmth of its breath against her face, the metallic taste of her own blood against her lips.

And then she felt it. Something hard and cold beneath her cheek. The knife. The dog's jaws were around one forearm, but somehow she pulled her other arm free. Her fingers closed around the handle, and with one final burst of energy she thrust the blade upwards, blindly, in the direction of the dog. All at once there was silence. She felt the animal waver and then fall, with barely a sound, against her shoulder, where it lay, its body twitching, the knife in its windpipe.

Chapter Twenty-one

It happened again in the next village. They had pitched their camp, as was their custom, on the edge of an olive grove just a little way outside a small town by the shores of the sea.

It was Ilkai's sister, Yoanna, who found them. She had got up at dawn and stumbled upon the gifts of food already laid out on the ground: the fruit, the little loaves of unleavened bread, five new eggs, an earthenware crock full of olive oil. Yoanna lost no time in coming to tell Maryam.

There they were, sure enough, just as before, carefully arranged in a neat pattern on a bed of freshly picked leaves.

Maryam did not like it. Someone must have stolen up the little path that led to their camp while it was still dark; someone must have been rooting around nearby while they were asleep. The fact that strangers could get among them so easily without any of them knowing about it made her uneasy.

But Yoanna was elated at their good fortune, and so was her sister Ilkai. They ran to get the others, who came out from their tents sleepily at first, but were soon noisily disputing among themselves how to share out the food. Only Elena, watching the scene from the shadows behind the thin muslin curtain of their tent, guessed what Maryam was thinking.

She took the loaf that was their share, sprinkled it with oil from the earthenware crock, and went to sit next to Maryam in the shade of a tree. It was still early, and in the dappled light of the ancient olive grove the air was deliciously cool. In the little town below them they could hear the sound of a cockerel crowing; through the whitewashed houses the sea shimmered.

'You are troubled, Maryam,' Elena said gently. 'Was it that dream again? I heard you cry out in the middle of the night.'

When Maryam did not reply she broke the little loaf in half and handed it to her silently, together with a handful of the olives. Elena turned to look at the view. The bright blue of the sea, the white of the houses and the dust in the road; it almost hurt her eyes. In the distance, on the other side of the town, came the tinkling of a flock of goats being led to pasture; while out to sea a little boat appeared on the horizon, its white sails billowing in the wind.

Elena tried again. 'These people are poor, why do you think they are giving us this food?'

But Elena's questions only seemed to annoy Maryam that morning. She stood up and without a word walked off down the hill in the direction of the town. Elena watched her go with resignation. She was used to Maryam's moods. It had been an idle question, anyway: who cared why they should be leaving them these gifts? The traditions of hospitality in these southern lands were very strong: that was all surely? Elena was too hungry to care. She bit into the bread with a sigh. The oil was bitter, slightly green, the very best; the olives were sweet, their flesh thick. This day was going to be a good day, Elena smiled to herself as she ate.

Their luck was changing; she could feel it in her bones.

It was then that she heard it: the tiny tinkling of bells. Only this time it was not coming from the other side of the town, but from somewhere very near. She looked around, thinking that it must be a goat that had become separated from the rest of the herd, but then she realised it was a different sound altogether, smaller and lighter than the one she had heard before.

Elena began to walk further into the grove of trees, following the sound, and was surprised by how dark it became, and how quickly. What she had taken to be an olive grove was in fact a dense copse of trees, perhaps even a wood.

Some of the trees seemed very ancient; lichen, green and silvery-grey, clung to the trunks like cobwebs. Elena walked clumsily, her feet sinking into the thick, sharp humus of dead scrub underfoot, stumbling on hidden roots and vines. Compared to the already hot day outside, the air in the wood felt cool against her skin. Behind her she could still hear the women's voices coming from the camp;

if she looked hard she could just see them through the trees. There were her little daughters, Nana and Leya. In their brightly coloured dresses they looked like butterflies, flame-yellow and flame-red. Elena had almost made up her mind to turn back, when she heard the sound again: the tiny bells. It was near now, very near.

Almost despite herself, Elena walked on. The trees grew more thickly here; were so close together that little sunlight penetrated this part of the wood at all. It was not just cool now; the temperature was positively cold.

Elena shivered; hesitated. She heard a sound; a stick cracking underfoot; felt her heart jump. She turned around, expecting to find that Maryam or one of the other women had followed her – but there was no one there.

Or was there?

As she turned, Elena caught sight of something out of the corner of her eye, something that shone. But when she saw what it was, she almost laughed out loud. By Our Lady, what a fool you are! She put a hand to her thumping chest, chastising herself for her own jumpiness. The shining thing was nothing more sinister than a beam of sunlight, which at that moment had broken through the canopy. Motes from the forest floor danced in the light like diamond dust. In the dark forest that one sunbeam seemed more beautiful to Elena than anything she had ever seen in her life.

It was only then that she caught sight of the shrine.

Elena knew at once what it was. A simple thing, no more than a rock in a little clearing, but even from a distance she could see signs that someone had once fashioned it crudely. Cautiously she took two paces towards it: could make out a shape like a crescent moon, another like a hand, a third like a plant or a flower with three stems. Whatever it was, it seemed to her like some very ancient thing that she had come across, no doubt long forgotten by the people of the town.

Elena crossed herself quickly.

Around the base of the rock thick green moss and grasses grew, so she guessed that it must be the source of a hidden spring. Curious to see it for herself, she approached the rock, moving slowly, and on tiptoe, she was not sure why. And there, sure enough, bubbling up from a deep crevice came a trickle of water. By the purest chance the sunbeam fell upon the rock and the water, illuminating it, so that the water shone like crystal. Tiny rainbows danced among the moss, shedding their colours – red, violet, indigo, orange.

For a few moments Elena stood staring at it, her mouth slightly open. She was so entranced that at first she did not notice how silent the wood had become: a silence so profound it rang in her ears. Not a creature stirred, not a bird sang. She did not notice that she could no longer hear the voices of the women in the camp; and that, had she stopped to look, she had lost sight of her daughters, too.

All that Elena was aware of was a sudden and terrible thirst. Her mouth was dry, her throat was parched. She must drink some of the water, she must. But she still hesitated to approach the rock too closely. *Panayia mou!* she admonished herself again. *There's nothing there, don't be a fool* . . . She went up to the little pool which had formed at the base of the rock: a tiny pool, no bigger than a man's hand, but filled with the purest, most crystalline water she had ever seen. Elena dipped her cupped hand in and drank. The water was so cold it hurt her teeth. And the taste! Never had she tasted water like this. She drank and drank, until her teeth ached and her lips were numb. And then she heard it again. Unmistakable. The tiny tinkling sound of bells.

Only this time it was coming from behind her.

Elena turned to look over her shoulder and straight away something shining caught her eye: a piece of silver hanging from the branch of a tree. She went over to take a closer look. It was an amulet. Elena knew better than to touch it. She peered at it closely. A figure of a double-tailed mermaid looked back at her. From its tail hung a bunch of tiny bells.

And there was the ringing again. And again and again. Even in the short time that she had been inside the wood, the position of the sunbeam had shifted slightly, and was now shining on the tree with the amulet. Elena saw that there was not just the one amulet, but many amulets glinting in the watery sunlight. Each showed the same figure, a double-tailed mermaid, tied to the branches with coloured thread. Some were swimming on their backs, others were blowing a horn. Although most were in the shape of female mermaids, their long hair streaming behind them, a few depicted mermen, with little crowns on their heads. In each case, a tiny cluster of bells hung from the bottom of the amulet. Although there was not a breath of wind in the wood, they stirred and spun on their threads like living things.

Her faint feeling of unease began to grow. She should not be here at all, of that she had absolutely no doubt. This ancient grove she had stumbled into was a sacred place. Instinctively she crossed herself again; looked nervously over her shoulder, thought she heard a faint sound like a cough coming from behind a tree. Was there someone there after all? What would they do to her if they found her here? She had drunk from the spring! The silence that had seemed so peaceful was beginning to feel oppressive. She thought she could sense someone watching her through the trees. There were eyes – eyes – everywhere, she was sure of it now, watching her from the bushes . . .

Elena began to run.

Chapter Twenty-two

'That's it –'

'Careful with her head.'

'Take the little ones, can't you –'

'That's it, gently does it – no not there – over here – yes, that's more like it.'

When Elena came to, she was lying in the shade of their tent's little canopy.

'What happened?' Maryam was leaning over her; her face looked pinched. 'Did someone try to hurt you?'

At first Elena could not speak, could recall nothing of what had occurred. Then, in her mind's eye, she saw again the little silver amulets, the mermen and merwomen, on their coloured threads, spinning in the airless wood. For a moment that same feeling of dread came over her again; that same sense of being watched by unseen eyes. She clutched Maryam's hand and shivered.

'Tell me, you can tell me.' Maryam's normally bronzed and weatherbeaten face was drained of colour. She held Elena's hand tightly in her own. 'Did they touch you?'

'No, no, it was nothing like that.' At the sight of Maryam's anxious face, Elena managed a small smile. 'It was dark. I gave myself a fright, that's all.'

'Woods,' Maryam cast a nervous look over her shoulder, 'I've never liked them –'

'But Maryam, we can't stay here, we must leave this place at once.'

When Elena told her what she had seen in the wood, Maryam became very silent. Then she reached into one of her pockets and brought out the silver amulet that Bocelli had given her.

149

'Was it something like this that you saw?'

Elena took the little silver mermaid, held it delicately between her long fingers. For a while she said nothing.

'I'm sorry, I should have told you before –' Maryam watched her anxiously.

Elena looked up. But whatever Maryam might have feared she showed no anger, only curiosity.

'What does it mean?'

'I'm not sure – Bocelli did not tell me much. Only that in these parts mermaids are thought to have magical powers. He said you could find amulets such as these all along the coast . . .'

'But in that case why did they want to be rid of her?' Elena's quick mind went to work immediately. 'Why didn't they want to keep her for themselves?' Her brow furrowed. 'That man paid us a fortune – two horses – to take her away . . . it doesn't make sense.'

Elena was right. It had never made sense. Maryam thought back to the filthy stable where Bocelli had first showed her the mother and child. Was it because it had reminded her so much of the miserable years she had spent in the Grissanis' bear cage that Bocelli had been able to persuade her to take them on? Perhaps. It hardly mattered now. The fact was she'd brought a whole peck of trouble on their heads, and no mistake.

'Is this why they are bringing us gifts? Because of the child?'

'I don't know, I don't know any more than you do. A good-luck amulet is one thing, a real mermaid is quite another. I know that's what Bocelli thought. He knew they were afraid.' She took the amulet from Elena again, holding it so the little bells tinkled in the breeze.

'But how do they *know*? The people here, I mean. No one has seen the child except us.'

Maryam shrugged again, and fell silent. Studied her nails. Looked down towards the little town on the seashore beneath them.

'Mary-*am* –?' Elena began to sit up. 'What is it? Is there something else?'

'Yes –' Maryam hesitated, 'I think I –'

'What?'

'I think I saw him.'

'Who?'

'Bocelli.'

'You saw that man Bocelli again?' Elena blinked her sandy eyelashes with surprise. 'Where?'

'In the last village, when I went to buy bread. I wasn't sure, I thought I must be imagining it. But then today, just now down in the town, I saw him again. I came back to tell you,' she ended lamely, 'and found you like this. I was going to tell you everything, really I was.'

'Bocelli again!' Elena said, mystified. 'The man from Messina. What can he be doing here?'

There was a pause. Then Maryam said, 'I think he's following us.'

'Following us?' Elena almost laughed. 'But why? What can he possibly want with us?'

'I don't think it's us that he wants.'

They found the mermaid woman in the back of the cart. Maryam had rigged up a makeshift shelter out of a small piece of old sailcloth that she had found washed up on one of the beaches along the coast. She lay beneath it, very still, with the baby beside her.

Elena approached them, as she always did, speaking softly in a sing-song voice, as though they were wild creatures that needed to be gentled. She had brought water with her and a cloth, and while Maryam carried the mother a little way off from the straggling camp to a place where she could do her ablutions, Elena unwrapped the infant from the napkins in which it had been wrapped and began to clean it.

When Maryam came back, she knew at once that something was wrong. 'What's the matter, is the child sick?'

Elena said nothing, just carried on looking at the child on her knee. 'No, not sick,' she said at last in her calm way. 'But – something's not right either. Look at it – still so tiny, like a newborn.' She picked the infant up, held it in the bowl of her hands. 'No heavier than a little leaf,' she said, shaking her head sadly. 'I fear for it, Maryam. It does not thrive.'

The two continued to look down at the baby for some moments.

'It never cries.' Elena kept her voice low so that the mother would not hear her.

'Why?'

'I think . . . I think it's too weak to cry.'

151

The baby's tiny ribcage was rising and falling rapidly, as though it were struggling for breath.

'D'you think . . . is it a boy or a girl?' Maryam was almost ashamed to ask the question.

Elena looked at where the baby's two legs should have been, where instead was a single limb; two tiny feet, perfectly formed, but joined at the ankle and turned outwards like the tip of a fish's tail.

'Neither,' Elena said with pity. 'Or both. Either way . . .' But whatever it was that she had been about to say she stopped herself, shook her head sadly, 'Well, we'll see. Come, let's do what we came to do.'

She went and sat down next to the mother, where Maryam had put her under a tree to enjoy the sun. The ground was rocky, but smelt of aromatic herbs, mint and wild thyme. A piece of carved marble, the column from an ancient temple, lay on its side amongst the undergrowth. Elena sat down on it, then took out a comb from her pocket and started to comb the girl's hair.

'She likes this,' Elena said softly. 'You like this, don't you?'

'I thought we were going to make her talk to us, not spend hours dressing her hair.'

'Have patience, Maryam, you'll see.'

And she was right. After a while the young woman seemed to relax; she shut her eyes and turned her face to the sun. A small breeze had got up, and below them little white wavelets now appeared on the blue horizon. Her hair blew about her face, shimmering like red gold. Soon Elena stopped combing and took her hand between her own.

'Thessala!' she called to get her attention, shook her arm. 'Thessala?'

The girl, who had been gazing at the horizon, looked round. Her eyes were as blue as the distant sea.

'What is your name? You must have had a name, before you came to us? *Pos se lene?*' she said, shaking her arm again, a little less gently this time. '*Onoma?*'

'Does it matter what her real name is?' Maryam said gruffly. 'She doesn't hear you. She doesn't hear anyone. It's as if she's asleep.' She put her hand in her pocket again. 'Perhaps we should just put them both back in the sea and have done with it. Here, see if this will wake her up.'

Elena took the amulet and held it up for the young woman to see.

'Look!' She shook it so that the silver caught the sunlight, and the little bells tinkled. 'It's for you, for your baby.'

She placed the silver charm on the upturned palm of the mermaid woman's hand, closing her fingers round it, but the girl seemed not to notice. The amulet slipped out of her slack grasp and on to the ground.

'It's no good – I don't know why we're bothering. She's simpleminded, and there's an end to it.' Maryam picked up a stone and lobbed it impatiently down the hill. 'Probably always has been.'

But Elena was not so easily deterred. 'Look.' She picked up the amulet again and held it between her fingers. 'Look, Thessala. Now you see it –' she waved her hand, closed the hand with the amulet in it, 'and then, *ha!* –' she opened it again quickly '– now you don't!' The amulet was gone. 'And then, look, what have we here?' Smiling, she leaned over and drew the amulet from behind the girl's ear.

'You're wasting your time.' Maryam picked up another stone and threw it high into the sky, so it bounced and clattered down the hill towards the sea. 'She's never going to be able to tell us anything, I tell you –'

'Maryam –'

'Not about Bocelli, not about anything –'

'*Maryam!*'

Something about the sharpness in Elena's voice made her turn around.

'Did you see that!'

'What?'

'The girl. Something's happening to her –'

And it was true. Maryam could see immediately that there was something different.

'What is it?' Maryam was kneeling down next to them on the rocky ground. 'What did you do?'

'Nothing, I swear.' Elena sat back on to her heels. 'Just one of my illusions –'

'Again, again, then, quickly.'

So Elena repeated the trick. She took the amulet, made the little mermaid swim between her fingers, so fast and dexterously it really did look like a silver fish; and then, when she was sure of the girl's attention, made it vanish, made it appear again, once, twice, three times, from behind her head, from inside Maryam's boot, from a crook in the tree behind them.

'It's her eyes, look at her eyes –'

As she watched an extraordinary transformation came over the girl's face. As if a mist, or a veil, were lifting. As if the person inside were slowly waking after a long, long sleep.

'Quick, where's the water, give her something to drink.'

Maryam handed the girl her leather water bottle, but she pushed it away, and instead reached out and put her hand gently on Elena's arm, looking round at them both with a faint expression of bewilderment, as if she were seeing them for the first time. Her lips moved faintly.

'*Ach . . . Panayia mou!* I think she's trying to say something.'

The girl's lips moved again, but at first no sound came. She blinked rapidly several times, raised a hand to her throat with the same faintly puzzled look. Elena drew closer, put her ear to the girl's mouth. And this time she heard something, just one word, a little hoarse, but distinct.

'. . . *name* . . .'

'I think she said "name".' She turned to the girl again. 'Do you want to tell us your name?'

The girl gave a small nod.

'Yes?' Elena smiled at her encouragingly. '*Onoma?* Tell us, your name? What – is – your – na-me?'

And then, after what seemed to both Elena and Maryam an eternity, the faintest whisper fell from her lips, whipped away so quickly on the sea breeze it was almost as if it had never been.

'My name . . .' the girl whispered into the wind, 'my name . . . is Celia Lamprey.'

Part II

Chapter Twenty-three

They say lots of things – don't they? – about what it's like to drown.

That you will see the whole of your life flash before you as you pass into nothingness, or into the next world.

But now, now that it was all over, Celia Lamprey knew that it was not like that at all. All that remained, all that you had to cling to, were the tiniest of fragments, the random squares of a mosaic: confused, babbling, terrible. Something that sounded like the echo of her own voice screaming *not this not like this not the sack* the muffled voices of the men *come along you boys get on with it the sooner we finish the job the sooner we can go home* the rush of water in her ears . . .

Then, suddenly, another rushing sensation, as if coming up for air, spinning upwards from some deep dark place, sparkling and dazzling and tumbling like sunlight through sea foam.

Like a baptism.

Like a rebirth.

Chapter Twenty-four

She was sitting beneath a tree on a hot cliffside.

The air was warm and smelt of herbs. Overhead was a sky the colour of gentians; below, a blue, blue sea. A fallen column. Someone had just spoken. She could hear the words hovering in the salty breeze.

My name is Celia Lamprey.

It was only after some minutes that she realised it was her own voice that spoke.

There were two women looking at her. At least, she thought they were both women. One was taller than any man she had ever seen, the height and girth of a prize fighter; the other was pale and delicate-boned, with a long sad face. They regarded her anxiously.

My name is Celia Lamprey. When she said the words for the second time she could taste the salt on her lips.

The two women exchanged glances as though something miraculous had occurred. Celia looked from one to the other. She found that she was not frightened, only curious.

'Do I . . . do I know you, *kadın*?' she said, and it was so strange to hear her own voice again that she almost burst out laughing.

'*Kristos!*' The sad-faced woman crossed herself quickly; she looked completely stunned.

'*Kristos!*' she repeated, as if she hardly knew what to say; and then, in a voice that was no greater than a whisper, 'She's . . . she's awake; quick, get her some water, Maryam.'

'Why?' Celia looked at them again, her brow furrowing as she began to realise, although only vaguely at first, that she had no knowledge at all of how she had come to this clifftop. 'Have I . . . have I been asleep?'

'Have you been asleep?' the woman echoed. She looked up at her giant friend again, put up a hand to cover her mouth, but not before Celia saw that her lips were trembling. *'Panayia mou!'* There was a catch in her voice. 'By the Blessed Virgin!'

'Elena, Elena . . .' The tall one put a hand on her companion's shoulder, as if to reassure her. 'Come, now, you'll frighten her this way.'

As she held a water bottle to her lips Celia could see that her eyes were full of tears. The other put her hand up to Celia's face, as if to stroke her cheek, but then took it away again, as though suddenly unsure what to do.

'But I do know you, don't I?' Celia said, for she was sure of it now. She picked up the little silver amulet with the bells on it and held it in the palm of her hand: a fragment of mosaic. 'Yes, I remember now –' She started to speak very quickly, the words gushing from her like spring water. 'You were the tumbling troupe who came to the harem that day, the women from Salonika – you performed for the Sultan, and his mother, the Valide – there were two little girls with you, I remember them especially, all the *kadın* liked the little girls – you made flowers appear, and then disappear again, from behind people's ears – just as you were doing a moment ago with this amulet –' She stopped abruptly, as if her chain of thought had been interrupted.

There was another stunned silence.

'Yes, Lord love you!' Elena and Maryam exchanged glances again.

'So – you were a lady . . . in the imperial harem?' It was Maryam who spoke.

Celia looked up at her, her face clouded. 'Yes. I mean, no. I don't know. I suppose I must have been.' She looked round at them, puzzled. 'Was I?'

With an ease that surprised them all, Maryam managed to get the women passage on a small, two-masted ketch, the same vessel whose sails they had seen on the horizon earlier that morning. The captain, who had pulled into the harbour for fresh water, said they were heading north-east up the coast of Dalmatia.

There had been no more offerings, and no more sightings of Bocelli – although Maryam was beginning to think she might have imagined the second one – but even so it was a relief to them all to leave that land.

The girl – Celia, as they must all now learn to call her – followed Elena with her eyes. Although she seemed terrified of the boatmen, she was quite happy, quite calm, as long as one or other of the women were with her, as though their presence reassured her. She seemed to have accepted the fact of her broken legs, even of the baby, with equanimity. The only thing that appeared to make her anxious was to be too far away from Elena, as if – like the little embroidered pocket she always carried with her – she were another fragile thread connecting her to her unknown past.

Only Maryam's heart was troubled. It was clear that Celia was a fine lady, of that she had never been in doubt. Nails that had never scratched the soil, a complexion so delicate it seemed almost unnatural to the swarthy-skinned women of the troupe. But a woman from the imperial harem? It was . . . too much to take in. What adventure – what dishonour – could possibly have brought her to that place? More than ever Maryam felt a great unease: as though she were a thief, as if Celia were stolen treasure.

Elena came and sat next to Maryam, who was leaning up against the mizzen on the deck.

'She seems quite happy, don't you think? She remembers her name. She remembers us, Lord love you,' Elena said. 'As for the rest . . . nothing. Not even the thing she keeps looking for in that pocket of hers.'

'And the infant?' Maryam remembered the night she had stared into the mermaid baby's eyes. 'What about the infant?'

And for once, Elena had nothing to say. She shrugged, spread the fingers of her hands wordlessly.

Both Maryam and Elena had watched Celia and the baby together carefully; she fed it, cleaned it, but with the same detachment as before. Nothing had changed. She never picked it up, or sang to it; it seemed to give her neither pleasure nor pain. Indeed, she seemed to have no feeling for it at all.

'No mother love –' Maryam shook her head. 'Are you sure it's hers?'

'Yes, I'm quite sure.' Elena, who had examined and cleaned Celia when Maryam had first brought her to their camp, and who had had

160

children of her own, nodded. 'She has some tears in her secrets, and her courses now are very heavy ones . . . yes, I'm sure.'

'It does not seem natural.' Frowning, Maryam picked at a hole in her leather jerkin.

'It happens.' Elena pulled one of her own little girls to her, and kissed her fiercely. 'But you know, Maryam, a child like that –' she glanced at her friend, and then away again quickly, 'well, it could be nature's way.'

'What do you mean, nature's way?'

'Maryam, Maryam,' Elena sighed, 'the child is not like to live. You know that as well as I. It gets weaker every day. Accept it.'

'I thought . . . I thought it might be different now, that's all.'

'But remembering won't make any difference to the child . . .' Elena shrugged. 'All the same we must do everything to help her.' Reluctantly she gave the struggling Nana a kiss and let her down from her lap. The young woman's fate seemed to her more terrible than ever, as if she were a person adrift on the deepest ocean, with nothing to anchor her to life.

'Perhaps.' Maryam shifted uneasily. 'Perhaps not. Perhaps it would be better for her not to remember, have you ever considered that?'

She thought of her own story: the things she had seen, the people at whose hands she had suffered. How much would she give not to remember. Besides, she knew in her bones that there had been some terrible violence against this woman. Her legs, the baby . . . Whenever she thought of it Maryam felt a sensation like a hand gripping her windpipe. *If I ever see Bocelli again I'm going to wring it out of him, the filthy, lying little tick. I swear it, on the bodies of Nana and Leya. If it's the last thing I do.*

On my own life, I swear it.

Celia woke with a cry; her heart racing.

In her dream someone had been coming towards her, a man whose face she could not see. She tried to run from him, but she could not; tried to scream but no sound came. There was a crushing sensation, as if a heavy weight were pressing down on her until she could barely breathe, let alone move; then a pain, both sharp and hard, between her legs, a feeling as if a claw, metal or bone, or a human nail perhaps, were tearing and ripping at her, prising her apart, opening her up. Her cheek was grazing against rough wooden planks, under her back was a pile of something hard like the coils of a rope, and the stench of something she vaguely recognised, but putrid and dead, fish perhaps? – *come on you boys get on with it* – and then another thing, something unseen, hard flesh or hard bone, stabbing clumsily at her and at the tops of her thighs *come on you boys get on with it the sooner we finish the job the sooner we can go home* round and round, closer and closer, searching out her secret place, torn and bloodied now, but missing the mark each time, until finally – a pause no longer than half a heart beat – he finds it. The strange catch in his breath, the smell of fish in her ear, on her cheek and even her lips, and she realises with horror that he is licking her with his tongue, licking her face, the side which is not crushed into the bottom of the boat *so this is it now oh god* he rams into her, no quarter given, *oh God the pain the pain help me help me God*, his breath in her ear again like a sob this time, far far in and deep deep down, and the feeling that if this goes on any longer, with any more of them, she will quite simply cleave clean in two . . .

Celia sat up, her shift soaked with sweat.

It was a few moments before she saw where she was. It was night and she was lying with the other women in a row on the deck of the ketch. They were anchored for the night in a small inlet. Umbrella pines grew down a steep slope all the way to the water's edge. Even on the open deck the heat of the night air was intense. The cicadas, so insistent by day all the way along this coastline, had quieted, but the small noises of the boat were all around her: the faint creak of wood, the scrape and groan of the anchor chain; the rustle of some night creature in the forest. A full moon shone, so brightly that she could see the red of Maryam's bandana where she had left it, hanging from a nail in the mizzen.

As she lay there, willing herself to shake off the shadow of the dream, she heard a sound. Something nearby was splashing in the water. Celia pulled herself over to the side of the boat and looked over. Out towards the deeper sea, where the moonlight silvered the water, she could see two dolphins jumping together.

She watched them for a moment, entranced. And suddenly, that same sensation again, of the rushing, tumbling, spinning, and there it was: another piece of the mosaic.

It was a hot summer night such as this one, and they were being taken to watch the dolphins sporting in the Sea of Marmara.

They were in a little boat – no, in a fleet of little boats – all of them lit up with lights like fireflies. The air was scented with roses. There was the sound of music playing, and of voices laughing together. Ahead of them was the Valide's barge, its poop inlaid with precious stones, shining with ivory and mother-of-pearl, seahorse teeth and gold. And Gulbahar was there, Turhan and Fatma. And of course Ayshe . . . Celia's heart leapt. Ayshe!

But Ayshe had another name, didn't she?

Ayshe. Annetta.

Annetta. Ayshe . . .

But it was no good. Just as suddenly as it had begun, the rushing stopped. The beautiful vision dissolved like a dream. The harder she tried to hold on to it, the more rapidly it faded. She was back on the creaking boat again, her hair and clothes stiff with sea salt, with the harsh breath of the tumbling women all around her.

Beside her, in its little bundle of rags, she could sense the baby stirring. It gave out a small sound, a tiny mewing more like a kitten than a child.

Don't wake, please don't wake, not yet. She reached out and picked it up, holding it awkwardly in her arms, not close to her chest, close to her heart, as a mother should. She hoped the movement would send it back to sleep, just for a little while longer.

She looked out at the moonlit sea, at the little harbour, the pine trees creeping down to the water's edge. Not a breath of wind. She looked at the baby and at the water. And then back at the baby again.

The child seemed to have quieted. She put the bundle down again, but on the other side of her, close to the deck's edge this time. A little too close to the deck's edge. She looked around. All she could see were the black lumps of the women sleeping together in a row. No one stirred.

Sitting on her own in the moonlight Celia had the lonely sensation that she and the baby were the only two creatures who existed in the whole of God's universe. A feeling of such utter desolation gripped her she thought she could hardly bear it. Below her the sea slapped softly against the side of the boat.

With difficulty she edged herself closer to the side and looked down. Beneath the silvered surface the water was deep and black. The child, in its little bundle of cloths, was dangerously close to the edge now. Beneath the swaddling she could just make out the form of its single limb, the fish-like tail. Celia reached out to pull it safely back – and for a moment her hand wavered.

There would be no one to see, no one to hear it fall. After all, I'll only be returning it, she thought, returning it to the deep. She imagined it: a tiny creature swimming free. Jumping across the moonlit seas like a dolphin.

Maryam woke sometime towards dawn. The space where Celia normally slept was empty, and when she looked she found that the girl had somehow shifted herself to the foredeck of the boat and was sitting, as Maryam had so often seen her do, with the little pink embroidered pocket open on her lap.

With an effort, her big bones creaking, Maryam got up, and went to sit down next to her.

'What is it,' she whispered, 'what is it that you are always looking for? Have you lost something?'

When Celia looked up, her expression was desolate. 'I don't know. At least – I think I had something in here, something I was supposed to keep safe; something very precious. But there is nothing here now. Do you know what was in here?'

Maryam shook her head. She picked up the little pouch. In her huge hands it looked so small, like something that might belong to a child or a doll.

'You had this on you when we first found you,' she turned the pocket inside out, examining the black silk lining, 'but there was never anything in it, except for an old stone. Do you remember where it came from?'

'The pocket?' Celia smiled. 'But of course, all the harem women had one, all the *cariye*, even the Valide. We always wore one tied to our belt. It's what we put our daily stipend into . . .' She stopped suddenly, as if the memory of so slight a thing had caught her unawares.

'Then it had money in it?' Maryam ventured. 'Some aspers perhaps?'

'Perhaps.'

164

Celia looked up at her. She wondered if she should tell Maryam about the dolphins playing in the moonlight, and the other memories it had provoked, but the truth was she was still a little afraid of her: the giantess in her crude leather jerkin, who stood so tall and spoke so little.

The sun was rising now, and there was a stirring amongst the others on the boat. In the pale light she could make out Maryam's face more clearly. Without the customary bandana tied around her head her black hair hung limply over her greasy face, a sprinkling of soft dark hairs on her upper lip. Maryam, it occurred to Celia, was almost magnificent in her ugliness. What must it be like, Celia wondered, to be a freak of nature?

Next to them, on the deck, came a small sound.

When Celia made no move towards the baby, Maryam turned to her. 'May I?'

Celia nodded; watched as Maryam picked up the infant. What an absurd sight it was, the giant woman and the tiny child. Maryam held the little bundle so awkwardly that Celia thought she would drop it; cradling it not in her arms, but in her cupped hands. Her broad face, with its pockmarked skin, gazed down so tenderly at the child lying in her hands that Celia felt suddenly ashamed. The baby let out another tiny sound; a fragile arm came loose from the cloth that swaddled it, waved ineffectually in the air. Maryam put out her finger; seemed to hold her breath as the child's tiny fingers fluttered, and then closed around it.

'Look!' she breathed. 'His little hand –' in the soft dawn light her face seemed to glow, looked, for a moment, almost beautiful '– like a moth fluttering.'

'His?' Celia frowned.

'But of course.' Maryam, who did not seem able to tear her eyes away from the baby, nodded. 'He's a boy, isn't he?'

As she spoke, another of the strips of cloth in which the baby was wrapped came loose, revealing the lower part of its body: the two tiny legs fused into one limb, tiny feet splayed like a fish tail. Instinctively, before she could stop herself, Celia averted her gaze.

'I – don't know,' she muttered, 'it's . . . hard to say.'

Maryam caught her look.

'There's no need to be ashamed.'

165

'Ashamed? I'm not ashamed –'

'Then why do you blush?'

And it was true. A rush of blood had risen to Celia's cheeks. But it is not only shame I feel, she wanted to say, it is revulsion. My flesh creeps and crawls at the very sight of it . . . And, although I know that God will curse me for it, there's not a day that goes by when I do not wonder what would happen if I were to return it to the deep . . . But there was such a tightness in her throat that Celia found she could say none of these things.

If Maryam could see what she was thinking she did not say.

'My parents were always ashamed of me.' There was no bitterness in her voice as she spoke. 'I was always big. They thought I was a freak,' she shrugged, 'I suppose I *was* a freak. At eleven I was taller than my own father, and he was a tall man, and nearly as strong. They tried to hide me away so our neighbours in the village wouldn't see me, wouldn't let me go out to play with the other children . . .' She moved her big head from side to side slowly, as though trying to shake the memory away. 'But this little one,' tenderly she tucked the cloth back around the fish tail, 'no one is going to be ashamed of him.'

Wrapped in its swaddling again the child was turning its head from side to side and making the same strange mewing sound.

'He's hungry,' Maryam said.

'He doesn't eat.' Celia looked at the infant sorrowfully.

'Let me try.'

She went off, and came back with a cup of milk.

She took the child in her arms again and held it in the crook of her elbow, and then, dipping her forefinger into the liquid, with infinite patience fed it, drop by drop.

'Look.' Maryam's face was shining, 'he eats!'

Celia watched the baby lying in Maryam's vast embrace. It was so small and weak, its skin still red and shrivelled like a newborn, and she realised then what Elena had known all along.

'I'm sorry,' she said, and the words were out before she could stop them, 'but I think it may be too late . . .'

'Too late? It's never too late – look.' Maryam put another few drops of the milk on her finger, held them to the lips of the dying child. 'He eats, you'll see. He will get stronger.' She looked down at it tenderly. 'We're going to the city, to Venice, they have doctors

there, at the *ospedale*, one of the boatmen told me about it, you'll see.
I'll look after him, always.'
    I swear it.
    On my life.

Chapter Twenty-five

It was only a few hours before sunset when Carew finally made it back to Constanza's *palazzo*.

He had travelled back from the convent in Ambrose's boat, at the Rialto Bridge they parted, and from there Carew carried on by foot. After the fresh air and breezes on the lagoon, the city's narrow back streets seemed even more noisome and crowded than they had done that morning. The heat at this hour was intense, radiating from the peeling plaster walls like bread ovens. Washing hung out to dry from the windows; he breathed in the stink of the canal water, the smell of frying fish, supper for the servants of some great household. Two children ran past him chasing a dog and carrying the ring-shaped bread rolls they called *simit*.

Carew walked and walked. Unlike Pindar, who normally travelled everywhere by water, Carew was used to the back streets of the city, knew them like the lines of his own hand: the tiny bridges and the dead-end *calles* with their peeling pink and yellow paint, the *sotto-passaggios* and the hidden courtyards; and, always, the stench of the black canals. But now even he seemed disorientated.

In his hand he held the little velvet pocket that the nun had dropped. Ever since he had left the island the same thought had been running through his mind, over and over again. Could it really be an identical pocket to the one that had contained the diamond, or was he just imagining it? It had been so dark in the *ridotto*, lit only by candlelight, and they had only seen the diamond for a few moments. Yet if it were an identical pocket, how on earth had the nun come by it? Could it be – Carew ran a disbelieving hand through his hair – could it *possibly* be that *she*, after all, had been the lady from the harem?

There was something else about her that nagged at the back of his mind, something familiar that he could not quite put his finger on. What was it? He could not for the life of him remember.

Eventually he found himself at the gateway that he had been looking for: the back entrance of Constanza's *palazzo*. When Carew put his hand up to knock for entry he found to his surprise that the iron gate was already open, standing slightly ajar. He pushed the door open cautiously and went in.

The little courtyard was more dishevelled than he had remembered it. The wood for the kitchen fires, normally so neatly stacked, lay in a disorderly heap where it had been delivered. Old pieces of broken furniture lay against the walls, and there were weeds growing up between the paving stones, and up the marble stairs that led to the balconied *piano nobile*. Ivy grew riotously up the brickwork, spilling over the top of the walls and out into the narrow *calle* behind.

In the centre of the courtyard was an old stone well. A woman was standing there with her back to him, pulling up a wooden pail of water. She wore high pattens on her feet to protect her shoes from the outside dirt, and the outer skirts of her dress were hitched up over her petticoats. It was some moments before he realised who it was.

'Constanza . . .?'

The woman turned, and when she saw who it was, she put her hand up to her forehead.

'It's only me . . .'

'John Carew!' She stared at him as if he were a stranger. 'You made me jump.'

Without comment Carew took the heavy pail from her and carried it into the kitchens. Constanza followed him slowly.

The kitchens, too, showed similar signs of neglect; the tiled floor was greasy, dirty plates and glasses piled on a dresser. The fire, Carew noticed, had gone cold long ago. At a glance he could tell that no one had cooked here for a long time.

'*Senti* . . .' Constanza started to say something but Carew stopped her.

'As I said, it's only me. You don't have to explain.'

'No one normally enters this way except the servants, my visitors always come to the canal entrance –' she began in confusion.

169

'Where are they?' He looked at her anxious face. 'Your servants, I mean.'

'Who knows.' With a shrug, Constanza pulled her skirts down to cover her petticoats again. 'Do you remember my maid, Tullia? She still comes sometimes, but not today. As for the rest,' she shrugged again, 'I haven't see any of them for months.'

Carew could not recall ever having seen her in daylight before, had never, to his recollection, ever seen her outside the magnificent room overlooking the canal where, like the jewelled phoenix of her youth, she held court to her visitors.

In the daylight, Constanza looked different; her face was older, there were lines around her eyes, the beginnings of a little crepiness at her throat. It occurred to him that perhaps it was deliberate on her part, the care that she always took to be seen by candlelight. Most of the men she knew, on whom she depended for her living, were unlikely to be so forgiving.

There's nothing so lamentably disgusting as an old whore, don't you think? Francesco's harsh words came back to him. Even so, the sight of her doing something as ordinary as hunt about in her own kitchens for bread and cheese seemed almost blasphemous.

Upstairs, enthroned once again in the shadows of the beautiful room, Constanza seemed more at ease. With the vast canopied bed at the centre, the little table covered with the Turkey carpet, the room seemed to Carew like an empty church, even bigger and more echoing than it had been before.

During the day a series of linen screens had been pulled down over the balcony windows to shield the room from the searing heat, and now Constanza opened them in the hope of catching an evening breeze.

'*Che caldo!*' She dabbed ineffectually at her throat and temples with a handkerchief. '*Madonna*, this heat. Have you heard? They say we'll have the plague again this summer.'

Evening light, reflected off the canal water beneath, danced on the ceiling above her head. For some moments Constanza gazed down into the canal, her back to Carew. Her dark hair hung down her back in a thick rope. She was wearing the same blood-red Ottoman sleeveless robe as when Carew had last seen her.

She leant her forehead against one of the cool stone pillars. 'Will he come, d'you think?'

Watching her, Carew gave a small smile. 'You asked me that before, remember?'

'So I did,' Constanza's eyes were closed, 'but what is your answer now, John Carew?'

At first Carew said nothing; then, as though reluctantly, 'I hoped you were going to tell me that.'

'Ah, so you're looking for him too? Well, here we are again then. Just like before. Waiting for Paul Pindar.' Constanza gave a small sigh. 'You can have no idea, my friend, how tired I am of waiting.'

Round her throat was a necklace of gold links set with a red jewel. She fiddled with it abstractedly.

'It's true that he was here for a few nights, after that time when you brought that Ambrose fellow, but I haven't seen him since, if that's what you were going to ask.' There was a pause. Then, with her back still to him she added, 'He's still in love with her, isn't he?'

'In love?'

'With the girl, with Celia Lamprey.'

'You can't be in love with someone who's dead.' Carew's voice sounded harsher than he meant it to. 'It doesn't make sense to me.'

'How do you know she's dead?'

'Dead to him,' Carew's eyes were like two stones, 'it's the same thing, isn't it?'

'Spoken like a true philosopher.' Constanza turned to face him. With an effort she had thrown off her sombre mood, was smiling, playful again. 'Bravo, John Carew! Come, drink some wine with me before you go.'

She crossed the room to the table at the foot of the immense bed on which she had placed some bread and cheese, and a jug of wine. Her footsteps made a hollow sound on the bare floor.

'And what about you, John?' She handed him one of her long-stemmed glass beakers. 'Tell me,' she looked into his face, serious suddenly, 'have you ever been in love?' But then, seeing his expression, she began to laugh. 'Oh, I've heard all about your nocturnal wanderings, the visits to the convents ... but you have nothing to fear from me.' She gave him her sleepy cat's smile. 'All I can say is that I pity the girl who ever falls in love with you, John Carew.'

To this Carew said nothing. He went over to the table. In amongst a disarray of paper and pens, an ink stone, a knife for trimming the

171

pens, was the pack of *tarrochi* cards that he remembered Constanza playing with the last night he had been here, the ones she used to tell fortunes. He looked at the inscrutable pictures on the cards: the Magician, the Moon, the Fool, the Hanged Man – well, that was probably him if he stayed here any longer. To avoid any more questions he picked up one of the pieces of paper which was filled with Constanza's writing.

'Does Paul allow you to read his papers like this?' With a raised eyebrow Constanza made as if to take it from him.

'I did not know you wrote poetry,' he said, handing the page back to her.

'One of my patrons particularly requires it. That, and the cards, of course. This one's for a party he's giving in his gardens on the Giudecca tomorrow.' She cast her eye down the page of verses and then put it carefully to one side.

Carew's eyes kept returning to the pack of *tarrochi* cards on the table, scattered across the Turkey carpet as before. Constanza followed his gaze. 'Remember the other day when I tried to read the cards for you? Well, there was something that always puzzled me –' Constanza sat down at the table, cut the cards, shuffled them, repeated the action several times, spread them all out in a fan shape. 'Here, pick one.'

Her characteristic playfulness seemed feverish all of a sudden, as though she were acting a part.

'As I said before, Constanza, I know only too well what my fortune is,' Carew began, but to please her, nonetheless, he found himself taking one, handing it back to her without looking. 'And I'll pick one for you too, if you like. Here –' He took a second card out of the pack, placing it alongside the first, face down on the table. She glanced up at him, and then at the downturned cards.

'Don't you want to know what you have picked?'

'No. I didn't come here to have my fortune read.' Carew flexed his fingers, making his knuckles crack. 'I really just came to leave a message. For Pindar.'

'Well, as you can see, he's not here.' Constanza was looking with great concentration at the cards, as if she feared to touch them.

Carew took a knife from one of the several hanging at his belt and pared off a piece of cheese from the one on the plate. He knew he must speak now, say what he had come to say, or it would be too late. He put the cheese carefully into his mouth.

'Pindar saw the diamond, the one you told me about. We both did.'

She became very still. 'The Sultan's Blue?'

'That's the one.'

An image of the extraordinary stone came back to him. Blue ice. Blue fire. Something from another world.

'You've seen it? So the stories are true then –' Constanza sat back in her chair. 'And where did you see it? Oh, no, don't tell me –'

'That fellow you mentioned. Memmo, was it?'

'Zuanne? Zuanne Memmo?' Constanza put her hand to the red spinel at her throat.

'There was another fellow there too. Francesco. A friend of Memmo's apparently. Didn't like him much either.'

'Francesco?' Constanza went pale. 'Francesco Contarini?' She looked as though the name might choke her.

'I take it you know him then?'

'Oh yes, I know him all right. And so does Paul. This is worse than I thought. He doesn't mean any good towards him, Carew, you mark my words.' Another thought seemed to strike her.

'But they didn't make him –?'

'Play for it? No, not yet –'

'Oh, thank God.' Constanza, who had half-risen to her feet, sank down into her chair again. 'Thank God! Francesco and Zuanne! Oh God, why didn't I stop him when I had the chance?'

'But, make no mistake, he's going to,' Carew said bitterly, 'the moment he can prove to them he's got money to lose.'

'Oh thank God, then there is still time –'

'For what?'

'To stop him, of course.'

'Stop him?' Carew looked at her as though she were quite mad. 'No one's ever going to stop him, not now.'

Quickly Carew explained to her about the conversation that he had been party to between Paul and Prospero Mendoza in the ghetto that night. The stories about the woman selling her jewels who was rumoured to have once been in the imperial harem; the mysterious man from Constantinople who had lost the diamond at cards and then disappeared.

173

'And does Paul think these two are somehow connected?' Constanza seemed puzzled. 'I don't see how.'

'He doesn't know for sure – no one does – but it does seem too strange to be just a coincidence. And there's something else you should know.' Carew told her briefly about the inscription. 'Prospero says the Sultan's Blue is not like other gemstones, that it's a magical stone. The fact that Pindar was able to read the inscription when no one else could –' Carew shrugged '– it's convinced him the diamond will somehow lead him to Celia, or to news of her.'

For a moment Constanza said nothing.

'You say that the man from Constantinople has vanished. But the harem lady?'

'It seems that this lady has chosen to continue her secluded life, and has taken refuge in one of your convents. That was the message I was hoping you'd give to him. Look.' Carew paused; feeling inside his shirt he brought out the nun's pocket. 'I think I've found her.'

'And yet you say you didn't speak to her?'

The little pocket lay in the palm of Constanza's hand – pink velvet embroidered with silver thread, after the Ottoman style. She examined it carefully. It had a drawstring top, a black silk lining, and long points by which it could be fastened to a girdle at the waist. The fabric was very stiff, as though it were lined with some other stuff, paper or parchment.

'No, not really.'

'What do you mean "not really"? Do you even know her name?'

Carew looked at the floor.

Annetta. He knew her name now, it was true. *Her name is Annetta.* But somehow he could not bring himself to say it out loud. All he could remember was that moment in the garden. How many times now had he played it over and over inside his head – the feeling that he was seeing her for the first time, the strand of dark hair and the mole on her cheekbone, and him standing to one side and letting her go – what had possessed him? – watching her walk away from him and out of his sight for ever.

'John Carew, are you listening to me? I said, then I don't see that you have anything to go on.' Constanza's words broke into his reverie. 'How can you be so sure it's her?'

'I wasn't – not at first.' He took the pocket from her again. Held it to his nose, sniffed at it cautiously. What had he been hoping for? That it would still have something of hers, some perfume, anything? But no, there was nothing.

'I am fairly certain this is an identical pocket to the one that Memmo kept the diamond in.'

'Is that all? There could be hundreds like this one.'

'And there is something else, although at the time I was not quite sure what it was.' Carew hesitated. 'It's the way she walks.'

'The way she walks?' Constanza stared at him as though he had gone mad. 'And how is that exactly?'

'When I was in Constantinople I saw some women in the imperial harem once. Through a hole in the wall –' he saw Constanza's look '– I know, it's a long story.'

'*Madonna!*' Constanza leaned back in her chair. 'A *monarchino* even then!' She seemed highly amused, but when she saw Carew's face she became serious again. 'And so: these harem women had a particular way of walking, is that it?'

'Yes, a sort of undulating movement, something about the way they move their hips – hard to describe – but very distinctive. I knew it reminded me of something, but it was only when I got back here that I remembered what it was.'

There was a pause.

'It's still not much to go on, is it?' Constanza said.

'No, but if we tell him what I've found out so far it might stall things a bit. Buy us some time. Deflect him from this new madness.'

'You really think he'll try to play for the diamond?'

Carew looked at her. 'You've seen him at the cards, I know you have.'

Constanza could only nod.

'He's like a man possessed by devils. It's like a sickness. He won't stop until he's staked everything he has on it,' Carew said slowly. 'He'll stake everything he *hasn't* got on it. And if he weren't ruined before, he will be this time, believe me.'

Constanza stood up again, moved restlessly to the window, as if she did not know what to do with herself.

'It's all my fault,' she said, stricken, 'I should never have let it slip that night –'

'He would have heard about the diamond anyway, and the game, from someone else.'

'But you don't understand,' she turned to him, 'I could have said something, if only I'd been . . . thinking straight.'

'What could you have said?'

'I could have told him –'

'What?'

'Something I heard from one of my patrons. The one who likes poetry, he likes the cards too – *primero*, *bessano*, all those vying games. I hear things sometimes, when men are in . . . how can I put it? in a sleepy mood . . .' she gave Carew a small smile, 'they let things slip that they would not otherwise. All I know is that he would not go near this game, not even for a prize as great as the Sultan's Blue. Zuanne, he does not have a very good reputation, you know. And as for Francesco – *ha!*' She flung her hands up in the air. 'Far worse. Someone was killed at one of his so-called games a while back.'

'What were his reasons?'

'Too many foreigners.'

'Too many foreigners?' Carew stared at her. 'What does that mean?'

'It means you're easy to cheat.'

'You mean they'll rig the game?'

'No I don't think so.' Constanza frowned. 'That would be too obvious. Too many people know about it, and there'll be too many spectators. But, mark my words, there will be trickery of some kind.'

There was a pause while Carew digested this information. He looked down at his hands, criss-crossed with silvered scars and the marks of old burns.

'If we tell him that, he'll only persuade himself it's a ruse to prevent him from playing,' he said eventually. 'He wants the diamond, Constanza. If I know him, there'll be no stopping him now.'

Constanza regarded him sadly. *Carissime Carew*. She did not try to contradict him. 'So, what are you going to do?'

Now it was Carew's turn to go to the window. How long was it since that interminable night when he had waited here with her for Ambrose Jones to show up? Well, his attempt to shame Pindar out of his gaming madness had not worked. What malign forces were at work here he could not tell. Perhaps he should have got Constanza to tell the cards for him after all. He felt exhausted suddenly, weary to his very bones. He had not been going to, but now he decided to tell Constanza.

'There's a merchantman leaving for England at the end of next week.'

'You're leaving?'

'Yes.'

'You can't leave him, not now.'

'You don't understand, he's ordered me to go.' Carew looked down into the black waters of the canal beneath him. 'Besides, there's nothing more I can do for him, I've done everything I can.'

'But you must go back there again, to the convent. There's still time. Find a way to speak with that nun properly, find out what she knows.'

Carew did not turn round. 'I can't,' he said.

'What?'

'You heard me, I can't go back.'

'Why not?'

At first he did not answer.

'You are afraid, then?' she goaded him. 'That's not like you, John Carew. I know the penalties are severe for men who transgress with our nuns, but I would have thought –'

'Afraid?' Carew turned to her angrily. 'Of course I'm not afraid. It's just – well – it's complicated,' he muttered. 'Get Ambrose to do it. He knows one of the nuns there. He was supposed to ask her when we went there today.' He realised in a flash that he had clean forgotten to ask Ambrose if the painter nun knew anything.

'Ambrose Jones?' Constanza stared at him. 'That self-important, puffed-up, yellow-headed –' she searched vainly for words that would express her utter disdain '– baboon! You really think Signor Jones can be trusted?'

'Look, I don't like him any more than you do, but it turns out he works for the Levant Company, collects intelligence for them.' Carew still felt the smart of humiliation at the thought of it. 'He and Pindar knew one another all along. It would be in his interests, if nothing else, to help him.'

'In his interests – are you sure about that? What are Signor Ambrose's interests exactly?' Constanza said drily. 'You might trust him, but I don't. Believe me, I've known men like that. There's only one thing that motivates them. *Avarizia*. Greed. Who else do you think he's collecting for? *What* else is he collecting? Those are the questions you should be asking. It won't just be for the Levant Company – or even for Paul's old merchant friend – that's for sure. No, no, no: there must be another way.' She seized Carew by the arm and shook him. He had never seen her so agitated. 'You have to go back, John. You have to go back to the island and talk to her again.'

Carew pulled his arm away from her, but when he did not reply straight away, she knew he was not going to refuse.

'Just promise me: no climbing over walls.' Her voice had softened again. 'For pity's sake, John Carew, use the front doorway this time.'

'The front doorway?' Carew managed a smile. 'And me with a lifetime's experience climbing over walls.' He saw the anxious expression return to her face. 'Constanza, I'll find a way. But in the meantime –'

'In the meantime I too will ask some more questions when I go to the Giudecca today –'

'And if you find out anything, anything at all –'

'I'll send you word.'

Constanza watched Carew go. His feet made no sound on the bare wooden floorboards. For a few moments, standing alone in the empty room, she felt quite desolate. She went to pour herself some wine, saw the *tarrochi* cards that he had left face down on the table. One for him, one for her. She put her hand out to pick them up –

And, for the first time, hesitated.

Found for the first time a breath of fear whisper down her spine.

Constanza shook herself. Foolish woman! It was just a game, wasn't it, a game that children played?

Quickly, without allowing herself to remember whose card was which, she turned them over. And there, just as she had feared, the same cards as before.

There was no mistaking them.

The Lovers.
Death.
But which lovers? And whose death?
With a shiver Constanza swept the cards back into the pack.

Chapter Twenty-six

The nun who summoned Annetta to the parlour the next day was not the usual gatekeeper.

'You have a visitor, *suora*.'

Annetta looked up with surprise from the paintbrushes she had been cleaning in Suor Veronica's workshop. She recognised Suor Caterina immediately as one of that group of nuns whom she had always thought of privately as the *contessas*: aristocratic women with no vocation at all for the contemplative life. Suor Bonifacia, the Abbess, as Annetta had recently learnt, was one such; Suor Purificacion another; and there were at least half a dozen others. Given the fame and beauty of its physic garden, and the relative ease – some would say laxity – with which Suor Bonifacia allowed the convent to be run, the many exemptions it enjoyed, on account of its working gardens, from the usual prescriptions governing conventual life, it was a popular choice among the families of the Venetian nobility.

When Annetta had first arrived back at the convent, Suor Caterina, with her gold chains and luxurious clothes, had seemed to her every inch a noblewoman. Annetta had been dazzled. Like the other nuns from high-born families, Caterina addressed her fellow noblewomen – which included one of her aunts, and several cousins – as *signora*, my lady, rather than the usual *suora*, or sister. Like them, she would not have dreamt of taking her clothes from the communal wardrobe as was stipulated by the convent regulations. Everything she wore she had brought with her in her *cassoni* when she first arrived: silks, lace and linen of the finest quality, like a bride's trousseau, beautifully stitched and monogrammed.

But it was not only the quality of her garments, it was the way she wore them that had most impressed Annetta. Against all the sartorial rules of their order, Caterina wore her black veil pushed back high over the crown of her head, showing the blonde hair beneath, two curls pinched out on each cheek. She wore high-heeled pattens on her feet, and a bodice pulled down so low it revealed the curve of her small breasts, and a ruby and emerald crucifix hung from a gold chain around her waist.

Of all the choir nuns Caterina was the one closest to her in age. Annetta had made the mistake, in the first few days after she had arrived back from Constantinople, not only of emulating her (the lace, the pattens, the silk stockings scandalously trimmed with gold, all these had been copied from Suor Caterina) but of trying to befriend her. Her advances had been ruthlessly repelled. It had been made abundantly clear by the *contessas* that they regarded Annetta, a former *conversa*, as little better than a servant still; an upstart who was never going to be good enough to mix with any of the choir nuns, let alone with them. No amount of dowry money – and at three thousand ducats, Annetta's was the biggest dowry that the convent had ever received – would ever make up for that fact. In the weeks that followed Annetta had learnt to be wary of the languid gaze, which concealed beneath it a proud and ill-natured temperament.

Now Suor Caterina was standing uncertainly at the doorway of Suor Veronica's room.

'You have a visitor, *suora*,' she said.

She was holding up the skirts of her robe, pinched fastidiously between her two fingers, so as to lift them out of the dust. In the other hand she held a small lace handkerchief, which she held to her nose to block out the smell of paint. From the way she peered curiously into Veronica's studio it was clear that she had rarely, if ever, penetrated very far into the working reaches of the physic garden. Annetta had noticed her in the evenings sometimes taking a turn beneath the lime trees, arm in arm with one of her cousins; but never, so far as she could remember, into the herbarium, let alone Suor Veronica's workshop.

'A visitor, *suora*,' she repeated, 'in the parlour,' and then, in answer to Annetta's enquiring look, she added, 'he says he brings a message to you from someone called Prospero Mendoza.'

Despite being half a head shorter than Annetta, Suor Caterina somehow always managed to convey the impression that she was looking down her nose. Beneath her black robes, Caterina's under-skirts of lace-trimmed silk made a soft whispering sound as they dragged along the flagstones. Even in this heat, Annetta thought enviously, she seemed spotless, cool as a lagoon breeze.

As she followed behind Caterina, Annetta wondered what had happened to the usual gatekeeper, Suor Chiara. Normally the *contessas* thought themselves too grand for mundane duties such as these, and were highly inventive in their efforts to circumvent them. Outside the obligatory hours of chapel they spent most of the time visiting one another in their cells, eating the fruit and sweetmeats that were delivered to them daily by their relatives from the mainland; they took no interest in the garden, and regarded their hard-working sisters, such as Veronica and Annunciata, with earth-roughened hands and paint-spattered robes, with some-thing approaching contempt. On the few occasions that they were obliged to participate in ordinary convent life, they were notori-ously careless about applying the rules.

Annetta had to hurry to keep up with her.

Although she did not have the faintest idea who Prospero Mendoza was, some deep instinct warned her not to admit to it – not yet, at any rate. The convent may have been more lenient than most about receiving visitors, but Annetta was morally certain that the usual gatekeeper, Suor Chiara, would never have countenanced the visit. This in itself was enough to pique Annetta's interest. She lowered her eyes demurely, so that the other would not see her expression.

'Where is Suor Chiara?'

'She is sick. She has a fever,' Caterina answered her shortly. 'Our Reverend Abbess, Signora Bonifacia, also; haven't you heard?'

They walked on a little way.

'And this Prospero Mendoza, what does he want?'

'How should I know?' Caterina looked bored. 'Isn't he the jewel merchant from the ghetto?'

She gave Annetta such a look that Annetta felt as though she had had cold water thrown in her face.

'You had to sell some of your own jewels, I believe. For your dowry?'

The barb was casually thrown, but it stuck. Annetta bowed her head and walked on in silence.

A jewel merchant? She felt a stab of apprehension. What would a jewel merchant possibly want with her? If Suor Caterina had been hoping to read her thoughts she would find nothing there. Annetta composed her face into a shining blank.

But Caterina was right. Annetta had at one time owned a considerable quantity of jewels. Some of them had been given to her by the Valide herself, who had always been generous to her most trusted servants. Most of them, however, she had acquired as part of her dowry after the Valide's death, when, as a free woman once more, she had elected to return to her native Venice. She had not known, until now, that the selling of these jewels was common knowledge.

All of them had been sold through a suitable intermediary found by the Archbishop of Torcello, to raise the money for her convent dowry. As for the jewels themselves, Annetta had never mourned their loss. For all her love of finery, she had never had much use for them; indeed, had rather despised the harem girls who squabbled and schemed over them; and who spent their hard-earned stipends on any sparkling baubles. These women thought of them only as, what? – consolation, perhaps. For Annetta – privy for so many years to the Valide's ways – the spinels and topazes, turquoises and pearls, had a different kind of value. She had come to see them as a means to an end, part of that wider, more subtle harem currency, to be used and traded for influence and power.

There was only one jewel – the Valide's great diamond, the Sultan's Blue – that could possibly be of any interest to her. But that was long gone, and she never expected to see it again. Traded for that ultimate prize: a human life. But for a common Venetian jeweller to have any knowledge of it? It was so implausible as to make Annetta dismiss the thought out of hand.

Prospero Mendoza? What could he possibly want with her?

Luckily Suor Caterina did not seem to expect a reply to her question. It was several hours before noon and yet already the day was broiling. With her long skirts still held between her fingers, Caterina seemed cool as a lily leaf in one of the physic garden ponds. She floated down the dark stone-flagged corridor, moving so fast Annetta had almost to run to keep up with her.

They passed the herbarium, with its peculiar smell of drying herbs and flowers; then took a short cut across the kitchen courtyard. Through an archway to one side Annetta could see into the herb garden; a pile of scarlet and orange pumpkins the size of cartwheels was stacked up against a wall; on the doorstep, as usual, Fat Anna shelling peas. From the kitchens came the faint smell of food cooking, onions and meat.

They reached the parlour through a side door. Annetta's eyes were still so dazzled by the sunlight outside that at first she could see no more than the dark silhouette of the man waiting for her behind the grille.

'The stupid fellow insists he must give the message to you personally.' Annetta could hear Caterina's voice behind her. 'Well go on then –' she felt an impatient hand on the small of her back '– just make sure he doesn't take all day about it, that's all.'

Slowly, Annetta approached the grille. After the heat of the garden, the air felt very cool. For a moment or two neither of them spoke. Although, in the sudden shadows, she could not yet see his face, she could feel him watching her. His whole body was tensed, and she knew he was wondering whether she was going to give him away. If she wanted to expose him, this was the moment she had been waiting for. This was the intruder in the garden; the *monarchino*, the seducer of nuns – the one who had run off in such an undignified hurry that he had left his own shoe behind in a flower-bed. It was common knowledge that the penalties for attempting to seduce a nun were severe: one word from her and she could destroy him.

And yet – and yet – something made her hesitate.

'*Suora*? Is everything well?'

Caterina, who in the absence of Suor Chiara would act as Annetta's chaperone, now spoke from the back of the parlour where she had positioned herself to wait. Annetta opened her mouth, but instead of the incriminating cry, heard herself say, quite calmly, 'Please, don't trouble yourself, *suora* – I mean, Signora Caterina – I'm just coming.'

And still she hesitated. In the darkness of the parlour his face was gradually emerging from the shadows. He looked pale; those eyes, which had once seemed so hard, were no longer like stones. She could feel his eyes on her; she held his gaze. And in that moment she realised that she had never really looked at him before now. All her sightings of him had been oblique ones: through the spyglass, through the shadows of the convent corridors, a reflection in the water. Even yesterday, when he had followed her in the garden and tried to talk to her, she had averted her eyes, tried to avoid looking at him for as long as possible. But never, until now, like this. Face to face.

Eventually, aware of the figure of Suor Caterina hovering at the back of the parlour, she knew that one of them had to speak.

'You have a message for me?' Her voice, sounding louder than she had intended it to, echoed across the flagstones.

'Yes, lady –' he began, '– a message from my master – er – Prospero Mendoza.'

They both knew he was lying.

In a low voice, so that Caterina could not hear her, she said, 'You really think I believe that? You were with that man, Suor Veronica's English collector, and he's nothing to do with anyone called Prospero Mendoza, or not that I ever heard mention.' She paused for a moment. 'Who is this Prospero anyway?'

In the same undertone as Annetta's he added quickly, 'Prospero Mendoza is a jewel merchant. I'm sorry, but it was the best I could do at short notice.'

So Caterina was right after all. Annetta's heart skipped a beat.

'The best you could do . . .? I don't understand. No one asked you to come here.' She took a step back from him. 'Who are you? What do you want?'

'Come a little closer and I'll tell you.'

'Why should I trust you, you of all people? Anything you have to say, you can say it from there.'

'As you wish.' His gaze flickered briefly towards the other nun watching them from the end of the parlour. 'My name is Carew. John Carew.' His voice was more pleasing than she had remembered it. 'And you are – Annetta,' he added in a whisper.

'I know what my own name is.'

Annetta felt a stab of the old rage towards him. Did he really think she was such an easy picking as the other one? The thought was so insulting she felt like spitting at him again; but she would not, she

185

would hold her temper. There were other, more effective ways to be revenged. She could still call out, even now; expose him as the *monarchino* – But for some reason – what was it, curiosity perhaps? – still she hesitated. What madness was this, that had brought him to take this risk? This was no cheap act of seduction; this was something quite other.

'Well, John Carew,' she said coldly, following his glance over her shoulder, to Suor Caterina who was sitting examining her nails, 'you'd better state your business quickly and be on your way –' she put on the kind of voice that she had heard the *contessas* use when they spoke to a servant '– there's a good fellow.'

For a moment he seemed crestfallen. He took a step back from the grille, and lowered his gaze to the floor. But Annetta's sensation of triumph was shortlived.

'Very well, lady,' he replied. 'My master sent me to say,' he announced in a louder tone, for the benefit of the invigilating Caterina, 'that he thinks he might have something that belongs to you –'

'What nonsense is this? I've never heard of your master. He cannot possibly have anything that would be of any interest to me –'

There was a pause.

'You are quite certain of that?'

'Quite sure.' And then, in a whisper again, 'And don't think that I'm not perfectly aware that this isn't one of your stupid tricks.'

'So I take it that you will not be wanting this?'

From the inside of his shirt Carew brought out the pink embroidered pocket.

Annetta took one look at it and lunged at him.

'*Ladro!*' She tried to snatch it away from him through the bars. 'Thief! Where did you get that? Give it to me . . .'

But Carew was too quick for her. Having held it out, at the last moment he pulled it back, dangling it tantalisingly just out of her reach.

'*Suora?*' Hearing the scuffle, Suor Caterina was wrested from her daydreaming. 'Is everything well with you?' she enquired.

On hearing her voice the two of them became immediately still.

'Yes, *signora*, all is well,' Annetta called over her shoulder, to where the nun had half-risen from the bench where she had been sitting.

'Why is he taking so long anyway, the stupid fellow?' Beneath her black headdress, Suor Caterina's bored face peered at them from the other end of the room. She seemed to vacillate, uncertain as to what she should do.

'It's ... it's a complicated matter.' It was imperative to Annetta, suddenly, that Caterina should be kept well away. 'About my dowry. You were quite right about it, *signora*. Please – I'm just finishing with him now.'

'Very well,' Caterina's natural indolence overcame her, and she sat down again, 'but really, *suora*,' her voice – thin, plaintive – seemed to come from a long way away, 'tell him to hurry up, I can't be sitting here all day.'

Carew passed the pocket through the grille.

'You dropped it,' he said, by way of explanation, 'in the garden yesterday. You ran away before I could give it back to you.'

Annetta took it from him. At first she said nothing, accepting it silently. He watched as she ran her hand over the stiff embroidery, flexing it between her fingers, then holding it up to her ear as though she were listening for something.

'I haven't taken anything from it,' he watched her face, 'it was empty when I found it.'

'Empty?' Annetta's fingers were trembling so much she could hardly undo the drawstring. 'You did not look hard enough then.' She regarded him with a dazed expression. 'Have you any idea how hard I've searched for this? I've turned the whole convent upside down.'

He watched as she plucked at a thread, unpicking part of the stitching and pulling apart the silk lining from the outer embroidered velvet. And then, slipping her forefinger and thumb into the hole she had made, she drew out a small piece of folded paper, held it up between her fingers for him to see.

'A piece of paper?'

'No, not a piece of paper. A poem.'

'A poem?'

All that fuss over a piece of paper with a few verses written on it! He could see faint lettering, in a hand so small it might have been written by spirit creatures. But he dared say nothing now that would alarm her. He knew that he did not have much time. He must ask the questions that he had come to ask, and then leave. It was reckless to have come back to the convent like this, in broad daylight, and on such a spurious pretext. He might be recognised at any time by the other nun. But somehow, he could not bring himself to the point.

He searched around for something to say – anything – so long as it would keep her here with him for a little longer.

'Did you . . . did you write it?'

Her nostrils flared slightly at the question.

'No.'

There was a pause. Feeling foolish, Carew racked his brains again.

'May I read it?'

To this she did not reply; merely held the paper briefly to her lips. Carew watched her insert it carefully back into its hiding place inside the lining of the pocket. He could not stop looking at her. The turn of her throat; the little mole, like a beauty spot, on the side of her cheek. Her eyes curiously formed in a way that he had not noticed before, long and almost almond-shaped.

'Whatever it says, it must be . . . very precious to you.'

'It was written by someone I once knew, someone who is now lost to me. She asked me to keep it for her.'

'Was she also a nun?'

'My friend, a nun?' she laughed. 'I should hope not.' Her tone was mocking. She had a way of half-tilting her head towards him when she spoke. 'I was to give it to the person she wrote it for. Her lover –' She spoke as if the words were somehow profane, and she was saying them for the first time.

'But you still have it?'

'Yes, I still have it, for the moment. He lives far from here. And I, well –'

As if for explanation, Annetta put her hand on one of the iron bars that separated them. And before he could stop himself Carew too put his hand out. She felt his fingers close over hers, felt the touch of his skin. Heard her own sharp intake of breath.

They stood looking at one another, face to face, saying nothing. She knew she should take her hand away, but she could not. She could feel his eyes on her, his gaze so intense it was as though he were touching her, tracing fingers over her cheeks, her hair, her parted lips.

188

'Stop.'

'What?'

'Just stop.'

She closed her eyes, but when she opened them again he was still gazing at her, at her lips this time, and the curve of her throat, saw there both hunger and tenderness.

'I won't hurt you, I swear ... not for anything, not for all the world.'

He was so close now she could hear his breath, feel it against her cheek –

At that moment there was a movement at the back of the nuns' parlour. Annetta jumped as though she had been stung. Behind them Suor Caterina had risen from her seat again; she had her back to them and was talking to someone out of sight, behind the door.

'I have to go ...'

Annetta looked over her shoulder at the two figures standing in the shadows. The presence of the second nun, the sound of their voices whispering together, filled her with sudden foreboding.

'I have to go,' she was desperate now, 'I have to go.'

'No, don't go, not yet.'

Now was his chance, his last chance. Carew knew that he must not put off the moment another instant.

'There's something I have to ask you –'

'There's no time –' Already she had half-turned away from him. 'Go quickly – please – no one else must see you here.'

'It's about a diamond,' he said. 'A diamond called the Sultan's Blue.'

It was not what he had meant to say. It was not what he had meant to say at all. He had only meant to ask her if she were the lady from the harem in Constantinople ... But the effect on Annetta at the mention of the diamond was instant. She turned around to him again, her eyes staring.

'*What do you know about the Sultan's Blue?*' She gripped the iron bars with both hands, her knuckles white.

But it was too late. He had left it too late. In the distance there came the sound of the chapel bell ringing dolefully.

'*Suora.*' Caterina, the stiff skirts of her silk petticoats whispering against the stone floor, was now approaching them. When Annetta did not turn around she repeated, more sharply this time, 'Suor Annetta! The bell for chapel is ringing, can't you hear it?'

But Annetta was still holding on to the bars. That she knew about the Sultan's Blue he could now be in no doubt. But what did she know, and how did she know it?

Carew watched helplessly as Suor Caterina led Annetta away.

Chapter Twenty-seven

Annetta was in such a daze when she followed Suor Caterina out of the nuns' parlour that it was some moments before she realised that it was unusually early for midday prayers. It was some time, too, before she noticed that the chapel bell was making an altogether different sound from the one that normally summoned the nuns: a long doleful peal which continued to toll mournfully long after all the nuns had filed into the chapel.

The interior of the chapel was perfumed and dark. As a rule Annetta derived some solace from the long hours spent here but not now. Now she went in with the other black-clad figures as though in a trance, hardly seeing, hardly hearing, through the doors and into her usual seat among the youngest choir nuns, between Francesca and Ursia.

The Sultan's Blue! It was incredible, impossible.

Francesca must have seen Annetta's strained face because she put her hand on her arm and gave it a sympathetic squeeze.

'You have heard the news then?'

'News?' Annetta stared at her uncomprehendingly. For a few moments she was unable to speak. 'What news?'

'About our Abbess, of course, I thought you must have heard.' She gave Annetta a worried glance. 'You seem unwell, *suora*. Your face is quite white.'

With an effort Annetta tried to concentrate on what Francesca was telling her. 'What about our Abbess?'

'You mean you do not know? Why, she's dead!' Francesca crossed herself quickly. 'Our blessed Abbess is dead. Just half an hour ago.'

'Suor Bonifacia?' Annetta seemed unable to take in even the simplest information. 'Dead? That's impossible! I only spoke to her a few days ago –'

'But it's true, it was so sudden. *Poverina!* A fever, I heard. Suor Chiara has it too.' There was a catch in Francesca's voice, she shook her head sadly. 'That good lady was a saint! May her blessed soul rest in peace.'

'Suor Bonifacia was old,' Ursia, of a more pragmatic nature, whispered back. 'The question is, who will be our Abbess now?' She nodded her head in the direction of Suor Purificacion who was already kneeling in prayer.

'It will be put to the vote, of course. In the chapter. Is that not how it is always done?'

'Well, she will never get my vote –'

The excited whispers of Francesca and Ursia were now joined by some of the other choir nuns. Annetta hardly heard them. There was a buzzing in her ears. She could not bear it; she had to shut them out. Needed to think. At this moment Annetta could not have given a fig for who would be the convent's new Abbess; could not even shed a tear for Suor Bonifacia. She knelt down and buried her face between her hands as though in prayer.

Although she should have been praying for the soul of the dead departed Abbess, her mind was frozen. She could only think of one thing. *The Sultan's Blue!* Was that what that man – John Carew – had come about after all? What could he possibly know about it? Had they found her out? She had promised herself that she would be safe back at the convent, that no one would ever think of looking for her here, but now . . . Annetta could feel the panic rise in her.

The priest had arrived at last; was standing at the altar; was leading the nuns in prayers, asking them to remember their departed sister. The sounds of the nuns' voices rose and fell, lamenting their dead Abbess. Annetta tried hard to bring her thoughts back to the present. Tried to imagine how Suor Bonifacia would look on her deathbed. Tried to imagine that face, beautiful even in her old age; her silver hair spread out against the pillows. But all she could see was the body of that other dead woman: the Valide.

She remembered her feeling of terror at the dead woman's eye when, half-opened, it had seemed to gleam and wink at her through the blue and green shadows of her sleeping chamber. Remembered her hand, hard and cold as a bird's claw, with the diamond clasped inside it, and how, in desperation, she had bitten and chewed on that dead flesh, forcing it to relinquish the jewel. And then the stolen diamond, heavy as a stone in a drowning sack, when it lay at last in her pocket.

But that, as it turned out, was only the beginning.

Chapter Twenty-eight

That night Annetta woke suddenly, to find someone shaking her awake.

'Goose?' With a start she sat up, looking round her wildly. 'Is that you?'

'Who you calling a goose!' a voice whispered sleepily from beside her. 'It's me, Eufemia. You was talking in your sleep again.'

'I'm sorry, did I wake you?'

'Was you dreaming about your friend Kaya again? The one who reminds you of me?'

For a moment or two Annetta did not say anything.

'Her name was not Kaya.'

'But I thought you said –'

'I did.' A pause. 'It wasn't her real name. Her real name was Celia Lamprey.'

'Sounds foreign to me.'

Another pause.

'Yes.'

'Is that who you've bin dreaming about?'

'Yes.'

'It's a good dream then?'

'I – it's –' Annetta hesitated '– it's a complicated one.'

The little *conversa*, with her peasant's sixth sense, lay quite still beside her, waiting for her to speak.

'It's not so much a dream as a memory. A memory of the last time I saw her,' Annetta said at last.

'Is it a bad thing?'

Annetta did not answer. She lay on her back, fully awake now, staring into the darkness. In the first few moments of waking she had almost believed herself back in the other place. Instead of the whitewashed walls of her cell, in a trick of the light she had seen once again the green and red tiled walls of the room she had shared with six of the other *kislar*. Lord only knew how she had battled, all those months, to keep the two of them together. But somehow she had.

And now, almost without meaning to, in the quiet of her cell, with just the candles guttering in the corridor outside, Annetta began to tell her story.

'Celia and I were taken captive in the same shipwreck, I think I told you that already. We didn't know what would become of us, but whatever happened we were determined to stay together. I am dark, as you know; but Celia was an English rose, as they say in that country; she had the white skin and reddish-gold hair that is so highly prized by the Turks. I would put my arm around her, put my cheek against hers like this.' Annetta bent towards Eufemia. '*The dark and the fair together, mistress. Look, we could be twins.*'

'And somehow it worked. We were bought as a pair by the same slave dealer in Constantinople. She was the one who changed our names from Annetta and Celia to Ayshe and Kaya. And it was she who in turn sold us to the Sultan's favourite, a lady known to us all as the Haseki, who gave us to the Sultan's mother, the Valide. Our years together in the harem were spent there as the Valide's personal slaves.

'Despite what you might think, it wasn't an unhappy time,' Annetta went on, 'at least not for me. Far from it. I had been living here, in this very convent, as a *conversa*, put here by my family when I was very young. I didn't mind the life, but it wasn't an easy one – you know better than anyone how the *converse* are treated, not much better than servants to the choir nuns. But in the harem, well that was a different matter. There no one cared what kind of family you were from – they didn't give two figs if your name was written in the Golden Book, or if your grandfather had been on the Council of Ten – all the *kislar* were the same.

'And I did very well, even though I say so myself,' Annetta smiled to herself. 'I might not have been beautiful like Celia, but I was very quick to learn. The Valide took to me. I saw how she was, and how she liked things done, and learnt how to anticipate her every need, and before long she selected me to be one of her four principal hand-maidens. It was the sort of thing I was used to, after all, fetching and carrying for other people, but how different it was there! In the harem, that was important work. I was given beautiful clothes, even jewels, to wear. All the other girls looked up to me then, I can tell you. I had the respect of everyone, even the older women – the harem stewardess and the mistress of the girls – because I was close to the Valide, and had her ear.

'But it was different for Celia. Celia could not get used to her new life at all. All she could think about was the home she had left behind; about her father who had died in the shipwreck, and the merchant she loved and had been going to marry. *Madonna!* Especially him,' Annetta frowned. 'All that weeping and mooning about, wondering if he would ever know what had become of her, or if he thought she was dead, sunk to the bottom of the sea along with her precious dowry chests.' She made an impatient sound with her tongue against her teeth. 'I wanted to slap her sometimes. She couldn't get him out of her mind; she would dream about him every night.

'*Better not to sleep, in that case*, I would tell her. *Forget your dreams. Forget everything, you stupid girl. The past is no good to you here,* capito? *Think of the future, goose, it's your only hope.*

'But it was no good. Even when she became *gözde.*'

'What does that mean?'

'*Gözde* means "in the eye". In the eye of the Padishah.'

'You mean if the Sultan wanted to . . .'

'Fornicate with her,' Annetta answered flatly, 'Yes, that's right. Nice fresh *culo* for a fat old man, that's what I used to say,' she added. 'That place was no better than a brothel, with one client. But anyway . . . one day Celia was chosen.'

'And so what happened?'

'Well, I don't have to tell you that her heart was not really in it,' Annetta said drily. 'A whole month's wages I gave her so we could bribe one of the old harem women into preparing her properly. But was she grateful? Oh, no, no, no. She kept clutching her sides as though the very thought of it gave her a pain. *Couldn't you go?* she kept saying. *Couldn't you go in my place?*'

Eufemia stared at Annetta, fascinated.

'*Are you mad?* I would say to her,' Annetta was warming to her story. '*Don't you know what this means? Haven't you seen how everyone looks at you, now you are* gözde? *We've been given this one chance, and you,* carissima, *are it. So you'd better get on with it – you'd better do it properly.*'

'And did the Sultan – like her?'

'Yes, but not enough. He asked for her twice, but each time she was . . . outmanoeuvred . . .' Annetta tailed off, as though uncertain of how to continue.

'And?' Eufemia nudged her to go on.

'Then something happened which put a stop to all our hopes for good.'

'What? What was that?'

'She found out that this man, her merchant, was actually in Constantinople. She knew that he had come there with an English embassy several years previously, just a little before she had set sail on her fateful voyage; but what she had not known was that the business of the embassy had been delayed. Instead of returning to England, as she thought, her merchant had never left the city.' Annetta shook her head wonderingly. 'But as if that were not extraordinary enough, somehow – *Santissima Madonna!* – somehow he had indeed found out about her. That she had not after all been drowned in the ship-wreck, as everyone must have thought, but was living in the palace of the Padishah, right under his very nose. Why, he must have seen the roofs and treetops that sheltered her every day from the place where the foreign merchants all lived, on the other side of the Bosphorus.'

'But however did she find out?' Eufemia interrupted eagerly. 'Did he send her a message?'

'A message! What madness would that have been – from a man, and a Christian! – to one of the Padishah's women! No, he was too clever for that. He must have known that if he sent a message, either written or spoken, it might be intercepted. So he sent an object, something that he knew she alone would recognise as coming from him.'

'And what was it?'

'A strange instrument that he always carried with him – a compendium, I think she called it. There was a secret compartment at the bottom, which she knew how to open, in which he kept a miniature

197

of her.' Annetta shook her head again, sadly this time. 'It was still there. I saw it with my own eyes.'

'*Poverina!*' Eufemia sighed. 'Unhappy lady!'

'Unhappy lady indeed.' Annetta too gave a sigh. 'So much for all my warnings. After that, of course, she could not rest. Her mind was so oppressed with thoughts of him that I really feared she might fade away completely.

'And then she made the worst mistake of her life. She showed the compendium to someone else. Of *all* people she had to go and show it to the Valide. Dear Lord! I do believe she must have confided everything to her.' Annetta put her hands up to cover her face, made a motion as though she were grinding her fists into her eyes. 'Of all the stupid things she could have done, believe me *that* was the stupidest . . .'

'Was that really so bad? What could the lady do to her?'

'What could the Valide do?' Annetta took her hands away and stared at Eufemia; in the darkness her pupils were enormous. 'You haven't understood anything, have you?

'Later that day Celia and I met, quite by chance, in the Valide's courtyard. Everyone else had been to see the great gift that the English merchants had presented to the Sultan that afternoon. I had been so worried! I knew the queen had sent for her, and that they had had a long talk, but I didn't know then what it was about. We went into her old apartment to talk. She looked strange, sort of . . . restless. Kept pressing her hand to her side as though something were hurting her there. I knew then that something had happened.

'At first she was reluctant to tell me. Poor Celia, she knew me well enough to know exactly what I would say.

'*She says I can see him, just one last time. Tonight, at the Aviary Gate.*

'*What?* I said, my heart in my mouth. *She told you that?*

'But she did not seem to hear me.

'*If I could see him just one last time,* she kept saying, *see his face, hear his voice. If I could do that I think I could be happy.*

'It was then that she showed me the compendium.

'*I have her blessing,* was all she said.

'The Valide's blessing to see and speak to another man! Poor deluded girl! I knew that it was a trap. I told her so, but she wouldn't listen.

'*She's testing you, can't you see?* I was almost shouting at her. *To see where your loyalty lies.* Loyalty was everything to the Valide. *If you go, you'll fail her test . . .*

'*But this is my chance*, she kept saying, *this is my only chance. I have to take it. The Aviary Gate, tonight. Look I have the key*, she had it on a chain around her neck, held it up for me to see, *she says he'll be there . . .*

'I used to wonder to myself afterwards: did she know that the Valide had set a trap for her that night? Surely she did. But I never found out the answer to that question. All I knew was that if she went, she would never come back. After everything that we had been through to stay together! At that moment I really thought I would go mad. *Don't go, don't leave me, please . . .* I was weeping now, terrified of what might happen. *Please! I don't think I can do this without you . . .* But she wouldn't listen.

'Dusk was falling. Overhead there was a small patch of sky visible. I remember watching the light dwindle, the sky turn from pink to grey. I remember watching as the bats began to swoop overhead. We sat there together in the deserted room for a long time, our arms round each other.

'*Is it time?* I kept saying. *Is it time?*

'And each time she would look at the sky and say to me, *No, we still have time.*

'She was happy then, I think –' Annetta broke off, as though stricken. 'It was I who felt as though I were going to my death.

'And then it was time. I remember watching her stand on the threshold of the little room; I remember thinking that she looked like a bird about to fly.

'*Be happy for me, Annetta.* Her face was shining.

'And then she did something strange. She took a piece of paper out of her pocket and gave it to me.

'*It's for Paul*, she said – that was her merchant's name – '*promise me you'll find a way to get it to him?* Annetta stopped again as though it were difficult to get the words out.

'I still have it.' She reached into her own pocket and took the paper out. She unfolded it carefully and held it up in the dirty early-morning light for Eufemia to see. 'It's a poem. A love letter, if you like. But it was also the answer to the question I had been asking myself all this time. I think, in one part of her mind, Celia knew all along that the Valide was trying to trap her. She did not take the poem with her because she knew that her lover would not be there. She knew that if she used the key, as the Valide had suggested – if she so much as set foot outside the Aviary Gate – that it would not be Paul who waited for her on the other side, but the eunuchs with their scimitars, waiting to cut her down.

'Then I realised what had happened: that a kind of madness had overtaken her. But when I looked up, she'd gone.

'And I knew then that I had to stop her.

Chapter Twenty-nine

'I ran after her.

'I ran so fast that I kept stumbling and almost falling over the hem of my robe on to the flagstones. My hair worked its way loose, and began to fall down over my face, until there were strands of hair in my mouth, and across my eyes, and I was running almost blind, following by pure instinct the route that I guessed she must have taken, the path to the Aviary Gate at the far end of the harem gardens.

'I guessed that Celia would not have chosen the route through the main part of the harem, skirting the Valide's quarters, where she might have been seen and stopped, but another, longer path, across the courtyard and then along the Golden Way, the great stone corridor down which the eunuchs take the Sultan's chosen women to his bedchamber.

'And by some miracle I had guessed right. I reached the corridor just in time to see her figure disappearing into the shadows ahead of me. If I kept running I might still be in time, I might just be able to stop her before she reached the gate, before it was too late.

'And then disaster struck. My foot caught against one of the flagstones. I fell hard, bruising my knees cruelly against the stone. How could I have been so clumsy, so stupid? I was weeping, not only with pain, but with fear and frustration. I had no chance of catching up with her now.

'But wait! – listen! – what was this? Suddenly I heard the sound of voices, and footsteps, and before I could get to my feet again two eunuchs came running up behind me. They were holding flaming torches in their hands. *Madonna!* What they thought I was doing there I don't know, but I decided to seize the moment. *Stop her*, I cried out to them, *stop her, stop her, the* kadın *is running away!* pointing with my finger down the corridor the way she had gone.

'To my amazement, that's just what they did. They seemed hardly to have noticed me at all, for all that I was lying sprawled there on the ground, but ran on past me as though I were as invisible as a palace djinn.

'I struggled to my feet and limped after them as quickly as I could. I found my way into the harem gardens, and there an extraordinary scene met my eyes. There was a moon that night, but it had passed behind clouds, and the gardens seemed very dark. At first I could see no sign of Celia at all. I looked everywhere, up and down. And then, yes! Glory be! There she was, running through the rose garden. All was not lost. I remember being struck by how small she looked, no more substantial than a moth fluttering there, only the paleness of her hair, her white sleeves glowing as she ran through the darkness. If we could just stop her before she got to the gate, she would have committed no crime.

'*There she is, over there!* I pointed my finger again and opened my mouth. *Stop her!* But I could tell that the two eunuchs had already seen her. And as I watched them running I saw to my amazement two more eunuchs emerging from the other side of the garden. And then two more. Six eunuchs in all, each of them carrying a flaming torch. The Valide had sprung her trap, without even waiting for her to pass through the Aviary Gate.

'They were big tall creatures, those eunuchs, for the most part, for all they had no *coglioni*,' Annetta gave a small shudder, 'and they gained on her rapidly. There was one who was nearly upon her. I opened my mouth to call out again, when the moon emerged from behind a cloud and I saw, quite clearly, what I had not been able to see before. In his free hand he was holding up an unsheathed sword.

'Eufemia! What had I done!' Annetta clutched at her arm, gripping it so tightly that the little *conversa* almost cried out. 'Eufemia! God forgive me! In that moment I realised he was not going save her. He was going to kill her, even before she'd reached the gate.

'*Wait!* I was screaming now, screaming and trying to run to her on my broken knees. I don't know what madness made me think I might yet be able to get to her before he did. *Don't touch her, don't hurt her, she's done nothing . . .*

'And then – it was as if some miracle were happening –' Annetta gazed around the cell, her eyes fixed sightlessly on that far-distant horizon in her mind. 'He caught hold of Celia, but on hearing my voice, the eunuch stopped. He lowered his sword. I was sobbing and running and screaming at him, all at the same time. *Don't hurt her, don't hurt her! She's done nothing!* He looked round to see who was shouting, as though uncertain now what he should do. I could see her face, her look of desperation. And at that moment she saw me.

'*You!*

'I had never seen an expression like that on her face before.

'*What?*

'At first I was bewildered. I didn't know what she meant.

'*You called the guards!*

'*No!*

'*It was you, after all!*

'*Celia . . . please . . .* I could hardly speak. *Listen . . .*

'But she would not. She pulled violently away from her captor and began to run again. Another eunuch, coming up just then, slashed at her legs with his sword as she darted past. He was so quick, so dextrous. Like a butcher with his knife. I saw the flash of the blade in the moonlight. Two quick cuts. One, two, like that.

'It was all so fast that I could hardly see what had happened at first. She simply fell.' Annetta was kneeling up on the bed now, her face a mask. 'Celia, felled. Like a tree, before my very eyes. The eunuch had severed the backs of her legs, cutting both her hamstrings.

'It's what they do to slaves sometimes,' she whispered, 'to stop us running away.'

There was a long silence. Somewhere a bell rang. In the other cells they could hear the nuns preparing themselves reluctant for the first prayers of the morning, but in an unspoken agreement neither Annetta nor Eufemia made a move.

When the last nun had gone, clattering down the stairs towards the chapel, and they knew they were alone in the dormitory, Eufemia turned to Annetta again.

'What happened to her?' She seemed almost as stricken by the fate of Celia as Annetta herself.

'It was a long, long time before I found that out.' Annetta lay back down in the bed and pulled the coverlets over her, shivering slightly. 'She was not dead – of that much I could be reasonably sure. I would have heard the guns go off. Someone told me she had been taken to the harem infirmary, but after that –' Annetta shrugged. 'Nobody seemed to know what had become of her. It was as though – *pouf !* –' she made a gesture with the fingers of one hand '– she had simply never been.'

On the windowsill the little sparrow began to fluff out its wings and chirrup in its cage. After a while, Annetta resumed her story.

'Life went on in the harem, much the same as before. No one spoke about Celia, or Kaya, as she was known there. Not even the *kislar*, like Gulbahar and Turhan, who had been her friends. I knew the Valide was watching me, just as she must have watched Celia all that time. I think even she was puzzled by what had happened. Had I really meant to betray my friend? But I had to go along with it, I had to let her think that. I couldn't show, not even by the smallest sign, how much I missed her, how desperate I was to know where she was, what had happened to her. So I kept my eyes open, but my mouth shut. I put on a perfect mask. But I swore that one day I would find her, and that I would get us both out.

'The years went past – four in all – each one very much like the next. And then two extraordinary things happened, almost on the same day. The first was that I found out where Celia was, at last.'

'How did tha' find out?'

'Of all the strange things, it was the Valide herself who told me.' Annetta shook her head. 'She had been on a visit to the Old Palace – the Palace of Tears, they used to call it, because when a padishah dies, it is the place where his women go to live. I was attending her in her private chambers, and suddenly I heard her say, *I saw your friend Kaya today.* She said it so casually she might have been talking about the weather. Eufemia! –' for the first time there was a catch in Annetta's voice '– can you imagine what I felt at that moment? I could hardly believe that my ears were not deceiving me.

'*I saw your friend Kaya.* Had I really heard her right? I could feel the blood drain from my face.

'Luckily, I was quite used to her little tricks – she was getting old and spiteful by then – and I had the presence of mind to keep my gaze fixed to the floor so she could not read my expression.

'*Majesty?*

'*I said I saw your friend Kaya today, in the Old Palace.*

'*Kaya? Yes – Majesty*. I could barely get the words out.

'Celia was alive! Not only alive, but she was living quite close by. All this time! The only thing I could hope was that my voice did not betray me too much.

'For a while the Valide did not say anything more. She had me bring one of her shawls, and I helped her to her favourite place by the window. How she loved to sit there. I had a sudden memory of the first time I had waited on her in that room. The boredom of it! There were four of us, her favoured handmaidens. We had to stand, of course. How our backs would ache! The Valide would sit there for hours, watching the water traffic on the Golden Horn, the merchant galleys coming and going: watching, dreaming, plotting some new scheme. But that day, after all those years, I felt as if I had never done anything else.

'*It was a shame really*, the Valide said reflectively after a while, still staring out at the view. *The Padishah always liked her.*

'She continued to stare out of the window, but I knew better than to relax my guard. I kept my gaze on the floor. She had the trick of somehow being able to watch you even when she was not looking at you. I don't know how she did it – through the pores of her skin, I sometimes used to think – and I did not trust myself yet to look up.

'*You are unusually silent today, Ayshe*, she said after a while.

'Silent? Dear God! My throat was aching so much I thought it would burst. I didn't know whether I loved her or hated her at that moment. I opened my mouth to reply but no sound came out.

'*Don't cry, Ayshe*, I heard her say, quite gently. *I know what it is to love a friend.*

For a moment there was complete silence in the little whitewashed cell. Eufemia sat quite still, not wanting to break the spell. And when Annetta spoke again her voice was quite steady.

'Those were the last words she ever said to me. Two days later she was dead.'

'The queen, dead?'

'That's what we all thought at first.' Annetta could not help smiling a little at the note of horror in Eufemia's voice. 'The Valide, dead! It didn't seem possible. But it was. She died in the night. And it was I who found her.'

Annetta turned on to her back, and lay staring up at the ceiling. She imagined herself back in the Valide's sleeping chamber. Could see the body lying there, the skin already yellowing, the mouth slack, the hands – their flesh already hard and cold – folded neatly on top of one another. The powerful sensation that some spell had been broken at last, and she was seeing her for the first time: that everything the Valide had been was just an illusion, all along, an act of will.

So this is death, she remembered thinking. *Is that all?*

Was it that that had made her steal the diamond?

The thought of it, even now, made the sweat break out on the back of Annetta's neck. The diamond so big that it did not even fit into the Valide's clenched fist. The Sultan's Blue!

How many times since then had she relived the horror of that moment, the struggle with the already decomposing body to free the stone; remembered, with a small shudder, biting down into that sweet-tasting dead flesh, the sickening snap of the finger as she finally prised the great jewel out . . .

As if to shake off the thought, Annetta sat up again and leant her back against the wall.

'Since I had been the Valide's personal slave, I was free now. She had given me my freedom,' Annetta said, choosing her words with care. 'And also something else. Something of great value. A diamond.'

'A diamond?'

'They call it the Sultan's Blue.'

'She gave it to tha'?'

'No, you numbskull. She was dead, remember?' Annetta snapped at Eufemia, more sharply than she meant to. 'I stole it from her.'

'Tha' *stole* it?'

'After what she had stolen from me?' Annetta's black eyes glittered. 'Yes, I stole it: I stole her precious diamond! And much good it did me!'

'What did tha' do with it? Does tha' still have it?'

'No! I used to think that it would take a king's ransom to get Celia out of the Old Palace – and now I had it! There was only one thing in the world that I wanted, and that was to buy Celia's freedom, along with my own.' Annetta sat back as though she were exhausted suddenly, pressing her fingers into her eyes. 'There was a *kira* I knew and trusted, a Jewess who sometimes carried out small commissions for the harem women. She didn't know what it was of course. I made up a parcel to look like a jar of oil, with the stone and a letter to Celia hidden inside. She agreed to take it for me to the Old Palace, and promised to deliver it into Celia's own hands. I paid her handsomely to do it. As for the rest – well, the rest was up to Celia.'

She put her hand to her breast as though something there was hurting her.

'It's been more than a year now and I've heard no news of her. I don't know whether she's alive or dead. Or what became of the stone. Until now. Until today. Until he came, that man I told you about. John Carew. Eufemia! He knows something, I'm certain of it! You have to help me find him!'

Chapter Thirty

When Carew arrived back at Constanza's *palazzo* it was to find that once again the whole place appeared deserted. He walked through the courtyard, then the kitchens and storerooms on the ground floor, then up the outside staircase which led to the *piano nobile*.

Here, too, he found Constanza's beautiful room empty. As before, the linen screens were half-pulled across the windows to shield the room from the heat. Debris from the day before – the plates with their half-eaten bread and cheese, the glass beakers of wine, barely touched; a pile of discarded *tarrochi* cards lying in a pool of candlewax. Without the candles burning, the stench of the canal – something putrid and black – seemed to fill the air. The place seemed even more neglected than it had the day before. Motes of dust stirred lazily underfoot. Clearly, Carew thought to himself, Constanza's servants had not returned.

Of Constanza herself there was no sign. But when he went to pull up the linen screens he became aware that he was not alone in the room after all.

Paul was half-lying, half-sitting in the darkness at one end of the bed. He was wearing a dirty linen shirt open to the waist, and his beard had clearly not been trimmed for several days.

'Well, well, look what the cat brought in.' He watched Carew through narrowed eyes. 'I see you've learnt how to make yourself at home here,' he remarked softly.

'And a very good day to you too, Master Pindar.' With a vicious snap of the wrist, Carew drew up the last of the blinds. He looked enquiringly round the room. 'Where's Constanza?'

Pindar shrugged. For a moment the two men contemplated one another in hostile silence.

'I thought you'd gone,' Paul said at last.

He leant back against the headboard. In the dirty canal light that now flooded the room he looked paler than usual, but this time at least he was sober enough. 'Ambrose said you'd already sailed. Gone back to England, he said. On one of the Company's merchantmen.'

'Well I'm sorry to disappoint you.' Carew stood square, facing him on the opposite side of the room. His expression was sour. 'Looks as though Ambrose isn't quite the intelligencer he's cracked up to be, doesn't it? If you ask me, the only thing he's really interested in is getting his hands on this mermaid baby for Parvish's cabinet. *Faugh!*' Carew shivered. 'He couldn't stop talking about it when I last saw him. "*It's not nat-ur-al.*" ' He gave a surprisingly good imitation of Ambrose.

'A pox on Parvish and his precious cabinet,' Paul said irritably. 'A pox on Ambrose, for that matter. What I want to know is, what did you find out about that little nun of yours? The nun with the pocket?'

'I take it you've spoken to Constanza then?'

'She was good enough to pass on your message.'

'Well, I did see one of the nuns,' Carew said slowly. 'It's not her, it's not Celia.' He paused, contemplating the utter impossibility of ever explaining – to himself, let alone to anyone else – what had happened in the convent that afternoon.

'You know something.' Paul was watching him carefully.

'No, I don't –'

'Well I think you do.' With surprising agility Paul leapt from the bed and came over to where Carew was standing.

'I haven't had the chance yet –'

'Think I believe that? I know that look, know it of old. I can see the whites of your eyes, and that always means trouble. You know something, you damned rat-catcher; you know something and you're not telling me.'

From a belt beneath his shirt Paul took out a short dagger. Carew felt the sting of its tip as Paul drew it the length of his cheek, tracing the outline of the long white cicatrice that led from Carew's jawline to his mouth.

209

'Tell me or I'll slice your ear off this time.'

Carew could smell his breath, rank after another night with too much wine and no sleep.

'That's all right, I've got another one . . . *Ah! Jesus!*' Clamping his hand to the side of his face, Carew pulled violently away. 'What did you have to do that for?' He could feel the blood, sticky and warm, running down the side of his neck. He put his hand up to his ear, felt a flap of skin hanging down. 'Sweet Jesus, you *have* cut my ear off!'

'You thought I was jesting? Well, I'd like to remind you that I never jest,' Paul said coldly. 'Don't be such a baby, it's only the lobe. Besides,' he wiped the blade clean carefully on his shirt tail, 'as you so merrily say, you've got another one.'

'Jesus . . .'

Carew went over to the folding table; he picked up the flask of wine and poured some on to one of the linen napkins, then held it up to his ear.

Paul, sitting down on the edge of Constanza's bed, regarded Carew dispassionately. 'Does it hurt?'

Carew did not reply. Instead, he took one of the kitchen blades from the belt at his waist and pointed it at his bleeding ear.

'You can't hurt me, Pindar.'

With a well-practised flick, as though he were fileting a piece of meat, he sliced through the remaining flesh of his earlobe. A piece of skin, about the size of a farthing coin, landed at Paul's feet.

Pindar regarded Carew's earlobe impassively.

'I'm sorry.'

Carew leaned his back against the wall and slid down so that he was sitting on the floor.

'No, you're not.'

For a moment they sat together in silence. The sun had shifted, and beams of sunlight beat down into the room, showing the patch where one of the tooled leather panels had been taken down from the wall, the frayed damask of the bed hangings.

'Look at you.' Carew pressed the linen cloth to his throbbing ear. 'Look at what you've become. What do you think your father would say if he could see you like this?'

'You leave him out of this.'

Another long silence.

'Ambrose thinks you have fallen into a melancholy.'

Pindar lay down on the bed again.

'A pox on Ambrose,' he said faintly, 'a pox on you all.'

'Why, Paul? Why do you hate me so much?'

'You're wrong, I don't hate you –' Paul tailed off. 'Not all the time, anyway.'

'What then?'

'Because you are the one who saw her. And I did not. Because you should have torn down that wall with your bare hands to save her. And you could not.'

'No one could.'

Silence again.

'I know. Do you think that makes any difference?'

Carew was still sitting with his back up against the wall.

'Come back to England with me. The boat sails in a few days – tomorrow, even, if the winds are right.'

For a moment Paul seemed to be considering it.

'I can't.' He gazed up at the ceiling. 'I can't show my face there, not like this. Not yet anyway . . . Besides –' a pause '– I'm pledged to play in the game.'

Carew closed his eyes wearily.

'And what game might that be?'

As if he did not already know the answer to that question.

'What do you think? Zuanne Memmo's game, of course. The big one.'

'I thought – I thought he wouldn't have you? I thought the stakes were too high.'

'What? Do you really think I'd let a game like that pass me by? What kind of a fool do you take me for?'

'Not that much of a fool,' Carew snapped back, 'not even you.'

'What do you think I've been doing for the last few days?'

There was another silence.

'Don't you want to know how I persuaded him to let me play?'

'Not particularly.'

'By using my jewels as surety,' Paul went on, speaking in the low rapid tone of someone in a confessional. 'I sold all my interests in the Levant Company to buy them. And now Zuanne Memmo has them.'

211

'Everything you own, to play in this one game?'

'Everything I own to possess that diamond. To own the Sultan's Blue. I have to have it, John, I have to –' Paul swallowed. And then he added, not quite smiling, 'All or nothing. I like it, don't you?'

'Didn't you listen to Constanza? Didn't she tell you –'

'Yes, yes, yes –' Paul waved his hand '– she would say that, wouldn't she? I know you put her up to it.'

Carew made an inarticulate sound.

'You'll be ruined.'

'I won't lose this one.'

'How do you know?'

'How do I know?' Paul said between gritted teeth. *'Because – I'm – feeling – lucky.'*

'You'll be ruined,' Carew repeated.

'You really don't understand, do you?' Paul turned his head towards Carew at last; his eyes had the glazed, out-of-body look of someone who has not slept peacefully for many months. 'Whatever happens, I'll feel alive.'

Ambrose's gondola came to rest on the steps of Constanza's *palazzo*.

His way was blocked by a second gondola just coming round the bend in the canal in their direction.

On the oily water, the stench of the canal was overpowering. Ambrose held a piece of cotton cambric drenched with attar of roses fastidiously to his enormous nose.

'Excuse me, *signore*, is this the *palazzo* of the lady what they call *Signora* Constanza Fabia?' the passenger of the boat, a young girl of no more than twelve or thirteen wearing a shabby black nun's habit, called out to him.

Ambrose regarded her without enthusiasm. Unless they had something to contribute to one of the paper museums or cabinets of curiosities for which he so ardently combed the world – an exquisite botanical watercolour, such as Sister Veronica supplied him with, or a holy relic purchased, not too many questions asked, from one of their chapels (a piece of St John's shin bone and a drop of Our Lady's breast milk were two particularly satisfying recent acquisitions) – Ambrose had little use for nuns.

But all the same: even in this city of continual and loathsome vice, a nun actively seeking out a courtesan? His interest was piqued.

'The *courtesan* Constanza Fabia?'

'*Si, signore. La cortigiana honesta.*'

'And who, if I may be so bold, wishes to know?'

'Eufemia,' the girl replied in the rasping, slightly high-pitched tones of the Venetian vernacular, an accent so thick, Ambrose thought, he could practically have stuck a spoon in it. 'Suor Eufemia,' she added with pride. When she named the island convent to whose order she belonged, one of Ambrose's sandy eyebrows gave a barely perceptible twitch.

'Well, my dear, you're certainly a long way from home.'

Although he perfectly well knew the convent – having visited both the gardens and Suor Veronica there many times – Ambrose thought it unnecessary to venture this information in return.

'Isn't it rather unusual for you to be out and about like this?' He blinked at her. 'I thought your order was strictly enclosed.'

'Bless you, no, sir, I'm a lay nun, *signore*, what we call *conversa*.' Eufemia grinned at him. 'Them rules don't apply to us, only to the choir nuns. Although if Old Pure Face . . . I mean Suo' Purificacion could have her way none of us would be allowed out at all . . . *She* says it leads to gross immorality and shouldn't be allowed, but none of the rest of us really care at all for what she thinks now that our sainted abbess Suo' Bonifacia has popped 'er clogs, may her soul rest in peace –'

'Well, well, no need to run on, thank you kindly, I think I get the picture.' Still holding the sweet-smelling handkerchief to his nose, Ambrose regarded her dispassionately.

'And tell me, sister –'

'You can call me 'Femia if you like.'

'Can I really? How kind. 'Femia.' Ambrose stretched his lips over his teeth into something resembling a smile. 'And tell me, how did you find your way here?'

It occurred to him that the little nun, sitting up so perkily in her shabby rented gondola, had the air of someone enjoying an unexpected holiday.

'Prospero Mendoza, *signore*. He told me to come here.'

213

'Prospero Mendoza?' Ambrose's eyebrows twitched again. He put the handkerchief down slowly. 'The jewel merchant from the ghetto?'

'That's right. He a friend of yours, an' all?'

Ambrose started to stare at the little nun now with a peculiar intensity, an expression she might have found almost chilling if she had not been so intoxicated, at that moment, by her own sense of importance. 'He told me I'd most likely find the foreign gentleman here.'

Eufemia was now gazing with undisguised amazement at Ambrose's nose. She seemed to recollect herself at last. Having listened to Ambrose's faltering use of her mother tongue, an idea occurred. 'You're a foreign gentleman, ain't you?'

'That is correct – uh, 'Femia –' if she could feel Ambrose staring back at her almost as hard as she was staring at him, she gave no sign of it '– so perhaps, if you'll allow me to, I can help you?' Ambrose composed his features so that he was smiling at her with the air of a kindly uncle. 'You're a lucky girl, I must say, I know *everyone* hereabouts. Might I be so bold as to ask his name?'

On hearing her reply, Ambrose threw his hands theatrically heavenwards.

'Great heavens!' he exclaimed, casting her such an admiring look that Eufemia could almost believe that their chance meeting had been entirely contrived by her own brilliance. 'John Carew! Well, will you fancy that?' Ambrose patted the seat next to him in the little cabin of his gondola. 'John Carew is my *particular* friend. Such an *intriguing* man, I've always thought. If you come and sit here for a moment,' he glanced quickly upwards at Constanza's window but all he could see were the linen sun blinds, still reassuringly closed, 'then you can tell me what it's all about.'

'Oh no, *signore*, I couldn't do that!' Eufemia shook her head most decidedly.

'Don't be silly, child, whyever not?' Ambrose tried not to sound annoyed.

'I'm to give him the message from the *suo*' and come straight home. Give him the message and show him the letter, that is, the one what her English friend wrote to her merchant in Constantinople.' She patted something concealed in the folds of her robe, somewhat in the manner of a person who has been entrusted with a precious object and is mortally afraid of mislaying it. 'That way he'll know it's really her.'

For a moment or two Ambrose was completely silent. His face, which was already flushed from the intense heat of the afternoon, had become suffused with an even deeper crimson blush. He seemed about to burst out with something – whether it was an expletive, or a song, or possibly both, it was hard to tell – but then just as suddenly he apparently thought better of it. The air went out of him, as out of a balloon, and when he spoke again he seemed quite unconcerned by what he had just heard.

'Oh, well, a lovers' tryst, is it? Of course I quite understand, just as you please.' Looking bored, Ambrose trailed one finger in the fetid canal water. 'And what a good girl you are, indeed. I only wish my servants would be so particular.' With his other hand he picked up a fan and began to flap it languidly. 'A lovers' tryst, how dull. If that *is* what it is?' He glanced slyly in her direction. 'Well for your sake I hope that is what it is and not something more important, that's all. And to think, I could have helped him. *Poverino!* Poor John!' Sighing loudly, Ambrose busied himself ostentatiously about his collection boxes at his feet. 'Well, I must be off.'

'Why *poverino?*'

'Well yes, he's gone, of course. Sailed. *Disaparu.* All this talk of the plague, you know,' Ambrose muttered vaguely from the bottom of the boat. 'I told him it was for the best.'

'What, left the city?' she said, crestfallen. And then, 'So tha' really does know him then, this foreign gentleman?'

'Well,' Ambrose sat up, his face red with exertion, 'I don't think the merchantman has sailed just yet,' his large pale eyes goggled at her sadly, 'but too late for *you*, I'm afraid, my dear – uh, 'Femia. Unless you've someone like me to help you, of course.'

'Too late? Why?'

'Well, you know what sailors are like about letting women on board boats. They think it's unlucky . . .'

'You don't say?' Eufemia's brow wrinkled suspiciously. 'I never 'eard that before.'

'English boats. Very different.'

'Poor *suo*' then! She'll never learn the truth about her friend and that diamond of hers now – *oh glory! –*' With a horrified expression, the girl clapped her hand to her lips. 'Me and my big fat mouth!'

'Did you say . . . did you say *diamond*?'

Ambrose was gazing at her now as though he had swallowed a goldfish.

'*Oh glory!*' Eufemia's eyes rolled. 'I shouldn't have said that now, should I?'

'No, my dear.' Ambrose shook his head slowly from side to side. 'I really don't think you should.' He fixed her now with a grave, disciplinarian look. 'This is clearly more important than I thought. Well, I wasn't going to interfere, it's really none of my business, but I suppose –' he gave another big sigh '– I suppose I really *am* going to have to help you now. It's a perfect nuisance, but I really don't see what alternative I have. Dear me, dear me, if that John Carew weren't such a particular friend . . .'

At that moment there came a sharp sound from just over their heads. They looked up to see that someone on the first-floor balcony was drawing up the linen screens. Eufemia opened her mouth to say something but Ambrose silenced her.

'*Shhh!*' He put his finger to his lips. 'Hush, child. Walls have ears, didn't you know. Come and sit over here. We don't want the whole world to hear our conversation, now do we?' He indicated Constanza's open window, and then patted the seat beside him again. 'Now,' he said firmly, 'I think we must start at the very beginning, don't you?'

'Well, *signore*, I'm really not sure . . .' Eufemia pulled back but Ambrose had a hold of her arm. Through the rough homespun of her *conversa*'s robe, his strong fingers pinched her flesh. 'I said *no*, sir . . .'

'Oh, fiddlesticks, girl! Do you want me to help, or don't you?'

'*Si, signore.*' A small voice.

'Well, get a move on then because I haven't got all day. And you can start by showing me that letter. I know you've got it hidden on your person somewhere . . .'

Outside Constanza's *palazzo* Carew became aware of the sound of voices talking together. Down below, on the canal, he could hear a departing gondola bumping against the walls, the cries of the boat-men. And then a familiar voice, English, cheerful, unmistakable.

Carew picked himself up from the floor and went over to the window. It was just as he suspected. Ambrose. Damn! He pulled away, hoping not to be seen, but not before he realised there was a second passenger in the gondola, with whom Ambrose appeared to be in deep conversation. Strange. He could almost imagine it was a woman. Cautiously, Carew peered over the balcony again to take another look. He could see Ambrose's familiar back view, stout, immovable; his interlocutor was blocked from sight, protected from the sun beneath the little awning.

He drew away again.

'It's your friend Intelligencer Jones.' Carew looked as though he had just tasted something sour. 'Here's a riddle for you: what's the difference between Ambrose and a dead fish? Answer: nothing. Both of them smell nastier and more rotten with each passing day.'

'Ambrose?' Paul sat up. 'Well he's certainly taken his time. I have some business to do with him, I sent for him to meet me here.' Standing up from the bed he looked at Carew dispassionately. 'Well, haven't you got a boat to catch?'

Carew put the bloodied napkin down. His ear had stopped bleeding at last. 'Is that all you can say?'

'If you want me to say I'm sorry about your ear, well – as you so rightly point out – I'm not.'

'So you really are determined to go through with it? With the game, I mean?'

'Am I going to play in Memmo's game?' Paul looked at him mockingly. 'Yes, I am.' As he spoke there came the distant scrape of footsteps on the stairs outside. 'And so much of a hint of this to Ambrose and I'll cut your other ear off.'

Ambrose burst into the room.

'Ah! Dear friends! My very dear friends! What good fortune to find you both here!' Stretching out both arms, he looked from one to the other with a beatific smile. 'Just the two people I wanted to see!'

'What news, Ambrose?' Paul asked. 'You shine upon us like a meteorite, as you always do, positively.'

'Paul, my dear, dear sir –' Ambrose went over and embraced him tenderly. 'I bring great news!'

'For the love of God, Ambrose – what? The entire Portuguese fleet is dashed on the rocks at Buena Esperanza?' Paul, half-amused, half-irritated, pushed him away. 'No, don't tell me, you've discovered a goose that lays golden nutmegs?'

'No, no, nothing like that.' Smiling, Ambrose removed his turban and wiped the perspiration from his sweating brow. 'Well, can't you guess? She's what we've all been looking for these many years.'

Both Paul and Carew were staring at him, transfixed.

'You mean you did not see me arrive just now? You did not perchance – either of you – hear me converse at the gondola steps?' He looked carefully from one to the other. 'I only enquire because I do so *hope* I have not spoiled the surprise –'

'Ambrose – for the love of God, get on with it.'

'As you wish. I think –' there was a catch in Ambrose's voice, '– I think I've found her – dear Lord, I can hardly believe it, after all this time.' He put his hand tremblingly to his lips.

'Found her?' Paul's face was ashen. 'What are you talking about?'

'The mermaid for Parvish's cabinet, of course. What else do you think I've been looking for all these years?' There were tears in Ambrose's eyes. 'She's here, Pindar. My mermaid. She's arrived in Venice at last.'

Chapter Thirty-one

Carew walked back to his lodgings, but his head was so full of the strangeness of what had passed between himself and Paul at Constanza's that he was almost at the Rialto before he was aware of where his feet were taking him.

Venice's market place seemed unusually crowded that afternoon. Crossing the bridge, Carew pushed through the throngs of pedlars and foreign merchants, the Jewish vendors of gold and precious jewels, an itinerant acrobatic troupe advertising their show. He had just reached the far side, when he bumped into an old man walking the other way.

'Ho, English!' protested a voice that sounded vaguely familiar. 'Where's the fire? Can't you watch where you go!'

Carew looked down to see the diminutive, bearded figure of Prospero Mendoza glaring up at him.

'Prospero!'

'You again, English!' The old man looked up at Carew disapprovingly. 'Always a scowl on your face. What, did someone die?' And then, peering short-sightedly up at the side of Carew's face, 'What happened to your ear?' Without the jeweller's loupe obscuring his features, his eyes were very bright. 'Looks as though a dog chewed it off.' He seemed to find the idea highly amusing.

'A dog?' Carew put his hand up to his scarred left cheek, scratched off some of the flakes of dried blood that still remained there. He had been so lost in thought he had almost forgotten about his ear. 'Something like that.'

'You English! What is it with you? Always fighting, always blood.' Prospero gave a shrug. 'Where are you going anyway?'

When Carew told him where his lodgings were, Prospero said that he also had business that way and the two fell into step.

They were walking through the market place now, on the south side of the Grand Canal, past the vendors of fruit and vegetables, their wares arranged in pyramids of jewel-like colours; took a short cut through the colonnaded space of the fish market, past the crates of live crabs, the slatted shelves of mackerel and sardine, and tiny anchovies overflowing from their boxes like shimmering silver bullion.

'And merchant Pindar, how is he? He came to see me again yesterday, asked me to value all his jewels. You'll remember, I showed you them when you came to my workshop that time, the ones he's always left in safekeeping with me.'

But Carew, who was not in a talking mood, did not respond.

After a few more minutes the old man went on. 'He brought someone else with him this time. A Venetian gentleman. No manners, but that's to be expected. And sort of dirty-looking. He said he was his friend, from sometime way back, but I didn't like the look of him.' The old man shook his head. 'He took all the merchant's jewels away with him, said he was going to keep them now.' Prospero looked round at Carew mournfully. 'Why, English? Your master wouldn't tell me anything. What it's all about?'

'Dirty-looking, you say?' Carew scowled. 'Well, that would be Francesco, sure as an egg's an egg.'

'Yes, that's the one. Francesco, I remember now.'

'Well in that case I'm not surprised he wouldn't tell you anything, for that's the last you'll be seeing of them,' Carew said. 'Haven't you heard? Your want-wit merchant friend is going to play in Zuanne Memmo's game.'

'*Ahh!*' Prospero stroked his beard as though this explained everything. He looked round at Carew with renewed interest.

'The diamond? You have seen it then?' Prospero was almost running alongside Carew now, taking two or three steps to each one of Carew's strides.

'The diamond? Oh, yes, I've seen it,' Carew said savagely. 'A curse on the day he ever set eyes on it.'

'He has the madness then?' Prospero looked at Carew sadly.

'Yes,' Carew said, 'I think we can safely say he has.'

With the Rialto Bridge and the market place far behind them now, the two made their way over a series of small canals and side streets into one of the poorer areas of the city. The streets grew ever narrower. The crowds thinned until the alleyways seemed all but deserted, but Carew was too busy brooding to give it much thought. Pale pink and red stucco crumbled from the walls; women shouted to one another from the upper storeys and hung their laundry out to dry from the windows. A group of children, their clothes so ragged they were all but naked, played in the dust. A woman, with the carmine-coloured cheeks and absurdly high pattens of a common courtesan, came out of a doorway. When the children saw her one of them picked up a stone and threw it at her. '*Puttana, puttana,*' they shouted in their high-pitched voices. The stone missed her, but glanced against Prospero's shoulder as he passed by. With his head bent, he walked quickly, but not before they had seen him. '*Ebreo, Ebreo,*' they danced around him, a flock of malevolent little imps, until Carew chased them away.

'By the way, did she find you?'

'Did who find me?'

'That little *monarche* who came to my workshop this morning.'

'A *monarche*? A nun?' Carew stopped dead in his tracks. He felt winded, as though he had been punched in the stomach. 'What nun?'

'I have no idea why she thought I would know how to find you, I said she should try the house of Constanza Fabia –'

'But I've just come from there, and I didn't see any nun.' Carew grabbed Prospero by both arms and shook him. Could it be, could it possibly be that she had come searching for him? 'What did she look like?'

'What did she look like?' Prospero's voice echoed back at him shrilly. 'What do they all look like? Black robe, black veil. She looked like a nun, you imbecile!'

'Come on, old man, you can do better than that.' Carew shook him again, so hard this time that he almost lifted him off his feet. 'Old? Young? Dark? Fair?'

Her face, that face, he realised, that was before his eyes every minute of the day. Constanza's words came back to him: 'I pity the poor girl who falls in love with you, Carew.'

'Did she have a beauty spot, right here,' he pointed to his own face, 'on her cheekbone?'

'What's this, a *monarche* with a beauty spot!' Prospero's voice rose, shriller than ever. 'I've heard it all now. No wonder you've only got one ear.' He tried to struggle free of Carew's grip. 'And will you kindly take your hands off me, young man.'

'No, it's not like that. Not like that at all.' Carew dropped his hands. 'I'm sorry, Prospero. But what did she want?'

'How should I know?' Prospero rubbed his shoulders resentfully. 'She wouldn't tell me. She said her name was Eufemia, that's all.' He glared at Carew. 'And, no, she didn't have a beauty spot.'

They were just about to turn into a small *campo* when Carew felt Prospero tugging at his sleeve.

'Wait a moment, English,' Carew heard Prospero's voice at his shoulder, 'don't go there.'

From the other side of the *campo* a masked man was making his way slowly towards them. He held a long stick in his hand and, despite the summer heat, a coat so long that it skimmed the ground, its skirts stiff as though they had been treated with tar or wax. His curious mask was shaped like a bird's beak, a raven or a crow. A bird of ill omen if ever Carew had seen one.

He made as if to walk on across the square, but Prospero held him fast by the sleeve.

'What's wrong with you?' the old man said in a whisper. 'You want to die, English? Look, don't you know a plague doctor when you see one?' He indicated the sinister masked figure. 'So it's here in the city at last, they said it was coming!' There was a tremor of fear in Prospero's voice. 'It would be madness to go by that route.'

'I have to. I have to collect my things.'

'Take my advice, leave them. You don't want to go there.'

'But my boat sails in a few days. It won't take long.'

Prospero sighed. 'Come, quickly then, come with me, I can show you another way. It will be safer.'

They went on walking rapidly, but in silence, Carew following Prospero now, the old man moving with surprising speed. The alleyways here were almost completely deserted, many of the houses, too, the crumbling tenements of the poor, seemed to have been shut up, their crude wooden shutters barricaded against the vapours of sickness and disease. Even Carew could feel it now, the strange atmosphere. Fear clung to his skin like sweat.

From somewhere nearby there came the doleful sound of a church bell ringing a funeral mass. Then they turned a corner and found themselves at the entrance of a second, much larger *campo*. Despite the church at the centre, the place had a shabby, almost derelict air. Weeds grew from the holes between the cobblestones. Unlike most of the churches in the city this one was quite plain and unadorned, a poor church for a poor people.

At the door was assembled a strange-looking group. A pale-faced woman with two small girls, and two others. Beside them, and also of the party, was a huge giant of a man, carrying in his arms a very small rectangular box. It was some moments before Carew realised what it was: a baby's coffin.

When Prospero saw the funeral group, he stopped dead in his tracks.

'This is as far as I can go with you, English. Are you sure you want to go on? You shouldn't stay here. It's not safe.'

'Don't trouble about me, Prospero. I have to get back to Constanza's house, I won't be staying long.'

'Well then, go under that passageway, along the canal until you find the Ospedale degl' Incurabili . . .'

But Carew was not paying attention. His gaze was fixed on the little funeral party.

'Are you listening to me, I said –'

'I know what you said. Look over there – it can't be – but is that *Ambrose* over there by the church?'

Carew pointed to one of two men who were also standing watching the funeral procession on the far side of the *campo*. The other man had a large leather knapsack over one shoulder.

'Don't ask me, I'm an old man, how should I see that far?'

'God's blood, that man is *everywhere*,' Carew said, astounded. 'How does he do it? I just saw him, he was at Constanza's only minutes ago.'

'Well, farewell then, I don't suppose we'll meet again.' Prospero began to walk away, but then suddenly he seemed to remember

223

something. He stopped, called out to Carew, 'One more thing, English –'

'What?'

Carew was already halfway across the *campo*.

'The *monarche*. I remember now she said she was from the island convent, you know, the one with the botanical garden –'

Had Carew heard him? He was not sure. He watched as Carew ran off across the potholed cobblestones. There was going to be trouble, he could feel it in his bones.

'You English,' he muttered, shaking his head at Carew's fast-disappearing figure, 'always fighting, always blood.'

Blood! It was true. The very instant Carew had set eyes on Ambrose standing there – so smug, so smiling, so infinitely sure of himself – he had seen it. Blood! And, if at all possible, Ambrose's blood.

A memory, clear and sharp as winter light, had come to him of the moment when he had looked from the balcony of Constanza's *palazzo*, had seen that all-too-solid, yellow-turbaned back view as he sat in his gondola. There had been a woman sitting next to him, just out of sight. He had heard her voice. Carew was as certain as he had ever been of anything in his life that woman was the nun – Eufemia – from the island convent. Certain, too, in a burst of mingled joy and despair, that it must have been Annetta who sent her. And yet not only had Ambrose not thought fit to give him the message; but he had not even mentioned her, had in all probability deliberately turned her away.

Carew did not stop to wonder why Ambrose wished him ill. He did not stop to wonder what he could possibly be doing in this poor and plague-ridden part of town. Such niceties were not on his mind. As he ran he had only one thought: to get his hands around Ambrose's neck and rip the fat bastard's head off, smash that smug smile into the cobblestones, wipe it off his face for all eternity.

But it looked as though it was not to be. Someone else was going to get there first. As he drew nearer to the group, Carew saw that some kind of altercation was taking place around Ambrose and his unknown companion. To his surprise it seemed to involve the huddle of mourners at the church door. The *campo*, which until a few moments ago had seemed all but deserted, was filling up, as though with spectators come to witness a show. The peculiar atmosphere seemed suddenly heightened, strained to breaking point.

With his street-fighter instincts, Carew knew that something was about to happen.

Chapter Thirty-two

The church door was closed.

'Open the door.' Holding the tiny coffin under one arm, Maryam banged against it with her free fist. 'We've come to ask for blessings for our dead.'

For a time nothing happened. She banged again. 'Just a blessing, please, Father. For our dead baby.'

Finally a muffled voice came from inside the church, but the door remained closed.

A murmur rippled through the crowd.

With a stricken look, she turned to her companion. 'It's no good, Elena, he won't open.'

At that moment a familiar voice – a man's voice – spoke from behind her.

'What do you expect? It's not as though it's human.'

Ambrose's companion, a man with a leather knapsack over his shoulder, now approached the little party. When Maryam saw him she drew back, a look of such horror on her face it was as though she had seen a ghost.

'*Panayia mou!*' Instinctively she took a step sideways, placing herself in front of Elena and the two little girls. 'You! What in God's name are you doing here?'

When he saw her reaction, the man seemed to swell in size, as though it gratified him in some way. He took a swaggering step towards them.

'See what I told you, sir.' He turned to Ambrose. 'Ugly as a hippopotamus!' He sniggered to himself. 'A moustache and all, I didn't remember that bit.'

Maryam found her voice at last.

'Bocelli!' There was a strange constricted feeling in her chest. So it *had* been him she had seen in the village after all. She had a bad feeling about this, as bad a feeling as she had ever had. 'What d'you want?'

'Never one to mince your words, were you?' Bocelli laughed, showing the blackened stumps of his two front teeth. 'What d'you think I want? I've come for that, haven't I.' He jerked his chin in the direction of the tiny coffin. And then, in a loud voice so that everyone could hear him, 'I've come to collect what's mine.'

For a moment Maryam stared at him in disbelief. 'You've come to do . . . *what*?'

'You heard me.' His tone was deliberate, insolent. 'I've come to collect what's mine.'

Maryam knew she had to think quickly. The small knot of onlookers were murmuring among themselves; others were coming out of their houses now to join them. Maryam knew about crowds. She took another step backwards, towards Elena and the two little girls.

'I don't know what you're talking about, Bocelli.'

'You delivered the . . . what's in the box . . . to Venice, and now I want it back.'

'That's not true,' she tried to keep her voice as reasonable as possible, 'you begged me to take them off your hands.' Maryam's heart was thumping in her chest now, so loudly she could almost hear it. 'You gave me a horse,' she said, knowing she must remain calm, give no sign of the desperation she felt inside. 'You gave me two horses, remember?'

'Yes, I did, didn't I? I paid you handsomely.' Bocelli glanced at his companion again, and then moved towards her. 'To keep it alive until you got to the Serenissima.'

'No! That was never our agreement!'

'You told me you were coming to Venice, and you'd get it here alive. Be reasonable now, how was I supposed to look after it? I could see that the mother wasn't going to live long.' He gave a careless shrug. 'Then I saw you in Messina. A pack of women, and freaks yourselves,' Bocelli sniggered again, 'it was perfect! Come on! You were glad to have the use of it, you know you were. You said it'd be good for business.'

'I said no such thing.' There was a tingling sensation down one of Maryam's arms; she clutched the tiny coffin to her chest. 'I would *never* have suggested such a thing.'

'Look here, you great clodhopping cart-horse.' Bocelli, more unnerved by the crowd than he liked to let on, began to lose patience. He was up so close to her now she could smell his onion breath. 'It was good for *your* business while it was alive,' he whispered to her in a furious undertone; 'it's good for *my* business now it's dead, *capito*? Now give it over . . .'

He reached out as if to take the coffin from her, but Maryam, towering over him by a good three heads, stood her ground. A sigh went through the crowd, uncertain as yet whether to laugh at these antics, or to howl.

'*It*?' Maryam's voice was so low it was almost a growl.

'You know very well what I'm talking about. Now don't be any more of a fool than you can help!' Bocelli gave a surreptitious nod in Ambrose's direction. 'See that man over there, the one in a turban? Well he's going to pay handsomely for this. Very, very handsomely.' In his desperation to get his hands on the coffin his tone was almost conciliatory. 'Look, I'll see you get some of it, pay you extra for all your troubles. But it won't be any good to either of us if it's started to rot, *capito*?'

'Signor Bocelli!' It was Elena who spoke now. She stepped forward, was staring at Bocelli in dismay. 'What does this man want with our dead child? Yes, a dead child,' she continued, addressing the growing throng of onlookers, 'a tiny baby, God rest his soul.'

One of the little girls, Leya, started to cry.

'We've come to get a blessing for him, to bury him according to the proper rites,' Elena said. 'Please, let us go in peace.'

'Shame on you!' a woman in a green headscarf called out to Bocelli.

'Yes, shame on you. Let the poor creatures go, let them bury their child!' A washerwoman with red chapped hands was leaning out of her window. A heavy round object, a rotted apple, thrown from an unseen hand landed at Bocelli's feet.

'Wait!'

Until now Ambrose had been standing silently behind Bocelli on the edge of the crowd. With ostentatious distaste at the squalor of his surroundings, he held a nosegay to his face – a linen bag filled with dried herbs, prophylactic against disease. Only his eyes, two unblinking, protuberant blue buttons, gave away the fact that he had been observing the proceedings with forensic concentration.

'Wait!' His voice, loud and calm, reverberated around the weed-filled *campo* like a stone in a pool of cold water. 'Good people of Dorsoduro, why waste your sympathies on them? These women are strangers in your midst. No better than gypsies ...' There was an uneasy silence. 'And we all know what gypsies are like.'

Compared to the raucous demotic of the crowd, Ambrose's tone, despite his clipped English accent, was quellingly patrician. It resonated through the hubbub with an icy authority. 'We all know what gypsies do, don't we?' he went on. 'They lie. And they cheat. And they steal –'

'They steal children,' a man with a goitre on his neck called out, 'everyone knows that.'

'Quite.' Ambrose twirled the nosegay slowly between his fingers. 'Babies too, I shouldn't wonder.'

He allowed a second or two for this thought to penetrate.

'Who is to say this baby – if that's really what's in the box – is theirs at all?'

He put the nosegay up to his nose again. In the carefully timed pause that followed, a hush fell on the *campo*.

'So tell us,' Ambrose said at last into the silence, 'which one of you is the mother?' His piercing gaze fixed enquiringly first on Elena, and then Maryam. All eyes were on the little group of women huddled at the church door. When neither of them replied Ambrose shook his head slowly from side to side.

'No,' he sighed sadly, 'I thought not.'

And then, like an exhalation, another murmur rippled through the crowd, but its quality was different this time, a sudden bubbling up of anger.

'Gypsies bring nothing but dirt and disease!' Now he was sure he had the crowd on his side, Ambrose risked speaking in a slightly louder voice. 'Who knows, perhaps even ... the plague!'

'*Madonna!* What did he say?' – 'Did he say the plague?' – 'Yes, the *plague* ... the *plague* ...'

Fear was in the air now, as well as anger. Maryam could almost smell it, could feel it lapping around her. There was that constricted feeling in her chest again. She could hardly breathe.

'Yes, that's right, the plague!' He looked round triumphantly. 'Why waste your sympathies on these vermin? When it is they – these dirty gypsywomen – who have brought this terrible affliction among you ...'

Ambrose was almost shouting now, intoxicated by his own rhetoric. But wait! What was this? A familiar English voice was speaking into his ear.

'Gypsies? They don't look like any gypsies I've ever seen, Mr Ambrose.'

Ambrose spun round. When he saw Carew his jaw dropped.

'You! Sneaking about! Why do you always have to creep up on one so?'

'My thoughts exactly, Mr Ambrose.'

Carew did not give a damn for the women or their dead baby, but he could see what Ambrose was doing.

'These women are not gypsies!' he shouted out. 'Do they look like any gypsies you have ever seen?' He took in the faces around him, faces made ugly by fear. 'Why are you listening to him anyway?' He pointed his finger at Ambrose. 'He's a foreigner, a stranger here. Who's to say it weren't him who brought the plague?'

'Carew!' Ambrose's pale eyes were almost popping out of his head. 'Have you gone mad? Yes, yes, I think you have. I think you have finally gone mad –'

With his superior dress and demeanour it had been second nature to the crowd to defer to Ambrose; but with Carew they knew instinctively that he was one of their own. To Ambrose's dismay an uneasy hush descended on the crowd once more.

'I know this man,' Carew was now pointing at Ambrose who was beginning to look satisfyingly nervous, 'and if anyone is a liar and a cheat it's him.'

'Carew!' Ambrose lowered his voice beseechingly. 'What do you think you're doing? They'll rip us to shreds ...' He looked about him, genuinely frightened now.

But Carew simply put his mouth to Ambrose's ear again, whispering so only he could hear. 'Well if they don't, I'm going to,' he murmured lovingly. 'And that's just for starters.'

'Wha –? You overreach yourself! I'll tell Pindar. I'll have you horsewhipped . . . keel-hauled . . . so I will . . .'

Carew ignored him. 'Why didn't you give me the message?'

'What?' Ambrose gaped at him. 'What message?' he spluttered finally. 'I don't know what you're . . .'

'Oh, I think you do.' Carew's expression was pitiless. 'Why didn't you give me the message, Mr Jones? You know, I think Constanza was right about you all along,' he said slowly. 'You know everyone's secrets, don't you? But none of us can be quite sure whose side you're really on.'

The thought of what Ambrose had done filled Carew with such murderous rage it was all he could do to stop himself wringing his neck right then and there. But if he were going to be robbed – albeit temporarily – of the pleasure of smashing Ambrose's great nose to a pulp, of crushing his great bald head into eggshells between his hands, it was only because another, possibly even more painful punishment, was now offering itself.

There could be no doubt about what was in the coffin. There could be only one reason, and one reason alone, why Ambrose wanted to get his hands on it. That it contained the mermaid baby Ambrose had lusted after for so long Carew was completely sure. But he knew that he had to act quickly now.

'Don't think I don't know exactly what you're doing. Don't think I don't know what's in that coffin. I'm going to turn you into heads and trotters, Mr Jones,' Carew was so close now his breath tickled Ambrose's ear, 'but before I do that –' he indicated the women still huddling by the church door '– I'm going to do something you're going to find *much* more painful.'

'Wait, no . . . Not so fast . . . you don't understand. You have no idea what it took to get it here.' He glanced at Bocelli, who was watching them with bewilderment. 'The mermaid is *real*, I tell you! There's never been another one like it. It's worth a *fortune*, John,' he pleaded. Ambrose was no longer smiling, his face distorted with a craven mixture of fear and greed. 'A king's ransom. More than the Sultan's Blue!'

'That's all you care about, isn't it? What were you going to do with it, Ambrose, that dead child –'

'Child? What are you talking about? It's a freak –'

'That's not what these poor women think,' Carew indicated the pathetic little group. 'They were planning to give it a decent burial. What were you planning to do with it, Ambrose? Bottle it like a pickled cowcumber? Cure it like a side of ham? Or perhaps you thought a good salting would be best? What would these good citizens make of that, I wonder? I don't suppose they know much about your cabinets or your curiosities. I know, let's ask them, shall we?'

'Stop!' Ambrose's voice was like the feeble quavering of a goose.

But Carew was already striding towards the church. The prospect of losing his treasure worked on Ambrose like a bucket of cold water. He turned to Bocelli who was standing next to him, open-mouthed. 'See that man?'

Bocelli nodded.

'Get rid of him!'

For a moment Bocelli looked nonplussed. 'But, *signore* . . .'

'Oh, just get on with it, man! I don't care how you do it,' Ambrose hissed into Bocelli's ear. 'Kill him if you have to.'

When Maryam saw Carew coming towards her she had no idea that he meant her no harm. She had tried to follow the exchanges between the two men, but much of it was in a language she could not understand.

Maryam stood there listening, holding the little coffin in her arms. Although the box was no heavier to her than a bag of grain, somehow it was more difficult to keep a grip on it now than it had been before. One of her arms, and the fingers of her hand, felt numb. She felt the little coffin begin to slip from her grasp. Elena was tugging on her sleeve; she could see her looking up, trying to tell her something, but Maryam seemed unable to hear her. She tried to speak, but no words came. There was a strange buzzing in her ears.

A crowd had almost filled the *campo*. She could see their faces, ugly with fear and hatred. See their mouths working, the sinews of their necks. But all around her she had the strange sensation that there was nothing but silence.

The silence had been the first thing that Maryam had noticed when they first reached the lagoon. After so many weeks spent on the open seas, the water was like glass. The banks of the islands were so low in the water they looked like rafts. There was not a breath of wind. The sails of the boat hung useless, the only sound was the slow dip of the oars.

They had been almost within reach of the city when the baby died. It happened very early in the morning, a dawn of such exquisite beauty Maryam thought she had never seen its like. She had stood on deck with the child in her arms, lost in the wonder of it. When she looked down she saw that the sleeping infant had woken. Tenderly, she tucked in part of the swaddling napkin that had come undone. With one clumsy finger she felt along the tiny head, to where his hair grew, no thicker than dandelion down. The baby turned its head, was mouthing for its mother's breast; no cry came from him, only a tiny exhalation of breath. Maryam's throat ached to see him.

'Look, *agapi mou*, look,' she murmured, 'we're nearly there. We'll find a doctor to help us . . . One of the boatmen knows a place –'

Maryam struggled not to remember Elena's words, pushing them away with all her might.

It is no good, Maryam, you must prepare yourself. The infant is too weak to feed any more. It can't be long now. She could hear the sadness in her voice; Elena, who had herself lost two of her own children as babies. *You must not blame the mother, it is a terrible thing to know your child is going to die, even one . . . even one such as this. It is God's will, Maryam.* Elena had put her hand on Maryam's arm. *But there will be others.*

But not for me! Maryam wanted to cry out. There is no God for the likes of me! And I will have no others!

Had she actually spoken those terrible, blasphemous words? Actually said them out loud? Perhaps she had; she realised that she did not care any more who knew it. They could laugh at her all they liked. She could see the disgust on their faces whenever they took the swaddling napkins off to clean the baby, she felt their horror when they looked at his deformity. But not Maryam. She saw only the perfect little feet, ten perfect little toes, the nails like flecks of mother-of-pearl.

But now, as they approached the city, her arms already felt empty.

'Nearly there, my sweetling, we'll find someone to help us, you'll see . . . I won't give up, I'll never give up . . .'

Maryam put her finger down, felt the tiny fist, softer than a cloud, close around it, thought she had never in her life felt this way.

She could hardly bear it, the pain of so much love.

She heard a cry from one of the sailors, and looking up saw one of them pointing at the horizon. At first she could see nothing. In the distance there were great mountains standing like sentinels behind the city, their peaks still covered with snow. But ahead was only mist and the glassy lagoon water the same colour as the sky. The man cried out and pointed again, but still Maryam could see nothing. With a lonely cry a flock of birds flew across their bows, twisting and dipping and skimming above the water.

And then, suddenly, there it was. The mist parted slightly and in the distance was the fabled city at last, glowing pink and gold through the dawn, a city which seemed to her at that moment as if it must be inhabited by angels rather than by men.

When she looked down again the infant's tiny ribcage was still; his eyes were open, but their surface was glassy and blank. It took all four of the boatmen to hold her down, before Elena could take the dead child from her.

Now, seeing the crowd still spilling into the little *campo*, Maryam felt wearier than she ever had in her life.

She thought she had been so clever, tricking Bocelli into giving her the two horses, but all along – she realised now – it had been the other way round. She was the one who had been tricked. It had all been too easy. The ketch arriving when it did; the boatmen, their unquestioning willingness to take the women all the way to Venice. Why, they'd even known to take the dead baby to the Ospedale degli' Incurabili, she saw it all now. All along she had been the unwitting pawn in someone else's plan.

And now, when Carew began to stride towards her, she did not see him at all; she saw instead the faces of those men all those years ago, the faces of her tormentors.

Maryam began to run.

Still holding the tiny coffin, she charged blindly through the crowd. Men and women scattered, sprawling on the ground in her wake. As she ran she could see their mouths working, see the sinews stretched across their necks, but the world had gone silent. The only sound was the pounding of her own heart.

234

She ran round to the back of the church, trying to find the alley-way to lead her back to the *ospedale*, but she took a wrong turn. She crossed a little bridge over a canal, but then realised she had never been this way before. There were two turnings ahead of her. She hesitated, then passed under a *sottoportego* to the left. Found herself at a dead end.

Ahead of her was nothing but a vast expanse of water. The men were only a few steps behind her now. There was nowhere to go, no way out. With some sixth sense she could feel rather than hear their footsteps. She turned, saw a flash of steel in Bocelli's hand.

She knew then what was coming; she knew she was going to have to fight. Had they brought dogs with them? There must be dogs somewhere. There was a taste in her mouth she could not identify, and for a moment she thought she might vomit. In her confused and grief-stricken state Maryam could almost imagine she was wearing the cow horns again. She shook her great head from side to side, but uselessly now, like a wounded animal.

She had not been able to save the baby in its short and troubled life. But she knew that, even if it took the last breath in her body, she would save him now, would not let those men take him.

Whatever happened they would not take her baby away. She had promised, hadn't she?

I swear it.

On my life.

But when Maryam turned to face them she realised that there was no fight left in her. It only took an instant for her to make up her mind what to do. Still holding the tiny coffin in her arms, she jumped.

Maryam and the mermaid baby fell together like a stone, down into the deep green waters below.

Chapter Thirty-three

The bells were still ringing when Carew came to. He was lying on the ground in a dank, dead-end alleyway, the smell of stale urine in his nose. There was a sinister, throbbing pain on the back of his head.

For a moment or two he did not know where he was. He sat up and put his hand to the back of his head, where an egg-shaped lump was forming under the sticky mass of his hair.

From somewhere nearby came the sound of someone weeping.

A woman was standing, a little way away from him, looking down into the waters of the Giudecca Canal. When she saw him stirring she looked round at him with a tear-stained face.

Carew found that he could make no sound at all. The two looked at one another speechlessly, survivors from a shipwreck.

The woman sank down on to the ground, put her face in her hands.

Carew pulled himself up into a sitting position. His clothes were completely soaked through. His ears were ringing.

Slowly things began to come back to him. He remembered the scene outside the church in the *campo*; the huddled group of women; the unexpected appearance among them of Ambrose and the other man who seemed to have been working for him. Then the woman – who at first he had taken to be a man – taller and uglier than anyone he had ever seen in his life before, with the tiny coffin under her arm, running, falling . . .

'What happened to them?' he called out to the woman on the ground, but she did not seem to hear him.

Carew sat up a little more, and winced. There was a pain in his ribs, as well as on the back of his head, as though someone had kicked him in the chest.

'What's your name?'

The woman was weeping silently now. '*To onoma mou inai Elena.* Elena.'

'Elena.' Why had he asked that, what good would it do? He had a vague memory that she had had two children with her in the *campo.* 'Where are your two little ones?'

'I sent them back to the *ospedale,*' the woman, Elena, shrugged hopelessly, 'someone had to tell the mother.'

'The mother?'

'The mother of the dead child.'

Carew digested this for a moment.

Elena looked up. 'The mother can't walk ... her legs ...' She seemed too exhausted to go on. 'She can remember some things now ... but not that.'

Christos! Carew closed his eyes. What was he doing here, for Christ's sake? *Left half for dead in some Godforsaken alleyway*, he could hear Paul's voice in his ear. No surprise there.

But he wasn't staying. What did he care about these women, about the dead child? They were nothing to him. He had been on his way back to the convent. He would be there now if only Ambrose had given him the message. He tried to move again, but the pain was too great.

Ambrose! Ambrose and his precious mermaid. Well, he'd never get his hands on it now. At the thought of what Ambrose's face must have looked like when he realised it was gone Carew began to laugh – stopped with a wince at the renewed pain in his ribs.

He decided to rest here just a moment longer, before standing up. Without opening his eyes he called out to the woman, 'Where did they go ... those two men? Did you see where they went?'

When she did not reply he opened his eyes again and saw that the woman, Elena, was looking at him. There was a calm, clear intelligence behind her grief-shrunken face. They sat in silence for a moment longer, staring into the green-grey, oily water.

'That man, Bocelli, I think he tried to kill you,' she said after a while.

'The one with the leather knapsack?'

'Yes, that's the one.'

Bocelli. So that's what he was called.

'The other one made him do it, the one in the yellow turban. I was watching them. He hit you from behind, and you fell into the canal. You were trying to stop Maryam from jumping.'

He stared at her. So Ambrose had tried to kill him. It seemed at once incredible, and entirely probable, that Ambrose should have wanted to do such a thing. The question was, why?

'The man in the yellow turban, are you sure?'

'Yes. The fat one. He gave Bocelli his knife –' From the folds of the curious long-sleeved garment she was wearing the woman produced a small bone-handled dagger. 'Luckily I managed to get it from him,' she added simply, 'so he used his stick instead.'

With some barely imperceptible movement the dagger, which she had been holding out on the palm of her hand for Carew to see, seemed to vanish into thin air.

For a moment Carew was too surprised to speak.

'How did you do that?'

Elena managed a weak smile. 'I'm sorry. Habit, that's all.' And before Carew's astonished eyes the dagger reappeared in her hand. 'It's what I do.'

'What you do? I don't understand.'

'My companions and I travel as a troupe of tumblers, all of us women . . .' her voice tailed off. 'Although I don't know what will happen to us now . . . now that Maryam . . .' Elena looked as though she might start weeping again, but she managed to govern herself. 'I specialise in illusions. Fairground tricks.' She gave another small smile. 'We performed for the Sultan once. In Constantinople.'

'Really?' he said without apparent interest. Scowling, he rested his forehead on his knees.

Constantinople! He was beginning to think he loathed the very mention of the place.

'You should find something to put on your head.' Elena was looking at him.

Carew put his hand up to the bloodied egg on the back of his head.

'I'm still alive, aren't I?'

'And whatever happened to your ear?' she added, frowning.

His ear. *Christos!* He'd forgotten all about his ear.

238

'You can come back with me to the *ospedale* if you like,' she ventured, as though reading his thoughts. 'We can get water there. I can wash it for you.'

'My thanks, but no.' With an effort Carew stood up. The last thing he wanted was to get any more involved with these women. 'My lodgings are round the corner – I think – somewhere –' he said vaguely. His head swam so badly he nearly fell over again. He clutched on to the wall to steady himself.

'Well, farewell then. I'm sorry about your friend.'

He knew he should probably quiz the woman about her time in Constantinople, but no sooner had this thought arisen when another replaced it: the recollection of what Pindar had done to his ear.

Harems. Jewels. Celia Lampreys. To hell with the lot of them! He felt a wave of nausea go through him. Why should he trouble himself about any of it any more? They could go hang, the whole lot of them. Let Pindar sort it all out for himself.

'Farewell, then,' he repeated, raising his hand unsteadily to the woman. But she seemed not to hear him. She looked so forlorn, with her long, pale tear-stained face, still sitting there at the water's edge as though she could not quite believe that her giant friend was gone, as though she had convinced herself she might reappear out of the water at any time.

What would happen to her now, he wondered, she and her two little girls? Would the troupe be broken up? Would a few fairground tricks be enough to keep them, or would she be forced to turn to other things to survive? He had seen women such as she all over Europe, he knew only too well what her fate must be.

Well, he shrugged to himself, it was really none of his affair. He would not get involved. He would try for the convent one last time, then in a few days he would be gone. In the distance, on the other side of the water, he could see the island of Giudecca, with its churches and pleasure gardens gleaming. He wondered vaguely if Constanza were still there, whether he was ever likely to see her again. Gondolas and other boats passed them by on the busy waterway. Ordinary life carried on, as if none of this had happened.

Without saying any more Carew turned and started to walk slowly back down the deserted alleyway in the direction of the church. He heard a voice behind him.

'*Kyrios*,' the woman called after him. 'Please, sir. That man Bocelli –'

Reluctantly, Carew stopped. 'What about him?'

'Do you know where I can find him?'

'After what you told me, I'd be sure to stay out of his way if I were you.'

'He's a liar and a thief.' Her voice was so faint he could hardly hear it. Mumbling, almost incoherent.

'Amongst other things,' Carew said drily.

But again Elena seemed not to hear him, so wrapped was she in her own thoughts. 'The baby's mother . . .'

'What about her?' He was impatient now.

'He stole it from her, I know it,' she said, suddenly fierce. 'It was him, it must have been.'

Carew did not know what to make of this, so he did not answer.

'She can't remember what it was,' Elena's face was so pale she seemed like a ghost, 'but she's never stopped searching for it.' She looked up at him, shaking her head sadly. 'She has a name for it, but it makes no sense to me –'

'None of it makes sense,' Carew said, almost to himself, 'it never does.'

He turned and started to walk away from her again. In his mind's eye he could picture Annetta's face; to see her again was all he wanted. To be out of all this ugliness.

'*Kyrios* . . .' he heard her voice, very faintly, calling after his departing figure. 'Please, sir, stay a moment . . .'

But the look of raw pain on her face was suddenly unbearable to him. Pretending he had not heard her, Carew kept on walking.

Chapter Thirty-four

Zuanne Memmo put a black velvet bag down in the middle of the table.

'My lady, gentlemen –' He looked around the little octagonal-shaped room, at the group of players assembled here for the first time. When he was sure that he had everyone's full attention, he slowly poured the contents of the bag out on to the table. With a hard sound a small and insignificant-looking faded pink pocket rolled out.

For a moment there was not a sound in the room. A silence borne of an anticipation so profound it was as if no one could breathe. Paul Pindar could feel the hair pricking on the back of his neck.

He had waited so long for this. He watched as Memmo picked the pocket up and weighed it carefully in his palm. For a few moments Memmo said nothing, merely held out the bag to the assembled group. His hand trembled slightly.

'My lady, gentlemen,' Memmo repeated softly, looking round at each one of them in turn, 'I present to you: the Sultan's Blue.'

A murmur, like an exhalation of breath, went round the room. In the reflection of a hundred candles the diamond shone, glittering with strange points of light, the colour of ice, or of moonlight, but so clear, so pure, that light seemed to be emanating from a source buried deep within it. Twice as dazzling, it seemed to Paul, as the first time.

Just then a servant came into the little chamber and whispered something in Memmo's ear.

'I beg your pardon, gentlemen,' Memmo excused himself. 'I will only be a few moments.'

With Memmo gone, an uneasy silence filled the little antechamber.

There were six of them in all: five men and, somewhat to Paul's surprise, one woman. Each was carefully masked. Their combined winnings at *primero*, together with tens of thousands of ducats' worth of property or money which Memmo had demanded they surrender to him in advance of the game, were to act as surety, to make good the enormous losses all but one player would face that night. Zuanne Memmo was taking no chances.

The masked figures, who had been sitting as silent and still as so many wax mannequins, now came to life. They began to whisper together, but softly at first, like conspirators. Only Paul Pindar, dressed in his customary black, did not join in the conversation; curious, rather, to discover all he could about his adversaries in the game to come.

The first player to speak was a man sitting to Paul's immediate right.

'By the saints,' he said, 'have you ever seen anything like it in your life? Three hundred carats!'

Paul regarded his neighbour carefully through the narrow eye-slits of his mask. On the thumb of one hand he wore a heavy gold ring with an intaglio seal. An older man, then; and, from his tone of voice, patrician certainly. A lover of fine things. Judging by the quality of his clothes – the fine lawn of his undershirt was shot with gold thread – quite possibly an aristocrat, the accumulated riches of some ancient Venetian patrimony his to squander freely at the gaming tables.

'Three hundred carats? The Sultan's Blue is three hundred and twenty-two carats. I saw it weighed in front of my very own eyes. A perfect diamond, flawless, *incredibile . . .*' said a second player, shaking his head as though lost for words.

'But where did Memmo get it from, that's what I want to know?' a third player, lolling in his chair on the other side of the table, now whispered across to them.

'A bad gambling debt, of course, how else would he come by it?' the first speaker replied with complete conviction. 'Some fool lost it at the card table.'

'Lost the Sultan's Blue at cards?' the third speaker, sitting almost directly opposite Paul, gave a dry laugh. 'He must have been in deep!'

The timbre of his voice, albeit muffled by his mask, and his slighter frame, suggested that he was much younger than the first two. Through his eye-slits Paul was able to watch him carefully. This younger player, too, had all the trappings of a nobleman, and his insolence. Paul knew the type only too well; had played them many times before: young men, mere boys many of them, gambling recklessly against fortunes they had not yet inherited.

'He's right, how do we know it's not stolen?' said the second speaker.

'Faugh! What does it matter? What I want to know is why doesn't the Cavaliere just keep it?' A fourth player, the only woman in their midst – a courtesan with the low-cut dress of her profession, and its flamboyant hairstyle, two horns of hair gathered up one on either side of her forehead – spoke now. Paul strained to hear her voice, wondering if he might recognise her by it, wondering if he had ever met her with Constanza, but through her mask her words were hard to make out. Paul was sure that she was as much a stranger to him as the other two.

'What, Zuanne Memmo keep the Sultan's Blue?' the man with the intaglio thumb ring answered with disdain. 'And what would a man like him do with such a thing? Zuanne has no use for beauty. Money is the only thing that matters to him.'

'But to possess the Sultan's Blue! The stone is worth a fortune . . .' Through her mask the courtesan's voice sounded breathless, as though in the candle-filled room she was fighting for air.

'And what would the Cavaliere do with it?' The old nobleman's tone was crushing. 'In itself the stone is worth nothing to him.' He gave a short laugh. 'That's just the point, madam: the Sultan's Blue is worth everything, and nothing.'

'So it's worthless then, is that what you're saying?' The young man was leaning back in his chair, his long legs thrust beneath the table. 'Not that I care,' he said with an air of bravado, 'I'm here for the cards, not some piece of coloured glass.'

Under the table Paul could feel the vibrations of one of his feet tapping restlessly against the other. Not quite so insouciant as he would like to make out, then. It did not take much to guess that he was playing a carefully rehearsed part; beneath it he was like a coiled spring of nervous energy. He would make mistakes.

'No, sir,' came the older man's cool reply, 'I did not mean to imply that the stone was worthless. Merely priceless.'

'What his lordship is saying, madam, is that the diamond is only worth what someone will pay for it.' Paul's neighbour on his left side now spoke up again. From the relative sobriety of his dress, and his slightly accented voice, Paul understood he must be a merchant, like himself.

The merchant now turned to the courtesan, who sat on his immediate left, and addressed her politely.

'I heard the Cavaliere tried to find a buyer, but no one would take it from him.'

'And I heard that he wanted to get rid of the diamond quickly,' said the young nobleman, twisting restlessly in his seat. 'He's afraid that the Council will get to hear about this *ridotto*; some say that they already have, that they might close it down at any time. You know how it is here in Venice. Everyone knows about the stone. I'll wager Memmo's afraid they'll get to him before he can get rid of it. That's why he's arranged all this so quickly.'

'Not quickly enough, if you ask me. How much longer is he going to keep us waiting?' said the older nobleman impatiently. 'Where has that idiot got to?'

He turned round and strained his neck in the direction of the heavy black curtains across the entrance to the little antechamber – but there was still no sign of Memmo.

For a few moments the players lapsed into silence again. On the table in their midst lay the diamond, marooned on its velvet bed.

There was one player who, like Paul, had said nothing until now. The sixth of their number was a dark-haired youth wearing a gold mask, if possible even younger than his lolling neighbour, who was sitting opposite Paul, between the courtesan and the young nobleman. As though on impulse this last player now put his hand out as if to pluck the diamond from its resting place, and would have done so had the courtesan not pushed his arm away before he could grasp it.

'Are you quite mad, sir? Hasn't anyone told you about the curse?' she said in horrified tones. 'Only the rightful possessor of the stone may touch it. It brings *sfortuña* – bad luck – very bad luck – for anyone else to touch it.'

'What, those old-women tales?' the old man with the thumb ring said scornfully.

'We've all heard them,' the merchant said. 'The stone brings great fortune to the person who possesses it, whether good or bad who can say?' He shrugged. 'But you shouldn't listen to everything you hear in the Rialto, madam.' From his tone of voice he seemed to be smiling at her behind his mask.

'But it's *sfortuna*, I tell you –' She let her hand drop all the same.

Paul saw that the young man seemed frozen, made no attempt to touch the stone again.

'Here,' Paul said, breaking his silence for the first time, 'I'm not afraid.'

He reached over and picked up the diamond, setting it carefully in the palm of his hand, felt the same strange tingling sensation on his skin as before. There was a small, shocked intake of breath from the courtesan. The others said nothing, watching him warily.

'If we believe those stories, which of us would ever touch it?' Paul challenged them. 'Who is to say to whom a stone like this should belong? One of our company will win the stone tonight, but will that make it rightfully theirs?' He looked round at them. 'We all know how the diamond got here – a gambling debt, so Memmo says – but how did that fellow come by it? You are right, sir, to say that the stone is priceless,' he turned to the man with the thumb seal. 'They say that great gems like this are rarely, if ever, bought and sold in the market place. They are given freely as gifts. Or, what is more likely, taken by force. Besides, do you think Memmo would tell us the truth even if he knew it?'

In his outstretched palm the stone glittered with its strange moonlight-blue fire. He looked down at the inscription, traced his finger over the tiny Arabic lettering. 'It says *A'az ma yutlab*, my heart's desire.'

There was a pause.

'Well, well,' the young nobleman started to laugh, 'so the English cadaver speaks after all.'

'Not a cadaver, but a philosopher,' said the older man, turning to look at Paul for the first time.

'So what are you saying, sir?' said the courtesan. She picked up her fan, waved it languidly in front of her face. 'Surely you are not suggesting that we should return the diamond to the Grand Signor?'

'No, madam –' Paul rounded on her with sudden brusqueness. He held the stone up to her, watched her shrink away from it as though she feared it might bite. 'The Grand Signor has many things in his possession that do not belong to him.'

He looked down once more at the diamond sitting in his upturned palm. His hand trembled slightly. He remembered Prospero's words. *They say that the stone will move on. There is no point asking why, or trying to prevent it.* For one long moment, Paul stared at it. Would it stay with him? He had staked everything on it, everything he had. And yet, studying the diamond sitting in the palm of his hand, what did he feel? The tingling sensation had stopped. He felt nothing. Was he mad, as Carew said? At that moment he thought perhaps he was. The diamond could not bring Celia back to him, how could he ever have thought it? In his upturned palm it seemed to him terrible suddenly. It gleamed like a living thing; ice-blue, malevolent. Quickly he put it back down, safe in its velvet cocoon.

There was a stir around the table. Zuanne Memmo was coming back.

'Are you ready?'

A servant was holding aside the heavy curtain, the players were up, preparing to follow Memmo into the main room.

'So, good sir,' the courtesan whispered to him as she walked past, 'if what you say is true, what should we do?'

'We do the only thing we can do. We play the cards, of course.' Paul took a breath. 'We play the cards. Let Fortune decide.'

There was no going back now.

Chapter Thirty-five

Afterwards, Paul was never quite sure how long they had played. It might have been two whole days and nights; it might have been three. Apart from Zuanne Memmo himself, he doubted whether any of them could tell.

In the world outside the beautiful high-ceilinged room, with its walls of mirrored glass, he supposed that life must have gone on much the same as it had always done. That world in which the sun rose and set, merchants went about their business, ships docked and sailed; that world in which men and women met one another, fell in love, died. But in Zuanne Memmo's *ridotto* it was always night; the heavy velvet drapes were always closed, a thousand candles always burning.

On that first evening, he thought he still had some sense of his body's natural rhythms. Thought he knew when it desired food, or drink, or sleep. But after that he soon lost all sense of himself, abandoned himself completely, luxuriated in the mind-numbing, soul-crushing exigencies of the cards.

Lift. Vie. Rest. Discard. Draw. Set. See. Fold.

Was he happy? He did not know. He could not think.

He was alive. It was enough.

Shuffle.

Lift to see who would deal.

'I did lift an ace.'

'I a four.'

'I a coat card.'

'And I.'

'And I.'
'And I a seven.'
Pass the cards to the eldest hand, the seven.
Deal.
One, two. One, two. One, two. One, two. One, two. One, two.
Cups. Coins. Clubs. Swords.
'Pass.'
'Pass.'
'Pass.'
'I set a hundred ducats.'
'I'll none.'
'I'll none.'
'Nor I.'
'I must of force see you. Deal the cards.'
The eldest hand deals again.
One, two. One two. One, two. One, two. One, two. One, two.
Each player now has four cards.
'I'll see as much as he sets.'
'See here my rest, let every one be in.'
'I am come to pass again.'
'And I.'
'And I.'
'I set my rest.'
'I'll see it.'
'I cannot give it over.'
'I was a *primero*.'
'But I a *fluxus*.'

And so on. And on and on. From time to time there would be a flurry of interest. In place of a *primero*, one card of each suit, there would be a *supremus*, or a *numerus*, or a *fluxus*. Only the highest hand, four cards of a kind – the *chorus* – evaded them.

And all the time the pile of ducats rose and fell in front of each player like the tides of the sea.

Occasionally a footman would bring a plate of cold meats, some bread and fruit, a glass of wine; occasionally one or other of them would absent themselves for a few moments to relieve themselves in the *po* behind the door. More servants would come in to replace the guttering candles, or to wet the rushes on the floor. At these times a desultory conversation took place between the players. Once, when Paul took out his compendium, he became aware of the others looking at him curiously.

'What is that you have there? Is that your lucky charm, English?' The old nobleman with the thumb ring leaned towards him.

Paul kissed the brass casing, with its design of twisted lampreys, and put it away without comment.

'Two eels! I hope it brings you better fortune than you've had before.' The old man stretched his arms over his head wearily, but Paul could hear the taunt in his voice. 'But not tonight, eh gentlemen?'

The dense crowd of spectators that had clustered around them at the start of play had soon dwindled to only a handful of diehards. In his efforts to concentrate on the game, to read his adversaries, and to conceal his own tactics, Paul hardly noticed them. Faintly, in the distance, he could hear the sound of bells ringing, a hollow green sound, now far, now near, across the city. Was it dawn outside already? He tried to imagine the beauty of the dawn as it broke over the lagoon. After the long humid night, the first exquisite breeze of morning faintly ruffling the surface of the water outside their windows, limpid and blue in the early light . . .

But the vision did not last long. No world other than this existed; he wanted no other.

Now, when he looked up, he was surprised to find that the six players were almost alone in the immense room. The mood had changed from the feverish, heightened one of carnival sport to one of extreme inertia.

As far as it was possible to tell behind the all-concealing masks, even the players looked bored. Zuanne Memmo dozed for a few moments on a chair. The young nobleman had brought a slim leatherbound volume of poetry with him, hardly looking up from its pages to study his cards, by which he seemed profoundly bored. And Paul might almost have believed this ruse were it not for the fact that he would occasionally find his own gaze drawn towards him, aware with some sixth sense that he was being watched, and for an instant saw the gleam of his eyes as it flickered between the players, resting on Paul as often as not, trying to read his cards, suck out his thoughts like marrow from a bone.

Each one had their little piece of theatre, invisible to a mere onlooker. The merchant brought out a piece of paper on which there were written columns of figures in a neat secretary hand and studied it closely. At one point, he could not tell how long into the game, Paul became aware that the older nobleman was lying face down on the table, not dead as Paul first thought, but fallen suddenly asleep, exhausted finally by the exigencies of the cards. Only the man in the golden mask appeared perfectly at ease, speaking not at all unless the cards required it.

At first Paul was intrigued by this silent player in their midst. Although he could not see any part of his face it soon became clear that the man must be older than he at first seemed; there was something about him – the way he sat, perhaps, or the manner in which he shuffled the cards – which at times was familiar. Paul thought he must have played him before somewhere, at the Sign of the Pierrot perhaps, or one of the other *ridotti* that he had so often frequented over the last months. Then the man would shift in his chair – or spread his cards in a certain way – and he began to doubt himself again.

At the beginning of the game Paul had occupied himself by trying to settle in his mind the nature of each person's play. The two whose games it had been easiest for him to decipher had been the merchant and the older nobleman. The first was all caution, playing too tight; the other, flamboyance and bombast. From the beginning he knew they were no real threat. The young nobleman on the other hand proved a various and subtle player, with none of the rashness that Paul had come to expect from a youth of his age and rank.

All of them, it was clear, found the presence of the courtesan unsettling.

'What do you mean letting that woman in, Zuanne?' the nobleman complained when the lady had absented herself for a few moments.

'What could I do? She has the surety.' Memmo merely shrugged. 'There's no law against it, monseignor.' He gave one of those smiles that did not reach his eyes. 'The Council, in its infinite wisdom, has issued a *parte* about almost everything else – but not this. Or not yet, if Your Eminence will forgive the observation.'

'Well, there should be,' the other said plaintively, 'someone should see to it.'

But there was nothing he, or any of them, could do.

From what Paul imagined must have been the relative cool of the early morning the room became hot again, the candles in the golden sconces hissed in the sullen air. The men were down to their cotton undershirts. The courtesan had removed her surcoat and her collar, even her sleeves, and was wearing only a chemise and bodice that barely covered her breasts.

In the heat Paul's mask was becoming intolerable. The ill-fitting wood pressed against the bridge of his nose, rubbed a raw patch on one of his cheeks. He felt like a man parched with thirst and dreaming of water in the desert; all he could think about was removing the mask. But there was no remedy.

Shuffle.

Lift to see who would deal.

'I did lift a six.'

'I a seven.'

'I a three.'

'And I.'

'And I.'

'And I a coat card.'

Pass the cards to the eldest hand.

Deal.

One, two. One, two. One, two. One, two. One, two. One, two.

Cups. Coins. Clubs. Swords.

They placed their bets.

Were dealt again the second round of cards.

And on. And on.

In the end it was the courtesan who broke first.

'Zuanne, I can't help it.' She turned to him. 'I can't stand it any more. I must remove the mask.'

'What say you, gentlemen?' Memmo looked round the table. 'For the lady, I think we can allow the rules to bend.'

But she had already begun to untie the ribbons that bound the mask to her face. The courtesan, whether by habit or design, moved slowly, perhaps more slowly than was strictly necessary, it occurred to Paul, her tired fingers plucking clumsily at the knots. Paul half-expected that one of the other players might object to this unveiling of the only woman in their midst, but they did not. He saw that they were looking at her thirstily. There was a tension in the room that had not been there before. They watched as her beautiful rounded arms rose and fell. A rivulet of sweat, like a tiny silver cicatrice, gleamed between her breasts.

She removed the mask at last, put her hands up to unpin the horn-shaped hair pieces, shook out her natural hair, ran her fingers through it with a sigh. When she turned back towards them Paul thought for a moment that he was dreaming. She lifted the heavy weight of her hair to cool the back of her neck, a gesture so familiar to him it was as though a hand were twisting itself through his gut. He half-rose to his feet.

A glass beaker that had been sitting on the table at his elbow fell. It shattered on the floor into a thousand pieces.

'My God ... can it be ...?'

Her undressed hair seemed to catch the light; it fell in waves to her shoulders, shining reddish-gold in the candlelight. But, in the same moment, he saw his mistake. It was a stranger who gazed back at him, a woman he had never seen before. It was not Celia Lamprey.

'Why, sir,' The courtesan looked from Paul to the shattered wine glass. Now that she was exposed to view she seemed suddenly, coquettishly, aware of the effect of her own flesh. 'What were you thinking? Do you know me?' Her face was flushed.

'I beg your pardon, madam –' Paul sat down again heavily. What was wrong with him, he must be getting tired. 'You are very like someone – but no, I don't believe we have ever met.'

In the room the mood had changed again. There was a tension now that was palpable. Paul tried not to look at the unmasked courtesan, tried not to become distracted – the desire to best a woman at cards almost always made men careless – but he could not help himself. He could not tear his eyes away. Her resemblance to Celia was uncanny. Was this part of some trickery to put him off his game? The thought, like a small worm, seemed to crawl at the furthermost edges of his mind. Had Carew and Constanza been right to warn him after all – but no, that was impossible. No one in this room – no one in Venice other than Carew and Ambrose – knew what Celia looked like.

It was the merest chance, surely; or was it? What were the chances that a woman looking so like Celia Lamprey should turn up at the big game for the Sultan's Blue? The thought buzzed round and round his head like a fly on a window ledge. At one point he thought he intercepted a look of understanding between Memmo and the courtesan; another time he imagined the same with the golden-mask man –

But this way madness lay. He thought he could not stand it. He could not breathe, could not think. His mask was driving him insane. He had to take it off, even if only for a few moments. Paul excused himself from the room and went into the little antechamber behind the curtain. He tore off the mask, his fingers fumbling with the ties. Next to the *po* was a basin filled with cool clean water and some linen. He began to splash water on his face, but then on second thoughts plunged his whole head into the basin. He felt his head clear a little.

It was fatigue playing tricks on him, it had to be. Lack of sleep could give men waking dreams, he knew. But however hard he tried to push it away, the thought kept coming back to him: a discordant note echoing somewhere in the room, a sound so small, so distant, it was almost inaudible, like the chiming of a tiny, cracked bell.

The unmasking of the courtesan had rattled them all. In some indefinable way, each player's game seemed to change; whether by design, or by Fortune, he could not say.

The merchant and the old nobleman, both of whom had already sustained huge losses, were soon almost at their limit. The merchant was the first to fold. He stood up from the table with a dazed expression, as if he could not quite believe what was happening to him, staggered from the room without so much as a word. The nobleman followed him soon after, his *fluxus* losing to Paul's *chorus* of sevens.

He stood up, removed his mask, bowed to each in turn with perfect dignity.

'I congratulate you, English.' Although, like the merchant's, his face was haggard, he gave Paul the ghost of a smile. 'It seems that eels bring good fortune after all.'

In silence the remaining four watched him go. When the door had finally closed behind them both, the young nobleman looked at Paul enquiringly.

'Eels?'

'No, not eels. Lampreys.'

'Lampreys?' Paul could feel rather than see the raised eyebrow. 'If you say so, my friend.' Rolling up his sleeves, the other gave an indifferent laugh. 'Come, what are you all waiting for, let's play.'

What was he waiting for? That was the question. How many times had Paul asked himself the very same. Waiting for the moment when he would know, finally and for sure, that Celia was never coming back? Waiting for that moment when some other kind of life could at last begin? Waiting to feel ... what? – something – anything. But what kind of life was possible for him outside the walls of this room? Whatever it was, he was not sure he wanted it any more.

He had put all his fortune in, to see what Fortune would give back. All or nothing. A kind of death. An expiation, even.

It seemed to him – whatever Carew might say – that nothing less was possible.

Now, towards the morning of the third day, it looked as though he would have his answer. The courtesan had been the third of their number to withdraw, so they were down to three: the young noble-man, the man in the golden mask, Paul.

The room was filling up again with curious onlookers; carrion crows, Paul thought to himself, waiting for the kill. At one point, out of the corner of his eye, Paul imagined he saw a familiar turbaned figure join the throng. Was that Ambrose? What on earth was he doing here? But when he looked again, the figure had gone.

And then, as though by a miracle, it seemed as though Fortune had begun to smile on him after all.

With a *fluxus* he won sixty-nine points, with a *numerus* fifty-five. The pile of gold and silver coins in front of him grew greater and greater.

The courtesan moved her chair so she could sit closer to him.

'Looks as though I am your lucky charm, English,' she whispered into his ear. After two nights without sleep her breath smelt stale, but he was too absorbed in the cards to care.

The onlookers were crowding round the table now, but Paul barely noticed them. He could feel his heart beating smooth and fast; could feel the blood coursing round his veins. Energy seemed to crackle through him, over the skin of his body, from his fingertips. He was more alive than he had ever been in his life before.

All was forgotten except the hard certainties of the cards. His fight with Carew. Celia. Even the Sultan's Blue. The distant voice of the warning bell had receded until he could no longer hear its discordant notes.

With a run of sixes he forced the man in the golden mask to fold. Fortune smiled on him. He was invincible.

Memmo brought new cards. Passed them to the young nobleman to shuffle. They lifted, he dealt. Now it was down to just the two of them. And then suddenly, out of nowhere, there was a commotion at the table. The man in the golden mask was on his feet, shouting something.

'I saw you, sir,' he had taken a glass of wine and thrown it in the young nobleman's face, 'these cards are false.'

Paul could feel the courtesan holding on to his arm; felt rather than saw the uproar in the room behind him. The table overturned, cards flying. The sound of broken glass.

The game was over. He had won.

Paul stood up. Took off his mask. A blackness passed before his eyes. He held on to the table to steady himself. A crowd had gathered round him, he felt the press and heat of their bodies. The feeling of superhuman energy was beginning to dissipate. It was over. All he could feel now was numbness. He could see their mouths working, but for a few moments he could hear nothing – nothing other than a roaring in his ears, a sound like the sea. Someone handed him a glass of wine. He drank it down in one; held the empty glass out for another, drank that too. Someone had pulled one of the drapes from across a window. He saw the daylight, reflections from the Grand Canal, come rushing into the room. It hurt his eyes.

He was aware that the young nobleman was being taken from the room. The courtesan too. But he was past caring. Someone – he did not know who – was talking at him; their tone was low, conciliatory, but somehow he could not take in the words, as though they were being uttered in a language he could not understand.

And then Zuanne Memmo was standing in front of him. He was holding out the pink velvet pocket in his hand.

'It's yours, English.' Vaguely he was aware that he was being handed the diamond. When Paul did not take it from him, Memmo picked up his hand and put it in his palm, folding his fingers over the little package.

'It's yours, English. The Sultan's Blue.'

Paul felt the weight of the diamond in his palm. He expected to feel something – elated, joyful – but he felt nothing. There was a hand on his arm; he turned and saw the familiar figure of Ambrose standing next to him.

Paul looked at him, blinking. Ambrose. What was he doing here? He was aware of the effects of the wine hitting him suddenly, like a blow to the head. It burnt through his veins like aqua vitae.

'Congratulations, Pindar.'

'Thank you.'

'It seems the stone has moved on.'

'Yes.'

There was a tiny pause. The two men looked at one another. Even in his befuddled state Paul could feel the hostility radiating from him.

'I'll toss you for it, Pindar.'

'What?' Paul was aware that he was staring at Ambrose, his mouth open like a country want-wit.

'I said: I'll toss you for it.'

Paul began to laugh. 'What in God's name are you talking about, Ambrose?'

'You heard.' Ambrose was not in a mood to mince his words.

'Yes, of course I did.' Still laughing, Paul wiped a tear from his eye; his head was swimming so much he thought he might pass out. 'You cannot – possibly – be serious.'

But one look at Ambrose's face told him otherwise.

'You owe it to me.'

'Owe it to you?' he repeated. 'How so?'

'After the injury that man . . .' Ambrose could hardly get the words out '. . . I won't say his name, indeed I will not, sirrah . . . but after the injury your *servant* has done to me . . . you can have no possible idea what you owe me.'

Paul was still staring at Ambrose.

That small discordant note again. If only his head did not swim so –

'But the Sultan's Blue –' Paul faltered, aware that the whole room had fallen silent. 'The stone is priceless, Ambrose,' he said slowly.

'And I also have something that is priceless.' Ambrose reached into his pocket and brought out a small piece of parchment.

'A piece of paper?'

'Intelligence, sirrah. It's what I do.' There was another small pause. 'Something that you want, far, far more than any stone.'

'What intelligence can you possibly have that I would trade for the Sultan's Blue?'

'Some information about Celia Lamprey has come into my possession. To be precise, a poem. It seems to have been written to you, Pindar.' Ambrose sighed, rolled his eyes. 'Some kind of message, in her own fair hand. All the way from the Great Turk's harem in Constantinople. Quite touching, really.'

He held up the paper just close enough for Paul to see the writing on the page. Pencil marks, small and feathery. Celia's hand. He would know it anywhere.

' "To My Love, Farewell." ' Ambrose read the title of the poem out loud, paused for maximum effect. 'Why, Pindar, you look quite pale. I'll warrant it's all in here, everything you want to know, everything you've tormented yourself about all these years.' Ambrose gave a small smile. 'It's perfect, isn't it? "Your heart's desire." '

Paul opened his mouth to say something but no sound came out. He shut it again. There was a long pause.

'How do I know you are telling the truth?' he said at last. He knew he had to play for time, think what to do, but his whole body felt heavy, his mind was numb.

'It seems there was a harem lady after all.'

'I don't believe you.'

'So God is my witness.' Ambrose's pale blue eyes seemed to bore into him. 'Trust me. Just one toss of the coin, that's all I ask. Whoever wins, the paper is yours. All things considered, it is more than generous.'

'And if I refuse?'

Ambrose moved the paper over to a candle on the table, the flames began to lick one corner. 'Don't imagine for a moment I won't do it.'

'Stop, stop –' Paul put his hand out. 'Not so close, I beg you.' He was sweating now, could feel his heart hammering in his breast. What could he do, what could he say? He had to think of something, quickly, before it was too late.

'The stone has moved on, Ambrose. I have it now.' He hoped his desperation did not show. 'You can't win. The diamond has chosen me.'

'Then you have nothing to fear.' Ambrose's voice was soft as silk. 'Go on, Pindar,' he whispered, 'think of the glory.'

When Paul did not reply he held out a coin, a silver ducat.

'Heads I win the diamond,' he said, business-like suddenly, 'tails you keep it.'

Paul nodded his agreement.

'Cavaliere Memmo –' Ambrose turned to the *ridotto* owner. 'You are my witness.' He looked around the room. 'All of you are witness. If I win the diamond it will have been in a fair contest. No one can say otherwise.'

There was a murmur of assent; a chorus of voices.

'Go to it, English.'

'Bravo.'

Memmo took the piece of silver. Made a sign that Ambrose should give him the parchment also. He turned to Paul.

'Signor Pindar, are you sure you want to do this?' There was a look – was it pity? – in his eyes. 'I know you are a gambling man, but this . . . for a piece of paper?'

'You don't understand.' Paul jerked his chin. 'Just toss the coin.'

'Very well,' Memmo shook his head, 'if you say so.'

With a long smooth movement he sent the silver ducat spinning up into the air.

Chapter Thirty-six

When Paul emerged from Zuanne Memmo's *ridotto* at last it was to find that it had rained in the night. The temperature had dropped sharply and there was a chill in the air. He stood on the steps of the wine shop blinking in the morning light. How long was it since he had first stood on this very spot with Carew and Francesco? A week; a month; a lifetime ago? He hardly knew. Had lost all sense of the passage of time. He sniffed the air. After the staleness of the curtained *palazzo* it smelt sweet. A gauzy mist, a rain so fine it was all but invisible – angels' tears, as the Venetians call it – hung over the city, obscuring everything, turning the golden dawn of his imagination to white.

In his hand he held the paper passed on to him by Memmo as Ambrose claimed the diamond as his own.

He sat down on the wine-shop steps, holding it carefully out of the rain. His hand shook. Perhaps the Sultan's Blue was a magical stone after all, perhaps you did not have to possess it for it to work its spell. Written on this paper were the words that would bring Celia back from the dead. Words that might finally unlock the past, set him free at last.

But now that the moment had come his heart failed him. He was frozen, unable to move. Suppose Ambrose had been lying? He felt a chill go through him. He thought he had recognised Celia's writing, but he could so easily have been mistaken. Suppose the letter had been written by someone else? Was something entirely unconnected with her?

There was only one way to find out. He touched the paper with his finger. It had been folded carefully into three. He lifted it to his face, sniffed it. It had a sweet, faraway smell. Slowly he unfolded it.

It was written in lead, in a hand so small and frail he had to bend his head to read it. A voice from the dead.

To my love, farewell

Whenas I saw you at the gate
Barred hence from my enslavèd fate
And knew in that one instant sore
I would not see you ever more:
Oh love! How my small heart did break
And tears course down for thy dear sake!

And now I think me where thou art
And with what weight of lonely heart,
And wish me where thou liest, to say
Perhaps hard fortune will one day
Relent its cruel division of me:
My sad heart here, its love with thee . . .

But in the darkest hours of night
When ev'n the moon has lost her sight
And from the dark mosques' tow'rs arise
The heathens' strangest midnight sighs,
I lie awake and hear truth speak:
Thou'rt lost, and never more to seek.

Oh love! Remember me, I pray,
When to thy eyes the English day
Sheds oft its soft and ruby glow
Upon the gard'n we trod below,
When all the world and time was ours,
Unnumbered in its bliss-thought hours;

Remember me, that on the beach
Of Bosphorus thy name doth teach
Beneath a bough of foreign tree
In whispers to my memory:
Who loves thee still, and ever will,
Though time's long grief my heart doth kill.

So she had known! All that time Celia had known that he was in Constantinople. Whether by Carew's sugar ship, or his own compendium, it hardly mattered. That much at least he now knew for sure. But as for the rest . . . It seemed that she had been led to believe by someone that she was going to see him again. She had waited somewhere, hoping to see him, thinking he was going to come to her – but, of course, he had never gone. Had she thought herself forsaken? Dear God! Would that he had never set eyes on that infernal paper. Far from setting him free, it had only served to increase his torment.

In an agony of mind Paul started to walk; twisting through narrow *calles*, across innumerable bridges. The water in the canals beneath them was black as pitch. He had no idea where he was going, or what he was going to do.

He stumbled into a tiny *campo* with a stone well in the centre; saw that two houses were boarded up, marked with black crosses. He stumbled out again in fear.

At some point he found himself walking down a broader street; and then, to his surprise, in the distance he became dimly aware of an ample, turban-headed shadow scurrying ahead of him through the mist. Could it possibly be . . . yes, Ambrose!

Paul began to follow him, although he had no very clear idea why; perhaps it was just the idea that he must have the diamond – his diamond! – secreted somewhere in the voluminous folds about his person. The thought of it seemed to lure Paul onwards like a will-o-the-wisp.

It occurred to him that he should catch up with Ambrose, stab him in the back with his rapier, and steal the diamond again – leave him to die like a stuck pig in some urinous-smelling alleyway. But all the days and nights without sleep, and then the wine, had unmanned him completely – and besides, he now realised, he had left his rapier behind at the *ridotto*.

If Carew were here – Paul could almost hear the satisfying sound of gristle on bone as Carew cracked open Ambrose's skull, mashing him to pieces with his bare hands – but Carew was not here, nor was likely to be again. *What had he done?* Even Carew had left him now. He felt a stab of something like grief at the thought of it.

By now Paul was shivering; whether with shock or cold, he could not tell. It was only then that he realised his rapier was not the only thing he had left behind. Unlike Ambrose, well wrapped up against the rain, Paul was still in his shirt. He had left the rest of his clothes – his doublet and sleeves, even his hat – at Memmo's.

The angels' tears seeped steadily into the thin lawn of his undershirt. It would not be long before he was soaked through, but he did not care. Besides, there was no going back now. In his confused state he doubted whether he would be able to find the mysterious *palazzo* again even if he wanted. Zuanne Memmo's *ridotto* seemed to him at that moment as fantastical as some lost land from a sailor's chapbook: a place of phantoms and shattered dreams.

Keeping the figure of Ambrose just within sight, he stumbled on and was surprised to find himself suddenly in an open space. The mist was so dense here that, disorientated, it was a while before he realised where he was. Then he saw the gilded domes, the mosaics of a church, a flash of pink and white, and realised that he was in St Mark's Square.

From somewhere nearby came the sound of music; a pair of cymbals, a reed-pipe, a drum. Their plaintive notes were half-muffled by the mist. A small crowd of onlookers, all dressed in long black cloaks, were gathered at the water's edge. Ambrose drew closer. Paul followed him, keeping out of sight.

A wandering troupe had set up their show in the square in front of the Doge's Palace. Paul had seen many of their number here before, fairground acts for the most part – minstrels and acrobats, magicians and feats of strength, and once even a tightrope walker; all made their way to the Serenissima at some point. Ambrose, who was now marching purposefully to a waiting gondola tied up at the waterfront, was level with them. Paul too, still shadowing Ambrose, followed the music to the water's edge, where the lagoon lapped the stone.

There, at the centre of the crowd, was the strangest figure he had ever seen: a woman with a long, sad face that she had whitened with chalk or some kind of powder. She wore a robe of brightly coloured cloth, every part of it stitched with silver spangles. At first Paul thought that she was dancing, but as he came nearer he saw that she was making her way rapidly in circles, round and round the little band of onlookers, gliding with a curious, smooth gait – not quite a walk, not quite a dance – rather as if she were moving on well-oiled wheels.

The mist began to dissipate; a ray of watery yellow sunlight pierced the whiteness. It caught at the spangles of the woman's robe until she seemed to shine like some angelic being.

So curious a sight was this that even Ambrose was drawn to pause and watch her for a moment. Paul did likewise, as he drew closer he saw that as she circled the crowd the woman was making objects appear and disappear mysteriously in her wake.

Feathers, flowers and pieces of fruit were produced from the robe of one onlooker, the sleeve of another. A rose was plucked from a woman's kerchief. From two men standing just in front of Ambrose she produced a pair of embroidered handkerchiefs, and then pushing each one down into her clenched fist she pulled them out again with a quick deft movement, magically knotted together in a streaming silk rainbow. From behind each ear of a small child standing with her mother at the front of the circle she plucked an egg; then throwing them both into the air made them vanish again, and the materialise in the lap of another child who was sitting nearby, in the form of two softly cheeping chicks.

The music grew louder and the drumbeat quicker. The woman came to stand in front of Ambrose now. She reached towards him, was taking something from his turban. Ambrose put up his hand as though to push her away but she was too quick for him. She held something in her hand, was showing it to the crowd on the opposite side from Paul. He craned his neck, but there was too great a throng in front of him for him to see easily. Then his eye alighted on Ambrose. His look of utter horror told him exactly what it was that she had found in the yellow folds of his turban. At that moment the woman spun past Paul and he saw, sure enough, that she was holding the pink embroidered pocket. The Sultan's Blue!

Ambrose's face turned from deathly white to crimson; his pale eyes bulged so much they looked as though they were about to burst clean out of his head. He opened his mouth to shout something but no sound came out. The woman was bending her elbow, arching herself backwards, making as if to throw the little pink velvet pocket skywards –

'Stop! Thief!' Suddenly Ambrose had found his voice.

But it was too late.

Before their astonished eyes the pocket simply vanished into thin air.

She held her hand out.

In its place was a small silver coin.

Ambrose took one look and with a roar dashed it to the ground.

'*Ladro!* Thief! Where's it gone?' He lunged at her. 'What have you done with my . . . with my . . . my property?' He seized the pale-faced woman by the throat, was shaking her like a rat. 'Why, you pickpocket,' he shouted, 'what have you done with it, vermin? Give it back to me at once.' He was bellowing at her now like an enraged bull.

'I'm sorry, *kyrios*, I didn't mean any harm . . .' she began.

But Ambrose had his hands around her throat. The musicians, three women, flung their instruments to the ground and rushed to help her.

'Stop, stop, let her go, let her go,' they cried.

Some of the men in the crowd came forward to pull him off. It took three of them to prise him away.

The woman lay panting on the ground. There was a graze on her cheek where she had fallen. From somewhere about her person, Paul was never quite sure where, she took the little pocket and threw it at him.

'Here's your pocket, *kyrios*,' she said. 'Take it. I meant no harm.'

Ambrose caught the pocket clumsily in both hands. His face was blotchy, ugly with rage and greed. With shaking fingers he drew the strings, looked inside, weighed it in his palm; was satisfied. He turned and, looking neither to right or left, scurried towards the waiting gondola.

Paul watched him go. Watched the black gondola tip and rock as Ambrose stepped inside; heard the slap of the lagoon water against the stone landing; watched the gondolier push off from his moorings into the lagoon, and the sleek black vessel disappear finally into the mist.

So that was it then. The show was over. Slowly the crowd dispersed. Paul sat down on the ground and put his head between his knees, too weary even to think.

It was a while before he realised that someone was standing beside him. He looked up and saw the woman with the pale face and the spangled motely. He felt in his pocket, but realised that he had nothing, not even the basest copper coin to give her.

'I'm sorry . . .' he began, but she interrupted him.

'Paul Pindar?'

Almost nothing now would surprise him. 'What?'

'Are you the English merchant, the one who goes by the name of Paul Pindar?'

He remembered thinking she had a pleasant, low voice; not Venetian. Greek, perhaps?

'Yes,' he said, fighting off the sudden, mad urge to begin laughing, although he thought that if he started laughing now he might never stop. 'At least, I think so – once –' he shook his head '– perhaps.'

'*Panayia mou!*' she said very gently.

She looked out on to the lagoon towards Ambrose's disappearing gondola. There was a ghost of a smile on her lips.

'Has he gone?'

'Yes,' Paul replied simply, for there was nothing more to be said.

And it was true, the last ghostly silhouette of Ambrose's gondola could no longer be seen. Paul felt strangely light, as though an enormous weight had been lifted off his shoulders.

'In that case I think it's safe for me to show you this.'

She was holding out something small and shining on her palm. He took it from her uncomprehendingly. It was a silver coin, the one that Ambrose had dashed from her hand just a moment or two ago.

'What's this?'

'Take a look.'

Paul turned the coin over in his fingers: there were heads on both sides. In silence, he handed it back to her.

'It's a trick coin he used to cheat you of the diamond. Your friend, John Carew, was convinced he would try something. Although it was the other one – the lady Constanza – who found out about the coin. You have a lot to thank them for, Mr Pindar. Especially John Carew. That time in the alleyway, you see, he turned back after all.'

Carew turning back? In an alleyway? Paul had no idea what she was talking about, and he did not care. For a long while neither of them spoke.

'It wouldn't have made any difference,' he said eventually. 'They say there's no point trying to prevent the stone moving on. If not this, then . . .'

'Ah, well,' for the first time the woman smiled, 'perhaps someone should have told your friend Ambrose that.'

Vaguely he wondered how on earth she knew Ambrose's name, or John's, or Constanza's; or his for that matter. His sense of dislocation was so great by now it was as though he were in some waking dream.

'What do you mean?'

'I mean that the stone has been moving on for many, many months now, Mr Pindar.'

He looked down to see that she was holding something out to him: a pink embroidered pocket.

'Take it, Mr Pindar. The Sultan's Blue.'

At that moment the three women who had been accompanying her on their instruments came up and surrounded them.

'It's time, Elena,' one of them said.

'Is she here?'

'Yes, look there, they're coming now.' Another of them pointed to the lagoon.

'Quickly now, help him up.' He could feel kind hands bringing him to his feet. 'Gently now, gently.'

'I have to tell you that she cannot yet remember everything, it's possible she never will,' the woman they had called Elena was saying to him, 'and that's a blessing. I know Maryam –' she broke off; took a breath '– I know Maryam was convinced of it.'

Paul stared at her, uncomprehending still.

'Her legs too. They were not broken, as I had thought. The backs of her legs had been badly cut and had not healed well. A miracle, so the doctor at the *ospedale* says, that they missed the tendons by a hair. *Panayia mou!* He has great hopes that she will walk normally again one day.'

'Her legs?' He grabbed her by the arm and shook her. 'Whose legs?' His heart was beating hard now. 'What are you talking about?'

But when she turned to him he saw that she was weeping silently.

'Why, Paul Pindar,' she whispered, 'can't you guess?' The look she gave was infinitely sad, infinitely sweet. 'Why else do you think the diamond has made its way to you?'

And the next thing he knew he was alone on the waterfront. The women had vanished; he did not know where they went. At first, gazing into the grey-green waters of the lagoon, he could see nothing. And then, through the mist, he made out the low sleek form of a gondola sliding slowly towards him.

Two people – a man and a woman – were on the deck: the man standing, the woman sitting at his feet. As they came closer he saw that it was Carew standing on the prow. Behind him was a woman wrapped in a cloak. The mist swirled around her, obscuring her face.

It can't be –

Had he spoken? He did not know.

Oh please God –

He could not hear.

Oh dear God, please –

His eyes were full of tears; he could not see.

But she had seen him now. Carew was helping her to her feet. She was calling to him. Calling out his name.

Oh please God –

He fell to his knees in the rain.

Celia. My Celia. My Celia.

Chapter Thirty-seven

When Carew finally reached the convent it was raining again. Angels' tears shrouded the ancient walls of the physic garden in a white mist, blurred the windows, the tops of the lime trees, giving them a melancholy aspect.

He presented himself at the main gateway this time. There was a nun whose voice he did not recognise.

'You can't have no business here, sir,' he could hear an uncertain, muffled voice on the other side of the door. 'You mun go away.'

But Carew was not to be put off so easily. He pummelled on the great wooden door with both fists. Eventually the hatch opened a crack and a pair of frightened brown eyes looked out at him.

'What's your business, sir?' When she spoke it was in a dialect so thick he could hardly understand her. 'We've no herbs to sell. They say it spreads infection. The archbishop has forbidden it, until the danger is past.'

'Danger? What danger?'

'Ain't you heard? The plague has come to this house. We mun't let no strangers in. By order of the archbishop.'

She was about to close the hatch again, but Carew was too quick for her. 'I don't give a damn about any of your archbishops,' he said, and with a quick movement he pulled out one of his knives, thrust its handle into the hatch, blocking it open. He heard with satisfaction her gasp of horror at this blasphemy. 'Open this door! I'll smash it down with my bare hands if I have to.'

There was a silence on the other side. Through the tiny opening in the hatch he could just see her still standing there, head bent, listening for him.

'Look, I don't want to get you into trouble, *suora*,' he said in a more conciliatory vein, 'I'll go to your lady abbess if you like, to ask her permission.'

'Our blessed Suo' Bonifacia is dead, sir; just four days ago; her servant, too.' The gatekeeper's voice was tremulous, high and thin like a child's. 'And Suo' Purificacion lies mortal sick, and we thought even the devil himself would never dare take her. Most of the old ones, too, the *discrete* . . .' Her voice trailed off into a helpless whisper. 'It all happened so quick. The *educande*, they're all gone and all sent back to their homes. I'm to tell tha' to go away, sir. Tha' mun't come in here.'

Carew thought for a moment. Despite his threats about breaking the door down, he knew there was no chance of getting through the main convent gateway without her help. He supposed he could break in through Suor Veronica's entrance, or scale the walls by the lime trees in the place where he had once lost his shoe, but somehow he had lost his taste for that kind of adventure.

He paused. Took a breath. 'Look, I'm sorry if I frightened you.' Patience did not come easily to Carew; but he was rewarded by a small sniff from behind the hatch.

'What's your name?'

'Eufemia, sir.'

'Well, look, Eufemia. This is very important.' He forced himself to speak slowly and calmly. 'I have urgent business with one of the *suoras*. Do you think you can help me? Her name is Annetta.'

'Suo' Annetta?' He heard a sparkle of recognition in her voice.

'Yes, Suo' Annetta, of course.'

Dear God, he leaned his head against the wooden door, how could this have happened to him? 'It's important – can you get her – the *suora* – for me – please?'

For a long time there was no reply, and then suddenly he heard the sound of the bolt being somewhat inexpertly drawn.

Before the big gates had swung open more than the tiniest crack Carew forced his boot between the two doors. They swung open and a strange sight met his eyes. Standing nervously before him on the threshold was a very small nun – although when he looked at her more closely he saw that, despite being dressed in full nun's regalia, Suor Eufemia was a child no more than twelve or thirteen years old.

She wore an ill-fitting habit made of a greasy black homespun which looked as though it had seen many years of communal wear before the present incumbent; her shoes were rough wooden clogs.

On either side of her in the corridor of the gatehouse were two piles of still-smoking straw, an ineffectual attempt to cleanse the pestilence from goods or clothing going either in or out of the convent walls.

'You want to see Suo' Annetta?' she said.

'Yes,' Carew replied.

'Tha' must be the one, then,' she said, looking up at him curiously.

'The one?'

'The one I were supposed to give the paper to at Prospero Mendoza's workshop.' She gazed at him, her eyes innocent as a child's. 'The one she's been crying after these last few days.'

Carew stared at her for a moment in silence. 'The one she's been crying after?'

God's blood, what was the matter with him? Carew wanted to kick himself. Did he really have to repeat everything the girl said like some country dolt? But mingling with his annoyance at himself were some of the strangest sensations Carew had ever had in his life before; feelings that he could not possibly have put a name to; a feeling of wild, mad elation; as though the wind had entered his soul.

She's been crying after *me*? he wanted to say to her; wanted to take her by the arm and shake her and say again, *she's been crying after me?* Just to make her say the words over, so he could hear them again, possibly even more than once, and be sure, absolutely sure, that he had not misheard and that was what she meant.

But he did not, because at that moment he could not trust himself to speak.

'Well, she says it's because I lost the paper she gave me,' she went on in her high-pitched voice, 'gave it instead to that great fat man, he said he knew you, the one with the funny yeller 'at. That and a nose like a prize *zucchino*. Well, he *tricked* me,' her eyes narrowed, 'he *tricked* me to give it to him instead and now she says she can't keep her promise to her friend . . .' she tailed off again. 'But when you didn't come, when she couldn't think how else to find you – well, I knew it weren't the only reason for the crying.'

'Please, *suora* ... Eufemia ... can you find her?' Carew cut in through the stream of words. 'I have good news for her, about her friend.' He looked at her encouragingly. 'And for you too, here –' he put his hand inside his shirt – 'I brought the paper back, to prove to her I mean well.'

Eufemia regarded him suspiciously for a moment or two. 'How did you get that?'

'You know that man – the one with the nose like a prize *zucchino*?' he said gravely. She nodded. 'He gave it back to me. In a manner of speaking.'

'Alright, I'll get her for tha',' she said, decisive all of a sudden. She turned and motioned him to follow her into the courtyard. 'But I tell you this, sir, I wouldn't do this for no one else.'

Carew followed Eufemia from the gateway into the courtyard, and through a colonnaded passageway into the visitors' parlour. He recognised the iron grille separating the visitors' parlour from the nuns' parlour, remembering the last time he had spoken to Annetta. To his surprise Eufemia did not seem to want him to stop there, but led him through the door, which had been left swinging carelessly open, and into the main part of the convent.

It was only then that Carew began to notice that a curious hush had descended. Normally the convent was all bustle and activity – *educande* laughing and running in the corridors, the sound of water trickling in the great garden behind the walls, the nuns at work with their hoes and their watering cans, the aroma of cooking meat and onions drifting in from the kitchens nearby – but no longer. Now it had taken on the dark, dank feeling of a deserted place.

They met no one on that journey, and the little nun cut a solitary figure as she scuttered along through the two parlours, her wooden clogs clattering loudly on the stone. About halfway down the corridor they came to a doorway where she stopped. Carew looked in and saw that she had brought him to the one place that he had somehow missed on his nocturnal wanderings.

The convent refectory was a large high-ceilinged room, panelled in dark wood. A simple crucifix hung on the wall opposite him; above it, almost in the rafters, was a dingy painting of the Last Supper. In the middle of the room, about a third of the way across, someone had placed an ecclesiastical chair with a high carved back of the

271

kind bishops sit in. Opposite, about a third from the other end of the room, was a similar high-backed chair. In between was a row of partially burnt straw, and he guessed that some sort of interview must previously have taken place here.

'Tha' mun stay here until she comes.' Eufemia indicated that he should sit in the chair closest to the door. 'Tha' mun't move from the chair, *capito*?'

'*Capito*.'

Carew sat down on the edge of the seat and looked round him. Long trestle tables were ranged around the walls on three sides; in front of each place setting was a small dish of salt and a bottle of olive oil, but here the impression of comfortable domesticity ended. When he looked more closely he saw that the white cloths on the tables were all stained; pieces of stale bread, the remains of some long-ago meal, were still scattered on the trestle tops. Small brown sparrows flew and cheeped between the rafters, swooping down unchecked to feast on the crumbs.

It seemed scarcely possible that so great a change should have come to a place in so few days. Carew wondered what he would do if one of the other nuns should come in and discover him sitting here, but although he strained his ears he could hear no other sounds, not even distant ones, of footsteps or voices.

At last, at the other end of the room, he heard a door opening. And when he looked up she was there. Her normally fine complexion was a little paler than normal; she wore the black robe but not her headdress, her dark hair hung loose about her shoulders.

At first she merely stood there, as though hesitating whether to approach him or not, but the sight of him seemed to make her almost angry.

'What madness is this?'

When he did not reply she advanced a few paces into the room.

'Don't you know the pestilence has come to this house?' She indicated the still-smouldering straw strewn across the middle of the floor. 'You should not have come.' She had reached the chair, and was standing facing him with one hand on its carved back.

'You should not have come,' she repeated, softly, almost in a whisper, 'not here, not now.'

'I had to come,' he stood up, 'I had to tell you. Celia Lamprey is found. She's here, in Venice. Not a league from where we sit.'

272

'Celia?' She seemed to frown. 'How do you know that name?' She spoke the words slowly, like one in a dream. 'Found?'

'Yes, found.'

'Goose? Found?' He saw her grip tighten on the chair. 'It can't be true. But . . . what . . . how do you know?' She seemed confused.

'I am Paul Pindar's servant.'

'What –?' She stared at him. '*You*? The *monarchino* . . .'

'Yes,' Carew said. 'And you are the lady from the harem. The one we were looking for all that time. I never knew –'

But she interrupted him.

'*You!*' She seemed scarcely able to believe her ears. 'No, no, no, no, it's not possible. When you asked me about the Sultan's Blue I thought –' she stopped '– the truth is I did not know *what* to think, that's why I sent Eufemia to find you –' she seemed at a loss for words '– but that you should be the merchant's servant – all this time . . .'

They stared at one another.

'And so – he must be – is he here too?'

'She is with him now.'

Annetta made an inarticulate sound and put her hand to her chest, as though the thought of it were so sweet it almost hurt her.

'Please, won't you sit down?' He indicated the chair, but she shook her head.

'No, I can't stay.'

He saw the tears well in her eyes.

'She says you stole the diamond from the Valide, and gave it to her –'

'– so she could bribe the eunuchs, so they would find someone to bring her here to Venice. But that was a year ago now –' She was clutching the back of the chair, as though her legs would not longer hold her. 'In all that time, I didn't know – I never knew what had become of her –' her voice was very small '– in all that time – you've no idea.'

Her eyes were searching his face. 'But how is she?' She seemed to detect some hidden anxiety in him. 'Is she quite well?'

'She will be well – in time,' Carew chose his words carefully. 'But I must warn you that her journey here has been long and hard.'

'How so?'

'She says they tried to drown her. The diamond saved her life.'

Annetta put her hand to her mouth. 'My poor goose.'

'That much, at least, she can remember.' Carew paused for a moment, wondering how to go on. 'But whoever it was to whom she gave the diamond forced her to lie with him – either he or some other along her way –' Carew held her gaze steadily '– and she bore a child.'

Annetta stared at him. 'She has a child?'

'She had a child, although from what I heard it was never like to live.'

He related then, so far as he was able, the story of Celia's journey, the strangest tale either of them had ever heard told. The story of the mermaid baby and the stolen diamond; a story about the greed of men and the kindness of strangers. He told her about Ambrose Jones and his factor, Bocelli, about Elena and Maryam and Constanza. He told her about the great game for the Sultan's Blue.

He even told her about his own small role. How by some miracle he had turned round after all, turned round and gone back, that day in the alleyway.

When he had finished they stood gazing at one another.

'I can't believe it's true,' she said after a while.

'On my life. I swear it is all true.'

What was the matter with him? He could not tear his eyes from her face. Was afraid to move, in case he startled her again, startled her into getting up and leaving him. He did not think he could bear her to leave him just yet. For a long time neither of them spoke. The only noise was the sound of the sparrows in the rafters.

'What happens now?'

'She asked me to find you. She wants to see you –'

'Well, she can't see me,' Annetta said angrily. 'Can't you understand? No one can, not now.' She looked around her at the deserted refectory, at the line of burnt straw separating them. 'Nor should you be here,' she whispered. 'What utter madness made you come?'

Why had he come? Perhaps he was a little mad. He did not feel himself, it was true. Ever since that day when he had picked up the dropped pocket in the garden. He knew what he wanted to say, but how could he – John Carew – ever utter such words? 'I came because I . . . because I could no longer bear to stay away.'

But there, somehow the words were out, and he had the strange sensation that it was as though someone else entirely were speaking through him.

She turned her gaze on him, her eyes luminous. 'But I – I fear –'

'Don't fear!' He was in a torment now. 'That time in the garden, I would never have hurt you. I swear to God you have nothing to fear –'

'But I do –'

'What – what do you fear?'

'That I am just like the others – some kind of game –'

'No, never – I swear it.'

'I could not bear to be just some kind of game to you –'

'Never – on my life.'

He had the impulse to throw himself on his knees in front of her. He could no longer bear it. He took two steps towards her before he knew what he was doing. She jumped up.

'No, you must not! You must not come any closer.'

They were standing no more than a foot away from one another now, only the line of straw between them. He could see the long smooth length of her neck, the curve of her beautiful upper lip, her cheekbone with its tiny brown mole; in his eyes even Suor Veronica could never have painted anything more heartbreaking.

'Go away, John Carew,' her voice trembled. 'You must go away from here. Go now.'

'I cannot.'

'Just go!' When he did not answer her, she repeated, 'You know you must.'

'How can you tell me to go when you have been crying after me all these days?' he whispered.

'But how could –?'

'Because I have been crying after you.'

Standing there, in that lonely room, it seemed to both of them as if they must be the last two people in the world.

'I thought you weren't going to come,' a single tear was running down her cheek, 'I thought I would never see you –' she put her hand to her breast as though something hurt her there '– but this is worse.'

'I won't ever leave you.'

'Don't be absurd, John Carew!' She dashed the tear with her hand. 'Get you gone now. Before it's too late.'

'Let me hold you, let me kiss you just once.'

In all his life he had never wanted anything so much as to hold her body in his arms, to feel her flesh melt into his, to feel her heart beating beneath his. He felt as though he could tear up whole forests, rip down walls, cleave boulders in half with his bare hands to reach her – but it was no good. They were so close now he could almost imagine he could smell her hair, the secret place behind her ear – and yet an unbridgeable divide, fathoms deep, separated them.

'No!' She shook her head.

'I can't leave you here.'

'You must.'

Carew looked around him, desperate now. 'Come with me.'

'Now I know you're mad.'

'I mean it, come with me. Look, the door lies open,' Carew pointed towards the nuns' parlour, 'there's no one to stop us. Come with me, I have passage on a merchantman that leaves tonight.'

'No! I can't listen.' Annetta put her hands up to her ears as though to block out his words. 'I won't listen! If you stay here any longer you might die.'

'And if *you* stay here you will die.'

'I might. I might already have the plague. But supposing I should live?' She was crying now. 'I need –' she could not get the words out '– I need –'

'What do you need?' He strained to hear her. 'Tell me – tell me what you need – anything –'

'I need something to live for.'

And somehow Carew was walking away. He was walking back down the echoing corridor, through the parlour, across the court-yard, and out through the doors of the gatehouse with its piles of smoking straw, into the outside world, where the angels' tears were still falling.

As he walked he could think of nothing; only that he felt a pain, as though something had torn, deep inside him. And for some reason that he could not quite fathom he could not think of Annetta, or of Celia, or even of himself just then, but of Paul, and the sight of him falling to his knees in the rain as Celia had come towards him, weeping as though his heart would break.

And at that moment he finally understood what he had never really understood before: what it might be like to lose the person you loved more than any other.

John Carew stumbled out into the rain.

Acknowledgements

I would like to thank Al Alvarez, for the gift of his books and for some exhilerating conversations about poker, and Thomas Leveritt for taking me to play it at the Grosvenor Victoria Casino. I am indebted to the 1623 edition of John Minsheu's *Pleasant and Delightfull Dialogues in Spanish and English*, which helped me reconstruct the *primero* game in this book.

Grateful thanks are also due to Ken Arnold for his scholarship on cabinets of curiosities, to Michael Gibson, Melanie Gibson, to Sarah-Jane Forder for the copy-editing, and especially to June-Anne Hare for our visits to Hatton Garden and for all her many kindnesses to me over the years. I am grateful yet again to Alexander Russell for his good-humour in providing me with suitable Greek vocabulary; to Abdou Filali-Ansari for the Arabic; and to Andrea Chiari-Gaggia for his advice on Venetian Italian. any errors that remain are of course completely my own.

My warmest thanks us always to everyone at Bloomsbury, both in the UK and in the US, but most especially to Katie Bond, Alexa von Hirschberg, Kathleen Farrar, Penelope Beech, Erica Jarnes, and of course my peerless editor Alexandra Pringle. At Rogers, Coleridge and White I would like to thank Cara Jones, Stephen Edwards, Laurence Laluyaux, and of course my agent Gill Coleridge.

Nearer to home a really special thank you to Libbi Seymour for being my completely invaluable helper over the last year. And last, but by no means least, my husband Anthony, for all his love and support, and of course for Celia's poem.

Reading Group Guide

These discussion questions are designed to enhance your group's conversation about *The Pindar Diamond*, a novel of fortune and romance set in Venice at the turn of the seventeenth century.

About this book

The Pindar Diamond picks up four years after *The Aviary Gate*'s adventures in Constantinople. Now, in 1603, Paul Pindar and his servant, John Carew, are in Venice, where Pindar, still mourning the loss of his beloved Celia Lamprey to the Sultan's harem, tries to forget his grief at Venice's gambling parlors. Desperate to bring Pindar to his senses—and out of debt—Carew calls upon Ambrose Jones, a sinister collector who has other dealings in Venice. Ambrose is determined to secure two priceless treasures: the Sultan's Blue, a diamond rumored to have been stolen from the Sultan's harem, and a live mermaid.

A giantess named Maryam has just discovered that mermaid: a stranger thrust the frail baby and its dazed, amnesiac mother upon Maryam's troupe of female acrobats. Maryam is determined to bring the mermaid to Venice, where a doctor might be able to save its life.

Meanwhile, Annetta, now living a pious life at the Convent of Santa Clara, is about to meet her match: Carew has been sneaking into the convent, at first for secret liaisons with nuns, but now to track down the elusive Sultan's Blue. When the diamond is finally found, Pindar decides to risk everything to win it—his instincts tell him that the diamond will lead him to his long-lost Celia.

For discussion

1.   Describe Paul Pindar's state of mind as the novel opens. Are his fortunes in as bad a state as Carew and Constanza fear? What are the sources of his desperation, and how are his friends able to guide him through his dark days in Venice?

2.   Consider how *The Pindar Diamond* brings early-seventeenth-century Venice to life. What sights, sounds, and smells of the ancient city does the novel evoke? Which characters suffer most from the dangers of the city: its temptations, debaucheries, and illnesses?

3.   Many of the characters in *The Pindar Diamond* strive for two types of fortune: money and luck. Who is successful in the search for riches? Who finds talismans of good luck? When does luck fail, and another force—love, fate, or even rash behavior—take over? When does a game of chance become a swindle for fortune?

4. As Carew returns to the Santa Clara convent, he wonders, "Why was it … that nuns always held such a peculiar fascination?" (123–24) Compare the Santa Clara convent to Annetta's previous home, the Sultan's harem. Which place hides more secrets and intrigue: the convent or the harem?

5. In a flashback, Maryam reveals the violence and horror of her childhood. What troubles did Maryam endure as a young giantess? How does Maryam's past influence her present, as she tries to rescue the mermaid baby and its mother? What makes Maryam so determined to protect her two charges?

6. Ambrose Jones is the most sinister villain in *The Pindar Diamond*, causing trouble all over Venice in a few short days. What motivates Ambrose's ruthless search for the Sultan's Blue and the mermaid?

7. As Constanza deals a deck of tarot cards, two images keep reappearing: the Lovers and Death. Whose fates are revealed in these cards? Who represents the lovers, and whose ultimate fate is death?

8. Compare the two short chapters that open each half of the novel: Chapter 1 (3) and Chapter 23 (157). What horrors at sea does the narrator describe? Why is the narrator voiceless in the first chapter, and what "baptism" and "rebirth" does she describe in the later chapter? What is the effect of the repetition between these similar chapters?

9. The actual location of the Sultan's Blue is unclear for much of the novel. Who seemed most likely to be hiding the precious diamond, before it appeared at the *ridotto*? How did it finally come into Zuanne Memmo's hands?

10. Consider the novel's description of the *ridotto*, Zuanne Memmo's secret gambling parlor. How does this room set the scene for the nerve-racking competition for the Sultan's Blue? Why do the players mask their identities? What double-crosses does Pindar face during this gambling marathon in the *ridotto*?

11. What does the inscription on the Sultan's Blue—"My heart's desire"—seem to mean? How does the meaning of the inscription change as the diamond changes hands? To whose "heart's desire" does the diamond ultimately lead? Who is deceived or disappointed by the diamond's powers?

12. Elena, the illusionist in Maryam's troupe of tumblers, plays a small but key role in *The Pindar Diamond*. What kind of relationship do Elena and

Maryam have? What effect do Elena's illusions—making items disappear and reappear—have upon other characters?

13.   Pindar risks his newly won diamond to read Celia Lamprey's last poem. What longings, regrets, and desires does the poem express? Do you agree with Pindar's interpretation of the poem—that Celia thought she would see her fiancé again? Or do you agree with Annetta's belief that Celia knew she would not make it to the Aviary Gate? Explain your answer.

14.   Discuss the relationship between Annetta and Carew. What is the basis of their attraction? Their budding love story ends on an ambiguous note—why does Carew walk away from Annetta at the end of *The Pindar Diamond*? Might they ever meet again? Does Annetta's health seem doomed by the plague that is sweeping through the convent?

15.   If you have read *The Aviary Gate*, Katie Hickman's first novel about Paul Pindar and Celia Lamprey, how does *The Pindar Diamond* compare to the previous book? What future adventures can you imagine for Pindar, Celia, Annetta, and Carew?

Katie Hickman is the author of six previous books, including two bestselling history books, *Courtesans* and *Daughters of Britannia*. She has written two travel books. *Travels with a Circus*, about her experiences traveling with a Mexican circus, which was shortlisted for the 1993 Thomas Cook Travel Book Award, and *Dreams of the Peaceful Dragon*, about a journey on horseback through the forbidden Himalayan kingdom of Bhutan. She was shortlisted for the *Sunday Times* Young British Writer of the Year award for her novel *The Quetzal Summer*.

Katie Hickman lives in London with her two children and her husband, the philosopher A. C. Grayling.

Suggested reading

Katie Hickman, *The Aviary Gate* and *Courtesans*; Christi Phillips, *The Rosetti Letter*; Marina Fiorato, *The Glassblower of Murano*; Donna Russo Morin, *The Secret of the Glass*; Tracy Chevalier, *Girl with a Pearl Earring*; Vanitha Sankaran, *Watermark*; Barbara Quick, *Vivaldi's Virgins*; Caroline P. Murphy, *Murder of a Medici Princess*; Michelle Lovric, *The Floating Book*.